Freedom

By: S.A. Wolfe

Dedication

For my brothers

They have both been there.

One
Dylan

"What has changed the most for you in the last five months, Dylan?"

I'm not getting laid?

That persistent question hangs in the air between us for a moment while I look around the room, trying to sum up how I feel without sounding like a repetitive loser.

I've been seeing Dr. Wang every week for months since I came out of the treatment facility, or The Cuckoo's Nest as my friend Imogene fondly refers to the place where I went to deal with my bipolar disorder.

I had met Dr. Wang before I went in the place, an emergency situation that warranted starting meds again, and then we'd picked up with regular sessions in January when I had returned from my stay at the rehab joint.

Rehabbing my brain is how I've seen it, and it has been interesting and frustrating to say the least.

There was no doubt that I had needed the intervention; I had driven one of our company delivery trucks off a bridge and had no recollection of why I had been so distracted. I was banged up yet not seriously injured. It had left me with scars on my head, but other than that, it had really been the sign I had needed to get professional help.

I don't remember a lot of my erratic behavior prior to going to Massachusetts and checking into the Willow Haven Center. They always give these places goofy preschool names to make it sound like we are running around with butterfly nets and sipping lemonade all day. I wish it could have been that simple, but mostly the doctors

1

and therapists wanted me to talk about my lifelong struggles and earliest memories of when things seemed to have gone wrong for me. It meant having to share the worst events—my mother's death and my father's suicide—with a room full of strangers.

Unlike other patients, I didn't tell long-winded stories, and I didn't take any comfort in the group empathy. I was blunt and to the point, showing no signs of grief when it was my turn to talk. I was so brusque in my first group session, telling my family history in about thirty seconds, that one guy laughed loudly and said, "Well, I guess you're done here. So much for therapy." That obnoxious guy became my best friend while I was imprisoned in Camp Happy.

Truthfully, my brother had been right to insist that I go into treatment. Last year, I was a mess. I mean, I might have been about to propose to Jessica, a woman who hadn't loved me, but that had just been the start of my downfall. You could say I wasn't operating at full capacity, and that would have been an understatement. I wasn't pining over her—I knew that much—because I had never truly been in love with her. It was merely a manic episode in my life where I had constantly been drifting in my own head and feeling pretty soulless. Unfortunately, I had used Jess as a filler in an attempt to get over the lousy emptiness that had surrounded me.

Jess was someone Carson and I had known briefly one summer when we were kids and she had been visiting her aunt in Hera. So, when she had come back last summer to collect her inheritance after her aunt's death, I had used the opportunity to make a move on her. She had seemed game for a fling. Apparently I foiled Carson's plan to do the same, though. I knew he was attracted to her, but I'd had no idea my brother was in love with her, and neither had Jess. At least, not until after she'd dumped me.

Of course, I've been the one that has come off as the

2

pariah in the whole fiasco because everyone blames it on my notorious philandering. And I take full blame for my behavior towards Jess and Carson. I expected that, as my lifelong protector, Carson wouldn't try to intervene if he thought it would hurt me, and it worked; he stepped aside. I played that card extremely well, and I don't know why since there is no one on this earth that I love more than Carson. However, I was also playing with Jess's feelings. I have a vague recollection of being attached to her in a desperate way, one that wasn't anything close to resembling love.

I had been blind to the fact that she was falling in love with my brother from the minute she'd moved to town almost a year ago. Somehow, I managed to create the biggest fucking mess for all three of us because of it.

Luckily, Jess is a smart woman and broke off our relationship, and Carson, despite the trouble and pain that I caused him, made me get help.

So, there it is; I agreed to go to a residential treatment program to get my bipolar behavior under control. It has helped that I was away from everyone in the puny town of Hera, namely my brother and the woman he loves, so they could have the relationship they both want and deserve. Yeah, I can be a good guy—just send me off to the crazy house to get a periodic tune up.

I finished my rehab stint in January, only to find myself as the best man in my brother's wedding. Who did he marry? Jessica, of course.

"Dylan?" Dr. Wang asks again. He is a slight, young man with a big, friendly smile and kind eyes behind black-framed glasses. He looks like he's sixteen even though he has medical degrees plastered all over his walls from prestigious schools.

He types quickly on the computer in front of him, taking notes on our session while watching me.

"Sorry, I got sidetracked."

3

"Is the medicine having any adverse effects?" Dr. Wang pauses in his speed typing and looks thoughtfully at me. "Are you more tired or anxious?"

"No, I feel fine." I look down at my hands resting on my thighs. I flex them, releasing my fists, hoping to find something to calm the nagging feeling inside me.

"Tell me what's going on." Dr. Wang is assertive even when smiling. "Are you still running?"

"Yeah, I run every day. At least six to ten miles, and I work out in the gym after work."

"You've been coming here since January, and you are different. You're more subdued in our sessions. Still restless, but I'm not seeing that high-energy, anxious side of you. I've noticed the change."

I nod along.

"And you've been weight training, excessively it seems," Dr. Wang adds. "I had your recent physical sent over from your GP. Everything looks fine. The blood work is good. You've gained more than twenty pounds. But that's okay for your height, considering all the exercising you do. It looks like it's all in muscle. Is that what you've been doing—spending all your time bulking up?" Dr. Wang smiles reassuringly.

"When I'm not working… yeah… pretty much I just work out. I don't know what else to do with myself. I don't drink anymore, so I don't go to bars with my friends."

And I'm staying away from women, too. Dr. Wang already knows that, though.

"So a typical day for you is to get up and run, go to work, and then lift weights at the gym afterwards. And you avoid everyone except people at work?" Dr. Wang's smile is replaced with a serious frown. "I've heard this scenario before. You do realize that you repeat this to me every time you come here."

"That's pretty much my life in a nutshell. Sometimes I run on my lunch break, too. It keeps me out of trouble." I

4

shift uncomfortably in the small chair.

Dr. Wang's eyes widen. I don't sound like a normal person at all. I sound like some freaking Schwarzenegger caricature. Running, lifting weights, working and avoiding people outside of work. Who lives like that except emotional wrecks like me?

"Is that what you're afraid of? Getting into trouble? Do you worry about what Carson thinks?"

"Of course. I've been raising hell for so many years, and now I'm finally the good brother. I don't want to mess that up for me or anyone else, for that matter. They've all spent enough time on me."

Dr. Wang gives an unhappy nod. He has heard this before—I'm not good at adding anything meaningful to our sessions other than to confirm that I am not on the cusp of another manic episode.

"There has to be something else. What do you do for fun? When you aren't working or exercising, what do you do to let go?"

"Not much. Sometimes I take long hikes on the weekends to get out of the house."

"Anything else? Do you ever relax at home and watch TV or go out for a movie with a friend? I'll accept any person here—you fill in the blank."

"No, I don't really go out at all. I hate being home alone, though. It's kind of…"

"What? Lonely?"

"Yeah. Being—living alone sucks. Leo is never home; he spends all his free time at Lauren's house, so I have the place to myself, and I've discovered that I don't like being alone. At least at Willow Haven I had friends who were in the same boat as me. Some of them were unbelievably bat-shit fucked up, but—oh, sorry."

Dr. Wang smiles. "It's okay."

I sigh. Sometimes I feel sorry for my doctor because he has to deal with miserable fucks like me.

"But you do this intentionally," he says. "You're isolating yourself from everyone except for the people you work with. What about Carson and Jessica? Do you see them?"

"Yeah, I've been to their house a couple of times for dinner and there's nothing weird between us. Jess is like a sister. I don't think of her in any other way."

"So why don't you spend more time with Jess and Carson and your other friends? What's stopping you?"

"They all look so happy that it makes me feel miserable." I rub my palm over my forehead.

"You feel like you're missing out?"

"Sure. Sometimes."

"Are you feeling depressed at all? I'm talking about the extreme low points you felt before the therapy and medication."

"No, it's not like that. I don't feel depressed, and my moods aren't flying all over the place. I feel kind of… numb and dull."

Dr. Wang doesn't look satisfied with that response.

"You just turned twenty-four. Did you have a party or celebration of some type?"

"Nope. I met Carson for a quick dinner at the diner and then headed home."

Dr. Wang looks at his monitor and continues to type away before turning back to me. "Listen, Dylan, you've been coming here for months. Contrary to your concerns, you're not an alcoholic or a sex addict—that was established in the treatment center—but you're treating yourself like someone who can't control himself if you're around others. I don't see an inability for self-control on your part. You've been doing well, even if it seems like very little progress to you.

"How about this? The next time your friends ask you to join them for dinner or a night out at a bar, you accept? You can drink seltzer or something. And stop thinking you're not allowed to date women. If you're not ready, don't do it. That's fine. But, for months, you've been hinting at or telling me directly that you're ready for more, and I'm telling you it's okay to move on."

Two
Emma

Finally, I'm out of there. I couldn't take the past year of living back home, working for my father again in the corporate office of his retail chain.

My father, Daniel Keller, has built his own little empire of mid-quality, dingy, auto repair and supply shops, promoted daily with low budget TV ads and the company's mascot—an obnoxious, shrieking spokesman portrayed by a has-been pro linebacker. It's an unglamorous job, but it's a paycheck.

My parents offer a nice home and decent employment, however I have to move on and have a real life of my own. With the exception of going away to Syracuse for college, I have never been separated from my parents or "the business" for very long. I don't come from a mafia family in the way that the rest of America glorifies it in movies or television, but unfortunately, I am surrounded by the real deal. My family is embedded in the culture to an extent; we have suffered because of it. It is not entirely my father's doing, either.

He had no idea that building a successful company would put us in this situation. I think he always believed that we would be set free, given the opportunity to stop paying off extortion fees to guys who came to visit him every month. That never happened, though, and the more money my father's retail chain made, the more he paid and the more I got involved with the types of kids my parents wanted me to stay away from.

And then there was Robert. To put it mildly, he

enchanted me. He was my first hard crush. I watched him grow up from a tough street fighter—the leader of the cool kids that all the young girls fawned over—to a smart, Princeton grad who polished his image as his father moved up in the ranks of *the family*. Robert Marchetto was a few years ahead of me and too handsome and popular to be in my circle. He was out of my league... until one day when he wasn't.

I was working in my father's office on summer break from college when Robert showed up at the company with his father, Vincent Marchetto. I saw the discomfort in my father's face as Robert walked right in and started talking to me. He had recognized me from when I was a freshman in high school and recalled who I had hung out with. He was charming and beautiful, just as I had remembered. Only right then, he was a man and I, too, had changed dramatically in those five years, enough so that Robert was very interested.

In hindsight, if I could go back and alter time, I would. There's no use lamenting over the impossible, however.

My new home and job in the little town of Hera, New York are the perfect opposite of what I had in New Jersey. The furnished cottage I am now renting is a very cozy, little one-bedroom hut with full-on 1980s décor, not far from the center of town. Plus, in nice weather I can walk to my job at Blackard Designs. In contrast, my parents' suburban neighborhood is not far from the Paramus strip of retail stores, businesses, car dealerships and other notorious establishments. I am used to density and traffic; Hera is quiet and wide open without a single traffic light. I can breathe in peace, and there's no Robert here.

I am fortunate that Lauren, one of my good friends from college, hooked me up with this job. She and Imogene—also one of my college buddies and a lifelong resident of Hera—knew I was going crazy with interviews in New York City and getting rejected for every single position. Young, inexperienced college grads flood the streets of New York like confused locusts, swarming into each other with no real direction. I am no different than everyone else in our generation; I can only assume that I have some spectacular hidden talent to take on the world, yet it is hidden so well that I have no clue how to figure out what I should be excelling in.

At the age of twenty-three, I seem to be highly skilled in pacifying unsatisfied wholesale customers even though it is terribly unfulfilling to have people gripe at you all day about automotive parts.

I do credit Lauren with saving me from another year of living with my bickering parents and working in my father's miserable offices. However, at least I can say that working for him over the years has given me the opportunity to wear a lot of hats, so I am qualified to do something beyond fetching coffee and filing.

My father is a difficult boss with all of his employees. He is fair, but he manages his staff like they are roaming, mindless herds that need constant prodding and shouting. As the underling assistant to the *real* marketing assistant in his wholesale department, I wasn't spared his infamous wrath. Behind his back, everyone refers to him as Genghis Khan, and I couldn't agree more. Often, my father would yell at me more than other employees as if to prove a point that I wasn't getting any breaks for acquiring my job through nepotism. It was incredibly exhausting to play that role. Day after day of being his verbal assault target would wear down my nerves. Between his management style, and my mother's breakdowns over wanting to flee New Jersey, I was suffocating.

After I interviewed with Carson Blackard at his furniture factory last week, I knew he would be so much more pleasant to work for than my father, and I already have Lauren and Imogene here as friends—people that have no connection to my Jersey life and the *other* family I

10

am trying to forget about.

In my interview, Carson mentioned that the office is casual unless they visit clients out of the office. Nevertheless, I want to make a good impression on my first day, so I wear a charcoal gray pencil skirt that falls just above my knees; low black pumps; and a fitted, white silk blouse with a relaxed neckline. It's not casual, but it's not too conservative, either. I consider wrapping my long hair up into a loose twist, then decide that will look like I am trying too hard. I have seen the shop—guys wearing flannel and covered in sawdust and the receptionist wearing jeans—so I don't want to look ridiculously out of place. I leave my hair down in loose waves and put on some mascara and lip gloss before heading out the door.

When Carson gave me the tour, I paid strict attention to the details of the process—from weathering the wood in the ovens to the actual craftsmanship that takes place in the studio. I took copious notes like I was in chemistry class, repeating everything he said and writing it down like I expected some big test on all the material. Carson kept glancing at my clipboard and smiling, probably because I was clearly so nervous and overzealous in my all-business attitude.

Once in town, I drive off the main street and around the building where others have parked behind the factory's extension that houses new equipment. The employees' vehicles are parked any which way on the dirt area, so I wedge my little car up along the far back wall, parking parallel to the side of the building and close to the side door. I have the smallest car on the lot, so it seems like the best spot for me.

I grab my huge leather satchel, which only holds my wallet and cell phone, hoping it makes me look more professional despite its sparse contents. I take the side entrance inside and walk through a hallway of offices that leads me out to the front desk where Daisy, the receptionist,

11

sits.

"Good morning, Emma!" Daisy says, jumping out of her chair. "It's so nice to see you again." She is a very chipper person, the kind you want greeting everyone who comes through the front door.

"Hello, Daisy. It's nice to see you, too. Where should I put my bag? Carson never showed me where I'd be working." I step behind the receptionist counter to join her.

"That's because we had to clean out the back office to make space for you and Dylan. He's really a sweetheart. You'll like—"

Daisy is cut off when a tall, broad-shouldered guy comes striding around the front of the receptionist's counter. "Who took my spot?" he demands. "Someone parked in my bike—"

"Cool it, Rambo!" Daisy snaps and tosses her headset on her desk. "This is Emma Keller. She's starting today. Emma, this is Dylan Blackard. You two will be working together." She shoots Dylan a look that says he needs to play nice.

"Huh?" He sounds like Scooby-Doo, and I would laugh except he looks like a trained assassin, though a handsome one, in my humble opinion. Still, he looks tough. Actually, he's very attractive despite a dark sandy buzz cut that shows off long, thin, white scars on either side of his head. He has aqua-blue eyes that complement his sculpted features, and there's a fierce, rugged quality to him, like someone who has spent a lot of time outdoors. It doesn't hurt that he is wearing a gray sleeved Henley that hugs his thick chest and his beefy biceps.

Beefy biceps? Since when do I care about guys' arms? That's not like me. I must be a little over-excited about starting work to let a guy like this unnerve me. I have worked with bigger guys than him, frigging goombas; I am not going to be intimidated by this guy. Damn, he is big, and he keeps looking at me with a confused expression like

12

he can't decide how he is going to kill me. Will that be quick and easy, or slow and torturous?

Obviously, I have spent too many years in my father's male-dominated business and have seen my fair share of shady characters come and go from his office. Watching my father muttering angry expletives under his breath when one of those creeps would come around to give him problems was another reason why I wanted out of the family business. The smell of burnt coffee, stale cigars and motor oil is even less appealing when it comes at a steep price tag, like a mortgage you can never pay off.

Blackard Designs is hip and new, and it's bursting into a more glamorous world of home design and eco-friendly development. It is a move *up* rather than the uninspiring lateral move I would take if I stayed in my father's outdated business.

"Dylan, Emma is Carson's new marketing and sales assistant. She's helping with the clients. Remember, this was all discussed at the last company meeting?" Daisy looks at me with a roll of her eyes and shakes her head.

"Hi," he says to me in a softer tone.

"Hello." I wait for him to offer to walk me to our office, yet he just stands there, so I grab my bag and walk around the reception counter to follow him.

As he glances at my legs and my bag, he doesn't even attempt to hide the fact that he's checking me out.

"He's recently been replaced by a surly, alien pod person," Daisy says to me as she waves her hand in Dylan's direction.

"This way," he says and turns. I notice he is wearing faded, relaxed jeans as I follow his splendid butt down the hall to our office.

Opening the door, he leans against it so I have to squeeze by him to enter the room. I sense him looking down at me, getting a good view of my cleavage and my own rear end. That's fine. I am used to working with men, and I work out for a reason. Sure, it's a healthy activity, however I won't lie, I like getting noticed, too. Better this guy than some of the middle-aged married men that I used to have to deal with in my father's business.

The room has two desks with brand new computers, a couple of filing cabinets, and some nice chairs for visitors. One wall has two windows that face the side of the building where I've parked my car. Behind it, I see a shiny Harley has blocked me in.

"Oh," I say, looking at my little Honda.

"So, you're the one who took my parking spot." He leans against the desk that has stacks of papers and a personal coffee mug.

"So you're a Harley guy? A Super Glide?"

"How did you know?" His blue eyes narrow a bit.

"Don't look so surprised. My dad has some vintage bikes, and he's restored a few Harleys, so I know something about them."

He scoffs and looks out the window, which gives me a good view of his profile consisting of a strong jaw and nice cheekbones.

I kept hearing how this guy was all baby doll charm and sweetness with a womanizing past; there is nothing sweet about him, though. He looks like he eats baby goats for breakfast. Lauren has filled me in on the accident he had a few months ago and his treatment for depression, but he is nothing like I've imagined. I expected a kind, quiet guy, not this tightly wound bundle of nerves in a hot package.

"If it had been marked as *reserved*, I wouldn't have parked there." I drop my bag on the floor next to the bare desk.

"Huh," he grunts. "I didn't know you were coming today. I didn't even know my brother had hired you yet."

I shrug. "Then I guess this is a surprise. Surprise!" I splay my hands open against my fake smile, yet his face

14

remains impassive.

"Good, you're here." Carson stands in the doorway and gives me a warm smile.

The Blackard men sure got more than their fair share of the *handsome* gene, and from what I understand, they aren't even related by blood. You won't see me complaining about the view, however. These guys make my father's employees look like trolls.

"Dylan, sit down with Emma and bring her up to date on all the accounts. Jess installed the new software last night so it's a lot easier than the old system. You'll see all the account tabs are easy to find, and if you have any trouble, Jess said she'd come in and give a tutorial."

"I think I can figure it out," Dylan responds as he drops his large frame into his office chair and leans back so his long legs stretch out under the desk.

Carson looks at Dylan quizzically for a moment and then turns to me. "Emma, stop by my office if you have any questions. The door is always open. Literally. There's no door. Dylan managed to demolish it a while ago and we never replaced it. Why don't you tell her that story to break the ice?" Carson smirks at Dylan.

"Another time," Dylan replies, glancing down at his large, callused hands.

I look at his hands, too. Who rips a door off its hinges, and why do I have to share an office with him?

"You have my permission to kick him when he's being a jerk," Carson says. "I'm just down the hall if you need me."

"Thank you." When I sit down on the end of my new desk chair, Carson smiles and then leaves me alone with the mercenary.

"Okay," Dylan says, standing back up, and with a finger, he rolls his chair next to mine. "Move over, and I'll show you the set-up."

He is terse and doesn't seem pleased with me taking up

space in his office. Fortunately—or not—I am used to this kind of guy. It would be easier to laugh it off if he had a potbelly and doughnut sugar sprinkled across his chin. He doesn't, though.

I scoot my chair to the right and he slides in next to me. It's a tight fit with both of us squeezed into the u-shaped desk area.

"Excuse me." As he leans over my legs to reach the power switch under the desk, his hard chest pushes against my shins and I feel his breath on my bare skin.

"Hey!" I shove him aside so his chair slams into part of the desk.

"What the eff was that for?" he growls in a deep, booming voice.

"For touching me. Hello?" I snap. "You could have asked me to flip the switch."

"Fine. Go ahead." He glares at me, and I swear the guy's lips barely move when he talks, like he's one of those weird ventriloquists.

I bend down to the floor and scramble on my hands, pulling the chair forward so I can reach the damn switch. I must look like a silly crab with my ass in the air, which I'm sure is what Jackass is looking at.

"There. Got it." I swing my body back up and whack my head on the bottom of the desk. "Fuck!" I grab the back of my head and cover my mouth at the same time. Out of the corner of my eye I see Jerkoff smirking.

"And all because you couldn't stand me touching your leg. Was it worth it?" His tone is dripping with sarcasm as his mouth curves into a slight smile of satisfaction.

"Don't be a smug bastard. We have to work together. Now show me the accounts. And move over. Seriously, you take up so much space that your leg is on my chair."

As I talk, I rub my head. It gives me a good excuse to avoid seeing his goddamn handsome face. I hate good-looking pricks. I like when an ass looks like an ass. It

16

makes the work environment easier. This guy is buckets full of testosterone along with all those attractive, badass hormones that I don't need anywhere in my vicinity. Give him a shoulder holster and a pair of black Ray Bans and he could go work for my father as an intimidating bodyguard.

"I need to get to the mouse, so I can either reach in front of you or reach behind your back," he says. "It depends on which body parts you're afraid I may accidentally touch."

"Oh, you think you're funny, don't you?"

"Not really. I just want to get this over with."

"I can handle the mouse. You can direct from there," I reply and push him back hard in his chair so his arm isn't touching mine.

He laughs, and the transformation in his face is remarkable. It is a real laugh, not a smirk or scoff. His cheeks turn into rosy, little apples and his eyes sparkle. It's fleeting, however his smile is quite a thing of beauty, and I can't stop staring at him. When his laughter subsides, he looks at me for an extra beat, and a blush heats my face.

I turn back to the computer, and for the next couple of hours, we both manage to talk without actually looking at one another. The computer screen and all the charts and spreadsheets make the perfect buffer, so I don't have to face him even though the warmth from his presence and the mild scent of his soap and deodorant is a little too exhilarating.

Three
Dylan

I really could leave her on her own with the accounts. All of these spreadsheets are familiar to her, and she doesn't need me to read the vendor files since the sales numbers speak for themselves. I don't move away, though. I keep myself jammed in behind her desk with my right arm across the back of her chair as she scrolls down the computer monitor, so I can take in her shiny, wavy dark mane of hair against her creamy skin.

Processing these absurd thoughts makes me want to laugh. Then again, I really wouldn't mind catching another close-up of her big, brown eyes, either. However, she seems pretty determined to keep them averted from me and on the task at hand.

Great, she has me thinking about sex again. If I've thought my senses were numb and dull before, they sure as hell aren't now. From the minute I saw her standing behind the reception counter, a brick of lead surged from my stomach to my throat, leaving me mute. I meet a lot of ambitious, smart, attractive women in this business, but I wasn't prepared for Emma. I could barely say hello to her when we were introduced. I'm certain that I came off like an oaf.

Daisy was right, we did talk about filling this position at the last company meeting, and while I was in California on business, Carson mentioned that he was interviewing one of Lauren's friends. It was a brief conversation in which Carson explained the need for this woman to get out from under her father's business. Fair enough. I knew a bit about the interview, but I didn't know she's already been hired, and I didn't know she looked like... this.

The last woman I was with was from the catering staff at Carson's holiday party before I went off to my "special" therapy program as Lauren puts it, like I am some kind of wayward boy. Although I agreed to see Dr. Wang and prepare in advance for moving to the treatment center, I had other priorities on my agenda. Getting laid seemed critical at the time, it didn't matter who the woman was—it felt like it would be my last feast. The woman I was with, well, we were on the same page about that, and I can't even recall her name.

Unfortunately, the catering server and other women have come back to haunt me. As I went through my various group sessions in the treatment center, I started to conclude that women were a bad vice for me. I listened to the other guys in group talk about their depression and mood swings, and how it coincided with extreme promiscuity, alcohol abuse, or drug use. Some of them had multiple addictions, and it made me wonder if I had the same problem with women and alcohol. My doctors at Willow Haven said I never fit the profile of a sex addict or alcoholic, however I was so unsure at the time that I decided to give everything up; women, booze, and anything that resembled fun. Whatever it would take to show Carson that I could beat the destructive alter ego I have had living inside me for years.

But, *fuck*. I've known *this* woman for only a few hours, and all I can think about is what her soft, plump lips would feel like if I ran my tongue against them and then down her neck to her spectacular cleavage. Yeah, I've got a perfect view of Emma's tits since I am more than a head taller. She has no idea that I keep glancing down at the top of her loosely buttoned shirt. I can see all the way down her bra and estimate the size and feel of those mounds of flesh. *Shit.* This isn't the time for a hard-on—at work with a new employee. It is going to be impossible to share an office with her.

I lift my right leg and cross my steel-toed work boot over my left leg to hide the bulge growing in my crotch. The space is too confining, but I'm not ready to leave her desk. My right leg brushes against her thigh as I try to get more comfortable. Her hands smooth her skirt down to keep it in place while her eyes stay locked on the computer monitor.

She is all business. That's good because I have managed to stay away from all sexually appealing women for months, yet if she gives me any indication that she would jump into bed with me today or let me screw her on this desk, I don't think I'd be able to resist her. Any part of her. I have to get out of this situation.

I probably should call Dr. Wang for an emergency consultation about this. I've thought I had everything under control. Work has always been a safe zone for me. It's feeling pretty iffy at this moment, though.

"Okay, I think you can handle this on your own." I stand up abruptly.

I have a lump in my throat, and it worsens when she looks up at me with those sultry, dark eyes and slightly parted lips.

"I'll fill you in on clients as we go along." I kick my chair back to my desk. "No need to cram everything into one day."

"Fine by me. I'll take the laptop home, too, and catch up on accounts over the next few nights."

This is good. I can handle this awkward feeling. I just need to get out of the room *now*.

"I'm going to the studio to talk to Noelle about an issue she's having with one of the new table designs. If you need me, text me. It's easier than using the PA system. No one can hear over the machinery. I'll put my number in your cell phone." I hold out my hand to her.

"Oh, sure." When she pulls her phone out of her bag, unlocks it, and hands it over to me, her fingers graze my palm and I flinch. I am nervous as hell. This is a first; I've never been anxious over any woman. Pushing those thoughts aside, I tap in my cell number and return it.

As I am about to leave the room and escape the unbearable arousal I get from being around her, Cooper fills the doorway. Carson hired him the day he interviewed when I was out of town last week.

Cooper is very vocal about his single status and the women love him. I'm not sure if I like him, though. He's got that overdone biker look going on with thick, shoulder-length blond hair, beard stubble, leather vest; the whole Harley package that women fall for. He's cocky, and sometimes I want to punch him for being the witty office charmer, a character I used to play well.

I want him to leave *now*.

"Hey, Emma, we're going to go grab some food. Can I treat you to a first-day-on-the-job lunch?" Cooper gives her a big I-love-screwing-pretty-new-girls grin. I would know.

He makes Emma smile.

Fuck, no.

"Oh!" she exclaims as if no guy has ever asked her to lunch.

"She can't," I snap, surprising myself. "She's having lunch with me. We still have some business to discuss."

Emma turns to me, and her smile for Cooper is replaced with a furrow between her arched, dark eyebrows and a tilt of her head. There is something very feline about her, and I wonder if my brain is screwing with me, envisioning a sexy Catwoman.

"Okay, well, a few of us are heading over to the diner now, so we'll probably see you there," Cooper responds before leaving.

I wasn't going to let some other guy zero in on the woman that has just woken me out of a long winter slumber of nothingness to an electrical firestorm. Even if it is proving impossible for me to tell if this is normal or if I am one sick fuck who is desperate for a female.

"You're taking me to lunch? I thought you had to talk to Noelle about the tables?"

Emma swivels her chair so she is facing me, crossing her ankles and tucking her legs under her chair. *As if that will prevent me from fantasizing about her bare skin and what I'd like to do with those legs.* I chuckle inwardly, knowing that I am on a fast track up shit creek if I don't slow myself down. I can't screw around with my brother's new employee.

Emma seems like a sincere, hardworking girl trying to make it on her own without Daddy's money. I can't drag her into my screwed up world, and it wouldn't be fair to put Carson in the middle of another one of my epic disasters.

"I'll talk to Noelle after lunch. Let's go grab a bite."

***

She sits across the diner booth from me, nibbling on a grilled cheese sandwich while I scarf down two bloody burgers smothered in guacamole.

"You sure you don't want something more than that little sandwich?" I ask. She's eyeing my plate, so I assume she is hungrier than she let on. "Bonnie's burgers are the best. I'll get one for you." I am about to raise my hand to flag down Lauren to order it when Emma shakes her head.

"No, I'm a vegetarian."

"Oh." I look at what is left of my second rare burger oozing red juice into the fries. "This carnage on my plate must make you ill."

She smiles and shakes her head. "No, I'm used to it. My parents live on steak, the kind that's so rare it's ready to walk off the plate. I am astounded by your appetite, though."

My appetite. Coming from her perfect lips, it sounds sexual to me. "I get a lot of exercise," I say, suddenly

22

losing interest in my food.

Lauren stops by our table and her bubbly hyperness clues me in to what will follow. "Time to make a wish," she says while rubbing my buzzed scalp. I am used to it from the women that know me, although it got old months ago, and now it's an embarrassing display in front of Emma.

Emma smirks at me.

"How is your first day, Em?" Lauren asks. "Is Dylan behaving?"

"I've been a perfect gentleman."

Emma looks at me pointedly before resuming the little nibbles she has been taking of her sandwich.

"Uh, gotta go, kids." Lauren scans the door as more customers come in.

I am relieved. I wonder how much Lauren has told Emma about me before she accepted the job from Carson. Have I been made out to sound like a sad sack of problems or a despicable womanizer? Lauren has been my friend since we were kids; she's seen almost every heinous thing regarding me. I suspect a good friend like Lauren would warn her girlfriend well in advance, and that's why I am getting this scrutinizing vibe from Emma.

"So why did you leave your family's business for Carson's? What makes this place so special?" I push my uneaten food away.

"Carson's business isn't on Route 17 somewhere between Satin Dolls and Crate and Barrel, my personal highway to hell."

I chuckle. "I know that area. Very lively."

"Right. Bada Bing," she says dryly. "Let me guess, you've been to Satin Dolls."

"Never. I've only driven past on my way to make deliveries."

"Sure. Men always drive past it, never to it." She smirks.

"Honestly, those clubs aren't my thing. Tell me more

23

about your dad's company and why you wanted to leave it."

"Let's just say my dad's business won't be around much longer. He wants to sell, and my parents plan on leaving Jersey and moving to Florida for an early retirement. It can't happen soon enough, in my opinion. Really, I don't want to talk about my father's business, it's not an exciting topic. Besides, there's no future there, so what's the point? It's tough to find a job in this market. I'm lucky Lauren put my resume in front of your brother. He could have hired anyone—he gave me a huge break." She says this as if she's escaped something terrible as she glances down at her unfinished meal and pushes it away.

"Did Carson tell you that I'd be handling the biggest accounts? They're high maintenance and want direct attention from us instead of going through our sales group, Mercer. I won't be available to help you much with client issues and on the sales end here. I'll need you to become very familiar with the Mercer people and make more trips into the city to work with them on distribution."

"I don't need you to babysit me, Dylan." There's defiance in her tone and a stony expression across her countenance. "You can trust me to work hard and do a good job."

But you probably can't trust me, Emma, especially my unedited imagination that has you in several very creative positions.

Four

Emma

For the rest of the week, Dylan doesn't laugh once. I guess that boisterous outburst I witnessed on my first day has been the laugh he allots himself once a year.

I am past the point of thinking of him as a jackass or a scary assassin. Now he just seems like some arrogant, hot guy who sits five feet from me every day. When he is in the office, he's constantly on the phone talking to clients. When he is not here, he is roaming the building, conversing with other employees. He talks to everyone except me. He mumbles and grunts some information periodically my way, however he seems to be working awfully hard at preventing any lengthy conversations between us, which is just fine.

I keep my crackling hormones in line, even though they spark constantly when Dylan is near me. I regularly catch an unnoticed observation of his profile or the back of his broad shoulders and well-packaged jeans when he leaves the office. For holy heck, when he throws on a tool belt to work in the factory, there is a pull in my center and I get unbelievably fluttery excited; I have to exit any room quickly when we have prolonged contact.

Sometimes, he looks rather uncomfortable around me, too, and perhaps all that tinkering and woodworking he really doesn't have to do anymore is because he likes to busy himself in the factory to get away from me.

Then there's his lunchtime running. I have a bowl of soup every day at the diner to catch up on the girl chat with Lauren and Imogene, who both work that shift. They sit with me between serving their customers, and I always manage to catch Dylan running by the big booth window.

Today, Archie sits with me, wearing a three-piece suit and polished wingtips. He's impeccably groomed, and I find this both refreshing and amusing in this small town where everyone else dons jeans and t-shirts most days. But then, Archie is the only attorney in town and seems to handle a lot of clients across the county.

"So, I'm going to skip my usual burger and try the vegetable soup that Emma is having," Archie says to Imogene who scribbles his order on a pad before her head jerks up to the window.

Lauren dashes over, giggling.

"Oh, here comes Ironman!" Imogene says, picking up a fork and using it as a microphone.

Archie looks at me and shakes his head at our juvenile hilarity, but I can't stop myself from laughing along with the girls.

"And he hurdles the fire hydrant! Excellent. Now, will he run around Karen and her stroller or will he hurdle the stroller? Oh! He runs around it," Imogene continues.

Lauren and I are laughing so loudly that other customers turn to watch. The truth is, I can't tell my friends that I think Dylan looks magnificent and that I look forward to these lunches everyday just to see him in action, sprinting shirtless.

"Bill Jamison just cut Dylan off with his truck!" Imogene continues in her mocking, sportscaster voice. "And now Dylan is giving Bill the finger, and wait, yes... Bill is laughing and he's giving the bird back to Dylan. It doesn't slow our Ironman down one bit... And he's off!"

"Oh my," Archie says, watching the finale.

Imogene plops down next to me and Lauren sits next to Archie as we continue laughing until Archie's disapproving sigh shuts us up.

"Where does he run to?" I ask.

"He takes the county road as far as he can and then

doubles back," Lauren replies.

"He needs it. It helps take the edge off all of his... edginess," Imogene explains as she scrunches up her face and shakes her shoulders to demonstrate.

They both leave to serve their customers, and I notice Archie's stoic face regarding me with a questioning seriousness.

"How are you and Dylan getting along at work?"

"Well, he seems to be very good at his job, and I'm doing pretty well with my new projects and clients, if I do say so myself. But, truthfully, we don't talk much. He's good at working with other people in the company, but he also seems like a loner."

"That's interesting," Archie responds, and I wonder if my comment made him slightly sad because of his tone. "I think he's trying to get used to his new situation. He's had to overcome some difficult issues."

"I know. This town talks."

"Yes, it does. Dylan happens to be one of my favorite people. I don't think I've ever told him that, though. But as an old man, I have always envied Dylan's perseverance and enthusiasm, despite some of his poor choices."

"You wish you could run like the Tasmanian Devil?" I smile.

"That, and I wish I could go back and grab the second chances I stupidly dismissed. It's merely an old man's musings." He has a kind smile that reaches the wrinkles around his eyes. "I'm glad you're working with Dylan. It's good that he has someone to contend with besides Carson." Archie chuckles.

"You make it sound like we're opponents. We work together. Sort of."

"Yes. I meant it's nice that he gets to have you in his office, sharing the workload. I saw you two having lunch here together the other day, you seem to have hit it off."

I bark a laugh so suddenly that I surprise myself.

"You're kidding, right? He took me out for lunch on my first day, and that was more than a little tense. This whole week, we've worked pretty much independently of each other. We're working around one another, but I wouldn't say we're hitting it off."

"It's just my observation." Archie winks with amusement.

"Maybe you need glasses," I tease him.

"I don't think so." He chuckles. "Don't let those young women lead you to believe that Dylan is worse off than anyone else. He's a good person."

"All right." I say nothing more about Dylan Blackard because it's clear that Archie wants the last word on this man who is very dear to him.

Naturally, I am not going to let on that I like these lunchtime festivities. I can't wait to see Dylan in his element, whether it's running through town or meandering through the factory at work. I have caught myself at the big, glass partition that separates the offices from the factory, watching him stroll around to different workstations, talking to the designers and craftsman, while I stand there stupidly with paperwork in my hand, gaping at him.

However, it is those images of Dylan running that I find extremely distracting. I can be talking on the phone with a customer when I'll start daydreaming about his incredibly muscled chest and abs and his powerful, corded legs, pumping fast as he runs. He is breathtaking when he moves like that. Though, at the same time, I have to wonder how lonely it must be to run so far away, out in the middle of nowhere, with no one for company.

Despite the rocky start to our first day, and the tension that leaves me wondering if it's attraction or friction, I would like it if he spoke to me more. I want to get to know him.

One morning I can't resist taking things further. We both finish calls to clients and there is an awkward silence between us before Dylan jumps up from his chair, grabs his tool belt off the filing cabinet, and begins securing it around his trim waist.

"Are you a salesman or Bob the Builder now?" I ask rudely to provoke him.

"Wow, you're a feisty wench," he replies without a trace of a smile.

"Wench? How about I'm an awesome salesperson because I work these phones all day while you run off to play with your hammer," I retort, waving my hand at his belt.

He pauses and glares at me. Then he's practically on me in two steps as he puts two big fists on my desk and leans in towards my face. "I can't sit in a chair all day, so I like to alternate between the office and the factory and the studio. Besides, I take care of my clients," he bristles.

Why did I start this tiff?

My head drops from his face to his hands where I notice a long thread hanging from his sleeve. I immediately seize the opportunity to change the subject.

"Give me that," I say, jerking his fist towards me.

I reach into my purse and pull my compact knife out. I push a lever and the blade shoots out.

"Shit. You carry a switchblade?"

As I pull the loose thread taut and cut it clean from his shirt, my swiftness startles him.

"Is that thing even legal?"

He looks quite alarmed, and I want to laugh at the fact that I shocked him so easily.

"It's legal for hunting, and we are in the country, and I happen to be hunting loose threads that annoy the heck out me."

"Haven't you ever heard of scissors? Really, who uses a switchblade to cut a piece of thread?" He pulls his wrist towards him and inspects my work.

"People who don't like scissors." I close the blade and

throw the knife back into my bag. "You have more dangerous things hanging off that belt of yours. I didn't think a little knife would bother you."

"It doesn't. It's the woman holding it that bothers me," he says and then leaves the room with a big, sexy swagger.

Whatever. I am here for a job and a chance at a real career. I am not here to moon over a guy who has a past of setting world records in one-night stands. At least, that's what Lauren has said about his college days.

From what I can tell, and from Lauren's unedited gossip, Dylan has become a temple unto himself, eschewing women and drinking since he got out of the mental hospital or whatever they call it these days. He looks pretty sound to me with the exception of all his excessive running and weight training. I wish all that physical activity would kill the pheromones he gives off. That would really help me concentrate on my work.

Sometimes, when I think I sense him staring at me, I'll turn to catch him looking away. What the hell kind of cat and mouse game are we playing here? I can tell myself that I am not mooning over him, yet the rest of me would disagree.

Aside from a new job I like, a nice aspect of living in this little town is that there are not many ways to blow my paycheck. I haven't ventured out for any social events yet. Archie, Lois and Eleanor—the sixty-something town yogis—have invited me to join their weekly poker game, but I don't know how to play poker, and I suspect Lois is a real card shark and a heartless one at that. Lauren and Imogene, who were a blast to hang out with in college, have invited me to their home as well to have dinner and watch movies with them and their boyfriends, but so far, I've declined. Yeah, being the unattached fifth wheel is always *fun*.

Until I get my bearings on the job, the social life will have to wait. The benefit of this is that the small, inexpensive rental cottage combined with my boring nightly entertainment of knitting and watching television will keep my bank balance at a livable amount. I have turned into my grandmother, and my vagina will surely shrivel up with this stale lifestyle, however I won't have to live paycheck to paycheck and eat rice and beans for every meal.

Friday afternoon, as I get ready to leave, I pass by the makeshift employee gym down the hall where I hear Dylan arguing with Carson. Curious, I'm unable to stop myself from peeking in. Carson is standing by the bench press with his arms crossed, looking annoyed while Dylan is shirtless, in sweat pants, flat on the bench and gripping the bar weighted with several huge plates. I don't know what this guy benches, but he looks amazing doing it. I jerk my head out of view and stand flush against the hallway wall so I can eavesdrop.

"Why didn't you wait until I was back from California before you interviewed her?" Dylan is pissed, and I have no doubt that I'm *her*. Well, that explains the cold shoulder treatment this week. He really doesn't want me here. In that moment, I realize those hot sparks I've assumed were a budding sexual attraction between us are merely the short-circuiting in my own conflicted, sexually deprived body.

"She's a perfect fit for this job." Carson uses a calm, steady tone with his brother.

It is probably familiar territory, given their turbulent childhood and history of brotherly conflicts. Lauren has told me quite a bit about their parents' early deaths and Dylan's destructive years while Carson tried to raise both of them.

Dylan doesn't respond. He just lets out a loud, deep grunt, and when I sneak another peak, he is consumed with that angry assassin look again as he pushes the weight bar up and lowers it several times against his chest. His legs are up and crossed at the ankles, and his repetitions get faster

31

and look more painful as it goes on.

"This is overkill," Carson comments, watching Dylan power through his set.

I move back to hiding against the wall and think about how I am going to work with a guy who really doesn't want me here. Maybe we could have separate offices.

"Overkill, my ass. I need this. What I don't need is an assistant who needs me to help her," Dylan grunts.

Assistant? Fuck him.

"She's not your assistant. She works for me just like you do, so let me tell you how we're going to operate. Emma is taking a big load off your shoulders, and she already knows the ropes. She has a lot of wholesale experience, so you are not training her. You're not her boss. You two will work together, and you will get your head out of your ass and start being more polite to everyone around here. Got it?"

"I heard every fucking word," Dylan growls.

On one hand, I want to cry for being spoken about in that manner. On the other hand, I want to walk in there and give Dylan a good, hard right cross against that handsome face of his.

Defensive moves are probably the only thing of value I learned from some of my father's bodyguards who taught me how to fend for myself without breaking my knuckles. My father's best guy, Sean, always says my preeminent defense tactic is to grab a guy's groin and squeeze the hell out of his nuts, and when he buckles in excruciating pain, I should ram the base of my palm up against his nose to break it. Sean says the fun part is when you get to watch a guy crumble and fall, howling in pain. I've done that before, and it is *not* fun. Besides, I shouldn't be entertaining these types of thoughts about Dylan. He hasn't physically attacked me; he simply gave me an emotional sucker punch to the gut.

Not wanting to hear any more of the conversation, I

flee down the hall and grab my sweater and bag from my office and bolt out to the back parking area.

Damn. I took Dylan's favorite spot again and he's parked his bike next to my car, boxing me in. Now I am going to have to go back inside and ask Dylan to move his bike so I can make a U-turn to get out of this jam. I don't want to face my angry officemate, but I don't have much choice unless I just leave the car and walk home.

No way. I am not letting this guy intimidate me.

I storm back into the building, down the hallway and into the gym where Dylan is now alone. He's standing and rubbing a towel over his sweaty chest.

Nice, hot stuff, now move your frigging bike!

"Hey," I say and he pauses his movements to stare dumbly at me. "I need you to move your bike so I can get my car out." My demand is terse, and I accentuate it with a little hands-on-hip action before leaving the room angrily.

You better be following me soon, buddy. I clomp down the hall and back out to my car.

In less than a minute, Dylan is outside revving up his bike—still shirtless. He moves it away from the driver's side door of my car and loops around back to the far side of the lot. I inspect the distance between Blackard Designs and the building next door, trying to judge how to turn my car in that tight space so I can drive out the back end of the lot, too. Instead of going back inside the office, Dylan saunters up to the other building and leans against it, casually watching me.

This can't be too difficult. I have a compact car. It can make a tight U-turn. I get in and start the car, feeling his eyes on me. I crank the wheel all the way to the left and pull out. I inch back in reverse and go forward again, each time trying to get the car to turn more. After too many attempts, it is like the silly golf cart scene with Mike Meyers in *Austin Powers*. I thought that movie scene was hilarious, though on me, not so much.

33

Dylan lets out a rumbling laugh that grows louder with each curse I mutter then finally approaches the car with a giant grin plastered on his face. He's cute and sexy, and I am furious with him.

"Move over," he orders as he opens my door.

"I can drive a car," I snap.

"Not like me you can't. Move."

I scramble to the passenger side and then he lowers himself into the driver's seat and adjusts it, rolling it back as far as it will go so his legs can fit in. Before I can say a word, he whips the car in reverse, turns quickly into the spot I started from and guns it. I mean, he *guns* it like a rocket launch. My hands clutch the dashboard, and I let loose the most awful, piercing shriek as the car flies backward at top speed to the open area of the dirt lot before Dylan slams it into a hard stop.

I stop screaming, still breathless, staring at the distance we've covered, then look over at Dylan who is leaning on the steering wheel, gloating.

"How was that?" It is a devilish grin that turns into a beautiful smile.

"Terrifying!" If it were anyone other than him with me, I'd probably vomit into my lap.

"You're out, aren't ya?"

"I think you left my spleen back there." I slow down my breathing, but I'm still shaking.

He chuckles.

"What the hell was that? You could have given me a little help and just directed me to back the car out myself."

"You seemed really determined to do it the hard way. Why didn't you think of backing out in the first place?"

"Because I've been driving out head first every day, so I was a little flustered. Forget it." I am not going to tell him that he makes me nervous, that my body trembles with little earthquakes when he is near me.

I get out of the car and walk around to the driver's side

on my wobbly, shaky legs and yank the door open. What is with this guy? He either shuns polite conversation with me or he acts like a madman.

"Sorry," he says as he gets out of the car.

He puts his hand on my shoulder, and for the first time, I notice a small tattoo on the inside of his wrist, a word that I can't make out. The warmth of his heavy hand makes me heady, especially since I am inches from his naked chest, nicely defined muscles and all; not to mention his low-slung sweat pants that sit below the rim of his briefs.

Look away, look away, my brain screams.

I push his hand off me and it startles him. "You listen to me." I do everything in my power not to tear up. "I heard your little tirade in there with Carson. I'm sorry you don't like this new working arrangement, but I like this job and I need it. Let's make a deal to get along because I cannot afford to go back to New Jersey. My family's business won't exist for much longer, and I don't want to work with any more goombas. I'm good at this job and I'm a people person, goddammit! I'm more of a people person than you are, and I can sell the shit out of anything! So don't you dare try to mess this up for me and screw me out of this opportunity!"

His blue eyes stay locked on me a moment longer without blinking. "I won't," he replies in a soft, deep voice. "I'm not going to screw this up for you, Emma."

"Okay then. Good night."

Without another word, I get in my car and drive away. As I do, I check the rearview mirror and find Dylan watching me.

Five
Dylan

I wasn't necessarily honest with Carson. I don't dislike having Emma here. I dislike feeling on edge, as though I am going to lose it around her because I like having her here *too much*. It's caused me to be a shit to her, letting her think that she's the problem.

This whole week has been about me working very hard to avoid her and everything that is appealing about her. That is hard to do when she sits a few feet away and wears a goddamn skirt every day, so of course, I have to watch her cross and uncross her legs every ten minutes or so. One day, I was on the phone with a client when I couldn't resist taking out my phone and using the stopwatch app to clock her leg action.

There is the sexual aspect—I can't deny that—but I also like hearing her talk.

I am scared shitless about this. I am not going to let her get too close to me, yet that doesn't stop me from observing her with others and catching her light-hearted laughs or no-nonsense conversations with clients. I want to say that her presence is good for me because I notice the differences in my own attitude. I've gone from numb to actually looking forward to my day. When was the last time I felt that way? When was the last time my emotions were genuine and not orchestrated by a chemical imbalance?

I think about her while I run in the morning, and when I get to work, I hope she is the first person I see when I walk in the door. My problem is that I don't know if this is happening for the right reason, and my self-doubt has made me more short-tempered than usual with everyone, especially Emma.

Jumping in her little car and then putting my hand on her shoulder, well, that just made my whole damn day. It doesn't take much—just her.

***

Speeding up the empty, dark road, I consider not going back to the house. It's a tomb. Maybe I need an all-night drive on my bike. It is Friday evening, so I don't have to be anywhere in the morning.

Before I can consider that thought further, I see flashing hazard lights up ahead. As I get closer, I notice it's Emma's midnight blue Honda on the shoulder of the road. I park my bike in front of her car and walk back to her. The front left wheel is flat and I can't help but laugh. I can't believe how many times I have laughed or felt like laughing in this one week alone, all because of this woman.

She gets out of the car, frowning at me. "Yeah, I know. It's hilarious." She's pissed.

"So after razzing me with your big speech, and burning rubber out of the lot, here you are, stranded on the side of the road." I chuckle and take my helmet off.

"I didn't burn rubber. I'm not that kind of driver."

"You're some kind of driver, that's for sure."

"Are you going to stop laughing and help me?"

"Pop your trunk. I'll get the spare out."

"Um…"

"What? I'll change your tire for you."

Emma puts her head down and groans another snappy curse word.

"This was my spare," she says. "I had a flat a few months back and I never got around to putting a new spare in the trunk."

"What?" I start laughing again. "Your dad owns auto supply stores all over the tri-state area. You couldn't pick up one little tire on your way out the door after work?"

My laughter isn't endearing me to her in the least.

Frustrated with her predicament, she leans against the car and sighs. "I can see you think this is a hoot, but please stop laughing."

As if my body is willingly deciding what I should do, I lean against the car next to her and rest my right arm on the roof as close as I can get to her glossy hair. If I have bad instincts about getting that close to her, I ignore them.

"I don't think we can get a tow this late," I tell her.

"That's fine. I don't want to deal with this now. I'd be happy to push it off the shoulder and leave it until morning. The house isn't that far. I can walk."

"You're not walking on a county road in the dark." I gently give her back a nudge away from the car. I hold the door open and reach in to release the brake then push the car and steer it off the shoulder onto the grass. Emma runs behind the car to help push with a little too much enthusiasm, and the car rolls faster than necessary.

"Whoa, hey, baby, that's enough. I'm not going to chase this car downhill." I chuckle, grabbing the brake and stopping the car.

I let her grab her bag then lock the door and slam it closed. When I turn around, Emma has an odd expression as she stands in the tall grass. Her legs must be cold, and... oh, crap. I called her *baby*. My instincts suck.

"Come on; I'll give you a lift home." I pretend as if I'm not getting too friendly with her. Let her believe I say *baby* to every woman.

"On your bike?" She glances suspiciously at my Harley and then down at her skirt. I look, too. She's got great legs and I wouldn't mind having them pressed against me on the bike.

"Yep. You need my helmet." I move in close to her and put my black, half helmet on her head and adjust the straps to tighten it. When my fingers touch her hair and graze the soft skin on her cheeks, it sends warning flares to alert my dick.

She looks up at me as if she knows this. Her dark eyes have their own magnetic force, and if I haven't totally lost my mind, they are showing a little interest, too. Damn, her eyes are beautiful. I am tempted to kiss her now for the hell of it to see if I'm right except I already said I wouldn't screw this up for her.

I take off my leather jacket. "You need this, too. Your little sweater isn't enough."

"Then you'll be cold," she replies.

"Don't worry about me." I put it on her and she shrugs her slender arms into my extra-large jacket. It's huge on her, and with the helmet, she looks adorable and sexy. I am so fucked.

I swing my leg over the bike and pat the back bump. "You're sitting here. Climb on and hold on tight."

She hefts her leather bag onto her shoulder and pulls her skirt up a few inches to swing her leg over the bike. "You're not going to speed, are you?"

"No," I answer as she leans against my back and barely holds onto me with just her fingertips. When I pick up her wrists and pull them tightly around my waist, she lets out a small *oomph* as I pull her flat against my back. "Hold. On."

It's less than ten minutes to her house, and it turns out to be the best damn ride I have had in years. Having her arms wrapped around me, tightening against me when I take turns and climbing the road to her bungalow, feels unbelievably good. I don't want this to end.

I drive right up to the front door and park the bike. Instead of letting her off and leaving, I get off and follow her the few steps to her door.

"I haven't been in these cottages since I was a kid. I forgot how tiny they are." I hover behind her on the small porch as she jiggles her key in the door.

Her eyes meet mine. "Thanks for giving me a ride home. You don't have to see me in. I'm good."

Yes, this is the point where I should go and leave her alone, but the thought of going back to Leo's empty home and spending the next few hours thinking about her before I can fall asleep sounds like misery.

"Well, I think you owe me," I say, contemplating some way to stall my departure.

"What?" She sounds a little peeved, trying to decipher my meaning. I guess my reputation does warrant her to question if I am making a sexual implication.

Her hand is keeping the front door closed.

"Dinner. You owe me dinner. I saved you and your car twice today. I'll take anything, even a can of soup and some toast."

I really don't give a crap about dinner at this point, however I'll say any lame ass thing to keep hanging out with her and that little smirk she gives me.

"Dinner?" she questions as she opens the door and leads me inside. "I suppose I do owe you a little favor."

"Jesus, this place is small." I walk inside and feel the urge to duck my head since the ceiling skims so close to my scalp. "My summer friends' families used to rent these cottages when they were strictly for the tourists. I don't remember these doorways being so low." I have to bow my head as I enter the miniscule kitchen.

"Well, you're a giant," she remarks, walking down a short hallway to her bedroom. "I'm going to change out of my work clothes."

That gives me a lot of fresh new images of her naked as I peruse her cramped kitchen.

"These appliances could fit in a doll house. Nothing is full size," I say loud enough for her to hear on the other side of the wall. "This would be perfect for a hamster."

"Shut up!" she shouts, however I can hear amusement in her tone. "I like this place. It's the right size for me and it's affordable." She returns barefoot, dressed in stretchy black lounge pants and a little white t-shirt that shows off her trim waist and that nice rack I notice every day at work. Her hair is flowing carelessly around her face and she looks relaxed for a change, and if possible, even prettier.

Sometimes, I worry my gaze may appear as a leer, so I avert my eyes before I get sucked into her vortex. *Too late, buddy.*

I pull open the fridge. "What are you going to make me for dinner? Because there's no food in here."

"I have food," she scoffs and joins me, ducking her head under my arm to peer into her pint-sized fridge. "Pickles, cheddar, water and yogurt. That's dinner."

Her self-assuredness makes me smile.

"You're kidding."

She steps back and puts her hands on her hips. "I didn't have time to go to the store, and I definitely didn't know that you'd be inviting yourself over for dinner. So pickles and cheese it is."

I slam the fridge door. "New plan. You come to my house, and I'll make dinner for you."

As I quickly think of vegetarian dishes I could drum up on short notice, Emma's face contorts as she stares at the refrigerator door. She doesn't even hear what I am proposing.

"Oh, my God," she whispers as she removes a magnet and pulls a note off the fridge door. It's a white napkin like the ones stacked in a basket on her kitchen counter.

"What's wrong?" I step closer to her and instinctively put my arm on her shoulder.

"He found me. Oh, my God. He already found me." She bites her lip and begins to tear up a little.

Six

Emma

"Who, Emma?" Dylan demands as he holds my shoulders firmly.

"My ex," I whisper. I can barely see through my watery eyes.

"You have an ex-husband?" Dylan asks, astounded.

"My ex-boyfriend, Robert." I shake my head. "I can't believe he was here. The door was locked when we got here, but somehow he got inside."

Dylan takes the napkin and mumbles the brief message to himself:

Missed you, babe. See you soon.

Love, Robert

"Are you saying he doesn't have a key? He broke in here?" he questions angrily. "Who is this guy and when did you last see him?"

"I broke up with him last summer. We dated for two years, and we've known each other for longer. It's a long story."

"Did he hurt you? Is that why you're scared?"

Dylan's bellow startles me, and I pull back from his hands.

"No. He didn't hurt me. The last time I saw him was around Christmas time at a bar. It was at my father's holiday office party. Robert showed up because no one, not even my father, has the authority to make Robert leave. His family... they have a lot of power. We spoke for a long time and he said he'd let me go, like it was his decision. I haven't seen him since. And no one, not even my parents, have my new address here. They call my cell phone when they need me."

"Carson mentioned something about your dad having issues with some mob guy. Are you telling me this guy is one of them?"

"I wouldn't say Robert is one of them. He was born into the business. His father is *the guy*."

"Business," Dylan scoffs at my delicate term for an organized crime syndicate. "That explains why it was so easy for him to find you. He probably has a network to track you. Hera is a small town. If he found out you were hired by Blackard Designs, then finding your home would be as easy as walking into Bonnie's Diner and asking anyone there if they know where Emma lives."

I gulp down the fear and anger lodged in my throat and dry my tears with a paper towel. I've never been afraid of Robert. It's the thought of him coming back into my life that scares me. All the drama he creates, his persistent need to be with me all the time, and the smarmy people that come attached to him.

"Emma," Dylan pulls me towards him, "we have to get you out of here. You can't stay here."

"What? No. Robert would never hurt me. This is my home. I'm not going on the run like some crazy *Bourne Identity* movie." I laugh nervously.

"You're crying and you're scared. I don't know shit about this guy, but Carson told me a little about your dad's situation with them. You moved here to get away from those people, so you're not staying in this house." Dylan's deep timbre is so soothing that falling into his arms would be incredibly easy. Melting into him, a regular small town guy, sounds like heaven compared to what I've had with Robert.

"I was crying because I thought I was done with Robert and all his possessive, controlling behavior. I thought he moved on, and I assumed I was free."

43

"So you're going to call the police and get protection from this stalker guy who leaves love napkins?" Dylan says sarcastically.

"No. They can't touch Robert. They could easily say it was forged. Robert knows how to break and enter without leaving evidence."

"That's my point, Emma." Dylan has me in a partial embrace and presses his hands into my back.

"I'm not afraid of Robert; I'm tired of him. All of them. Even my own family. I came here so I could be done with every last one of them."

Dylan's serious blue eyes capture me in a hypnotic vise. *This is a good place,* I tell myself, staring up at his demanding yet thoughtful expression. I want to reach up and touch his cheek and the light brown scruff that runs down to his chin. I want to run a finger along one of his white scars that snake around his scalp. I want to stay in this spot with him holding me. I should be thinking of how to deal with Robert, but I'm not.

I have spent the last week blissfully entertained in my new job, including being around Dylan's intensity. If he has the past that Lauren claims—a revolving door of women—I wonder how he would respond if I inched my hand down his chest to his rock hard groin pushing into me now.

I can't believe I am having sexual thoughts about him when I have this new nightmare with Robert to deal with, however I *am* thinking about Dylan. Maybe it is the way he looks at me and avoids me at the same time—all week! Maybe it's because he's very attractive and I'm listening to my lonely, stupid hormones.

I am not normally the type of woman to make the first move. I used to let Robert and others before him woo me like a silly schoolgirl because I was too chicken to take the lead, but in this second, I am so tempted to make a move on Dylan. He's hot, sexy and tough all wrapped up in one very fine package.

He hisses, and as if he can read my mind, he moves back a few inches. It doesn't sway my desire; if anything, I am more attracted to him and his action hero side. I have to get my stupid thinking cap on now.

Don't screw someone you work with, Emma.

Dylan moves back farther from me.

"Even if Robert does return, he's not dangerous. He's always been good to me. I gave you the wrong impression about him."

"Really?" he asks in angry disbelief. "Let's see. One, he's part of a mob family. Two, you said he was possessive and controlling—that's a bully. Three, he broke into your home. Four, his note is a reminder that he's watching you—a subtle threat. And you don't have a deadbolt, Emma. It's a little push button lock that anyone can open with a paper clip. Even if you did have one, the door is a piece of thin plywood that I could kick down with no effort, and don't get me started on the cheap windows. So, no, you can't stay here."

"I was upset because I was surprised, that's all. Stop blowing this out of proportion."

"This guy could come back while you're sleeping and stand at the end of your bed. What would you say then?"

"Hi?" I shrug and bite my lip, suppressing the urge to laugh.

"This isn't funny," he responds, and I'm rather surprised at how invested he is in my welfare. He is doing a damn good job of making me swoon a little.

"No, it's not funny. I'm pretty ticked off that he came here, looking for me."

"Good, then let's grab a few things and leave. We can get the rest of your stuff tomorrow when I can come back with my Jeep." He sounds so sure of his plan.

"Where am I going? The Red Roof Inn out on the interstate is the cheapest hotel in the area and even that is

45

too steep for my budget."

"You're coming to my house. Well, actually it's Leo's, but he stays at Lauren's place."

"I can't stay with you; I work with you." I can't believe my own ridiculous statement. I have spent the last five days inhaling his scent like a wolf in heat when he swooshes by me, and now I'm turning down his invitation? What is wrong with me? Not that I am scared of Robert, however the image Dylan has given me of Robert standing at the foot of my bed, watching over me while I sleep, does make me uncomfortable.

"The house has three bedrooms. You can have the guest room. It's an old house and a little shabby, but it's safer than this place." Dylan's right hand squeezes my shoulder.

"And it has you, right?" I ask, wondering if he is really trying to protect me or if he's making a play to get in my pants. At this point, I'm not sure that I care what his strategy is—I am all for it.

There's a moment of silence between us while Dylan contemplates my meaning. "Right. I'll be there, so I can make sure you're safe if this guido comes around."

"He's not a guido. Trust me. If you saw him…" I decide it's best not to qualify Robert's incredible good looks. He's handsome with endless buckets of charm. I was one of the many women that worshipped Robert's Italian gorgeousness before tiring of everything that came along with the pretty package.

"If I saw him… what? You still hold a torch for this guy?" Dylan removes his hand from my shoulder.

"No, not at all," I muse. "You must get all your ideas of organized crime families from TV and old movies. If you saw Robert's family, you'd think they are a nice, suburban family. He doesn't look like a guido."

"You were the one who called them goombas."

"Yeah, some of the guys on the bottom rungs, the ones

I consider the street thugs, look like goombas. Not the guys at the top."

"Fuck. If the guys at the top are paying the guys at the bottom to be thugs, then they're all goombas, guidos or thugs." Dylan is getting more than a little riled over this Robert business and I kind of like it.

I chuckle. "Okay, you're right. They're all thugs."

"You laugh, but I can't believe you would get mixed up with someone like that. I can understand your dad being coerced, but why you'd date a guy like that—"

"Okay!" I snap. "I don't want to talk about it right now. Robert was my mistake. Don't you have anyone you think of as a mistake?"

Dylan pauses and averts his eyes from me with obvious shame. "I was a mistake for a few women," he mumbles and then turns away to pick up his jacket from a chair.

"Huh. Not the question I asked, but very interesting." I follow his movements, willing him to look at me so I can decide if he is bullshitting me with this sudden *I'm-an-unlovable-sad-mercenary* act. "Fine, if we're going to your house, I'll go pack a bag with some necessities for tonight."

"Oh, we're going. You are not staying here."

And Mr. Action Hero is back.

I throw some clothes and toiletries into a tote bag and grab my satchel with my company laptop, and then Dylan and I hop back on his bike. He's wearing his leather jacket, and I have on a wool pea coat and the black helmet. I sling the satchel across my body and tuck it behind my back while Dylan crams the tote in front of him.

This time he doesn't tell me to hold on; he grabs my arms roughly and pulls them around his torso. I am more than happy to hug him tightly with my hands clasped under his jacket, pressing against his hard abdomen. As his t-shirt inches up and I feel his warm flesh, I turn my head and rest it against his back for the ride to his house.

47

Over the last five days, this guy has been mostly standoffish with me, and now I am falling into a vat of marshmallow fluff over him. Yes, I feel all fluffy inside. Dylan may not be aware that I am developing some kind of crush on him, however I'm either suffering from a serious medical condition, or my organs—especially the big one in my head—are turning into mush.

Contentment is easily defined when you are holding onto a big, warm, sexy male body, which is making me reconsider my rule about not fooling around with this particular man.

Seven
Dylan

Having her wrapped around me on my bike makes me want to ride all night long. Her warmth triggers all kinds of crazy ideas and emotions. I'm not the kind of patient that makes an emergency phone call to his shrink—especially to inquire about whether or not it is safe for me to get involved with a woman—however Emma has my neurons going haywire, firing mixed signals at me.

You like her, go for it.

Retreat before you put yourself and everyone around you in another tailspin to hell.

I must be a walking medical miracle with all the third party conversations going on in my head at this point.

We lean into a left turn, and Emma's hands tighten and push into my stomach, so I place my right hand over her hands and give a gentle, reassuring squeeze. It's one of those moments when you recognize that someone trusts you. It may be a singularly brief point in time, yet it's important to me. There are very few people that have trust or faith in me. No, I get nice little well-meaning pep talks from people close to me like Carson.

Speaking of Carson, I have no idea how he is going to react when he finds out I've brought Emma to my house. Not only have I just met this woman, I am putting her under my roof, and I also have to work with her.

If this is fucked up, then why does it seem like the right thing to do? And why do I feel alive for the first time in months? I mean, really alive and invigorated. Every part of my being is strumming along with a great buzz. My meds don't make me high, so it has to be her.

That's still no reason for her to trust me.

My house is dark when we pull up in front and I park my bike next to my Jeep. Emma gets off the bike, and it gives me a twinge of anxiety at losing her touch when she lets go of me. I am also getting a little too optimistic about what could happen next.

As Emma stands in front of the house and looks up at it, I wish Leo and I would have spent more time last summer working on his house and filling it with new furniture. Instead, I put most of my effort in with Carson, working on Jessica's Victorian she has inherited from her aunt.

Leo and I only got around to the necessities on his home, such as putting on a new roof, refinishing the wood floors, and installing all new windows. It was a lot of work, but we never got around to replacing the shabby old couch and putting a dining table in place of the antique billiards table. It looks like a bachelor dump, and there's no excuse for that with two guys who make furniture for a living.

"So you have a little farmhouse out in the middle of nowhere? It's so dark out here. I've never lived in a place without street lamps and houses in every direction."

"Everything out here is in the middle of nowhere. And everything shuts down early, which is why there's no tow service after dinner." When I grab her tote and take her leather messenger bag from her, she follows me up the steps to the porch.

"What's stopping Robert from coming here to see me?" she asks, amused.

"Me."

I see her smirk in the dim glow of the single porch lamp.

"What?" I ask as I open the door and flip a light switch on.

I motion for her to walk in then stare at her perfect,

little ass and get a little pissed thinking about her ex.

"Are you going to get out your shotgun and shoot him if he crosses the property line?" she asks as she chuckles and twirls around my living room like Tinkerbell.

She's so businesslike and remote at work, yet here, she's flirty.

"I don't have a shotgun, but if I he knocks on the door, I'll escort him out of town."

"Oh, really? A few hours ago you were yelling at your brother for hiring me, and now you want to help me?" She puts her hands on her hips, and I am already onto that move of hers. That's what she does when she's serious, and in my case, doubtful.

"That wasn't really about you." *Yes, it was.* "I wasn't pleased that Carson left me out of the hiring process, that's all."

I can't really tell her that I've been off women and sex for five months, and although I work with a lot of women, I'm not attracted to a single one beyond friendship or work relationships. Until Emma. If it was just horniness caused by sex deprivation, then I would be all over every single woman in the county as well as all those pretty sales reps that I work with.

"And now you're fine with the whole thing?" she asks, holding her arms out wide. "Just like that, you don't mind working with me? In fact, you're giving me a bedroom."

When she says it like that, it does sound strange. It also reminds me of some of the spontaneous decisions I've made in the past that got me into heaps of trouble. Emma *should* be suspicious of my motives. I have no idea what I am doing.

Dr. Wang thinks I'm doing well and keeps encouraging me, saying it is time for me to step out of the cave I have put myself in and start spending time with people again. I reek of isolation, and most likely, loneliness. I try to cover it with an impenetrable exterior, nothing too harsh, however I have replaced the old, outgoing Dylan with a more reserved one. I don't know how else to do this. I keep thinking of myself as two people; the guy who has to keep the past under lock and key, and the guy who used to live it up *too much*.

Whenever Dr. Wang brings up dating, I get a little hopeful, but I'm not sure he comprehends how terrified I am of regressing back into the manic Dylan. Dr. Wang is a brilliant doctor. I am beholden to him for bringing some semblance of structure to my thought process so that I don't torture myself the way I used to, however I have convinced myself that being with any woman would be the tipping point that sends me over the edge again. So why am I inviting a woman into my house? Either, I'm trying to prove myself right that Manic Dylan never went away and I am about to sabotage my progress, or I really do like Emma.

"I am fine with you at work, and I'm good with you being here. I wouldn't sleep at night knowing you're down in that cottage surrounded by empty summer houses and a stalker on your tail."

Jesus. I always take it too far. *I wouldn't sleep at night?* My face heats from saying that to her, so I quickly busy myself with her two bags. "Let's get these into the guest room upstairs."

I make a beeline for the stairs and she jumps to follow.

"So you wouldn't be able to sleep at night, huh?" she says softly behind me.

As I start taking the stairs two at a time, she huffs behind me, trying to keep up.

"Like I said, the room isn't fancy. It's clean and comfortable, though." I walk down the hallway to the last bedroom.

We will have Leo's bedroom between us, therefore I won't have to listen to her gabbing on her phone or moving around her room at night. I flip on the light switch and am relieved to see that the room looks better than I imagined. It's sparse but nice since this room has the good furniture from the Blackard workshop. It's the room Leo has his relatives stay in when they visit.

"Wow. It's lovely," Emma says, entering and circling the queen-sized platform bed. She touches the plain white, down comforter—part of the Belgian linens that Leo has purchased. I put her bags on the bench at the foot of the bed while she runs her finger appreciatively over the dresser. "Your furniture looks wonderful in here, and the simplicity of the room and the décor is beautiful." She points to a clay vase as she speaks.

I shrug, wishing I could take credit for this room. I'd like to be the one to impress her rather than Leo.

"Thanks," I mumble. "Ah, there's only one full bathroom. It's across the hall, and we have towels in the linen closet."

"Okay." She beams at me widely, and I want to take the four steps between us and kiss her.

That's what the old Dylan would do.

Instead, I am partially paralyzed as she removes her coat and then a fitted workout jacket that matches her yoga pants. Her skimpy t-shirt that's stretched across her chest and baring her belly button is speaking lulling words to my dick. I feel my groin getting excited again, so I make an escape for the door.

"Hey! Are you going to make me dinner?" She is several feet behind me. I hear the patter of her quick steps and her little breathy puffs as she tries to keep up.

"Oh, I'm making dinner. Absolutely," I call out as I jog down the stairs. I head for the kitchen, figuring she'll find me soon enough.

"Oh, my God!" she shouts from the dining room. "I can't believe you guys don't have any furniture down here. A pool table?"

I pull food out of the fridge and lump everything on the

counter next to the griddle on the stove.

"Honestly," Emma says, coming into the kitchen. "All you have in the living room is a giant flat screen TV and that pitiful couch that looks like it's from a frat house. And a pool table in the dining room? You guys make gorgeous furniture for a living. Why the heck is it only upstairs?"

"We haven't gotten around to it. Besides, it's Leo's house. He fixed the important things first. You know, like plumbing and the leaky roof?"

She scoffs and then hops up on the counter with her ass next to the butcher block. Great. I get to chop vegetables and admire her ass at the same time.

"So, Dylan."

"Yes, Emma?" I respond as I slice some apples.

She grabs my wrist and turns it over to look at the word tattooed on the inside of my arm an inch down from my hand: *Freedom*. As she whispers it to herself and then studies it in silence for a moment, I find myself hoping she doesn't ask me about it. Not yet.

She puts my hand back on the butcher block.

"What's your story?" She chooses an apple slice and starts nibbling on it.

Her and her goddamn nibbling. She knows how to get a guy to zoom in on her mouth.

I put my head down and focus on chopping. "There is no story. At least, nothing interesting. What's yours? How did you end up dating a scumbag? And how long did it take for you to realize you're too good for a guy like that? Did he cheat on you?"

I sure let it rip. I let it all out.

She stops chewing, swallows, and frowns. "Well, you certainly said a mouthful. No, Robert didn't cheat on me. Why do you care? Are you speaking from experience?"

"What did Lauren tell you about me?" I put my knife down and lean against the counter. "And don't bother denying it; I know Lauren very well. She talks about

54

everyone and everything."

"Yes, she does. She said you had to go into a treatment place for a while because you are—"

"Bipolar. Yeah. I went to the funny farm a few months ago." She looks a little stunned at my choice of words. "What else?"

"Lauren said you were a ho in college," she whispers apologetically. "Her words, not mine."

"Shit." I laugh in spite of the unflattering label. "I guess I deserve that."

I shake off that weighted voice that keeps trying to pull me down. The one that constantly reminds me that I've blazed a trail of fuck-ups, and they don't disappear just because I think I'm on the straight and narrow. I get back to the business of food and feeding my vegetarian houseguest. I slap together sliced apples, onions, Gruyere, mustard, and some butter on rye, and press the sandwiches on the griddle with the back of a spatula.

"Even if you were a womanizing, sexist pig, that sandwich looks good, and it smells divine."

"Did Lauren say I'm a sexist pig?" I ask, astounded.

Holy crap. I still have that shitty reputation, and I'm not getting any action whatsoever.

"No, I added that part for fun." She tilts her head and laughs. "Gotcha." This ability of hers to let go and laugh uninhibitedly, her whole body shaking with delight, is pretty cute and too captivating for me.

"Nice. Real nice," I say, plating her sandwich and handing it to her.

I lean against the counter again and watch her take a bite. Not a nibble, a big, slobbering bite with butter drizzling down her chin. Old Dylan is telling me to lick it off her chin. Or maybe it's New Dylan because he's got a thing for Emma. He wants to screw her, too.

"Oh, my God, Dylan. This is heaven," she says.

That's exactly what I'd like to hear you say to me in

bed.

Ah, man, I need willpower for this damsel in distress. And she's hardly in distress; she seems to hold her own just fine. Maybe I did blow this out of proportion so I could play the rescuer for a change. But what kind of guy breaks into his former girlfriend's house? A piece of shit I'd like to pummel, that's who, and that's all I need is to get into another fight.

"I'm glad you like it." I start eating my sandwich, sensing her eyes on me. "Let me get you a drink."

It's merely a good excuse to open both the fridge and freezer doors to chill down my cock. I grab two cans of seltzer and seriously consider throwing some ice cubes in my briefs. I crack a can open and hand it to her then polish off the rest of my sandwich in three bites.

"This is great." She takes a swig of her drink. "Do you cook like this every day?"

"I can," I say, knowing damn well I am trying to impress her and give her another reason to stay here.

"We should probably discuss this set up." She puts her empty plate down next to her and leans forward with her hands gripping the edge of the counter.

I stash the cutting board and pans in the sink for later and then return to my position of leaning against the counter approximately three inches from her small hand. "What do we need to discuss?"

"How long am I staying here? I have to get my car fixed. Plus, I have a lease on the cottage, so I have to move back sometime. Do I pay you rent while I'm here?" She rattles this off like it's a business deal.

Emma is not a business deal to me, though. She's already under my skin, embedded where the bad stuff used to dominate and still partially resides. I think she could knock that shit out of me.

"You can stay here as long as you need to. I'll get your car towed and fixed; my friend owns a repair shop in the next town. We'll get your lease cancelled; I know Joe, the man who owns those cottages, and he won't have a problem when he hears that you've got some asshat ex breaking in whenever he feels like it. So you are not moving back to the cottage, and you're not paying rent here. There, are we done with that?"

She crosses her ankles and swings her legs out, back and forth like a kid. "Why are you doing this? You've known me five days and most of that time you weren't speaking much to me. I got the impression that you were rather aggravated having me in your space at work. When I overheard you with Carson, it pretty much confirmed what I thought. So why would you want me living here?"

"I told you why I was tearing into Carson. It's not you. I'm glad he hired you, and since we'll be working together, helping you settle in Hera is the least I can do."

"Except I'm not settling. You just moved me out of my new home. I can't settle in here; this home belongs to Leo."

"He's busy settling into Lauren's house, and that belongs to Jess, so I guess, we're all settling where we can."

"I don't think that's the whole story," she says with a sly smile. "I think you're a nice guy. Although, it may be hard for you to admit it to yourself because it's apparent you've been dealing with some tough personal issues for a long time."

I close my eyes and hang my head with a sigh. That is exactly what I don't want to hear; a woman I am attracted to feeling sympathy for me and attempting to reassure me like I'm her new friend. That's a mood killer. I consider doing the dishes to top off my night when she places her hand on my arm.

"Thank you," she says sweetly and leans in close, kissing me lightly on the cheek.

I am so still that all I hear is my own breathing. She's lit the fuse. I want to kiss her. Hard. I don't want to talk; I

57

want to touch what I haven't been able to touch for months.

She doesn't move back; she hovers there next to my face with her lips a whisper away as her hand slides up my arm. I don't wait for another sign; I move swiftly and cup her face with both hands. I'm so hungry for her that I collide into her mouth. I keep the kiss slow and firm. I am not going to woo her with soft kisses and tenderness when I have spent five days living like a raging bull, thinking of her.

As my tongue caresses hers, exploring every part of her soft mouth, she runs her fingers up my arms and over my shoulders. Her soft hands are all over me. She caresses my head and traces my scars while her other hand runs down the back of my neck. This touch—her hand stroking across my scalp—is different than all the women who have been touching my buzzed head for months. The other women felt like intruders; Emma doesn't.

Then she opens her legs and I push myself between them. I use one hand to grab her ass and pull her towards me, and she wraps her legs around me. That's when I really begin to come undone. Any part of my body I thought I was controlling is succumbing to her. I hold her waist and move my hands slowly up her rib cage and cup the sides of her breasts before my mouth takes over her neck and works its way down to that hollow dip in her collarbone. She moans softly. This is too good. I don't want to stop touching her, feeling her heightened passion each time my hand or mouth moves across her skin, tasting and smelling with basic animal instinct.

"Dylan." Her voice is soft but insistent.

I stop kissing her and bury my face in her neck. "Damn."

Her legs drop their hold on my waist, and I remove my hands from her. We languish in that awkward moment when you both know you have crossed a line.

"That was…" she begins, trailing off.

"Sorry, I'll never do that again," I say hoarsely.

"I was going to say that was great." She looks at me with disappointment. "Seriously, I know a great kiss when I get one and that was a great kiss."

"Hell, don't say things like that." I put another foot of space between us. "Don't encourage me to lead you on. I don't want to be a prick. Not to you."

She gives another one of her light-hearted laughs and covers her mouth. "You're actually sweet and funny. Don't worry about me. No one can hurt me unless I let them, and I'm not that kind of woman."

"What about Rocky, your Italian stud? You cried over him."

"I didn't cry because we broke up. I wanted the break up. I cried because the thought of having to deal with Robert again is too much for me to handle."

"Then it's good we're not going to let this go any further. I'm not worse than Rocky, but I've got a shitload of baggage that no one deserves to get stuck holding."

"His name is Robert, and I think you *are* better than him."

"I'm damaged goods, Emma."

She groans and gives an exaggerated eye roll. Her perfect eyebrows scrunch up for a second before she shakes her head then grabs my wrists, gripping them tightly to maneuver me closer to her.

"I hate when people use that corny line."

"It's true. There's no other way to describe me."

"Dylan, why do people who think they are damaged goods believe they are protecting others by shutting them out?"

"It's the way we're wired—poorly—or maybe we're just different. I can't change that."

"If we were all wired the same way, life would be very boring."

"Except, sometimes my mind is stuck in high gear. It's

59

fucked up. My brain doesn't always let me downshift to a lower gear. Sometimes, it's like a never-ending race, and I don't know where the finish line is. This may be impossible for me to explain to you."

"Well, that does sound difficult," she says softly. "But I'm no angel, either. I've certainly made my mistakes. Doesn't youth allow a certain degree of bad behavior before we grow up and evolve into full-fledged, tax-paying adults who put real tables in their formal dining rooms instead of old pool tables?" She smiles and then laughs.

Her witty quip tugs a stubborn grin out of me. It doesn't last long, though. I have to give her a dose of my reality. "I can't be involved with anyone, Emma."

"Oh, you mean it doesn't work?" she says, pointing to my groin.

"It works fine, thank you."

"Yeah, I thought so. Your special someone made an appearance when I kissed you."

"I would hope so. It's been a long time."

Why do I keep giving her personal information like that?

"So what do you want to do now?" she asks. "Watch TV? Tell me your deepest, darkest secrets? Do you want to kiss again?"

She's definitely flirting with me, and I like it.

"No to all of the above. I get up early to go running, so I need to get some sleep."

"It's barely ten o'clock. Isn't there a fun local bar we can go to?"

"I don't drink."

"Oh, come on. You're going to bed this early on a Friday night?"

"You're welcome to watch TV, but I have to sleep."

"Boy, all that exercise and pumping weights makes you a tired grump. I guess I'll read a book or visit some chat rooms with perverts. That'll be entertaining for a few hours, I suppose."

"Goodnight, Emma." As I head out of the kitchen, she's on my heels again.

"You sure don't know how to throw a sleepover. Maybe I'll go through the Mercer file. I'll call you if I need help," she says as she walks up the stairs behind me.

Fortunately, my room is the first one at the top of the staircase.

"Sleep well," I say. "When I come back from my run, I'll make breakfast."

She shakes her head and walks down to her room at the end of the hall, muttering, "Sounds like an exciting Saturday."

I close my door and do a face plant on the bed. How am I going to sleep with her down the hall? I hear her grumbling in the bathroom before singing some twangy country song. I wait until I hear her walk back down the hall to her bedroom and close the door, then I dash to the bathroom and take the coldest shower of my life.

Eight
Emma

It's ten thirty-two and I am still awake, lying in the dark. Back in Jersey, my friends and I would be out drinking and dancing on a Friday night. It is one thing to live alone and spend some quiet weeknights knitting and watching TV, however it seems pretty pathetic to go to bed this early when I have a new, hot buddy down the hall who would rather sleep than talk to me. The laws of attraction are not working in my favor.

I take my phone off the nightstand and check the time again. Ten forty. This is going to be a very long night. I might as well call Lauren and Imogene to see what they are up to and live vicariously through them.

As I scroll through the phone list for Lauren's number, I come across Dylan's name. I forgot he added his phone number to my contact list on my first day at Blackard Designs so I can reach him when we are at work because the sound of machinery drowns out the PA system.

Okay, hot stuff.

I start texting. *r u awake?*

My action hero is probably sound asleep. Building muscles and running endless miles to nowhere makes even the mightiest very tired.

The phone in my hand pings.

Go to sleep.

I can't help smiling, knowing he's having trouble sleeping, too.

I respond. *I'm bored.*

That's because you're supposed to be sleeping.

62

I laugh out loud and respond. *Sigh.*
Stop.
Still bored.

There's no response, however I hear heavy footsteps pounding down the hallway, coming my way. Dylan throws open my door and has a knee on the bed, one foot on the floor, and his hands on either side of my head before I notice he is only wearing boxer briefs. In the dark, his face is unreadable above me as I clutch my phone to my chest.

"I'm going to kiss you," he says in a raspy voice as he holds his face a couple of inches from mine.

"Okay," I whisper.

When Dylan's lips greet mine with a tender stroke, my heart begins racing from their slow assault on my mouth. His tongue darts in and out, touching my lips with soft flicks. Unlike our furious, hungry kiss in the kitchen, this one creates a burning need inside of me as his mouth tastes me, slowly at first and then deeper.

He lingers on my mouth and all I can think about is how Dylan makes kissing a work of art. Then his lips graze my cheeks and circle around my temple, down to my chin, taking his time to cover every part with sweet kisses. When the stubble on his chin strokes my cheek, shivers run down my body from my hard nipples to my center. I am going to soak my panties.

I drop the phone at my side and kiss his mouth again at the same time that I run my hands up his hard chest, feeling every punishing muscle he has created. He moans as I touch him, and our kiss deepens before coming to a lingering end.

His mouth is slightly parted while short breaths escape as he looks at me. In the moonlight, his blue eyes glow whiter with a distinct intensity. I slide my hands back down his flexed arms to his hands, covering them with my own before I clasp his wrists. He has a hungry yet indecisive look about him.

As much as I am attracted to him and beginning to like him a lot, I am just as confused as he is about what we're doing. My job and being self-supporting is important to me, and getting mixed up with Dylan may cause conflicts I have not thought through as of yet. How can I think about being practical when I have this hunk hanging over me? We're both frozen in time, deliberating what we should or can do next.

"I'm going back to my room, and you need to go to sleep," he says finally. His tone sounds regretful, and I am thankful for that. I'd hate to think this is easy for him, that I am just another prospective notch on his bedpost.

"Are you sure? You can stay here for a while; we can just talk," I whisper, wondering what I am opening myself up to.

"I can't do that." He sits on the edge of the bed with one leg on the floor, but he doesn't pull his hands away from my grasp.

"You can't talk?" I'm completely taken by his hulking physique coupled with his forlorn expression cast in the shadowed light.

"Emma, I can't talk to you while you're in that little nighty and... not want to do other things." He actually reaches across me and grabs a pillow and then rests it on his lap to cover his bulging erection.

I would laugh, yet I don't want him to leave.

"I have an idea." I jump off the bed, grab my robe off the door hook and wrap myself in the oversized, thick terrycloth that covers all exposed parts of my body in a very unflattering way. Then I grab the giant, decorative bed pillows from the floor and line them up down the center of the bed. "There," I say. "You get on that side of the bed, and I'll stay over here."

"That doesn't work for me. I know what you have on under that robe, and I've already kissed you, so a few pillows are not going to deter the temptation." His voice is deep and rather somber.

"Dylan." I almost sound like I am pleading, which is not my intention.

"Get some sleep," he says, standing up. He tosses the pillow on the other side of the bed and strides quickly out of the room.

Oh, damn. Damn him. Damn Robert. Damn everything.

Why couldn't this job come with a fat, balding, funny guy instead of Dylan? On top of my uncertain feelings for him, I have to figure out what to do about Robert. I have to call my parents and discuss this new wrinkle in our plan of me starting over somewhere new and their focus on selling their business and moving to Florida. I don't want to deal with Robert anymore, though. I want to spend more time with Dylan and figure out why he is giving me pretty butterflies in my stomach while Robert started giving me sickening goose bumps, the kind that make you realize you can't be with someone anymore.

***

I am showered and dressed, drinking coffee from the pot Dylan has left for me, when he arrives back from his run. He is wearing what looks like biker shorts and he is taking his t-shirt off as he comes through the back kitchen door. Egads. I get to watch him half-naked again. He doesn't notice that I am sitting at the little two-chair, kitchen dinette set, working on my laptop—observing him.

"Oh, hey," he says when he finally realizes I am across the room.

"Morning. Thanks for the coffee."

"We offer more than coffee at Chez Leo. I'm going to take a quick shower and then I'll make you breakfast."

He tosses his shirt over his shoulder and walks towards me. He has no choice since it's the only way out of the kitchen. It's a struggle to drag my bulging eyes back to my computer screen.

"You could run your own little bed and breakfast

65

here," I joke. "People sure would get a *lot* of sleep." I click my tongue.

He stops at my wobbly little table.

"I barely slept at all last night." His tone is firm. "Besides, I like having one guest."

I glance up at him and his mouth curves slightly before he leaves me alone with those confusing innuendos to ponder.

I'll over-think this until my head implodes. It's just as well. I still don't know how my new boss will react to this situation, and I also have to worry about Robert. Was he just stopping by to say hello and be on his way? Yes, rich, handsome lawyers always drive their luxury cars out to the dusty boondocks to give a friendly howdy to ex-girlfriends.

Dylan returns in loose fitting jeans and a long sleeve t-shirt, looking happy. Maybe he just jerked himself off in the shower. I have no idea what's come over Mr. Split Personality this morning. In the last twelve hours, he's kissed me like he wanted more, then he begged off, and now here he is all sunshiny again. Regardless, I sure love looking at him.

I am glad I put myself together this morning. Even if it did take a lot of effort to blow out my hair with the low-wattage hair dryer I found under the bathroom sink. I am assuming it is one of Lauren's old cast-offs. I wanted that salon look and my arm started to ache holding the ancient hair dryer that only blew semi-warm air. I had no choice with wardrobe since the only other outfit I brought to Dylan's house is a pair of low-rise jeans and a dressy, green t-shirt that has a ruffled, scoop neckline, showing a little bit of cleavage. I've been told the green looks nice against my dark features. I hope that's what has put Dylan in his good mood.

"What are you working on?" he asks. "Picking up more assholes and perverts online?"

You would think he'd crack a smile at his own joke.

He doesn't, though.

"No. I don't need to pick anyone up. They come to me." Oh, great, here comes my stupid banter I usually reserve for when I am drinking at a bar.

"Oh, do they now?" He raises an eyebrow and puts a hand on the back of my chair and the other on the table to lean down to see my computer.

"I'm looking at the sales revenues of a few competitors and comparing where their peaks are geographically." I try to sound very serious even though his cheek is a couple inches from mine, and he has just activated the marshmallow fluff machine churning inside of me.

"Hmm." His eyes flick from the screen and back to me, then down to my lips and back up to my eyes. The marshmallow machine is shooting fluff everywhere. He better kiss me or move the hell away. His lips part as if he's considering just that.

"Breakfast?" I end the nonsense.

He stands up. "Yeah, coming right up."

"Good, 'cause one of the appeals of this ramshackle B&B is the food."

"One? What's the other?" he asks, smiling.

"The scrumptious bed."

"Ah, yeah, okay." He smiles and starts gathering the food and pans to cook for me.

I find this to be amazing—the way he works his way around the kitchen with a natural confidence—although I suppose any big guy who benches a gazillion pounds a day looks more innocent and endearing when he is whipping up eggs and setting the table in a homey kitchen. I move my computer to the pool table in the dining room and pretend to be working very diligently.

"Come and eat," Dylan calls loudly.

I return to my seat at the kitchen table and he places an omelet in front of me with freshly chopped tomatoes, basil, and a side of toast.

"Oh, shit," he exclaims. "Do vegetarians eat eggs?"

"This one does."

"Aren't they part of the meat group on the food pyramid?"

"Most likely." I take a forkful of the cheesy omelet. "I eat eggs and dairy. I just have some type of aversion to animal flesh. My mother says it started when I was four and connected the dots between my chicken nuggets and the chicken in my toy farm set." I shrug.

"So you like it?" He watches me intently before starting on his own food.

"It's excellent," I answer with a mouthful of food.

"Good. The first two meals are on the house. After that, you owe me."

"I don't even know how to take it when you say things like that. Are you joking or are you expecting…"

"I'm joking, Emma," he says softly.

He digs into his food and polishes it off before I can even finish half of mine. Well, he did run a gazillion miles, so he should have a voracious appetite. I even like watching him eat; the way his strong jaw jerks, and the way he devotes himself thoroughly to the food without talking.

I help clear the table and Dylan washes the dishes while I dry and stack them on the counter.

"See? You can work off your rent," he says, taking my dishrag and snapping it against the counter.

"Seriously? There you go again."

"What?"

"I can work off my rent?" I am hoping he says I can pay him in kisses because I think I would be really good at that.

"I'm joking. Jesus, woman, I meant you can do dishes, not—oh, forget it."

Wrong answer, Dylan.

"Let's go get my stuff." I grab the towel from him and snap it hard against his butt.

"Hey," he grins, "you're a good shot."

"You have no idea," I mumble.

***

When we take Dylan's Jeep Wrangler to my cottage, he drives like a lunatic. Not the best description for a guy who actually did time in a mental health rehab, but there is no other apt description for his high speed turns with one hand on the wheel and the other on the gear shift. I grip the door handle and my seatbelt like someone who is about to be accidentally ejected from a fighter jet. I have no idea what that's like, however I imagine it's horrifying. I didn't experience this on Dylan's Harley—hugging him and not being able to see what's in front of me helped there. From now on, I will have to insist on driving if we make any more excursions together.

As we get closer to my rental cottage, we see an SUV parked in front. Oh, *craptastic*.

"Who's that?" Dylan asks as he slows down and parks next to the Mercedes.

"It's Robert," I answer, and then, as if on cue, Robert walks out from under the shadow of the front door awning.

"You stay here," Dylan says angrily, whipping off his aviator sunglasses and tossing them on the dashboard before jumping out of the Jeep and slamming his door.

"No, Dylan!" I jump out and catch up to him as he charges towards Robert.

"Hey, beautiful!" Robert smiles at me. He's dressed impeccably in black tailored pants and a fitted grey shirt. His dark hair is shorter but still long enough that it has that sexy, just-showered look. He's handsome and he likes to flash megawatt smiles to win people over. It generally works, yet I can see that my maniac roommate is already in berserker mode.

"You!" Dylan points a finger at Robert as he strides towards him. "What the hell are you doing here?"

Robert steps back to protect his space, but he doesn't

look too concerned.

"Dylan! Stop!" I pull his arm back.

"What's going on here?" Robert asks, putting his hands low on his waist and spreading his legs slightly apart as if he's ready to pounce into a fight position.

Watching males get defensive when all their territorial blood rushes to their cocks is rather humorous. This is when they say and do moronic things. This is also when Robert's back-up man usually steps in, yet I don't see anyone else in the vicinity. I also know that Robert is always packing. Since he's not wearing a suit coat, I assume his gun is strapped to his calf. I am not going to tell Dylan this, though; it will only inflame the situation. Besides, Robert carries the gun, but he doesn't use it. He is not a trigger-happy guy. He may throw a punch, however he doesn't pull his gun on people. It's not his nature. His gun is purely for protection. At least, that's what I used to tell myself while we dated.

Dylan steps right up to Robert's face. He's got a good three inches on Robert and a lot more muscle than Robert's lean form.

"You broke into her house yesterday. Why the fuck are you here?" Dylan's anger makes Robert step back a little bit, though not enough to show weakness or fear.

"Emma and I are old friends. Who are you?" Robert keeps his tone very measured as he glares at Dylan.

"I'm her new friend, and I don't like that you're breaking and entering."

"Dylan, let me talk to him," I say, trying to come between them. I actually have to push against Dylan's chest with both hands to get him to move back.

"Robert, why are you here?" I hold my palm up behind me as if that will keep Dylan at bay.

"Emma, it's been a long time. I missed you and wanted to see how you're doing." He rakes a hand through his hair and eyes Dylan.

"She was doing fine until she found out you broke into her home," Dylan snaps.

"That was a little unsettling, Robert. Why didn't you call me like normal people do?" I inquire.

Robert smiles. "I thought I'd surprise you. You don't exactly have a real lock on your door. I used a credit card and jiggled it to open it. Baby, anyone could break in."

I hate that he's calling me baby in front of Dylan.

"And I noticed your old number doesn't work."

Right. I got a new phone for my new life, and Robert is not supposed to be part of this equation, but seeing him brings back a flood of conflicting emotions; the agitation that comes with his circumstances and our recent history as well as the dying spark from our old history. I am done with Robert and acknowledging that makes me sad to think of how our story played out from beginning to end.

"I've heard enough." Dylan moves in front of me to confront Robert. "You need to leave now."

Robert steps forward, too, and I can see that they are about to do the Neanderthal fight dance. "Look, I don't know who you are, but I'm here to see Emma."

"No, not now, Robert. This is a bad time. Dylan and I are moving my stuff out of here today. I don't have time to talk to you and rehash whatever it is that's brought you out here."

Robert's dark eyes take me in, and I hear Dylan's breathing escalate above me.

"All right. I understand. How about we meet for lunch or dinner later this week? I'll swing by your new office and pick you up. We can have dinner up at that Mohonk resort?"

"Are you fucking kidding me?" Dylan says. "I don't think she wants you here at all."

"Emma?" Robert's voice is crisp, a tone I recognize as one he uses when he's keeping his anger in check.

"Robert, I'll call you. Maybe next week after I get

71

settled into my job and my new home."

Dylan puts his arm around my shoulders. "You need to leave now."

Oh, boy. This won't help. This is the kind of behavior that makes Robert more determined to win. I know Dylan is trying to help me—I adore him for that—but this is how you turn Robert into your competitor and ensure that he'll definitely be back.

Robert scoffs. "Fine. Emma, I'll be in touch soon." He studies me for a second and then grins.

Please don't give me a goodbye kiss on the cheek, Robert. That is standard operation for him, and I don't want him to do that in front of Dylan. Thankfully, instead, Robert walks by me and heads back to his SUV.

I turn to watch him go, and just when I breathe a sigh of relief, he turns around and says, "Emma, you really do look gorgeous. I'm looking forward to catching up. But let's leave your guard dog at home."

Before Dylan can think of charging at the three-ton Mercedes, I block him so he rams into my back and I grip his groin and apply a lot of pressure.

"What are you doing?" he grits through his teeth.

"Preventing you from doing something you'll regret."

"Jesus Christ, woman, you're giving me a major boner," he says with a slight groan.

"That's the point. With all the blood rushing to Mr. Boner, you won't have the energy and desire to stop a moving vehicle with your bare fists."

As Robert drives off, I release my hand from Dylan's crotch. "There, that's done. It worked out fine. Let's go pack."

I turn around and Dylan is partially bowled over, both aroused and angry. "I don't think I can walk," he spits out. "What are you doing to me?"

"I'm sorry. It's the only way I could think of stopping you from doing something stupid."

"Stupid? You just made a date with that jerk. Why?"

"I didn't make a date with him. I said whatever I had to say to appease him so he'd leave."

"He's going to come back, and when he does, I'm not letting him on the property. And if you had any idea who I really am, you'd know I'm trying real hard to be the pacifist here. But if he shows up at work, I'm going to beat the shit out of him."

Nine

Dylan

I am so fucking pissed that she agreed to see that guy again that I throw her belongings into moving boxes she's had stored in her closet. I grab a bag of yarn and fling it in with the other stuff, causing knitting needles to fly across the room.

"Dylan! Be careful! That's a blanket I'm working on. You just lost my needles," she huffs, running across the room to retrieve them. "What's wrong? I got rid of Robert, didn't I?"

"You made a date with him." I want to put my fist through the cheap drywall to get some satisfaction from hitting the shit out of something at this moment.

"Stop calling it a date. I'm going to meet him for lunch and resolve whatever he thinks needs to be said."

I drop the moving box and rest my forehead and palms against the wall.

"What's going on?" She stands behind me and puts her hand firmly on my back.

"I'm counting backwards from one hundred with very deep breaths so I can stop the urge to smash my fist through this wall," I reply angrily.

"Does that work?" Her voice is an octave higher as if she's afraid I'll do it.

"We'll see." I don't want her to fear me, to worry that I am a loose cannon. I am supposed to have this under control and know how to deal with these situations when they arise.

"Dylan, it's not a date, and I wouldn't put myself in a

dangerous situation."

I take my last deep breath and turn around to face her. "When you do meet him, I'm going to be there. You're not going without me. That's the only way I'll know that you're safe."

Emma doesn't say anything as she scrutinizes my demeanor. I'm not certain what she's thinking, but I do know that seeing her ex has made me realize I am most definitely dragging her into my life. It's not because I am ill, either; it's because I like her. I want to be around her.

I can't get her knitting crap, books, and Magic 8 ball packed quickly enough. I need her out of here and back at my house. This is exactly how I felt the night before, having her on the back of my bike heading to my home. I knew it then; that I was going to get in deep with her. Even when I was bitching to Carson, I was already gone after almost a week of being lost in her high-pitched laughter with the other people at work, her doe-like eyes, and her razor sharp wit when she gets annoyed with me. From the minute Daisy introduced us, Emma has come at me hard, whether she realizes it or not, and I have thought of no one or anything else since I've met her.

"You're not supposed to go out with old boyfriends. When a relationship is done, you move on," I say.

"Really? Haven't you ever gone out with an ex-girlfriend to catch up and see how things are going?"

I am about to say no. I didn't have steady girlfriends in high school or college; I had a notorious reputation as a screw-around-guy that I didn't mind at the time, yet then there was Jessica. Shit. How could I forget that detail? After Jess broke up with me, and before she was officially dating my brother, Jess and I would regularly meet for lunch to talk like real friends. Then I went off to my boot camp therapy, and Jess and Carson got engaged while I was gone. It's not like I can ignore Jess or stay away, she's my sister-in-law, and we actually are friends. However, I don't see this Robert creep being a friend to Emma. I am no saint, but that guy is something much worse.

"I don't make dates or lunch plans with women I used to go out with." It's out before I can think of how I will backtrack over that lie when it's exposed. These are the kinds of secrets you can't keep under lock and key in Hera, and we are talking about my brother's wife. I am so fucked on this one. I don't see how this can play out well for me unless Lauren has already told her every detail.

"Well, I agree. It's best to move on, but I'm not going to get rid of Robert by trying to avoid him. A talk won't hurt."

"I don't see how it's going to help, either. I'm guessing Mr. Gigolo doesn't take no for an answer."

The sound of her giggle softens me a bit. "Told ya he was handsome, not a goomba."

"A good-looking dickwad," I mumble and Emma laughs again.

When the Jeep is loaded with the few belongings she's brought to Hera, she holds out her palm to me.

"I need to drive. I can't take your kamikaze action," she says.

I chuckle and hand over my keys. "This should be interesting. I've already had to bail you out of two driving situations."

"Yeah, whatever. Buckle up," she retorts as she struggles to adjust the seat so she can reach the pedals.

"Mind if I help?" I ask, smiling. I am ready to be the calm, cool guy now, not the tornado of raging jealousy.

She sits back and lets me adjust the seat, sliding her forward until she can see over the steering wheel.

"Are you going to be okay there?" I laugh. This is an old Jeep and the seats are practically concave. "You look really tiny in the driver's seat. You know, I can run back inside the cottage and grab that fat dictionary for you to sit on. Can you even drive a standard shift?"

She glares as me before putting her sunglasses on. "My family is in the auto business. I used to move the cars from the garage to the lot all day long. I can drive anything."

Three minutes into our drive back to my house, and I can't hide my laughter.

"What?" she snaps.

"You drive like a granny. Kids on bicycles are passing us." I grin as she looks at me defiantly.

"Well, good, 'cause my grandmother is an excellent driver. She's never had an accident. At least I don't go plowing off bridges." She glances my way.

"Bingo. You got me there." I smile.

So Lauren did tell her the details about my terrific dive off the old, wooden bridge near Carson's house last fall. Everyone has assumed I was scarred or devastated after seeing Jess leave Carson's house. That wasn't the case, though. I was in some kind of mental fog and took a turn too hard and too fast. Poor Jess thought I was suicidal because of our break up. I had to confess to her later that I wasn't broken-hearted over her, and that crashing the company delivery truck was nothing more than an accident. She was relieved.

"I shouldn't have said that," Emma says. "I'm sorry." She glances over at me to see my reaction, but I can't help smiling.

"Don't be sorry. It was a good comeback, and I was the idiot that drove that truck off the bridge. It's kind of nice to drive at this granny pace."

"Shut it." She smiles.

I'd like to keep making her smile.

When we get back to my place, Leo is putting a laundry basket of clothes in his truck, and Carson's truck is there, too. As he comes out of the house carrying Leo's computer, I guess my cover as a friendly roommate is about to be blown. Carson puts Leo's computer in the truck and then walks up to my Jeep as Emma rolls into the slowest stop ever.

"I don't think that drive has ever taken longer," I say, climbing out of the vehicle.

Emma hops down. "Slow and safe. That is Grandma's motto."

"Hey," Carson says. "Hi, Emma. So what's going on?"

He eyes me taking a box of girly things, knitting supplies, and a hairdryer out of the back end of the Jeep.

"Hi, Emma!" Leo walks over and joins us. "Dylan told me you moved into the guest room. That's great. You shouldn't be alone down in those cottages."

Carson's eyes grow wide as he looks at me.

"I gotta go, guys," Leo rambles on as if I just brought home a stray cat and not a woman to live in our house. "Jess is setting up my computer and Imogene is cooking. Life is good over at that house."

Leo hops into his truck with the smile of man who knows he's lucky. As he drives off, Carson turns back to me. Emma stands on the other side of the Jeep, unusually quiet for her.

"So, you're moving in here, Emma?" Carson questions. I am guessing he's being very careful with his tone. He still feels like he needs to watch over me in case I combust.

"She can't stay in the cottage. Her ex showed up unannounced and broke in," I begin to explain.

"Carson, I know this looks bad," Emma interjects, rounding the Jeep to face Carson head on with that spunky conviction of hers. "Dylan is my work colleague and you're my boss and this looks unprofessional, but I want you to know, I have a personal situation that I will not let interfere with my job. But the cottage is a problem, and Dylan came up with the only affordable solution for now."

Humored and intrigued, Carson raises his eyebrows at me. I feel a little downgraded at being referred to as her "work colleague," especially after dealing with the gigolo.

"If you're fine with staying here, it's none of my

business. What two consenting adults do outside of the office isn't my concern." Carson is trying awfully hard to sound open-minded, though his jugular looks close to rupturing. "You know, you could always stay at my wife's old house. It's a huge Victorian, and Jess rents it quite cheaply to Lauren and Imogene. I bet they'd like having you, and there are plenty of bedrooms and more amenities than this place."

"No, it's too crowded there. With the guys there all the time, they've got four people in that house already," I say, knowing I am making Carson more suspicious.

"I don't mind staying here," Emma says. "I've discovered that Dylan has absolutely no social life and goes to bed before the cows, so it's very quiet. I can even get some work done here."

Carson isn't falling for this bull. He laughs and slaps me on the back with extra force. "So you're that boring?"

"Are you sure you're okay with this, Carson?" Emma asks.

"Yeah, it's fine." He shakes his head in disbelief. "And before I forget, Jess and I are having a dinner party soon and you're both invited. I'll give you the details when Jess comes up with the spreadsheet on how she's going to pull this off." I can envision his neurotic wife organizing a social event using her computational and programming skills.

"A dinner party?" Emma's face lights up.

She has no idea that it will be a dinner party of townie gossip with all eyes on us. Emma may hate this part of small town life.

"It's casual. Jeans. Nothing special. Lauren and our usual suspects will be there," Carson says and then gives me a little sigh.

"That sounds fun. I can't wait." Emma looks very girlish with her enthusiasm over a simple dinner invitation as she grabs the box from my hands. "I'm going to take this in and start unpacking. See you Monday morning, Carson."

Carson gives a single wave to her and then swings his hand down to rest at the base of my neck. He is two inches taller than me, and even though I have caught up in the muscle department with him, he still packs a powerful grip.

"Brother, what's going on?"

"It's true." My words are bitter as I replay the image of Robert's arrogant expression. "She had a flat tire last night, so I gave her a ride home, and we found her place had been broken into by her ex-boyfriend. Some guy... well, I'm betting you already know about him."

"Yeah, I know everything. I did a background check on Emma, like I do with every employee. She's clean. Lauren told me about her family's issues and the ex-boyfriend, and I actually spoke to Emma's father. He doesn't think she's in danger, but he wants her away from the guy. The Marchetto family is another story, but I'm not going to hold that against Emma."

"Why would you hire her if you knew all this shit would follow her?"

"Because Lauren is like a sister to us, and she wanted to help her friend get a good job. And I can't forget what Lauren's family did for you and me. Can you?"

"No," I respond, remembering the time after our parents' deaths when Lauren's parents regularly brought us groceries and paid utility bills so we could keep living in the trailer we ended up in after my mother's medical expenses caused my father to lose our house. Carson was a teenager then and taking care of me, making sure we went to school and were fed and sheltered.

"I know you, Carson, you worry about everyone and everything. Why would you take a chance on bringing these characters to town? I don't mean Emma. I mean the guys she's associated with."

"I've done my homework. Even Robert Marchetto, the ex-boyfriend, is pretty tame. He's only guilty by association from what I can see. Believe me, I had to think about this before hiring Emma. When Lauren told me about Emma's situation, I made a lot of phone calls before I would even interview her. If I thought there was any risk to our family, our friends, or our employees, I wouldn't have hired her. Besides, we have..."

Carson's voice trails off and he shakes his head.

"We have what?"

"Nothing. It's nothing," Carson says, looking away. He's not telling me something.

"You always like taking care of people." I fake punch his shoulder.

"Me? You're the one who brought her to your house."

"Well, this piece of shit, Robert, showed up again. Not only did he break in last night before she got home, he then had the nerve to be there when we showed up today. Emma seems to think she can talk to him and he'll be on his way, and she said he's never been violent with her."

"What's your take?" Carson's voice is thoughtful and guarded, and I know he trusts my opinion most of the time.

"I don't like it."

"You don't like it because you like Emma, or you don't like it because you think the guy is up to something?"

I look off at the house and imagine Emma finding the perfect place for all of her things.

"I know you, too, Dylan. Yesterday you were reaming me about hiring her, unconvincingly I might add. Today you're playing knight in shining armor and moving her in with you under the guise of protecting her. Don't think I haven't seen how you look at her."

"It's not like that. I was just trying to help her and then this happened. I couldn't leave her there."

"I'm not saying it's wrong. It's okay if you like her, but please be careful. Don't rush into anything. Oh, fuck, what am I saying? You have her living in your house." As Carson laughs nervously, I'm honestly surprised he isn't

81

yelling at me. "Is the feeling mutual on her part or doesn't she know how you feel?"

"I don't even know how I feel about this. I'm a little worried about... regressing."

"You've been better this week, well, except for yesterday's drama. I'm guessing it has to do with her. Are you two going to be able to work together or will it be awkward?"

"I'm fine," I mutter, tired of being reminded of my past issues.

"Yeah, you are fine," Carson replies, putting his hand on my shoulder. "I think you're doing great. Maybe this is one of those subjects you can bring up with your shrink. But just so you know, I have complete faith in you. I think you're on the right track, and whatever there is between you and Emma, you two are adults."

"Ah, man. Tell me I'm not fucking up."

"So far, you're not. Do you think we're going to have a problem with her ex?" Carson is a serious guy, it's only since he's married Jessica that we've seen the content, cheerful side of him. If he has any concerns about Emma's ex, Carson will circle the wagons around Hera and protect everyone in the five-mile radius of our little pit stop.

"That's what I'm going to find out. I'll be watching out for this guy like a hawk. We all will." Carson scowls briefly before he sighs again.

"We? Who else knows about him?"

"I mean her friends... and me. She's in good hands."

"Hey, what about a background check on Cooper? That guy annoys the shit out of me."

Carson laughs. "Cooper is as clean as they come. Trust me. I like him. He was looking for a new career move, and he's a hard worker, so stop complaining. Don't you think he's kind of funny?"

"No, he makes me want to punch him."

"Ha! You're just jealous because he flirts with all the

women and makes everyone laugh. Lighten up, man. When you and Emma drove up, I saw you smiling. I haven't seen you do that in a very long time. It's good to see you smile. We'll help Emma, don't worry, and I'm sure you'll stop Cooper from flirting with her."

I'm not worried, Carson. And this time, I'm the one who will be helping Emma.

Ten

Emma

"Dad, I'm fine," I say into the cheap, prepaid phone.

I am lounging on the couch, and Dylan is leaning against the hallway wall watching me with his arms crossed, bunching up his thick muscles. He resembles a hit man at this moment. Again, a very sexy one in my opinion.

"No, Robert didn't bring anyone," I tell my dad, looking up at Dylan who is scowling.

"There was no funny business, Dad." I want to laugh at my father's old-fashioned term.

I listen to my father go on about updates on the business, prospective buyers, and my mother's condo hunting trip in Florida with my grandmother as I feel Dylan's unwavering gaze on me.

His friend fixed my car up with a new tire and then Dylan and Leo picked it up. When Dylan drove up to the house in my car with the new tire, and the spare in place as well as a nice little detail job, my stomach did a little flip. It's a little act of kindness, yet coupled with his brawny protectiveness, I am beyond comforted.

When I finish the call, I try to lighten the tense mood a bit. "That went well. My dad has someone interested in buying his company, and—"

"Why are you using that phone?" Dylan asks. "That's not your cell phone, at least not the one you usually use."

"This is a prepaid phone. My dad gave me a bunch to use when he and I need to talk." My family isn't something out of the *Sopranos* as Dylan seems to think, but we are far from being a *Leave It To Beaver* type of family. "It's his

84

idea of a safety precaution. No biggie."

"Oh, God, woman. Do you hear yourself? How can your father not be worried about your sleazy ex showing up?"

"Because I'm living with you. You've got my back, right?"

"Funny, you never mentioned me to your dad. I heard the whole conversation, and you never said a word about where you live."

"I'm trying to spare him a second heart attack, okay? One was enough. He doesn't know you. He thinks I'm staying with Lauren."

"And you staying with a skinny cheerleader will give him better peace of mind than me?" Dylan shakes his head and walks slowly over to the couch.

"It will all work out," I reply, hoping I'm convincing. I am beginning to worry about Robert's intentions; either because Dylan is right that I am delusional about continuing to engage in contact with someone like Robert, or because there is something different about Robert that I can't pinpoint.

"So you have a stash of these disposable phones to talk to your family, and you have a sleazoid determined to see you. There's a whole lot of information you're not telling me, Emma."

"It's part of my old life. Like you, I'm starting fresh."

He sits down next to me and leans his forearms on his knees. "Were you involved in anything illicit yourself? Something you're running from?" His tone is one of concern rather than anger.

"No," I snap. "I told you. My family has been victimized; not in a violent way, but we've had to pay a small fortune into the crazy-ass system that the law doesn't do anything about. They either look the other way, bust the small-time scavengers at the bottom, or they're on the take, too. My family has done what it has to in order to survive, to keep our business afloat, to keep over a thousand people employed, and we don't have blood on our hands, if that's what you're implying."

"I never thought your family did; I just had to ask. Carson told me he already knew about your situation when he hired you. He got enough info from Lauren and your dad. It's good he knows, too. Carson is someone you want to have on your side." Dylan clasps his hands then pauses, though I know there is more to his speech.

"Have I shocked you?" I ask softly. "Do you think less of me coming from this scummy life?"

"No, of course not. It sounds like you have a decent family, and that they happened to get strong-armed by the wrong people. I can't blame you for that."

"You blame Robert. He's only three years older than me, and he didn't have a choice in the matter, either. We both grew up with this as a part of our lives—it chose us."

"Why are you apologizing for that guy? He's an adult. If he's involved in his family's dirty dealings—"

"He isn't. That's why Robert went to law school. His parents are rich and they put all their kids in very good colleges and pushed education. I started dating Robert when I was on summer break from college. He was in law school at the time, and he talked about what kind of law he wanted to practice and his future didn't involve *the family.* I do believe he came here to see me as a friend. I was one of the few people—aside from his college friends—that were part of the real world. Unlike his classmates, though, I knew what Robert had to deal with growing up. I think I'm one of his few connections to normalcy."

"He's certainly snowed you, baby."

I like the endearment coming from Dylan, however I could do without the patronizing remark.

"If he's legit and practicing law—how ironic by the way—then he can find normalcy someplace else, like with his interns or clients. I don't give a shit how he pulls his life together except when he thinks it's okay to come back into your life," Dylan says, leaning back. He rests his arm across the back of the couch, barely touching my shoulders.

"I think he's trying to do the right thing," I add.

Dylan chuckles in disbelief. "Oh, man, you come from a colorful place, that's for sure."

"I guess my life sounds awfully nutty to people who grew up with typical families. Lauren never trusted Robert and was never friendly with him the whole time I dated him in college. She constantly tried to fix me up with nice guys at school. It's hard for her to accept where I come from. She has such a nice, normal family. My family and I are trying really hard to detach ourselves completely from that life, Dylan."

I inch closer to him, so we're touching from my shoulder all the way down to our knees, then curl ever so slightly into him. He responds by lifting a thick lock of my hair and wrapping it around his hand. His gaze drifts from my hair to my eyes with a fascination that makes my heart do a little dance. Not any old dance—these are not feather light twirling ballerinas—I have heavy-duty, clog dancers pounding out their approval.

"I just got out of Crazyville, and I don't want to go back there, but I will do anything to help you, Emma."

I've had sweet promises from boyfriends before—including Robert—but none of them have ever seemed as authentic as Dylan's funny yet touching declaration.

"Why would you put this kind of trouble on yourself? You barely know me, and I'm not a defenseless ninny." I smile because I don't know if I am making his intentions out to be more serious than they are.

"I like you a lot," he says emphatically with an expression of complete seriousness. There is no beating around the bush about feelings and shielding himself from my strange past.

I can't resist. I slowly trace the loopy scar on the soft

fuzz of his scalp and run my finger down the razor stubble on his cheek. "I like you, too. But I thought you were against this going any farther. Does it stop here because you think I'll drive you back to Crazyville?"

"I'm re-thinking this as we go along," he replies with a grin.

He leans in to kiss me gently, his beautiful lips urging mine open, making me visibly weaken. My breath quickens and I feel a sense of urgency as a heat rises in me and pleads with me to get naked with Dylan. All sorts of images of his nakedness, those muscular arms and six-pack abs— or are they called eight-packs now? Who cares? All I know is that I want to be with him and not just groping on the couch, making out.

Dylan lowers me onto my back and our kissing amplifies, with tongues discovering new body parts as if I have never done this before. I spread my legs and he rolls himself between them, propping his weight on his elbows as he works over my neck and sensitive spots with his mouth. When I moan and yank his t-shirt up, he helps pull it over his head and flings it across the room. Then, after I arch and pull my shirt off, Dylan stares eagerly at my lace bra.

My hands rove across his chest and up to his neck before I pull him back down to me. We have finally gone over that safe point of exploration, and there is a hungry brutality to his kiss, which I return fully. I wrap my legs around him and arch up so I can feel his hard-on through his jeans, rubbing my center. I moan as he pulls down one cup of my bra and works his tongue over the hard nipple.

The couch is not wide enough to hold our rocking bodies, but I am not about to let this stop so we can move to a bed. I want his pants off, so I work my hand underneath his jeans and cup his erection through his briefs.

As I imagine his next moves and the highly anticipated, sweet, explosive orgasm I so desperately want with Dylan, my phone rings.

The Dad phone.

Dylan groans.

"No," he growls in retaliation. "Goddammit. Can't you let it ring?"

"No, then my father would worry and he'd keep calling until I answered."

As I reach for the phone on the floor, Dylan rolls off me and stands up to adjust himself.

"Fuck," he mumbles.

"Dad?" I answer as I watch Dylan walk into the kitchen. Seconds later, I hear the fridge door open and close, and then Dylan walks back into the living room holding a cold can of seltzer to his groin.

"The car again? The car is fine. It was taken care of... Dylan's friend has a shop, and he replaced the tire and gave it a tune up... Dylan is Carson's brother. I work with him... I know, I know... Okay. Bye."

"Yeah, Dad," Dylan mimics. "Dylan is Carson's brother and I'm giving him some mighty big blue balls every half hour or so. Soon, he'll be dead. Bye!"

I start giggling as he waddles over to me.

"You think it's funny?" He grins devilishly. "Try this on for size." Before I can move, he straddles me, pulls down my bra and places the cold can directly on my breast.

"Ah!" I try to jump up, but he has me pinned. He tosses the can on the couch, and cups my face with both hands and then gives me a gentle, loving kiss.

He stands up again, and I adjust my bra and hold my shirt over my chest as if I am suddenly bashful.

"I like you, Emma. It's good your dad interrupted us. We're like horny teenagers screwing around on the couch. I don't want to rush into anything with you. Seriously, I've been there and done that. I think we need to take this slow. It's going to be really difficult to manage that with you living under the same roof, though."

"If this is too much for you, I'm sure Lauren will let me rent a room in their house. Jess's house. Whatever." I sound a little defensive.

"No. You're staying here," Dylan responds and holds out a hand to me. After I slip on my shirt and take his hand, he pulls me swiftly into an embrace. "Your hairdryer is already here, you might as well stay."

I give him a playful slap on his chest and one of those big, Dylan-cutting-loose laughs makes an appearance, making me feel good all over.

"What are you afraid of, Dylan?" I ask in all seriousness, considering we have an obvious chemistry, and I am ready for more with him.

"You."

Eleven
Dylan

Brian—my closest friend at Willow Haven—sits on the weight machine next to me. For five weeks we have gone to every group session together, we work out in the gym every day and take runs through the snowy woods several times a week. Anything to ward off the reapers as Brian calls our various mental issues.

Brian is twenty-nine and his life has been pretty fucked up until this point. From what he's told me about his drug addiction since the age of thirteen, and his alcoholism on top of his sixteen-year battle with depression—including an attempted suicide at twenty-one—it's a wonder he is alive.

"You've got to lift more than that, bro, if you want to improve your numbers," Brian says, watching me bench press.

"I don't want to get bigger than you and make you jealous."

"Ah, I'm already jealous of you." He smirks.

Brian is so easy-going and nice to everyone, the kind of guy you expect to be eternally content.

"How so?" I am waiting for the punch line.

"Dylan, you haven't figured it out yet, have you?"

"What do you mean?" I sit up on the bench and wrap the towel around my neck.

Brian stops doing his ab crunches.

"You're not bad off, kid. You're going to do just fine when we leave here."

"You can tell that by the way I bench?" I laugh.

Brian is a husky guy. Not tall, but thick with muscles.

He rubs his towel down his sweaty face. Even on meds and with regular exercise, sometimes he looks panicked. Since he has been somewhat of a mentor to me in this place, it drums up some fairly severe insecurities when I see him like that.

"You'll stay strong, and you'll beat the reapers. I know you will. You're not as fucked up as me."

"You're doing just as well as me, so we'll both leave here and the reapers won't follow us. Okay?" It's not very convincing coming from me. I look up to Brian as a big brother, a temporary replacement for Carson while I am in rehab.

"I've done this before, and the statistics are not in my favor."

"So be the outlier and don't be a number," I retort, a little angry. I can't handle people in group falling apart. I definitely can't handle Brian telling me he is going to slip up.

"I have so many fucking regrets," he says, shaking his head.

"The drinking and drugs are in the past. You never have to do that again".

"No, I'm talking about getting married and having a kid."

"Bullshit. You love your wife. I hear you talking to her every day. And your son, too. He loves when you video chat with him. You look like a pretty happy family to me."

"I do love them. That's why I wish I'd never had a family. Katy is the best thing that ever happened to me. She's also the worst thing because I worry about my responsibility to her. Then she gave me a beautiful son. The worst thing you can do to a family is put this kind of burden on them. I've never conquered my depression, and Katy has had to live with this hell since we were nineteen. I don't see how it will change. I've been on every fucking med, and for the past ten years, I've talked to shrinks until there's

92

nothing left to say. They stare at me and then write me a script. Is that all there is? Prescriptions and talking? Do we ever conquer this? Because I feel like I'm that brainless, caged mouse running in circles on a wheel."

"Maybe we don't conquer all of it, but we manage it and get rid of the worst parts. We have to. You have to. Your wife and kid want you home, not here hanging out with me."

"Yeah. I know."

"So, you'll conquer and manage. We have no choice," I say, deciding I have to change his attitude.

"But do we ever get our freedom from this hell?"

I need Brian to be my cheerleader, not my patient, and he is freaking me out. I need him to be the proof that I can battle this disease and eventually have a normal family life.

***

"You're living with her and you're trying to keep it platonic?" Dr. Wang pauses his typing and squints at me.

"Am I screwing up?" I ask. "I really like Emma, but I don't want this to go to crap. I don't want to do what I did to Jess… I don't want to get in deep and then find out I'm on another bender."

Dr. Wang smiles at my term for going manic. "I've been seeing you for months and you're doing well. There's nothing wrong with being attracted to Emma and dating her, if that's what you're suggesting, although living and working together so soon may be a challenge. However, if it's comfortable for both of you, it doesn't mean you're doing anything wrong. Although, you seemed to have rushed right in to living with her, the circumstances are unique. Dylan, no one—not even your brother—expects you to never have a relationship with a woman again. This choice of celibacy was yours. Did you plan on living like that forever?"

"I'm not sure. I suppose I thought I could pull it off and keep it together."

"Do you really think it's realistic?" Dr. Wang leans back in his chair and looks at me. "You're young, you're healthy, and for the most part, you've got your depression under control. You sound indecisive about it. Tell me about that."

"I'm indecisive about what to do with her. I don't know what I'm allowed to do." I get nervous just talking about Emma and my hands start fidgeting on the armrests.

"Allowed? You keep referring to these rules you think someone has established for you. Tell me more about what you're feeling with Emma."

"I like her a lot."

"You've said that at least six times since you walked in the door." He smiles. "From my perspective, I can see you're different. You're happier. Is that all because of Emma?"

"Yeah. When I'm around her, I think I actually feel my blood pumping, and I start feeling optimistic. It's like every part of me has finally been woken up from a coma. It's very vivid and that's what's scary."

"So you're in love?" Dr. Wang asks thoughtfully.

"No, I like her a lot, though." I have to downplay my feelings for her. If I say that I think I'm falling in love with her, I really will sound like a nut job.

"That's seven *likes*." He smiles again. "Okay, I see where this is going. I'm going to ask you two questions, and I want you to give me the first thing that comes to your mind. A quick response without deliberating. Understand?"

I nod and think of Emma back at the office, probably wondering why I have been keeping my hands off her for the last two days since our hot and heavy, near-sex episode on the couch. We drive to work together and spend our days dealing with accounts, and then when we go home, I cook dinner and we watch TV while she knits. We're like an old married couple that never has had sex, not even the consummation part. That's my fault, of course. She is not shy about what she wants, and I would want it, too, if I knew that my crazy head couldn't possibly put us on the road to ruin.

"Go ahead," I say.

"Why do you like Emma?"

"She makes me feel fantastic." I sound remorseful rather than thrilled.

"Why are you afraid of being with Emma?"

"Because she makes me feel fantastic... and I might turn into the old Dylan again. I might lose all this self-control I've been managing for months."

"Okay, this is what I want you to hear. *Fact*, you like her a lot and she makes you feel fantastic. You worrying about losing control and turning into the old Dylan are *speculation* and *fear*, not fact. We have to work with facts. If you keep letting your fear dictate how you live, you will miss some very big things in life."

His words provide some relief. It's like my shrink is handing me a golden ticket.

***

When I return to work, Emma is at her desk, giggling at Cooper's voice speaking over the PA system, projecting throughout every room in the company.

"Gemma and Emma, we're waiting for you two lovely ladies to join us for lunch." Cooper's flirting comes across loud and clear on the speaker system. We can hear Daisy's voice in the background, attempting to wrestle the microphone away from him. He's got a confident laugh. "Come on, girls; we're all out front waiting for you. Again, Emma and Gemma. Gemma and Emma, we need you two awesome chicks to join us."

"Knock it off." We hear Carson's voice and then a loud whack on the microphone. Carson must have taken the mic and given Cooper a good thump on the head with it.

"Good, someone shut him up," I say.

Emma laughs.

"You don't fall for that guy's schmoozing, do you?"

"He's nice." She smiles. She's wearing her long hair down in that sexy, loose way I like, and her skirt shows off her bare legs. Again. I tried not to stare on the way to work when we drove in together in her little car because she says I drive my Jeep like a madman. She doesn't censor herself around me when it comes to using every version of "crazy," which is fine by me. She's beautiful, and I definitely don't like Cooper's flirting, no matter how innocent it may be—she lives with me, she's *with me*.

"Where are you going?" I ask, watching her stand and gather her purse and sweater.

"To lunch. Duh. I'm going to get Gemma because I'm sure she didn't hear the siren call back in the factory."

"You're going to lunch with Cooper?" *Way to not sound jealous, buddy.*

"Remember, you're the one that wants to take it *slowwwww*. So, slowpoke, I'm going to lunch with Cooper and the rest of the staff. Everyone thinks we're just office mates who happen to rent rooms in the same house. This is what you wanted, Dylan."

"Not really." Knowing no one is around, I take two steps and engulf her in my arms. When she gasps and drops her purse, it hits the floor with a loud thud. "If you think I'm ignoring you, I'm not. If you think I don't want to touch you, it's not by choice. It's complicated."

"Shut up and kiss me," she says as she wraps her hands around my neck.

I kiss her, ravaging her mouth like I have been caged and starved for three days. She's soft but forceful, and I am immediately hard. My hands roam her back down to her ass, and all I can think of doing is yanking up her skirt and plowing my dick into her. Every crude image of fucking her on the desk or the floor comes to mind.

I will not be that guy, though. I will not fuck her like we are teenagers doing it for the first time in the back of a

96

car. I will not be the old Dylan that could meet a woman at a bar, and within a half hour, have her spread against a back alley wall while I impale her with my eager appendage.

Our kiss ends slowly as I take one last tug at her lower lip.

"You're always nicer when you kiss," she muses.

"That's because I like kissing you, and it stops you from saying anything irritating." I think of my golden ticket from Dr. Wang.

"Me, irritating?" she scoffs, and I reluctantly let her go so she can smooth out her skirt and top.

"You drive me crazy with your secretive family connections and those legs. Jesus, why can't you wear jeans like everyone else around here? But, yeah, I like you, and it's a little annoying when I see Cooper coming on to you."

"My family's so-called secrets are a giant ball of grungy wax you don't want to get involved with, and Cooper has never hit on me. You're imagining things. Besides, you can't complain about secrets when you haven't exactly divulged much about yourself. In fact, you never even told me where you went this morning."

"I was at the doctor." I have never talked to anyone about my visits with Dr. Wang except Carson.

"Are you sick?" Emma asks, her playful sarcasm turns to concern as she touches my forehead.

"No, not that kind of doctor. I saw my shrink."

Well, that embarrassing cat is out of the bag. She already knows about my screwed up bipolar past, however talking about seeing a shrink on a regular basis is pretty emasculating for me. I like being the strong guy who can do heavy work with my hands, and seeing Dr. Wang and talking about my feelings doesn't really fit that image.

"Oh," she says, sounding intrigued. "How did it go?"

"Good."

Shit, I don't want her to look at me as some weak, little

boy now, but I had to tell her. What I want from her—or hope to have—has to start out on the right foot. She has to know about my doctor and what I am dealing with at some point, though there is a fine line between revealing something important about yourself and saddling someone with your daily struggles; the shit you want to hide from everyone.

"May I ask what you talked about? I know it's personal, but… did you mention me?" Her smile is adorable and sexy, and my brain screams, *You've got a winner; don't screw this up.*

"Yeah," I mumble sheepishly. "I mentioned you."

Her big brown eyes pin me down with their delight and wonder. *You're a goner*, I tell myself.

"I can tell you more about him if you want, but there's really nothing interesting to tell. We just talk." I cast my eyes down, worried I am saying too much by unlocking the boogeyman.

"I think it's good," she responds, trying to catch my wandering gaze. "Really."

"How about I make dinner tonight and we can talk then if you want?"

Her sharp laugh startles me. "Oh, Dylan, you make dinner for me every night. We're not going to have more of those lousy TV-watching nights while I knit the never-ending blanket, are we?"

"No. I can't take any more of that, either. Come on, I'll take you to lunch and keep that pesky Cooper away from you."

"Good, because if you hadn't just kissed me, I was ready to invite Cooper up for a quickie at the Red Roof Inn."

"Don't even joke about that." I take her arm and escort her out of the office.

Before we reach the diner, a cell phone goes off in her purse.

"Oh, darn." She fumbles through her bag, and I notice that there are several more burner phones tangled in the contents.

"Don't tell me this is one of your Bat phone lines to Gotham. This is getting ridiculous."

"Shhh," she hisses at me while answering the offending phone.

"Hello...? Robert?" she asks, looking away from me.

"You're shitting me," I mumble.

Twelve
Emma

"I can't talk now. I'll call you this weekend and we can set up a time to get together." While I talk, I meet Dylan's angry glare as he leans against a mailbox waiting for me.

"I know it's important to you, but I'm at work and I have things going on..." My voice trails off, listening to Robert's insistent tone.

I used to fall for this; for Robert, for the drama, the excitement he provided, and the relationship I thought it was seductive and loving. I glance up at Dylan's scowl that evokes something much more appealing than anything Robert could offer. If telling Robert to never call me again would be effective, this wouldn't be a problem. He'd be out of my life. I tried that last summer, though. I was foolish enough to think we were done and I could move on, get a job and have a healthy relationship with a regular guy.

Obviously, however, Robert still gets to disrupt my life whenever he wants to. He could easily replace me with another woman, yet he's holding on to me because I'm a familiar person from his past—one of the few he trusts. I don't want to be that woman anymore, and I may have to call in reinforcements to end this twisted Romeo and Juliet scenario that's never quite played out the way I fantasized about when I was a teenager and had a major crush on Robert from a distance.

When I finish the call, Dylan is silent as he studies me thoroughly.

"Where is he? Where did he call from?" Dylan asks skeptically.

"I don't know. I assume his house in Jersey."

"He is one of those things we need to discuss, Emma. Sooner, rather than later."

"Tonight," I reply. I am not confident that I can talk about everything—not when it comes to Robert—but I am more than willing to try to win over Dylan's trust and possibly more.

If I tell him about what went down over the last ten years of my life—growing up in and around the world my father's business got us sucked into—I don't think he would take it easily. No kidding, he's pissed; the veins in Dylan's neck are popping from just the idea of Robert. So how do I explain my relationship with a man I defend as good at heart despite my own questionable testimonies and the inherent violence of that life I've belonged to?

It's a completely different kind of baggage than what Dylan brings to the table. A guy who has a history of mental illness and sees a shrink? Big fucking deal; I can handle that, especially since I am already falling for the other sides of Dylan that are everything I was hoping to get from Robert but never did. Me, on the other hand... What guy wants a woman who comes with ties to a disgusting world of organized crime and an ex-boyfriend who is like a chronic illness she can't shake? No shrink can get me out of the Robert situation. It's all on me, and I am afraid Dylan will walk away from this along with the potential of what could be something nice between us.

"Don't play games with me. This guy is not something you can stay secretive about."

"I'm not playing games. I am trying to resolve this."

"You're not doing a very good job. Maybe you really don't want to end it with him."

That sends a little pang of hurt through me. Dylan's jaw is clenched and his crossed arms show how much he is closing himself off from me at this moment. I understand that. He has been through enough and has to protect himself.

"No, I'm definitely done with him," I reply, looking around to make sure no one is on the sidewalk and can hear us. In a lower voice, I tell him, "I wouldn't be in your home, doing those things with you if I still had feelings for Robert. That's not who I am."

"Let's eat lunch and then we have the conference call this afternoon. After that, we're going home." He puts his hand firmly on my back and guides me into the diner.

"What about the gym? Aren't you going to meet Carson after work?"

"I'll work out at home—with you," he says quietly so the diner patrons don't hear.

"Is that the excuse you'll use with Carson?"

"I don't have to say anything to Carson. He's got me all figured out."

***

We are going *home*. I am thrilled with the way it sounds as if we are a couple. We have managed to stay off everyone's radar at work. After a couple of weeks, they are used to seeing us drive in to work together and the little showdown debates we have over clients in our office, yet they seem oblivious to our mutual attraction.

As I pull my Honda out of the lot with Dylan laughing at my cautious, repetitive looks to the right and left—as if this country road is the same as entering onto the highly competitive on-ramp of the 495 deathtrap in Jersey—Cooper zooms in front of us on his Harley, smiling as he guns it and roars down the road.

"Ass." Dylan shakes his head.

"Oh, stop. He's nice."

I drive us home at a leisurely speed.

"I'm going to take a nap. Let me know when we get there," Dylan says, feigning sleep. "Maybe it's about time we start taking my bike into work."

"I don't know about that," I say sarcastically. "People

102

might think we're a couple if we show up with me holding on to you for dear life. You wouldn't want that."

"Says who?"

"Right." I look back at the road. "I think you just want to out run Cooper on your big, bad bike. You guys like things between your legs, and you'll look cooler with a girl hanging on to you, especially if it's me." I smirk.

"Damn straight." He laughs.

"Are we moving into new territory? Out of the friends who kiss zone?" I ask as I park in front of the house.

"I don't think we were ever in the friend zone; do you?" Dylan retorts as if I've said the worst thing possible to him. I know that, if he said that to me, it would be a slam against my ego and ever-growing feelings for him.

"No, we weren't friends. Remember, I thought you were kind of a wise-ass jerk."

Dylan chuckles. "I kind of was, although I did reign in my attitude with a little heroic action on your clown car."

"And my unscrupulous visitor," I add.

"We still have to talk about him, Emma," Dylan responds, getting out of the car.

"Dylan, you're repeating yourself. Go make me dinner. I'm going to change."

My demand evokes a deep, sexy chuckle from him. I don't think he has any idea what he does to me. His voice, his body, his steely blue eyes. He is more charming and sexy than any man I have ever known. I want to curl up naked with him and do things that make me blush. How can he not see that? Watching him cook even turns me on, and I never get that from watching any of the celebrity chefs on the cooking channel.

Before I turn myself into a horny mess, I bolt for the house. I quickly clomp up the wooden porch steps before Dylan whirls me around for a damaging kiss. He heats me up in every crevice, and my nipples harden and strain against my bra while I unabashedly grind myself against the bulge in his jeans. I am so aroused, completely ready to skip over any foreplay and let him screw me here on the porch. His hand slides under my skirt and down my panties where he grabs my bare butt cheek.

Holding onto him, I wrench away from his kiss. "Is this dinner?"

"No." His voice is raspy and there's an extra beat where he considers this.

Say yes, hot stuff.

"No," he reaffirms, and I'm wondering if a good, hard slap across the face will shake him out of this frigging Prince Valor mode.

"Fine," I say, slouching against his chest. "Then your dinner better be out of this fucking world because I'm tired of you getting me all worked up and then dousing the flames."

"Then we're even. I have to look at your naked legs all day long, crossing and uncrossing them at work. You have no idea what's going through my mind when I see that, or when you talk to clients on the phone and you play with the top button of your shirt. Unbutton, button, unbutton, button. Jesus, I can't believe Carson put us in the same office. I feel like he's testing me."

"Really?" I ask, laughing. "I didn't realize I was exposing myself at work. You think Carson is testing you?"

"No, he wouldn't do that." Dylan's mouth curves and he leans down for a warm peck on my cheek. "But sometimes I do catch glimpses of your bra and what's underneath."

"I'll be more careful."

"Don't," he says in a sexy, deep voice. "I'm enjoying it."

"God. Stop it. I'm going to go change." I charge through the front door. "And you better make something spectacular for all this sex talk you keep using. My head is spinning."

I hear Dylan's baritone laugh all the way up the stairs as I race off to my room for a reprieve.

Thirteen

Dylan

That was a close call. I was ready to drag her into the hallway caveman style and have at her in a quick and thankless fashion. Something she would find completely forgettable.

She comes back downstairs in a clingy, short, black t-shirt dress thing, something that shows me more leg and scoops down to expose some cleavage. Clever woman. She is barefoot with her long, dark hair flowing all over the place like an exotic gypsy.

I try to continue with cooking the meal, however she keeps dancing around, taunting me with the sexual tension we've built up to epic proportions.

"Would you set the table, please?" I ask with a tight voice, acutely aware that I'm thinking about my constrained dick that is begging for something else.

She starts humming as she twirls around the kitchen collecting utensils.

"Have a seat, Tinkerbell." I place a salad and grilled mushroom sandwiches on the table.

"Yum," she says, sitting down.

"I kind of miss steak," I say out of the blue, not because I am thinking about steak but because she is so damn distracting.

"Like you miss sex?" She takes a bite of her sandwich and chews slowly, staring at me.

"Excuse me?" Of course I am thinking about sex.

"Lauren told me. You've chilled on women, or rather sex, drinking, and socializing all together. I bet you miss sex."

"You think?"

"Dylan, she told me everything."

"Huh. Right. Lauren."

Lauren told her everything and she still wants to be here with me?

"Is that why you're interested in me? It's been awhile, and geographically speaking, I'm the nearest available female."

I drop my sandwich and stare in disbelief.

"Does that seem plausible to you?" I am a little ticked off she would believe that. "You think that, with all this time we've spent together, I can't tell the difference between someone I like being with and someone who I just want to screw?"

"Sorry. No, I don't think that. I'm trying to get some confirmation of what this is for myself," she replies.

Her tone is sincere, and I guess I have to be impressed that she doesn't back down from my harsh question. Not many people would go there, most people are afraid of the truth.

"I thought I was doing it right for a change, taking it slow and not starting something with you based on sex as the opening act."

"Dylan," she takes my hand, "it is right. Do you think, if Cooper or someone else offered me a place to stay, that I would be so quick to move in with them? You don't have to try so hard to win me over. You've won. I'm here because of you. I haven't been shy about that."

"Then let's have dessert now," I respond.

She looks confused. "Oh, sure. What did you make?"

"Nothing. I'm tired of holding out."

I quickly stand up and grab her waist then easily hoist her over my shoulder. She lets out a sharp gasp and then a laugh as I carry her in a fireman hold through the living room. As I make it to the staircase, someone begins pounding on the front door.

"Oh, no," Emma says, hanging from my shoulder. She gives my ass a slap.

"This is unreal," I bark. "Why do I think this has something to do with you?"

I set Emma down and she brushes her hair back with her fingers. "I'll get the door," she says in disappointment.

"No. I'll handle this. It could be your stalker," I say angrily.

I swing the door open to find a huge guy about to bash his meaty fist on the door again. We quickly scrutinize each other. He is my height but built like a tank. Judging from how he fills out his suit and the earpiece he is wearing, I would say he's someone who knows Emma. He looks like a secret service agent and ex-military bodyguard all rolled into one. He is at least thirty with a buzzed scalp—practically bald—and underneath his shirt collar and sleeves, he has a myriad of tats; symbols, foreign words and images I can't make out.

"Sean!" Emma squeals and pushes past me to hug the guy.

"Hey, girl," he says, grinning as he sweeps her off her feet into a big bear hug.

Fuck. This is *so* not going well for me. I am falling for this woman, and I was about to take her upstairs to bed before this tattooed refrigerator showed up at the door.

"Sean, this is Dylan," Emma states, pulling him inside and closing the door.

"Hello, Dylan," Sean replies with a slight Irish accent. He gives me a bone-crunching handshake. "Good name. I have a younger brother named Dylan."

I nod apprehensively. His timing sucks—I am not in the mood to entertain a strange guy, especially one that Emma adores.

"How did you find me?" Emma asks. "My parents haven't even been out here."

Sean tilts his head and chuckles. "Em, come on."

"Yeah, right," she mutters. "No one can ever really disappear."

I feel like they are part of a secret club, and I am completely in the dark. "What's going on?" I ask Sean.

"Come and sit down, Sean," Emma demands, leading him into the living room.

He and Emma sit on the couch while I stand against the wall, anxious and too frustrated to sit.

"Your dad sent me to check on you. He's worried about you with all this crap Robert is getting into. I heard about him showing up here." Sean sighs and leans back, crossing his legs and spreading his arms across the back of the couch.

"I can handle Robert. There's nothing new there," Emma responds.

I ignore her remark and direct my attention to Sean. Fathers don't send guys like this to check on their daughters unless something is very wrong, and I suspect this guy is carrying at least one weapon under his expensive suit.

"What's going on with Robert? What have you heard and why does he keep contacting Emma? He even called her on one of the prepaid phones she carries. How did he get that number?" I ask Sean sternly.

He sighs. "Robert can get pretty much any number or address he wants. There's always someone who will tip him off. And Emma knows enough people that could easily inform Robert, even if it's unintentional. Robert has his ways."

"What does he want with Emma?" I push. I'm sick of these roundabout excuses that have no definitive answers.

"Old ties are hard to break," Sean says while looking sympathetically at Emma.

"I've put him in my past," Emma tells Sean.

"I know that, but Robert doesn't think so, and when a

man is down or running scared, he tends to turn to those who make him feel safe," Sean responds. "Vinnie is having problems with the organization and the Feds. Some think he may turn on his own son. Unthinkable that a parent would do that, but Vinnie's desperate, and it's ugly."

"I can't believe this," Emma says sadly.

A moment ago she was happy and ready to go to bed with me. Now—with this turn of events where she pouts over a former flame—it's infuriating; this conversation is beginning to turn my stomach. I want to take Emma in my arms and make her feel safe, yet I have no clue what they are talking about, and this Sean guy has the upper hand on me—a history with Emma and her trust.

"Who is Vinnie? And why do we give a shit about Robert?" I am getting angrier.

"Are we good to talk here?" Sean asks Emma.

"Yes, Dylan is my… my roommate and we work together. His brother hired me and knows a little about my situation. He spoke to Dad before hiring me because every girl loves having a prospective employer call her daddy for a reference." She snorts.

Sean chuckles and then turns to me. His gaze lets me know that he's aware I'm the roommate that wants to screw his beloved Emma. He looks at Emma's skimpy dress, and realizing she is revealing a little too much, she throws one of her knitted blankets across her lap.

"I suppose you should know who I am," Sean says to me. "I was hired by Emma's father when Emma had just became a teen. His auto business was growing and he was getting shaken down for more money, and he began to worry about Emma's welfare. And, well, because she was taking an interest in Robert and his friends and spending a lot of time around those kids. I'm a hired gun—protection for Emma's family. I'm one of the good guys." He smiles.

"Oh, great. So you *are* carrying a gun."

This is so far out of my realm in the furniture business.

I am pretty sure Carson already knows about this guy, too, which means Sean knows about me. Wonder what he thinks about a former resident of Willow Haven Treatment Center hanging out with his precious, little Emma.

"Everyone carries." Sean regards me carefully, trying to sum up where I fit in with Emma and if I am trustworthy.

"I don't." Emma adds quietly, "Not anymore."

I scoff and take a moment to study the woman who moments ago reminded me of a gypsy Tinkerbell.

"Jesus. What about Robert?" I ask Sean. "When he came around here... I can assume he's packing, too?"

"Always," Sean confirms.

"Robert is old fashioned, but he likes to carry a Glock," Emma says, as if this is helpful.

"What the fuck does that mean 'he's old fashioned'?"

"He would never shoot someone," she adds quickly.

"Em," Sean says wearily.

"Then why does he carry it?" I glare at Emma.

"He likes to carry something longer than his penis?" she jokes, looking at Sean with a gleam in her eye.

"Jaysus," Sean chuckles.

"You're scaring me." I point my finger at Emma.

Sean laughs more loudly and then I crack a tentative smile. It's all too weird—I have to smile. Besides, I am majorly hung up on her, and I want to be with her all the time, especially if she needs protection.

She shrugs apologetically with a look of embarrassment in her beautiful eyes that practically knocks the wind out of me.

"I'm not sure I find this humorous for the right reason," I state. "Seriously, Emma, you're all kinds of crazy."

"Doesn't that make you feel normal?" She smiles and Sean catches the look between Emma and me. I don't want to have a personal conversation in front of him.

"So, who is Vinnie?" I get us back on topic.

"Vincent Marchetto is Robert's father," Sean explains. "He's running the show. Without going into all their business dealings, he's been snagged on a few big Fed sweeps. Some of his guys got caught in a major drug bust, and some of it can be traced back to Robert."

"What? Robert doesn't work for his father. He joined that big deal law firm. He was never in the family business," Emma pleads Robert's case with too much love as far as I'm concerned.

"Em." Sean shakes his head.

"What did you think Robert was involved in—cupcakes?" I say too harshly to her.

"Robert was let go from the firm, Em. He's on the run because even he thinks his dad is going to make him the scapegoat."

"Vinnie cut him loose, didn't he? That's why I didn't see another guy with Robert when he was out here. He came by himself," she says.

"Afraid so."

"What does he want with Emma?" I question. "How can she possibly help him out of this jam?"

Sean shrugs. "Either he's looking for a friend or he thinks Emma can help. Any ideas about that, Em?"

Emma shakes her head. "I haven't had a lengthy conversation with Robert since the Christmas party. I don't want to even see him, but he's been insisting on meeting with me."

"Goddammit. This is so fucked up," I say.

"Robert is not about hurting Emma; she's right about that. I've studied that guy for years, though something is going on in his head that only he knows about."

"So you think we have a rogue mobster hiding in the woods, looking for Emma?" I ask.

They both look pretty calm for two people who are talking so casually about criminals and a possibly dangerous stalker. I try to breathe slower and count

112

backwards, so I'm not tempted to strike an inanimate object out of rage.

"Robert is not the type to hide in the woods. He has a network of contacts that are untouched by his father, which means he's probably with one of them. He's not hiding in this town, either. It's too small. Don't worry about that," Sean says reassuringly, at least to Emma.

"Jesus, Emma, why couldn't you have a Dr. Seuss life? Why this Godfather crap? Shit." I pace the living room.

"I would have preferred a Dr. Seuss childhood, but it wasn't exactly my choice." Her words are clipped.

"Who wouldn't?" Sean adds. "I love The Sneetches and that Circus McGurkus kid. I read those books to my niece all the time. Great books."

Emma smiles and pats Sean's large hand.

I am out of my element here. This news is pissing me off, and these two are acting like we're simply talking about a bad weather system coming to town.

"Listen," Sean stands, "I just came to check on you and make sure you're doing okay so I can report back to your dad."

"Wait a minute. What about Robert?" I question. "If I see him, do I just beat the bloody shit out of him?"

"Sure, you could do that." Sean smiles. "He deserves it."

"That's it? We're winging it?" I ask.

Emma stands and puts her hand on my arm as Sean watches closely.

"There's not much we can do right now. Do you want a gun?" Sean inquires, beginning to reach into his jacket.

"No. No guns. I can handle this guy." I look at Emma, and she gives a slight smile.

She trusts me enough to be here instead of in her father's armed fortress with Sean and his arsenal. That counts for something, but it doesn't mean shit if I get killed trying to be the hero in a game I have never played before.

"Em is fairly well-trained in defensive moves," Sean adds.

I look at her with surprise. She shrugs again.

Interesting. All this talk about her background has her suddenly clammed up.

"She has a great roundhouse kick, and her specialty is something she calls the Vulcan Grip." Sean chuckles as he says this.

"I think I know that one," I state pointedly to Emma.

***

After Sean leaves, I sweep the house, checking windows and the doors, thinking of anything I can do to improve our security while Emma quietly sits on the couch knitting. I don't know how she can be so calm about this.

I head into the kitchen and pull my meds out of the cupboard above the fridge. I pop my antidepressant with a glass of water as Emma enters the room and watches me. Then I take out the Xanax I haven't used in ages, but the situation seems to warrant something for my growing anxiety.

"What does that one do?" Emma asks, appearing behind me.

"One is my antidepressant and the other is a mood stabilizer. I take them every day. And this other little orange one is for bodyguards who tell me we've got a gun-toting ex-boyfriend after you."

I swallow the pills while Emma watches me with sympathetic eyes. I hate sympathy.

She walks closer to me and puts her hand on my back. "I'm sorry I put you in the middle of this. I can move in to a motel if this scares you too much," she says softly.

Great, now she thinks I'm too weak to handle her problem. "I'm not scared, Emma. I'm pissed because that guy gets to run around and do this to you. You're not going to a motel."

I snake my arms around her back. "I'm certain you

114

think you know everything about me. Lauren has told you plenty, but I'm not taking strong doses that can make me zone out or flip out if that's what you're worried about. These pills balance me out so I don't have the urge to hunt down people and beat the living day lights out of them... Shit. I'm making it sound worse... They're low doses. The pills help me. That's all."

"I'm not judging you. I know you take medicine, and I know you see a psychiatrist. I understand that. But I don't want my situation to make your life harder."

I pull her closer. "It already has. Even without this asshole in the picture. The minute you showed up at work, my life became harder."

Her brows furrow at my remark.

"In a good way." I kiss her forehead. "Being the exercise-workaholic was getting boring. You're not going anywhere."

She puts her hands on my waist and leans her head against my chest. "I do wish I had a Dr. Seuss life and less drama."

"Well, I didn't have one, either, and for a long time, I made my life and Carson's worse, so we're even there."

She looks up at me. "Sean has always watched over me as much as possible. I kind of shut him out when I was at college and seeing Robert, but Sean always managed to be close enough to make sure I was safe. The only reason he left us here alone is because he trusts you. He must know that you're good."

"Maybe, but he sure is a mood killer. Jesus, my meds haven't affected my libido at all, but that guy kind of ruined the moment." I chuckle nervously because I can't believe I'm telling her this.

She purses her lips in a retrained smile. "So, how about a date? We can watch a movie?"

"I can't wait." I fake a smile.

***

115

We sit on the couch where Emma's legs are tucked to the side, resting on mine as she knits and watches the film. My legs are stretched out and I have an arm around her shoulders. My thoughts are elsewhere, thinking about what Sean has said and wondering about Emma, therefore it is a full twenty minutes into the movie before I realize we're watching *Goodfellas*.

"I can't believe we're watching this," I comment.

"It was in the DVD player." She clicks her needles together and studies her knitting.

"It's Lauren's. She always brings these mob movies and thrillers over when she hangs out with Leo."

Emma laughs. "I forgot about that. She was like that at school, too. Such a hypocrite. She'd lecture me on Robert and all his nefarious ties, and then she'd watch Godfather marathons."

"This movie is doing nothing for me, but that clickety-click sound you're making with those needles is kind of turning me on," I say, watching her knit.

She pauses and looks at me with a mischievous smile. "Really?"

I run my hands along her bare legs. Her skin is so smooth that, just like that, I am rock hard again. Her hands are poised in mid-air, holding her knitting needles as I lean in to kiss her. My lips push against hers and she eagerly opens them, letting me run my tongue inside. I know where I want this to go.

I immediately grab her needles and toss them before pulling her to her feet.

"You're not my roommate. Let's go to bed," I say, walking her briskly to the stairs.

"Technically we're housemates since we've never slept together."

"We'll fix that," I reply, scooping her up at the bottom of the stairs and carrying her to my bedroom.

116

Fourteen
Emma

I had every intention of seducing Dylan when I floated downstairs in that little black dress that barely covers my thighs until Sean waylaid those plans. I thought talking about Robert and guns would not only kill the mood but would turn Dylan off me for good.

I watch him quickly drop his jeans and step out of them before pulling off his t-shirt and flinging it. In his black boxer briefs, I can see every curve of every muscle, and all I can think about is running my tongue over every one of them. His firm abs narrow down into his briefs, and I stare at that flat, taut skin that I want to touch and lick. God, something about him makes me want to lick him all over. I shiver.

"Well, are you joining me?" he asks as he pulls the covers back on the bed. "Because if I have to throw you on this bed and strip you myself, I will."

"Uh-huh," I say but don't move.

He strides over to me and pulls my stretchy dress over my head and slingshots it across the room.

"Oh, yes," he says, admiring my black lace bra and matching thong. "Good thing I didn't know this is what you had on underneath, or I would have asked Sean to leave sooner. This is perfect." His voice is deep and seductive.

He runs his finger slowly underneath my bra, causing my nipples to bud, while he watches my aroused expression and his breathing becomes heavier. Then, when his finger trails down my stomach to my thong, he slips it underneath the stretchy fabric and traces just above my wet folds.

"Mmm," is all I can manage to say.

"Mmm, yes," he murmurs.

When both of his hands slip under the thong and caress my ass, one hand comes back to the front and sweeps across my clit, and I am about to collapse. Dylan hoists me against him by holding my ass. He drops me on the center of the bed and climbs on all fours, looking down at me with a bemused expression.

"Hi." His sexy voice causes my wet center to flex and tingle with anticipation.

"Hi, you," I respond. I reach up and pull his head down until our noses are almost touching. I am eager to have his mouth on me—all over me.

"I want you," he says gruffly.

You would expect, for our first time together, that we would rush and claw at each other, yet Dylan is keeping it slow and teasing. He kisses me leisurely, and no matter how aroused and wet I am, I can't get him to move faster. He has definitely taken over, keeping his kisses and finger action painfully slow.

As his hand trails up my torso and pulls down one side of my bra, his mouth descends on my aching nipple. He licks and sucks it hard before going to the next breast. I moan and arch into him. I could easily be satisfied if he would plunge his cock into me now. This has been building for two weeks, and I want it hard and fast. He seems to have other plans, though, and is exhibiting more control than me.

"Dylan," I moan. "I'm ready."

"I can see that." He smiles against my mouth as he slips two fingers into me and swirls them around the wetness that's building. "We're not rushing this. I'm going to touch every part of you until you're screaming in ecstasy."

"That may be any moment," I reply as I run my hands across his broad back.

He shuts me up with more kisses, this time going deeper, while his hand works over my clit. I am wriggling and pushing into him beyond any semblance of my earlier thoughts of a sultry seduction. I reach for his bulging erection and rub my palm slowly against the fabric. His breathing escalates and he moves my hand away, so my next assault is under his briefs. I am fast as I push under the waistband and wrap my hand around the silky skin of his cock and pull it out of his underwear.

"Oh, shit," he groans into my neck.

I enjoy Dylan's spontaneous expletives and groans, letting me know that he is losing control. I would hate to think that it's easy to manage his arousal with me; I want him falling apart like me.

He helps me push down his briefs, pulling them off and tossing them the way of the rest of his clothing. Then I unclasp my bra and throw it before reaching for his engorged cock again. He grunts and removes his hand from my wetness so he can yank off my thong.

"Damn," he whispers. I see that he ripped the thong completely.

"You'll just have to buy me more pretty, little panties," I whisper as I rub the head of his cock against me.

"Deal," he rasps. He kisses me hard while one hand rubs over a hard nipple and the other moves his cock aside so he can start bringing me to a drawn out orgasm with his fingers.

"Oh, I want you in me now." My hand slides up and down his cock more forcefully. I am panting. If he doesn't comply soon, I am going to change into some feral creature that is going to be less patient.

"We just got started, baby. I still want to do more things with you." His voice chokes and his veins are bulging in his neck and shoulders.

"I've been waiting two weeks for this," I say.

"Oh, yeah? You wanted me even when you thought I

was a jerk?" His low chuckle turns into a groan when I push his hand away and rub his cock against my wetness. "I had some pretty awesome fantasies about you, too."

I stroke his cock with one hand and reach under with the other to apply light pressure to his balls. He shudders at the contact.

"Dylan, get a condom," I whisper into his ear.

He flies off the bed and retrieves a condom from the nightstand without a second prompt; I guess he is Flash Gordon when it comes to protection. Watching him roll the condom on his enormous erection makes my body instantly react. I look down and notice my legs have already spread wide open for him, and my breasts are swollen and perky. My body is way ahead of my brain.

He comes back and crawls between my open legs and angles his cock until it is centered on me. I wrap my legs around him, and as he rubs himself against me, we begin rocking.

"You're torturing me," I groan.

"Emma," he says, unwrapping my legs from him and then kissing my stomach as he trails his tongue down between my legs.

"Torture," I whisper, placing my hands on his head when he circles his tongue around my center, lightly rimming the folds before sucking on my clit.

I gasp as the euphoric tingling takes over me. Dylan sucks harder and I dreamily open my eyes to look down at this huge guy between my legs. His lavish attention increases and pulls me into an orgasm so quickly my hands smack the sheets, and I grip them as I push my pelvis up into Dylan, greedily taking what he is giving me. He doesn't stop until my moans cease and my body stops shaking. The orgasm never really ends; it leaves tiny vibrations in my center, waiting for more.

He begins kissing his way up my stomach again, licking along my curves before descending on my breasts.

120

He sucks on one nipple and moves to another, sucking harder with his teeth biting into me. I am wetter than ever and feeling frantic to have him inside of me.

"Now," I moan and he groans, as if this was a test of patience and he's ready to throw in the towel.

He props himself above me and begins rubbing his cock against me again. His composure is fragile as his hand guides himself into me. When he slips, I realize he is a little nervous. I move his hand and grasp his thick length and push it partially into me.

"Good Lord," he moans, feeling the tip of his cock firmly positioned inside as he attempts to gain stability on the bed.

As I run my hands up his muscled arms and wrap my legs around him again, he looks at me with desire and excitement before he plunges into me and doesn't stop until he's fully embedded. I moan, and we both hold our breath as he stills his body.

"Good God. This feels so good," he barely gets out.

As he closes his eyes and throws his head back to savor the moment, I use the opportunity to run my hands over his soft, buzzed hair while I flex and tighten my inner muscles to get another moan out of him.

When he opens his eyes, he looks down at me and his mouth curves into a slight smile. "This is better than I imagined."

"Sex? Or me?"

"You. Sex with you. All of it. I don't want to move. I want to stay buried in you and feel this good all the time."

"If you don't move and get me off again, I'm going to rip your ear off with my teeth."

Dylan chuckles and it sends a rumbling sensation through me all the way down to the most sensitive places. He begins pulling out and thrusting back in, slowly at first. My mind careens into a tailspin, waiting for that delicious orgasm to peak and spill me into oblivion. I am practically thrashing underneath him as he sucks on a nipple and rubs my clit as he starts pounding into me.

"Yes," I hiss.

He removes his hand from my clit, which is still vibrating, and then braces himself up on both arms. His face is flushed and begins to bead with sweat.

"You're so wet and tight, and I haven't done this in a while, Emma," he rasps.

"I'm so close." I think I say it out loud.

I am being overtaken by those delicious shocks that roll from my center. I arch up as my body explodes with a glorious display of tingling spasms. I keep grinding against Dylan as he pumps ferociously into me with the kind of unflagging joy you would expect from a young guy who has broken his long sentence of abstention. He climaxes with a sudden laugh and grunts with smaller thrusts to empty himself. Another orgasm rolls through me and I whimper before my trembling body subsides and Dylan collapses on me.

We lie like that for a few minutes, connected and entwined, and I leave a trail of soft kisses down his head and cheek. He props himself on his elbows to take his weight off me and kisses me long and lovingly again. I cup his scruffy cheeks in my hands and return the adoring kiss.

This is more than I have ever enjoyed with any man. Whatever personal demons Dylan has had to slay to get to this point, he found me and I found him. That is all that matters. I need him and I will do whatever it takes to get Robert out of my new life, even if it means cutting off all ties with my former life so I can be with Dylan. People say and do stupid things during the haze of sex, however I think my growing feelings for Dylan are genuine and were solidified before he took me to his bed. I hope I am right. One mistake like Robert was enough.

"Are you okay?" Dylan asks, beaming, knowing that I am very content.

"I'm excellent." I smile. "How about you?"

"You've confirmed it for me. I don't like being celibate as long as you're around."

He grins as he pries himself off me before getting up to deal with the condom.

"I guess we're more than housemates," I call after him. "We're bedmates."

Dylan wraps the condom in a tissue and drops it in a wastebasket.

"I hope we're more than that." His tone is as serious as when he told Robert to stay away.

I pull a sheet over me, wondering why modesty always takes over after sex.

"I wish I didn't have this family mess on my hands," I say. "I hate bringing you into this. After what you've been through—"

"I can handle this," he cuts me off with a sharp tone. "I'm not going to let that guy keep this up. I'm not going anywhere. We'll fix this."

He climbs back in bed and gets under the sheet before bringing me in for a hug.

"How do we handle this at work? What do we tell people?" I ask, thinking of Daisy making an announcement about us on the PA system.

"At work, we work. We don't have to say anything to anyone; they'll figure it out on their own."

"So what are we?" I inquire, sprawled across his chest.

"Whatever we want to be."

"That doesn't answer my question. You saw the way Sean looked at us. And Carson, too. What do *you* think we are, Dylan?"

His beautiful blue eyes bore into me with a thoughtful gaze and then his mouth curves. How could I ever think he looked like a mercenary or that he was jackass? He is so sweet and strong, and there is an unexpected gentleness to him.

"You're my… we're exclusive, right? I mean, it's going to be difficult for you to date other guys if you're living with me and sharing a bed with me." He grins.

"Funny."

"Yeah, well, what do you think we are?"

"I think I like this a lot."

"You mean having a guy give you a home, cook for you, take you to bed?" He is perhaps fishing for more. I'm not sure, though.

"I like you, Dylan."

"Good." He gives me a chaste kiss on my lips.

I take his right arm and study his small tattoo below his palm. "*Freedom*," I read it out loud. "What is this for?"

"It's a reminder for me. That's why I put it on my wrist, so I can see it anytime."

"Freedom from what?"

"From myself, my self-doubt, my—"

"Your illness," I say, holding his wrist gingerly in my hand.

"Yes. The word is to remind myself that my illness doesn't have to rule my life if I don't let it."

I lift his arm to my lips and kiss his *Freedom*. His curious eyes watch me intently, and I believe there is a glimmer of both trepidation and hope in his gaze.

Fifteen
Dylan

Waking up with her in my arms is amazingly easy. I'm not worried about getting out of some woman's bed as if it is a regretful college tryst, and I am not panicked that she is in my bed, cocooned next to me as if she has no intention of leaving anytime soon. I don't want Emma to leave.

I wake early because my body is used to five a.m. runs, but this time, I stay in bed with her limbs wrapped around me. I don't want to disturb her sleep, so I watch her eyelids flicker in slumber and listen to her faint whistling snore. Yes, she snores, drools and grunts when she adjusts her position, reminding me of Carson's bulldog, Bert.

She oversleeps and we have to rush through a morning routine of a quick shower and toast as we bolt out the door before racing to work. She chides me for letting her sleep in and worries about arriving late to the office and who may be watching us. She has no idea that I could care less about being late for work. At the time, I was more interested in showering with her and staying in bed longer. That is a little worrisome for me, wondering if I am getting caught up in a physical relationship with her. However, in the end, I didn't wake her up with my morning erection and I didn't corner her in the shower. I didn't let any of my sexual fantasies about her come into play. I just watched over her, and that felt good.

It's different at work. I have a heightened awareness of being the guy that runs around talking to the design team in the factory and studio and clients on the phone. I am the guy that is fully aware of the distance between Emma and me at any given point during the day, as well. She is wholly her own person with her own agenda at work and the relationships she is developing with the other employees. She carries her own responsibilities with great confidence and professionalism. I admire that in her, even when she leaves a room as if I am just another employee and my instinct is to touch her as if she's mine; she scoots away before I can act on it.

It hasn't been stated and no one else may see it this way, but she is my responsibility. For the first time, I feel attached to a woman in a way that doesn't resemble anything I have had in the past.

If we can get past this point of her revisiting her ex-boyfriend and engaging in ties that she claims she wants to break, and I can fix my turbulent brain, we have a chance at being together in a way that may work. Inwardly, I laugh at that possibility and my wishful thinking like a kid on Christmas morning.

Early in the afternoon, I need a break from paperwork and phone calls along with salivating over Emma's legs. Today my stopwatch app has timed her at thirty-two leg crosses, enough to drive any man over the edge if he is sitting a few feet away. It's time to visit the factory and get lost in the noise from the table saws and the heat from the wood oven—anything to get my mind off her for a while.

I strap on my heavy, leather tool belt, its weight pulling the waist of my jeans down a bit. I adjust my gear, and as I am about to leave the office, Emma glances at me as she finishes a phone call. She tries to hang up the phone while she keeps her eyes on my… belt, I am guessing. When she drops the cordless phone on the floor, it causes me to double check my attire; I look down at the familiar tools I take on jobs to work with the crew.

"What?" I study my belt again and look back at her for an explanation.

"What are you doing?" Her voice is lower; it's not her

normal no-nonsense tone, and if I am reading her correctly, she is aroused.

Oh, damn.

I close the office door and lock it, and in three strides, I pull her out of her chair and drag her to the dark corner by the window, so no one can see us from the parking lot.

"Dylan—" she begins to protest as I claim her mouth.

It's too late for words. Her excited expression has put fuel to my fire, so we are going to get something out of this mutual desire. I pull one of her thighs up and run my hand down her leg to her ass, thankful her skirt makes this so easy. I then hold the back of her head while my tongue works over the sensitive flesh on her neck.

"Not here, Dylan. We can't… do this," she moans.

Pinned against the wall with a leg in the air, she pushes into me and holds my head against her neck.

I cup a hand underneath and feel her damp underwear. "You're wet for me," I murmur into her neck. "You totally want this."

"Wanting it and doing it at work are two different things," she whispers in halting breaths.

"Everyone is leaving for lunch, they won't miss us." I unbutton her blouse and then push down her bra, seeking out a hard nipple, sucking until she is writhing against my cupped hand. "You have me so jacked up right now."

"How good is that lock on the door?" she asks.

"Very," I respond as my tongue and mouth never leave her soft skin. "It's a deadbolt. This used to be a storage room before we put in the windows and turned it into an office—"

"Shut up, Dylan," she quips and cuts me off from rambling about the construction.

Her hands leave my head and begin quick work on my button-fly before yanking my jeans down. I reach to unbuckle my tool belt.

"No, don't." She stops my hand. "It's sexy. Keep it

on."

"You're kidding," I say as she pulls my briefs down, too.

"No, I'm not. It's hot. It makes you swagger. So hot."

I am still holding her thigh up, exposing her to me as I release her bra clasp and pull it down.

"I don't want anyone to get injured. I've got some sharp tools—"

"Condom," she demands to stop my stupid banter again.

I have to let go of her leg to reach into my back pocket for my wallet. She quickly slides her underwear down while I remove a foil package and drop the wallet on the floor. She takes the package from me and opens it swiftly, then slowly rolls the condom onto my erection; watching her hands on me drives all the blood to my engorged dick. She moans in approval and wraps a leg around my waist before rubbing my cock against her wetness. I need to be touching her, but I am hypnotized by how she rubs herself with my dick. Her head falls back and she moans before opening her eyes and looking at me.

"I'm going to fuck you right now, Emma." I try to suppress the urgency in my voice.

"Yes," she whispers, laughing. "I like how you announce these things as if I don't have any idea about what's going to happen."

"Just being clear," I laugh in return.

As I hoist her up by her ass, her other leg wraps around me as I simultaneously plunge deep into her warm wetness. I gain some footing and push her up higher against the wall so I can thrust into her. I do it slowly at first, but when she pushes up my t-shirt and starts sucking on my nipples, I am overcome by all the sensations. The friction and wet rhythm—with the added bonuses of the hammer swinging in my tool belt, knocking the wall behind her with each thrust—propels me into a mindless sex rampage. She bites and sucks on my chest, and I pound into her harder. I completely lose it when she touches herself and puts two fingers on either side of her clit so they rub against my cock as well.

"Emma, shit," I hiss. "I'm going to come."

"Yes," she utters, as we thrust against each other furiously until she lets out a small yelp followed by a low moan.

As she comes, her muscles tighten around my cock and her fingernails scrape across my back and around to my chest where she pinches my nipples again. I explode into her, and I am about to shout, but her hand covers my mouth to stifle me.

I let her slide down the wall to a standing position as I slip out of her.

"Christ," I say, staggering back to watch as our bodies separate.

Emma fastens her bra and begins to button up her shirt. I find a tissue and remove the condom. We're careful not to walk in front of the window, and hopefully, the machinery in the factory drowned out the sound from the banging hammer, although I don't give a shit any more.

"I lied to your brother," she says, straightening her skirt. "I said I would be professional. Screwing his brother at work is sooooo far from professional."

"Baby, you should get a bonus for making the boss's brother very happy."

"Don't say that. It makes me sound like I'm getting paid for sex."

"I didn't mean that and you know it." I'm having trouble working the button-fly over my semi-erect dick. My cock doesn't want this to end. Neither do I—I am just getting warmed up. "You surprised me, that's all."

"I surprised myself. It's not like I've ever done this at work." Her face is flushed and she looks incredibly pretty. I want to kiss her and start over with more tenderness this time. Then again, maybe not. Maybe I just want to fuck her again.

"Good. This is a first for both of us then. I'm glad," I tell her.

"It's also a last. We can't do this here. This was…"

"Insane?" I chuckle and pull her into my arms.

"Yes. Insane." She laughs. "What were we thinking? I hope nobody walked by our closed door and assumed that we were screwing."

"People close their doors here all the time so they can shut out the noise and make phone calls."

"Except Carson. You never told me why you tore his door off the hinges."

I sigh, embracing her tighter so I can kiss the top of her head. "That was a bad time. I don't want to talk about that now."

Emma tilts her head up and her eyes are like warm, inviting pools of chocolate with swirls of amber liquid that make me dismiss my doubts about myself and us, at least temporarily. I know this won't last. It never does.

"Any time you want me to nail you, or do anything else for that matter, text me."

"Dylan, we have to chill it on the sex-at-work. This is wrong." She shakes her head and that sexy, demanding voice from earlier is replaced with Miss Worker Bee.

"Hey, thanks for making my day. Now that I know this turns you on, I'm going to wear this tool belt everywhere. The grocery store, the gas station, in every room of the house."

Emma smirks and stands next to her chair, looking very prim and proper again. I walk over to the door, unlock it and swing it open. I lean against the doorframe as we both take in the obvious silence of an empty office that has gone to lunch.

"Yeah, everyone is lining up to see us." I grin.

"Shush, we got lucky, that's all," she whispers. "I'm

going to run to the restroom to freshen up. Give me a ten-second head start so it doesn't look like we're going together."

"Ah, geez. You're funny."

As she grabs her purse and sails out the door and down the hall, I am two steps behind her. She looks over her shoulder, scowls at me then quickens her pace to get to the women's restroom. I laugh as I enter the men's room. When I finish, I wait in the hall for her, leaning against the opposite wall. She exits the restroom and glares at me.

"You're not supposed to wait around for me—it blows our cover," she whispers.

"What cover?" I laugh. "I'm feeling very energetic for some reason. I think I'm going to check on some things in the factory and then I'm going to bring you back a sandwich since you didn't get all the necessary nutrients for a well-rounded lunch. How does that sound?"

She's about to say something when one of her damn burner phones rings in her bag.

"Unless it's your grandmother, I know this can't be good."

Emma pulls the phone out of her bag. "Yes?" she answers, looking at me.

I'm not leaving until I have a full report on that phone call.

She is quiet while she looks down at the floor. "Okay. That should work. I'll see you soon."

I hate the sound of that.

Sixteen
Emma

It was like any other day until Robby Marchetto saved me.

Behind Ray's Pizza, my girlfriends and I are carrying our pizza slices to an empty picnic table. A few tables away, Robby Marchetto and his friends are eating and laughing, capturing the attention of every girl and envious guy around him.

Robby is enigmatic, handsome, on the verge of being a man at eighteen, and I always notice him. I am fifteen, still an invisible wallflower to Robby's circle. I will never be tall and voluptuous, but my rail thin figure has finally sprouted some curves, and my face is blooming into a simple prettiness, giving me a hopeful boost that maybe boys will start asking me out.

As I follow my friends out of the pizza shop, I sneak peeks at Robby's gorgeousness—his dark hair that he rakes with his fingers so it flops carelessly around his pretty face; his tan, muscular body from days spent at the Jersey shore; and that impossibly perfect smile that makes girls fall in love with him and fantasize about being his girlfriend. I am no different than those silly, young girls. Robby Marchetto is my idea of the perfect boy.

As I carry my food to my table and glance at Robby letting out a rambunctious laugh, an older boy—a senior from a rival school—blocks my way. Startled, I attempt to walk around him.

"Hey, sweetness. You're pretty. Who are you with?" he says and I freeze, unaccustomed to having any boy talk

to me like that.

He's tall—another popular jock—and attractive with his own following, but nothing like Robby. I stammer, perhaps mumble an "excuse me" to get back to my friends, but the boy doesn't let me pass.

"I'm with my friends," I finally say and try to walk around him.

He grabs my arm in a hostile way, making me nervous.

"Why don't you come sit with me and my friends? I'd like to have a pretty, little thing like you next to me." He smiles, yet there is a cruelty in his tone.

"She's cute," one of his friends says, sitting at their table only a few feet from me.

"I wouldn't mind that sweet mouth going down on me," the boy in front of me says.

I panic. My friends' table is farther away, and they have no idea that I have been separated from them.

The boy's presence bombards my brain with all sorts of warning signs. I consider dropping my pizza and slugging his face with my backpack. Before I can react, the boy is thrown to the ground, and Robby Marchetto is sitting on his chest, pummeling his face with his fists.

"Don't you fucking touch her, asshole, or I'll damage you so bad that no one will recognize your face!"

I drop my pizza and watch as Robby defends me. I look around at the other picnic tables; all the students are watching Robby defend my honor. I feel sick to my stomach watching that boy get the beating of his life, however I also feel a joyful quickening, elated that Robby is doing this for me.

As Robby stands up, he gives the kid one final, swift kick in the gut. The boy groans—he's next to tears—and rolls over in pain, but Robby yanks him to his feet effortlessly.

"Apologize to her!"

The boy's nose is bleeding and his cheeks are swelling

133

into purple mounds. He looks at me and that cocky smugness is gone. He looks scared and demoralized.

"Sorry," he mumbles to me.

Robby shoves him back to his table where his shocked friends remain silent.

"Wait here," Robby tells me softly.

He goes to his own table, picks up a plate with a slice of pizza and comes back to me. He then puts his hand on my back and walks me to my friends who are gaping in awe.

"Sit down. You can have mine," he says, placing the slice of pizza in front of me.

I am too stunned and nervous to say anything, so I sit as instructed.

He leans in close to me, and I turn to see his beautiful features up close, an inch from me. Those dreamy eyes and the lips every girl fantasizes about kissing are right within my reach.

"Are you okay?" he asks quietly.

"Yes, thank you." I finally say something to show him I am a living, breathing girl.

"Good." His mouth curves into a slight smile. "If you ever have any problems with any of these guys, Emma, you let me know."

I nod, dumbfounded that he knows my name.

"Everyone calls me Robby. I hate that. You can call me Robert, okay?"

"Okay," I manage to reply.

He goes back to his table with the popular seniors and lunch resumes, yet I am in a delirious daze for the rest of the day, perhaps the week.

I know in a few months he'll be leaving for college and I will be stuck in high school, pining over a boy who will be dating girls his own age. However, I am in love with Robert Marchetto, and right then, I am the giddiest fifteen-year-old. I will hold this torch for him all through high school

134

and college, through boyfriends I compare to Robert because of that one day and his chivalrous act that left me wanting more.

***

"Emma," Dylan says as I hang up the phone.

As we walk back to our office, Robert's call makes my shoulders slump. I lean against my desk for stability while Dylan stands directly in front of me and crosses his arms, shielding himself from my bad news.

"It was Robert."

"And? Are *we* meeting with him?" Dylan spits the words out like it's something foul.

"Yes, but he didn't say when. He just said he'll see me soon."

"Christ. I've had it with this guy."

No sooner are those words out of his mouth than Daisy appears in the doorway, breathless and excited. "Emma, there is a gorgeous Roman god standing at the reception desk asking for you."

I glance up at Dylan and his expression darkens with anger.

Daisy whisks herself away to accommodate the guest who makes everything else seem irrelevant. I can see why. As I round the corner of the reception counter with Dylan's large presence behind me, I see Robert in a way that others see him. Impeccably dressed with a striking handsomeness that can be intimidating. His good-natured, easy-going charm is what reels people in. He is comfortable with himself and with anyone; it is an innate talent of putting others at ease to make them worship you.

"Robert." My voice falters.

"Emma." He glances at Dylan. "I was hoping we could go some place and talk.

"You can talk somewhere else," Dylan says, taking command of the situation. "I'm going, too, but I'll give you some privacy. Get your car and follow us out to Rupert's

135

Grill on the interstate. It's loud enough so no one can hear you and the locals won't be snooping."

Robert doesn't look too pleased with the arrangement, but he isn't going to argue. Dylan takes my hand and walks by Robert, opening the door and leading me to his Jeep, which we drove in this morning. Robert follows us in a black Camry with Connecticut plates. Clearly his many friends are helping him stay off the grid as much as possible.

Dylan and I don't speak on the way to the restaurant. He certainly wants to control the situation, and at the same time, he's trying very hard to be patient with me and give me some leeway with this uncomfortable problem.

The parking lot is virtually empty as we pull in. Dylan gets out of the Jeep and rounds the vehicle to my side then opens the door and holds my hand as I jump out. His hand tightens its grip on me as Robert follows us into the restaurant. Once inside, we choose the bar section where the music is louder.

We haven't shown any public displays of affection, but Dylan cups my face with one hand and kisses my cheek before walking two tables away where he can keep an eye on me and watch Robert's face, I assume, since he won't be able to hear our conversation. Dylan's sudden territorial mark catches me off guard and leaves me feeling branded. It is an effective move on Dylan's part. Robert's eyes narrow in displeasure.

When we sit, a waitress stops by and introduces herself, keeping her attention on Robert the whole time and only giving me a cursory glance. She recites some appetizer specials, and Robert says those will be fine and then hands back the menus to get rid of her. I glance over my shoulder at Dylan. His face is solemn with a fury skimming the surface and then he breaks it with a quick wink for me. My heart zings as I catch his mouth curve slightly.

Robert unbuttons his suit coat and rests his forearms on

the table. "Are you two serious? You've only been here a few weeks."

"We're not going to talk about that."

"Why not? We used to talk about everything, Emma."

"We broke up last summer, which was almost a year ago. It's over, Robert." I shake my head at the memory of the screaming match that led to soft, understanding murmurs and joyless sex. Then he let me go, though perhaps in his mind it was with the understanding that all things are temporary, even break ups.

"It's never been over for me. You know that." His eyes glint as if they are watery. I have never seen Robert shed a single tear. It must be the lighting.

"I'm not little Emma, the teenage girl that crushed on you for years. And I'm not college Emma—I'm not that person any more. What's wrong? Why are you here?"

"You're the only good thing I remember. Everything has gone to shit in my life. My family, my career, my friends, and those promises my dad made to keep me out were a lie. All of it was a lie. You were the only real thing in my life. You were the only good person. You loved me."

His voice still shows his strong will, yet there is an undercurrent, a hint of fear. This is a side of Robert that I have never witnessed before. A teenage girl always expects her knight to be bold and larger than life—forever; she never envisions something that could bring him to his knees because that isn't part of the fairy tale.

For years I only saw Robert through that teenage girl's eyes. When we dated, I was swept up in a tidal wave of love and lust, his kindness, and the way he protected me like he did for little Emma. Sitting before me now is a man who is breaking. He has kept the veneer in place, yet the breath of life seems to be seeping out of him. His eyes look sorrowful, and I can't help feeling a bit sad for him. I reach out and place my hand on his.

"So this guy must really care about you. He brought in

137

a team to keep you safe from me, I'm guessing," Robert says, tilting his head to his right.

I look to my left. At the bar I see Cooper settling onto a stool. He nods at me, and for the first time, he doesn't look like the cute, funny Cooper from work. I see him the way others see him: a tough, leather-clad, unshaven biker.

My surprise at seeing Cooper doesn't go unnoticed by Robert.

"I'm pretty sure there's another one behind me," Robert says with a little smile.

I lean to my left to look past him, and sure enough, Carson is sitting three tables behind Robert. Carson looks just as rough with his longish hair and scruffy face. He puts his sunglasses on the table and checks his phone but glances up at me. Our eyes meet, and I realize that, whoever orchestrated this army of support, is a unified front against Robert. It makes me feel that much safer.

I slowly pull my hand back from Robert's.

"I heard your dad is in trouble," I say, wondering where to begin.

"Good, old Dad. He's worse than… he's setting me up, Emma. Remember that drug bust from two years ago? The one that made its rounds in three different states?"

"The one that hit all those colleges and they questioned all those students?"

"Yeah, it was an eight-figure deal and some of my dad's guys went down in that."

"I remember," I respond, thinking back to that year at college and how I had become unhappy with Robert. He was anxious, short-tempered, and angry at his father, yet he refused to talk to me about it.

"It's nothing for you to worry about, Emma. I'm taking you into the city for a little vacation. We'll get away from school and forget where we grew up for a while. Just you and me. And we can talk about our future."

I remember that time very well.

Robert had just started working at the prestigious law firm. He thought he had unbound the chains that shackled him to his gritty childhood when his father had been working his way up in the organization. Robert had wanted to be as far away from it as possible and I had, too. The dirty money that paid for his family to live well and afford him an exceptional education weighed on him heavily with guilt, though he wouldn't talk about that. It's one of the things I admired about him—his desire to be better, and to do something legitimate with his life that wouldn't be an extension of his father's corruption.

This is also how I've justified being with Robert. I felt we were cut from the same cloth; we didn't choose to be in that bleak world of criminals, our fathers put us there. Together, Robert and I would expunge ourselves from the harsh reality of the violent organization that surrounded us.

We were dreamers, and the young Emma in me had still been in love with Robert. He had been my beautiful savior, the boy who would protect me. Five years after the pizza shop incident, when he saw me in my father's office and immediately asked me out, my heart slammed against my chest and did a back flip. I was twenty at the time and his attention had wiped out the memory of every boyfriend and date before him.

It wasn't just that he was a perfect specimen of masculine beauty; I saw the inner side of Robert, a good soul that wanted to be better than his father and the men in his family before him. The world saw him as a wealthy, handsome man who could parade around with a pretty woman on his arm and live a lifestyle of means that most don't acquire.

It's true—the expensive cars, clothing, restaurants and trips have come from blood money. I'm not going to kid myself into thinking it's anything less heinous than that. It is also true that Robert and I became kindred spirits in our decision to cut those ties and make it on our own.

When he had been hired by the law firm, Robert stopped accepting money and gifts from his father. He purchased a modest, one-bedroom condo in a Jersey suburb and visited me on weekends at college, taking me on nice but affordable getaways in the city. Sometimes he would book a room at an inexpensive hotel near campus and we would spend the weekend together, eating take-out and watching movies while I also caught up on my studies.

I had loved him. I had imagined that there would be a future of a blissful marriage, a home with children, and careers we could both be proud of. It was easy to love Robert then. He was the same starry-eyed romantic as me, and he'd treated me with loving care and a resolve to make things right against the twisted world we'd grown up in.

It didn't go as planned, though. Before the drug-ring bust, other incidents regarding the Marchetto family were splintering Robert's optimism and future plans. There were times he would show up at my college apartment to pick me up when he was quiet and removed, angry about something he refused to discuss. He would say he was protecting me from ugly truths, but what good is a relationship where someone is kept in the dark?

My idea that we were more than lovers, that we were partners, became increasingly difficult to believe as I realized Robert was becoming secretive, and with that, more needy for my attention and approval.

"All that matters is that I love you," Robert says, kissing me.

He has me pushed against his car in the isolated, unlit parking lot.

I love our spontaneous sexual encounters, thinking it makes us a romantic couple. However, his sudden desire is unwanted, especially since he is trying to silence me from

*talking about the recent news story about his father and
everything that worries him. His need to distract me with
sex in public only dampens my arousal.*

*He pulls my dress up and pushes my underwear down
before he whips out a condom and covers himself. He is
aggressive, thrusting into me before I am ready, making
love to me in a way that he never would have in the past—
without feeling. It's not love; it is a basic, desperate need to
fill some void.*

*He climaxes in a matter of minutes as I hold on to him,
hoping I am giving him some comfort. Yet, I don't want to
be the "void filler."*

*As time moves on, our relationship turns in a direction
I don't like. Robert becomes more elusive and I become
more resentful. He thinks he is keeping me safe by
withholding information about his father's criminal
activity, but it only makes me angrier. He is still kind and
loving, however the sparkle of humor and vitality of that
eighteen-year-old Robert who was so enigmatic is gone. I
am dealing with a different man all together, one who
sometimes seems paranoid and is most definitely not telling
me what is going on, and his neediness takes an ugly
transformation into possessiveness.*

*He calls me several times a day while I am rushing to
classes or study groups. He checks in to verify with whom I
am hanging out with, and suggests that he come upstate to
visit me during the weeknights, too. It is no longer a
relationship headed towards my fairy tale marriage; it's a
young woman managing the fears of a young man.*

*I play nursemaid, therapist, nurturing friend, and
regardless of how much I still care for Robert, I am no
longer in love with him. I feel like I've become his
comfortable safety net instead of his ardent lover. My
passion to be with him has withered away to an undeniable
pity for him, and a self-loathing for myself, believing I
could change him or us.*

"Robert, what exactly is your dad doing to you?"

"The feds are breathing down his neck, and I think he realizes that he's not Teflon Vinnie any more. Some undercover agents and informants have plenty of tape on my dad's guys, and even my dad, making incriminating statements. My father is getting scared, and when he gets scared, he becomes inventive."

"In what way?" I ask, noticing the tremor in Robert's hand.

"My father never leaves a paper trail, not in this business. He screwed up somewhere, and he's ready to throw other people under the bus to spare himself."

"You? He'd do that to you?"

"Not just me, but others."

"How?" I don't know the dynamics or the ins and outs of the Marchetto organization—I've never really wanted to.

"My fingerprints are on that drug bust," he whispers shamefully.

I stare at him in disbelief. That was a huge news story. One weekend, in a hotel room, we watched the constant news coverage of people being arrested and doing the perp walk to various courthouses. Robert and I had felt relief to be out of that world, or so I thought.

Angry tears begin to blur my vision. "How is that possible?"

"I'm not going to make excuses for what I did, but my dad assured me that he just needed me on one job. It was a simple exchange of funds. No guns, no drugs. I mean no one was hurt."

"Of course people were hurt," I snap. "It was an enormous distribution of heroin that went to not only addicts, but kids, students, mothers, and anyone else they could sell to. How could you be involved in that?"

"I made a bad decision. A deal with my dad. If I did what he wanted, I would be cut loose, free and clear. I wanted that so I could leave here, and to maybe go across the country to be with just you. I should have known that the only one who wins in deals with my father *is* my father. He made sure to mark me with evidence as future protection for himself. His guy was wired and has me making a transaction during that time. It's small, but it's strong enough to bring me in. I knew I was picking up a cash payment, but I had no idea it was tied to the heroin shipment. You have to believe me. I thought it was one small, dirty deed, if that's possible. Something insignificant."

"And if they bring you in, they'll cut you a deal to blow the whistle on the guys at the top—your dad."

"My father would never let it come to that." Robert looks down at his trembling hands. Strong hands that used to engage in street fights for kicks. Hands I used to kiss and hold.

"I don't understand. Your parents kept you out of most of this crap, and when your dad became the boss and made the money, he sent you to the best schools. He wanted you to succeed in the real world. This doesn't make sense. Are you saying he'd let you go to prison for him?"

"No, Emma. He didn't want me to succeed in the real world; he wanted me to serve him. He wouldn't let me make it to prison. He has leverage against me. If I squeal on him, I lose everything, too. He's counting on me not talking."

I can't take in all this grisly information at once. He has shattered my perception of this dark world I didn't want any part of, and he has made it worse.

"So, if you don't divulge information to the Feds, they send you to prison, right?"

"In theory, but you need to think about the odds of me making it to prison or staying alive once I'm there. There will be a hit on me, no matter if I'm in or out."

"Oh, God, Robert. I can't believe this." I drop my head

and start tearing up again. When the waitress places water and some giant fried onion thing in front of us, Robert thanks her so she will leave then hands me some napkins to wipe my eyes.

My face must look puffy and blotchy from the tears because Carson looks at me and stands up. I shake my head and wave him back to his seat. He then looks over my head and shakes his head at Dylan, I assume. I glance over at Cooper who is leaning back on his bar stool, watching us full on. That is what I like about Cooper, he is not hiding like he's on a stake out. He looks like he is ready to pounce into action if need be.

"I didn't want to drop this bomb on you, but it's not just about me. It's..."

I look up at him as he struggles to find the right words. He decides to say nothing and then my curiosity is more than piqued.

"It's what? Tell me."

"Nothing," Robert says quietly.

"I don't know why you're here and what you think I can do. What *can* I do to help you? I have no power in this situation with your father. My own dad has already paid an enormous fortune to the organization, and I'm hoping he can sell his business to a bigger operation and get out. Get out of Jersey all together."

Robert winces, and I sense he wants to say something important, something that he's meant to tell me at this meeting, yet he is beginning to shut down again. Those familiar walls are going up—the barrier—so I won't hear or see unbearable things, but what does he have to protect me from now after what he's just told me?

"I had to see you," he says, his face relaxes a bit, his beauty oozing out again; those alluring dark eyes matched with a fleeting grin. "I suppose I had a fantasy that you'd drop everything and come with me. We'd leave this place and go far away—forever."

144

I don't know what to say, and my heart breaks a little as I watch his long, dark lashes sweep down as he closes his eyes. I used to love this boy whose swoon worthy good looks and adoring attention were enough to sustain me, I thought, indefinitely. A part of me keeps Dylan's image firmly at the front of my mind because my heart is falling for him, although I believe Dylan would understand my reluctance to walk away from Robert and leave him to bear this alone. I don't know what I am supposed to do, however I do know that abandoning Robert isn't an option.

"I can't leave with you, and I don't know how to help you. I want to, though I can't go on the run like we're Bonnie and Clyde."

"I don't want you to live like that either." He smiles and takes a gulp of his water.

I stare at the onion blossom, the fried monstrosity sitting between us.

"How can your mother stand by and watch this happen?"

I try to picture Robert's mother with her pretty Italian features; her thick, black stylish hair and attractive figure. Would she be willing to let her son go to prison so her husband could keep the money stream coming in? Would she still look beautiful and stoic for news cameras, or would she break down at the thought of losing her eldest child?

"She'll do whatever *the family* needs. Emma, I didn't realize my parents were these kinds of people until recently. I tried to look at everything through rose-colored glasses in a way, like you."

"What do you mean, like me? I've never had any illusions about the people in your business."

"Right." His tone is unconvincing.

There is more to this nightmare that he is hiding from me.

"Where are you staying? Who is helping you? What

aren't you telling me?" I want to reach out and hold his hand again, touch his face to reassure him. I am afraid my gestures could be misconstrued, though, therefore I keep my hands in my lap.

"The less I tell you, the better. I don't want you to be a part of this. I'm okay, though. I have friends who are helping me and I'm figuring out what to do next. Please don't tell your father or Sean that you spoke to me. Can you do that for me?"

"Of course. I won't tell anyone."

"Except for your three bodyguards." He smiles weakly.

I want to cry and scream and shake him at the same time. How could he do this? Even if it was a mistake, nothing done for his father can be considered an innocent slip. If he has been threatened or coerced in the way my father has been subjected to extortion for years, Robert won't divulge it.

"They aren't out to get you. They're my friends. They want to make sure I'm safe, that's all."

Robert gives a deep, warm chuckle. "I love that about you. If you could see the look on your boyfriend's face right now, you'd know he doesn't think of you as his friend. The way he's been watching me since we sat down... Well, let's just say, he's made his point."

At those words, I want to turn around and see Dylan's reassuring, composed expression. Knowing he is behind me fills my chest with a new sensation, stronger and different than what I used to feel with Robert.

"Was there something else you wanted to tell me?"

"There are a lot of things I want to say to you, maybe things I wish I'd said sooner. It doesn't matter now."

He sounds so hopeless, like he is giving me an end-of-the-world send off. I will not accept that. We are intrinsically connected, defined by circumstances we never controlled, and ending our intimate relationship was not enough to sever my attachment to Robert. I am past the

146

crush, the heart-stopping love, the lust, the hope, but I am very much connected to him by an undying fondness and concern. I can't simply blot him from my memory, though it would make life easier if I could.

"Times up." Dylan's demand makes me pop my head up. "You saw her and now it's time to leave," he says to Robert.

"Yeah. It is." Robert gazes at me as he throws cash on the table for the bill. He rises while Cooper and Carson come to stand behind Dylan.

I am flustered for a moment. I don't have my answers. Robert came here to give me this horrific news, and I haven't pledged any kind of help. I want to go back to my cozy makeshift home with Dylan, yet I don't want to leave this unresolved. I haven't done anything to help Robert, and now he faces a worse fate than I've previously thought.

As Dylan takes my hand again and leads us out of the restaurant, the others follow. Outside, Cooper is silent as he gives me a gentle tap across my chin with his fist. He then gets on his Harley and zooms out of the parking lot. Carson pats my shoulder before he gets in his truck. He waits for Robert to get back in his car and then follows him out onto the interstate.

Dylan opens the passenger door of the Jeep, and I climb in. I sit there for a moment, replaying the dialogue in my head while Dylan reaches across me and buckles my seat belt and then kisses me gently on the cheek. Sometimes people feed off each other's sadness, and Dylan seems to be in tune with mine. His lips linger against my skin as if he knows that we can't always release people who have been under our skin for so many years, and that escaping disappointment is next to impossible. I seek out his lips and kiss him back as he wraps his arms around me so tightly it triggers a faucet of tears until I am gushing.

I don't know how long he stands there holding my sagging, crying body. By the time he gets in the Jeep to

147

drive us home, it is dark and I wonder if I will ever see Robert again, if he even has a chance at living.

Seventeen
Dylan

It took all my will power not to drag that guy out to the parking lot and beat the shit out of him. I don't know if I am feeling more anger than jealousy. I shouldn't be angry about someone Emma was involved with before she knew me, but I can be pissed as hell that he is making her feel sorry for him. He's a sleazy piece of shit, and Emma's heart is too big. I could see the pain on her face. She can't help a dangerous guy like that, and the sooner I get that through her head, the better.

When we get home, she goes upstairs and lies on her bed, fully dressed with her shoes on. I heat up some leftover vegetable stew and rip a chunk of bread off a baguette and then take up a tray to her. Her eyes are open, staring at the ceiling.

What is so special about this guy that he could leave her in this state? I pull off her shoes and then she sits up and leans back against the big decorative pillows while I set the dinner tray over her lap.

"Eat something, you'll feel better," I tell her.

I climb in on the other side of the bed and sidle up to her, putting a straw in the iced tea she loves. I brew it every day for her. Seriously, I am ready to spoon feed this girl until she comes out of this ex-boyfriend coma. He doesn't get to do this to her, and she doesn't get to mope and feel sorry for him.

"Emma, stop it."

She glances at her food and then meets my insistent gaze.

149

"I'm sorry. Thank you for dinner. I don't know if I have an appetite, though." Her mouth turns down into a pouty frown, and she looks like she's about twelve.

"He's got serious problems, and you can't fix them for him. You know his family and their line of work." I scoff for referring to it as work. "He wanted to meet. You met him. It's done."

I rip off a smaller piece of bread and hand it to her. She holds it tentatively over the stew.

"Why was Cooper there? And Carson? I didn't see you call them before we left the office."

"We had an understanding, that if this guy... if Robert showed up, they'd watch out for you, too."

"Cooper seemed different, like he's done this before," she says in a soft, tired voice.

"I don't know about that. I just know Carson had mentioned that he would be watching out for Robert, so he must have enlisted Cooper."

"I'm surprised you didn't frisk Robert first." She dips the bread into the stew.

"Believe me, I thought about it. Then I saw his face. He wasn't there to hurt you. Whatever he needed from you—to see you one last time—"

"Why do you say that?" she asks, suddenly alert. "Do you know something I don't? Even Robert was fairly cryptic."

"I only know what your friend Sean told us. I assume he's in a situation that will bury him deep."

"If you believe he's guilty, why didn't you and Carson call the Feds yourself?"

She begins eating the stew, and I'm relieved to have that at least.

"I don't know if he's guilty of anything. I don't have any facts, so I'm not about to get us, or him, entangled with law enforcement when I don't have the information in front of me. What did he say to you?"

"His father is probably going to be able to pin a huge drug bust on him. Robert thinks he's being set-up by his father. He was involved in a transaction that he had no idea was associated with a major heroin bust two years ago."

"Ah, Emma. You believe that he couldn't know what he was doing? Babe, this is all he knows. His father is running the show. How is it possible for him to not be aware of what he was doing?"

She puts her spoon down. Shit, I just turned her off from eating. I couldn't keep my mouth shut?

"He's not naïve, but he did believe his father loved him. I don't think he ever anticipated that this could happen. Neither did I, for that matter."

She moves the tray to the floor. "Thanks for dinner. I'm just not hungry."

She then stretches out on the bed and I pull her close to me. She leans against my body, and I take in long, slow, deep breaths to calm my overly-excited nerves at having her so close.

"Why are you so worried about him? You were pretty upset that he was trying to see you, so what's changed your tune?"

I try to mask my frustration and anger over this guy with a softer tone. I kiss her temple, tempted to take it further. I want to fuck her until she's coming and moaning my name, wiping any trace of this guy along with any residual feelings she has for him.

"When Robert left that note at my house, I thought he was coming back to get me, to push me back into our old relationship. Today, I saw a different Robert. He's scared and sad... and, I guess it brought back memories—some good, some not."

"You don't have any power to help him. Besides, he can call it a mistake, but he has to pay the price like the rest of us."

"Like the rest of us?" she asks, pulling back from my

151

chest so she can see my face.

"A lot of us have had tough breaks and we have to live with it."

"Most kids don't grow up with mobsters. His life is a bit tougher, I'd say."

"For the most part, I grew up without parents, and my brother and I were dirt poor. It screwed me up along with whatever problems I was born with. It was a bad mix and it made Carson's life hell. He had to feed us, keep us sheltered, keep us together, and deal with my violent behavior. I made a lot of mistakes as an adult, Emma. I'm responsible for them, just like Robert is responsible for what he's done. Having a bad childhood or a fucked up family doesn't give you a free pass as an adult."

"I know that." She pushes farther away from me and huffs out an exasperated breath.

"So why does it look like you're coddling this guy?" I prop myself up on one arm as she folds her arms and looks up at the ceiling with teary eyes.

"I don't coddle Robert. You don't understand. He was very important to me, and I hate to see him being framed like this. He deserves better from his father."

The fury builds in my chest and moves up to my face like gasoline being ignited with a single dropped match.

"Do you hear yourself? Your ex-boyfriend admitted to participating in a crime and you think he's being treated unfairly?" My face is directly above hers.

"I think, if he committed a crime, he has to pay the price, but that subjects him to death—a hit by his own father. I don't know what price he has to pay, but it shouldn't be death." She looks unbearably sad as she closes her eyes and her long, dark lashes plaster themselves with tears against her cheeks.

"You don't know that he's going to be a target. I think he's exaggerating his circumstances to get you on his side. Did he ask you to leave with him?" I can barely maintain a civil tone. I want to scream some sense into her.

When I met her, I knew she had street smarts and a tough, wise-ass mouth. What happened to that strong girl?

She doesn't respond, which pretty much answers my question.

"Emma," I demand, "did he give you a sob story and tell you he needs you?"

"Yes," she hisses, "but not in the way you're implying. He was trying to explain what was going on and why he wanted to see me. We have a history together—we've seen a lot of the same stuff. There's an understanding between us that other people don't get."

"Like me? Is that what you were going to say?"

"Sean is right; Robert is scared. He's in a bad place and he thought seeing me would help."

"Did it?" I am too loud. I plant my left arm on the other side of her, trapping her.

"Maybe it helped him, but it sure freaked me out. I never expected to see him like this. It… it's hard for me to see him falling apart and in danger. I broke up with him because I saw a change in him over that last year. It all had to do with the business, and I didn't want to have my future infected with his father's seedy organization. Robert and I both thought he could separate himself from it and we'd get to move on and have our own life. We were falling apart. He was acting weird, and I couldn't take it anymore. The bad stuff is just following him and me."

"You still love him, don't you?"

"No, not like that. I care about him, though. And I never thought it would ever come to this. There are things he's not telling me, and it's frightening to think that what he's hiding may be worse than what he's already told me."

"You're sure that this isn't that you're not thinking clearly because you're still in love with him?" I hate asking the question. I want her to sound more positive about her long, stowed-away emotions for this guy. That they have disintegrated to the point of being dead. I want any feelings she has for him now to be insignificant compared to what she may feel for me.

The urge to run my fingers through her long hair and take her body with every part of me brings out my more brutal side.

"You seem to have conveniently forgotten that this dreamy fuckhead of yours is also part of an organization that has threatened and shaken down your father for years. Why you'd ever get involved with him in the first place escapes me, and I have to question why you're here with me. Maybe I should ask myself why we're... together."

I sound like an ass. I figure it's my last chance to make her come to her senses or at least acknowledge that she can't keep seeing this guy or letting herself get emotionally strung out over him.

"Are we together?" she asks defensively. "Haven't we concocted a convenient arrangement to sleep together and pretend to play house? And another thing, my father was also given protection. He's gotten something out of it. It's not ideal, but it's what we have."

"First of all, we're not playing house, otherwise you'd be doing your share of work around here, princess." I am in her face, but she looks so angry and pretty I just want to kiss her and erase this argument. "Personally, I don't think your circumstances are very convenient for me—you letting an ex-boyfriend hang on. You think that works for me? And stop trying to rationalize this whole screwed up place you come from. It's not working for me." I now have her slender body and limbs pinned to the bed, and her lips are an inch from mine.

"I sound like I'm more trouble than I'm worth," she responds, her breath heating my face.

"You're worth it. It's already been established that I like you a lot." I soften my tone. I am not the most patient guy; I want her to cave in to her feelings and desire for me.

I refuse to let her eyes leave mine.

"I like you, too."

Emma glances down at my mouth, which is all it takes for me to swoop in and take her bottom lip before parting her mouth with my tongue. My mind retreats to that pleasant place where I get lost in her touch. She tastes and smells like sugar as I take her mouth more aggressively. As my hand slides under her shirt, pushing her bra up so I can run my thumb across a hard nipple, she moans and strokes my back with both of her hands and slides them under the waist of my jeans. She then inches under my briefs, running her nails against my skin before she squeezes my ass. My cock responds in kind and swells eagerly against her.

"Take your shirt off," she demands.

"Whatever you say." The t-shirt gets tossed.

"And don't ever call me princess again," she adds, splaying her hands down my chest and running her fingers down my stomach. "God, Dylan, you are..." Her breath hitches and her eyes roam over my chest and arms with desire.

Having her look at me with appreciation and lust makes me feel like both a self-conscious sad sack that needs to convince a woman he is the one for her and a selfish, greedy bastard who wants more of her in every way.

She begins stripping off her own clothes while I remove my jeans and briefs. I didn't plan on using her somber, depressing encounter with her ex as a way to get her into bed, however I am not going to pass up this opportunity, especially when she's taking the initiative.

I chuckle when she reaches into her nightstand and pulls out a condom.

"I took a stash from your room. Thought they might come in handy here," she says as she tears the package and rolls the condom on my hard cock.

I am too mesmerized with her actions, her hands and

how she looks naked beneath me, to say anything. As I admire her creamy skin and perfect tits with rosy pink centers, she literally slams me with a kiss and pushes her hands against my chest so that I fall over on my back. She quickly straddles me, holding my cock firmly in one hand while she braces herself against the headboard with her other hand. When she pushes up on her knees and begins rubbing herself with my cock, that image alone is enough to make me come.

I grit my teeth and try to hold everything in, but then she arches her back and pushes her perky tits out and I have to fondle them. I am rough, squeezing her soft flesh at the same time that I try to push myself into her. She manages to keep me from thrusting into her by moving up higher on her knees and keeping a firm grasp on my cock so it only grazes her wetness.

She is teasing me.

"Ah, fuck, prince—babe."

"Oh, you almost made a fatal mistake. One more princess and I would have stopped and you'd go poof." She smiles.

I hold her hips and use more force to pull her onto my hard, aching dick.

"I need you now," I grunt out.

"I know." Her voice is husky as she rubs the tip of my cock against herself, moaning. "And you're making me so wet."

I am ready for this cock tease to end. I consider tossing her on her back and plunging into her, yet she beats me to it by impaling herself on me in one move.

"Thank God," I groan.

She throws her head back and uses both hands on the headboard to thrust against me in a long, slow rhythm. I grip her hips, afraid I will come too soon then I move my hands back to her nipples and fondle them until she moans and grinds harder against me.

"That feels so amazing," she says, opening her eyes.

She looks down at me, her hair cascading wildly around her. She looks like a sexy feline creature, aroused beyond recognition. I am so fucking turned on; I need her to come this minute.

I rub my thumb against her clit. She is so wet I need to slip two fingers between our grinding bodies. I use my other hand to tease her nipples. She grips the headboard tighter and begins slamming into me faster, grinding and thrusting. She is losing control and, as she constricts against my cock, I know I am pretty much done, too.

"Come," I hiss. "Come."

"Hey, stud, saying it doesn't make it happen faster," she says breathlessly.

"Please," I grit. "Don't think guys have the ability to hold out longer when their dicks give the orders. There's a hierarchy here. Dick, dick, dick, Dylan."

She laughs and then her eyes glaze over as she climaxes. Her face flushes while she continues to gyrate with the orgasm rolling through her. She lets out a long, deep moan as her arms begin to lose their hold on the bed frame. I grab her waist and thrust up violently, and in a matter of seconds, my release is just as explosive. She is going boneless in her euphoric state, so I have to hold her up and finish driving myself into her.

I shout out as I empty every last bit of myself and then let Emma's body fold onto me. We are both breathing hard. My brain is attempting to refocus and come back to reality, but it is impossible with this beautiful creature clinging to me. I deposit her gently on her side so I can get rid of the condom. When I return to the bed, she is stretched out with one thigh crossed over the other as if she is posed like an acrobat. Her eyes are closed and she looks content.

"The answer is yes," I say, sliding in next to her and wrapping an arm around her waist.

She opens her eyes and turns her head towards me.

"Yes, what?"

"Yes, we're together. Whatever it is you think you owe Robert, you're not with him. I don't know where we're going, but we're together."

She runs the back of her hand gently up my cheek and then her fingers playfully trace the scars on my head. I am not sure I've said the right thing to her. She is quiet and contemplative as she studies the deformed gorges of flesh on my scalp.

"Look at me," I demand.

Emma's gaze wanders down to meet mine.

"Are you done with that guy?" I don't even want to say his name out loud.

"Dylan, I have no intention of being involved with him romantically, if that's what you mean."

"Seeing him, feeling sorry for him, agonizing over his situation—all of that does make you involved with him romantically because you are reminiscing with him, leading him to believe that you're there for him."

"Then you and I have a very different definition of a romantic relationship."

"Maybe it's not intimate… because then I'd have to kill him," I say and she chuckles. "But everything else you are giving him—your attention… and hope… that's romance, baby. And you can't be with me and have that with him, too."

She looks startled. "Is this an ultimatum? Because if it is, I can move out now and go live with Imogene and Lauren."

"No."

"Dylan," she starts angrily. "No, this isn't an ultimatum? What?"

"No, I don't want you to leave, but I'm not going to share you."

"You're not. Robert is… I may never see him again. After what he told me today, I think it was his final goodbye."

"And what if it wasn't?"

I saw how Robert looked at her. That appearance of hope that Emma could still belong to him. It made me twinge with anger that there is a part of her that belongs to him, those memories of when she was in love with him. If I could obliterate those memories, I probably would; yet I don't know if I would have ever met her if it hadn't been for the man and the life she was trying to leave behind.

Eighteen
Emma

My phone call with my father is short and useless. He sounds agitated and anxious to end our conversation. He also does a damn fine job of sidestepping my questions about Vincent Marchetto and whatever rumors are circulating through his underworld network. It sounds like Hades and his minions. I wish it were that simple. A little Greek mythology, I can handle; an evasive father who has a history with the mob, I can't.

He says my mother is well and having a nice time in Florida with my grandma, and he can't say any more about Robert or his father because it is in my best interest to be an ignorant boob. Of course, he didn't put it like that, however that's what it comes down to when any man tells me he is keeping information from me for my own good.

Fuck. Them. All.

While Dylan throws together our breakfast, I'm thankful he doesn't bring up Robert. He wolfs down his food with his meds, telling me to stop pushing my food around on my plate. He wants to work out and decides that he is not going to leave me alone in the house while he goes on his usual run, so I have to watch him exercise in the house, shirtless and sweaty, doing push-ups. I am thrilled.

The air is electrified as I knit some rainbow concoction and subtly watch him from behind my knitting needles while Dylan hauls his bench set and weights up from the basement and organizes them in the sparse living room.

"Great, now this place is going to smell like a gym," I

say, but I really don't mind.

There's not much else to do out here since our cable went out days ago unless, of course, we want to have non-stop sex. This naturally crosses my mind every ten minutes or so, and with the way Dylan periodically looks at me in-between his bench sets or on his strolls to the kitchen for water, I would say he is thinking the same thing. Besides, since moving to town, I had to give up my gym workouts and haven't committed to an exercise program of any kind unless you count sex as a legitimate workout, and I do. I have to work off all those home-cooked meals Dylan provides.

It's just us in this house with the scent of Dylan's sweat and the atmosphere's charged with the excitement of our new relationship, wherever that stands. If I weren't worried about Robert's safety, this arrangement with Dylan would be perfect. He glances at me, too, as if he is aware of my thoughts, and most likely, it leaves him with some uncertainty about me.

I left Robert because I finally received a wake-up call about the reality of our situation. If we were together, we would never be free of his father, and the sweet idea I conjured up of an idyllic marriage and family would never happen the way I had imagined. Robert is not the same boy I fell in love with, and I'm not the same girl.

It has occurred to me that I am also entering into unknown territory with Dylan. It's easy to get caught up in the early stages of flirting and sexual desire; it's another to live together and pretend it is casual, and including Dylan's issues into the scenario makes it that much more precarious.

I am falling for him, and even though we don't say it, our bond is growing. I hope I am not leading him on. I think about that every time I have a moment to recall Robert or have a flashback down memory lane, remembering when Robert was my knight. Girls don't need knights in shining armor, but it sure is nice when they show up, and I have had two in my life now. I hope Dylan is the real *long-term* deal, though.

"Oh, this is wonderful," Lauren *says over the phone when I call to tell her that Carson has offered me the job. "And you'll be working with Dylan. Good thing he's mellowed out."*

"He couldn't have been that bad," I reply.

"He's not busting heads anymore." She laughs, but there is no humor in her tone. "I told you, he and Carson had it rough, but there was a time when Dylan made everything worse. He'd get in fights over little things and would do reckless things."

"Like what?"

"He was easily provoked and would spin into these rampages. He was a straight-A student, but there was perpetual fighting, getting kicked out of school, college suspensions, and illegal motorcycle races. God, Dylan was all over the place, and I never saw him with the same woman twice." She laughs again uncomfortably as if it is for my benefit.

"But you said he's done with treatment and he's better." I am trying to picture Carson's younger brother, who I haven't met yet. Carson is so mature and professional; it's hard to believe his brother would be the complete opposite.

"He is getting better," Lauren explains. "It's kind of new for all of us to see Dylan this way. I grew up with the guy. His mother's illness and death was devastating for him because he was just a kid. And then his dad shot himself when Dylan was a teenager. Between puberty and the family illness, Dylan really needed a parent then. His parents' deaths absolutely destroyed him.

"His father's side had a history of mental illness, so it wasn't exactly surprising that Dylan was diagnosed as

162

bipolar, but he wasn't getting the right assistance. Carson was a teenager, so it's not like he knew how to help his brother. We saw a lot of Dylan's explosive behaviors when he was manic and out of control, and then he'd crash into a deep depression—sometimes vocal and angry, sometimes quiet and closed off. The crazy cycles went on for years, but we never got used to it. He could be kind and lovable one day and then moody and pissed off the next."

"You're making me nervous about this guy."

"I'm sorry. It's not an easy thing to describe. Really, Dylan has such a sweet side to him. He was so cute and used to have this adorable, curly hair. Women would fall over him. He's still sweet, though sometimes he forgets that we see him in that way. But Carson and my parents all think Dylan is doing great now." Lauren lets out a deep, tired sigh.

"You don't sound very optimistic."

"I am, but it's only been a few months since he cleaned up his act, so I'm not going to kid you and say it's finally over and done with. I hope it is. The important point I want to make is that Dylan is a good guy. He's smart about the business, and I think you'll get along with him. This job is perfect for you."

I sigh, wondering what it's going to be like working with this Dylan person.

What I struggle with is, how well do I understand the ramifications of Dylan's mental health issue? We joke about it sometimes and use it to lighten a mood, as if it makes us braver and easier to face it head on. The truth is, I wasn't living here when Dylan was at his worst. I didn't witness the volatile behavior during his manic stages, and I didn't know him before his accident and the weeks he spent living in the rehab facility. I have gotten everything second-hand from Lauren and Imogene along with bits and pieces from Dylan.

What if I am replacing Robert with another troubled man that needs more than I can give?

As Dylan secures two large plates on the weight bar, it stirs me from my reverie.

"Those are enormous. Carson is right. It's overkill," I say, watching him lock the weights in place.

He is wearing cargo pants, and his bare chest is slick with a sweaty sheen. His brutal workout regime has given him the most spectacular body, and I love staring at his broad chest that narrows down into rippling abs. I have always thought Robert was a gorgeous man, but Dylan is beautiful, both physically and the way he is driven to push himself to the extreme. I assume it's to chase away bad mojo.

When I put my needles down and analyze his process of aligning the weights, he catches my gaze and grins. I think he likes having me around during his workouts so he's not enduring his solitary torture in vain.

"Why do you work out so much, Dylan? Between the running and all the weight training... I've never seen someone work this hard on their body unless they're training for the Olympics. You're not hiding something big from me, are you? I mean, you haven't been recruited for a slot on an Olympic team, have you?" I am back to being jokey because I know the answer is more complex than what we have ever discussed.

I am curled up on the couch with my lap covered in skeins of yarn and knitting needles. Dylan secures another weight plate and stands up to look down at me with a calm reserve.

"I have to do this, Emma. I have to take medication and I have to see my doctor and let him *therapize* the hell out of my brain, but I also need the exercise. It may seem like overkill, but I have so much physical and mental energy that, if I don't do this every day, my brain becomes cluttered with too many thoughts. The meds take the edge

164

off, but sometimes my brain won't shut off or calm down, and that's when it starts attacking me. I've discovered the only way for me to burn off the negative thoughts is to have my body expel the bad energy by force."

"Oh," is all I can say. "It must be very hard to keep up this rigorous schedule."

"Outside of work, I have a lot of time on my hands, so I've gotten used to this and actually look forward to it. Does it bother you that I put all this equipment in the living room? If it does, I can move it back to the basement."

"It doesn't bother me. I like your company." For some reason, that little statement makes me blush. I have brazenly stripped him naked and straddled him, yet that comment is more telling than sex.

He smiles again, a lopsided, innocent grin. "The feeling is mutual. I like when you're in the same room with me—at work and when I'm cooking in the kitchen. My workouts are long and tedious; it's easier to do when you're sitting there watching me."

"I'm not watching you; I'm knitting." I hold up my mangled project.

"Okay." He laughs.

"You really think keeping me prisoner in the house and guarding me night and day is necessary? Are you afraid of Robert?"

"Baby, the only guy I've ever been afraid of is me." He's kidding again, but there's truth to his words, and I don't attempt to dismiss him with a laugh. "I'm only concerned for your welfare, okay?"

"And I appreciate it. I do, Dylan, but how long can you be joined at the hip with me? We may have seen the last of Robert, and you can't do this indefinitely." *As much as I love your undivided attention,* I want to say.

"Until there are new developments. Maybe we'll see something on the news or we'll hear from your dad. Until then, we work and we hang out here. And don't forget, we have a fun-filled night ahead of us at Carson's house."

He resumes lifting his weights.

"Oh, I haven't forgotten. I can't wait to get out and do something different and be around some new people."

Dylan pauses and glances at me with a mixed expression. I am afraid that remark has wounded him.

"I meant I haven't gotten to spend any time with my friends or anyone else in Hera, so it will be nice to see them. I... I really like living here, though."

"Good." He pushes himself off the weight bench and joins me on the couch.

He then picks up the mangy little blanket I am knitting.

"Don't you dare throw this across the room." I pull it from his hands.

His mouth curves ever so slightly. "Why do you make these things?"

"It keeps my hands busy. I don't play video games, and I'm kind of a restless person, so this helps, even if I'm not very good at it."

"Now you know why I exercise so much. I'm a very restless person, too."

He unfurls my legs and pulls them across his lap and then leans in to kiss me. It's a soft, tender kiss, his blue eyes watching me as he nips at my lips and then my cheek. The earnestness of his warm gaze leaves me slightly breathless as a little tornado of glee begins in my belly.

I drop my knitting and hold his face in both of my hands, pulling him closer so he sinks down into the couch with me. His expression is so serious. I kiss my way across his cheek to a place behind his ear where I lick his scar. His shoulders release a little shudder when my tongue touches his scalp.

"I hope you stay here for a while," he says hoarsely.

I wonder if he deliberately added *"for a while"* to that statement so it doesn't come across as a commitment.

"I'd like that," I whisper into his ear. "Unless, of

166

course, I'm forced into the Witness Protection Program."

"Of course." He chuckles. "We wouldn't want that."

He embraces me, and for that moment, I feel like the most important person to him. Perhaps I am reading too much into our strange situation, and that working together and sleeping together have clouded my judgment. I want to say more and tell him I think he is brave to talk about his illness and to get involved with my unattractive problem; I wish I could be more forthright with him. Telling him I like him is not the same as telling him that his presence floods my heart with joy. I don't say more, though. I suspect we are both too hesitant to use stronger words, considering our recent troubles and the safeguards we have put in place for ourselves.

***

My nerves are a jumbled mess thinking about the dinner party. In my mind, this is our first real date, and it makes me laugh considering we have been sleeping and living together.

Carson's large, modern home is unbelievable, and just as Dylan has said, most everyone is dressed in jeans, the atmosphere very casual.

Jessica greets us at the door, her wild, red hair steamed up in curls from the cooking she's been doing, I am guessing. She begs off and races back to the kitchen with a fat bulldog chasing her.

"Wow, she must be cooking up a storm. It smells great," I say, taking in the vast living room with its two-story high ceilings.

"She can't cook. Their housekeeper, Talia, prepared everything and Jess is trying to figure out how to heat it up." Dylan chuckles.

Archie looks so distinguished in his three-piece suit, and both Eleanor and Lois—the yoga mavens—are glammed up in dresses and fine jewelry. Only the under thirty crowd is slumming it in jeans.

I elbow Dylan in the ribs. "Why didn't you tell me I could dress up? It's a dinner party. No one should go to a dinner party in jeans."

Dylan studies my skinny jeans and my ballet flats and then lets his gaze fall on my low-cut blouse. "You look fantastic, Emma."

His voice drops an octave, and he doesn't move to enter the party area. The way he looks at me, you would think this is the first time he has met me. A smile crosses my face as I realize that's what it feels like with Dylan—he says something or looks at me and I begin crushing on him all over again.

"Thank you. You look like a sexy assassin tonight, and it's a good look," I respond as the heat rises in my face.

Dylan laughs, causing the others in the living room to turn to see what the fuss is about.

"No one's ever described me that way," he says as he puts his arm around my waist and walks me into the living room. "I guess my pretty boy days are over. I hope."

"Who called you that?"

"Lauren and just about everybody," he replies. "That was before my accident, though. Before the nurses shaved off my curly mop."

"Well, look at you two. You finally arrived." Imogene takes a big swig of her red wine, peering at us suspiciously.

"Are you drunk already?" Dylan asks Imogene.

He tightens his grip on my waist and then pinches my side, causing a small yelp to escape me.

Imogene catches it all. "Getting drunk is the plan. So what's the deal with you two? Em, care to fill me in?"

"I'd rather not. I'm sure you heard about Robert."

"Screw Robert. I want to know how it's going living with Dylan."

"Imogene, you're supposed to help me corral people into the dining room," Cooper says, coming up behind her.

He is dressed as he always is, in jeans and a long-sleeve t-shirt with black combat boots, and he has the same unruly, long blond hair and beard scruff, but he seems different to me. Since showing up at my meeting with Robert, Cooper doesn't come across as the comedian I thought he was; he is more mature than I gave him credit for. Or it's all an act. Nevertheless, he carries off the hot biker look effortlessly.

"Oh, no you don't," she says to Cooper as he tugs on her hand. "I want to know what Dylan is doing to my friend."

"Man, leave them alone," Cooper says to her, but he's looking at me.

"Oh, God, here we go," Dylan mumbles. "Imogene, I'm not *doing*... never mind."

"Let's go sit down," I suggest, moving around Imogene.

"Oh, sure, but you still have to fess up, Ironman," Imogene says to Dylan.

I giggle at her nickname for him.

"Well, that's not so bad. She's called me worse things," Dylan adds.

Lois intercepts us and affectionately grabs Dylan's face with one hand and squeezes his cheeks. "You look so good, dear."

"Thanks, Lois," Dylan replies. "I owe it to my Ironman lifestyle, right, Imogene?"

Imogene snorts and throws back another gulp of wine.

"Dear, I think you owe it to this lovely girl," Lois replies, taking my arm and leading me to the dining room.

I turn back to Dylan, my eyes wide. We are so busted by everyone. He mimics my surprise and laughs.

"Hey, Emma," Carson says, giving me a quick peck on the cheek as he carries two bottles of wine past us to the table. "And it's good to see you out of the house, brother."

"Emma is tired of living like a prisoner in her own home," Dylan says, pulling out a chair at the dining table for me.

"I never said that, and it's not my home. It's Leo's."

"My house could use some work," Leo chimes in from the other end of the table.

"A lot of work," Lauren adds.

"Hey, wait!" Jess comes rushing in from the kitchen. "Everyone get up, I have a seating arrangement planned."

"Seriously?" Imogene whines.

"Jess, we're having enough problems getting the food cooked, do we really have to play musical chairs?" Carson asks, filling wine glasses.

"Yes! We're not sitting willy-nilly. Archie, you're at the head on that end. Emma you sit next to Archie, and Dylan you sit across from Emma. Cooper, you're next to Emma and Imogene is next to you. Lois, you sit next to Dylan, then Leo. Lauren, you're sitting next to Imogene and Eleanor you're across from Lauren. Carson you sit next to Eleanor, and I'll sit across from you, and we'll leave this head chair empty. Okay, everyone got it?"

Everyone is staring at Jess in utter confusion. She's very insistent on this seating arrangement, though.

"For heaven's sake, I'll direct everyone," Archie pipes up from his chair at the head of the table.

"We wouldn't have an open seat if Jeremy didn't leave," Imogene mutters.

"You babysit her tonight," I hear Jess mumble to Lauren who agrees enthusiastically.

"Where did Jeremy go?" I ask Cooper who sits down next to me.

Cooper huddles close to me, so Imogene doesn't hear. He really has an adorable smile. "He accepted a job offer with one of our retail chains in California. There was an opening for a management position and he asked Carson to put in a good word. They flew him out there two days ago for the interview and he got a job offer right away."

"Wow, poor Imogene. He just left her?" I ask.

There is a loud thump under the table. "Ouch!" Cooper shouts. He looks across the table at Dylan whose stern face and pinched mouth are locked on Cooper.

"Don't touch," Dylan says calmly.

"Oh, settle, man. She was asking me a question. I'm not hitting on your old lady," Cooper says, and I laugh at his hippie remark even though he is Carson's age.

"Old lady?" Imogene asks, sounding tipsy. "I knew it. Dylan Blackard, are you schtupping my friend? You guys are all the same."

"Imogene, that was uncalled for," Eleanor says. "Honestly, Imogene, you have been extremely ill-tempered. You'd think you're the first woman to fret over a man. Please, don't ruin Jess's dinner with your gloomy attitude."

"Well, thank you for reminding me how lousy I'm doing," Imogene huffs.

"Oh, honey, you can fly out and see Jeremy. It isn't the end of the world," Eleanor retorts. "If he's that important to you, use some ingenuity and figure out how to be with him."

"He didn't invite me out to visit him in California. That bastard," Imogene says and glares at Dylan.

"Don't give me the stink eye," Dylan says. "You can't pin this one on me."

"Listen to you two," Lois adds. "Why can't you all be well-mannered like Cooper?"

Everyone turns to look at Cooper whose tan face suddenly turns a light shade of pink.

"Him?" Imogene points her fork at Cooper. "What's so special about Cooper's behavior? He's a good flirt?" she asks acidly.

Cooper recovers from his embarrassment and puts his arm around the back of her chair. "You like my flirting?" It is as if he's challenging Imogene, provoking her to say more.

Imogene scoffs. "You're as smooth as a... a bed of

daggers," she struggles with a comeback.

"Ouch." Cooper dials up his charming smile. He's winning this round; Imogene is certainly off her game.

"Guess you need a new tactic," Dylan says, chuckling to Cooper. "Maybe we should move you away from the ladies."

I shoot Dylan a glare for his childish remarks.

"Maybe we need a kiddie table, so the rest of us can enjoy ourselves," Lois adds and Leo nods in agreement.

"Let's have a nice dinner without the drama, shall we?" Archie says. "This is Jessica's first dinner party and she's a little frazzled if you haven't noticed, and Carson isn't much help."

"It's beeping again!" We hear Jessica shout to Carson.

They are both in the kitchen, hopefully assembling some dishes of food.

"What's beeping?" Carson asks.

Our table is silent as we listen to their odd conversation coming from the other side of the archway.

"That thing that beeps. There it is again," Jess says angrily.

"I didn't hear anything. Besides, I thought you said you fixed the beeping thing."

"Apparently not. I don't know where it's coming from. Carson, this whole house beeps. All day long, something beeps and drives me crazy. The dishwasher, the washing machine, the dryer, the security alarms—they all have different warning beeps, but they're low enough so I don't know which appliance is producing the beep, and they're loud enough to drive me insane. This is high-tech hell!"

"Ah, babycakes, it's the wine cave. You always slam the door too hard and it bounces open and stays slightly ajar. See? The beeping is a signal that the door is open," Carson explains in his loving husband voice, the kind you use to calm down a pissed off wife.

"I hate that damn wine cave," Jess says angrily.

Our table has been listening intently and suddenly bursts out laughing.

Dylan's big boot nudges my calf under the table.

"I guess marriage is high-tech hell," I say to him.

He shrugs and gives a lopsided grin.

Lois catches our little flirty exchange and smiles.

"How about boyfriend hell," Imogene adds loudly.

"Come on, it's not that bad." Cooper rubs her back and Imogene gives him a murderous glare.

"Don't get her started. Please," Lauren says.

"Carson, is the bread on the table?" Jess asks from the kitchen.

"Yes, I think so," he responds.

We all look around at the table that is definitely breadless.

Dylan shakes his head. "They are imbeciles in the kitchen."

"Be nice." Lois slaps his hand.

"Take the brown dish out to the table," Jess instructs Carson.

"Oh good, the brown stuff is coming," Imogene deadpans. "You know it's a good dinner party when they bring out the brown stuff."

Cooper laughs and gives her an adorable smile, but Imogene will have none of that. She groans and turns to Lauren on her right side just to avoid Cooper.

"Oh, my, maybe you girls should go in and help them," Archie voices, getting up to re-fill everyone's wine glasses.

"Hell no, I'm off duty," Imogene responds.

"Here's something," Carson says, coming into the dining room holding a large Dutch oven with potholders. "It's meat. I think." He looks around the table. "Jess, there's no bread out here and they don't even have plates!"

When Dylan covers his laugh with a hand, I admire his boyish smile. I like this side of him.

"I'll help you, honey," Eleanor says and leaves with

173

Carson.

"Thankfully, we have wine," Archie smiles.

Eleanor returns with a stack of plates and Carson has another hot casserole dish of food.

"Oh, good, now we've got green stuff to go with the brown stuff," Imogene remarks.

"Come on, everyone, start digging in or Jess is going to cry," Carson stresses. "You don't know what it's like to work with her in a kitchen. I'd rather pour concrete foundations all day than spend ten minutes in that kitchen with her."

I have never seen my rough and tumble boss unravel. It is rather amusing and sweet to see him out of the office, entertaining dinner guests.

"I think that's a Beef bourguignon thing," he explains. "And that's some kind of squash or spinach dish. I don't know. Talia wrote out the whole menu, but Jess is just bossing me around in there like she's Gordon Ramsay, and I really don't think she knows what she's doing."

"I'll get the food moving along," Leo volunteers and stands up to serve everyone.

"Good, there's more coming," Carson says.

"Yay. A color-coded dinner," Imogene waves her hands.

"Just be glad we got our pies from the diner, I don't think we can screw that up." Carson flips a dishtowel over his shoulder and returns to the kitchen.

"This is awesome," Cooper says, shoveling a forkful of beef into his mouth.

"It should be. Talia is a great cook," Dylan responds.

As Jess and Carson return with another hot dish, bread and a salad, they look exhausted. Meanwhile, Dylan is scooping every vegetarian item onto my plate like I am a kid who can't serve herself.

"I was supposed to serve this in courses, but I decided it would be easier to have it all at once, family style," Jess says apologetically as she sits next to Lauren.

"Next time we're doing hot dogs," Carson declares as he sits down.

"Deal." Jess smiles at him and they laugh.

"This is lovely, Jess." Lois takes a dainty bite and nudges Leo to say something.

"Very good. Really," he states, stabbing a green vegetable and inspecting it before shoving it in his mouth.

Carson wipes his brow with his napkin as if these adventures in cooking with his wife are tumultuous endeavors.

Everyone gives them accolades on the fine food, and it is quite good. I imagine Dylan could cook the same meal without much effort. I can't remember ever having a boyfriend who could cook really well.

I listen to the conversations around the table and enjoy the hominess of the company, yet my attention is completely centered on Dylan. We are separated by the broad width of table, so I speak mostly with Archie and Cooper while Dylan sneaks glances at me in between his interrogation from Lois. She wants to know when he is going to start attending the local social events again. He gives noncommittal responses, and I assume this has been his habit with everyone over the last few months.

After dinner, when everyone moves to the living room for coffee and pie, I use the opportunity to walk around the house and check out the art. There is a passageway with a cascading wall of water. With the low lighting, it's like a private, quiet sanctuary with the soothing sounds of trickling water.

"There you are," Dylan says, coming from behind me. He wraps his arms around me and kisses my cheek.

"This waterfall is so cool."

"Yeah, it's part of the gray water system Carson uses throughout the house."

"Gray water?"

"It's recycled water that's used for non-drinking purposes. This is my favorite spot in the house. I think of this passageway as the cone of silence. It's where people come to hide or talk in private. So are you hiding or did you want to talk?" He smiles and turns me around to face him.

"I wasn't hiding, just exploring. It's nice being in the house of a normal couple with a normal marriage."

Dylan chuckles. "I don't know if Jess and Carson could be classified as normal. They're weird in their own way."

"You know what I mean. It's not a dinner party with creepy men negotiating seedy deals, and no one has to turn in their gun at the front door."

"Ah, yeah." Dylan's smile fades. "You okay with all of this?"

"Being here with everyone else? Of course. Why?"

"You were pretty upset about Robert. I didn't know if you were still obsessing about him today."

"I am concerned about him, but I didn't think about him during dinner. This was really a nice evening. I'm glad we did this. I used to imagine marrying Rob..." I stop myself. I can't believe I blurted that out. Dylan doesn't want to hear about my old fantasies about marrying Robert.

"Were you two planning on getting married?" he asks, looking disappointed.

"We would mention it, but it wasn't on any formal agenda. It wasn't anything in our immediate future. Carson and Jess look really happy."

"Despite their discomfort with kitchen appliances, yeah, they are very happy." He keeps his hands on my waist. This conversation could become uncomfortable if we keep talking about the topic of marriage.

A painting on the wall across from the waterfall catches my eye. I realize it is a portrait of Carson and Dylan. The artist has captured them smiling in some sort of brotherly headlock.

176

"I like that. You two look so sweet together."

"Sweet?" Dylan scoffs. "Jess did that last year as a gift for Carson. It was right after my accident. I was partying it up at Carson's annual holiday party he throws for his employees and half the town."

"Sounds fun. Especially in this house."

"You'll see it for yourself," Dylan replies, capturing my chin and turning it back to him.

As he kisses me with an immediate fierceness, his tongue tastes like chocolate, and as his warm body presses against me, my body responds. *Hell, yes.* His tongue parries playfully with mine before pulling me in tighter to devour me. I forget about the room full of other people and get swept up in an aphrodisiac of Dylan.

"Do you think about him when you kiss me?" he asks once we pry our lips apart.

It takes me a few seconds to realize he is referring to Robert.

"God, no, never when you're—"

"What? When I'm what?"

"When you're... with me," I say, fumbling for the right words.

"Does being in this nice house make you think about what you could have had with a rich guy like Robert?" Dylan is a little defensive; it's apparent he isn't comfortable about asking such questions.

"No, Dylan. Being in this house makes me think about the people who have nice marriages. Robert isn't in the mix."

"Good. I just want to make sure you're not still daydreaming about him."

"Gee, thanks." I am a little offended that he thinks I can sleep with him, live with him and kiss him like that and still have romantic ideas about another man. "You must not think I'm very bright." I try to brush past him and leave, however he grabs my arm and pulls me back to him.

"Wrong. I think you're incredibly intelligent, and I also think you're very sentimental and you want to help someone who doesn't deserve your help. I want to know that, when you're with me, you want to be with me, and you're thinking only of me."

"Wow. Me, me, me. You certainly don't have an ego problem."

Dylan puts his head down and smiles. "I do have problems, and my ego wasn't necessarily in the best place. But it is now, and I do know what I can and cannot tolerate. You're a smart woman, and you should expect the same for yourself."

"You're right. I'd be pretty pissed off if you were talking about a former girlfriend as much as I have deliberated over Mr. You-Know-Who."

"So, you would be jealous?" He smirks.

Oh, big shits. Sure, I gave myself away on that one.

"Yes," I come clean.

"Let's go home. I want to go to bed."

"You should be tired after all that absurd exercising and three helpings of everything at dinner and two slices of pie. That was hard to miss."

"I want to go to bed. I didn't say I want to sleep." He takes my hand and leads me back to the living room to say our goodbyes, but Lauren blocks us.

"So, are you done with Robert?" she asks. She has never understood Robert's appeal to women. She has always been attracted to the nerdy, quiet types like Leo.

"I think so," I mutter. This isn't the time or place to discuss my ex-boyfriend and the gossipy stories about his family.

"She's handling it," Dylan addresses Lauren while giving me a pointed look.

Lauren says something derogatory about Robert, and as Dylan listens, my gaze wanders over to the dining room where I have a partial view of Jess and Carson. I feel like a peeping Tom on their private moment. Carson pulls her into a big bear hug and she looks delighted as she throws her head back and smiles up at him. Then they fall into a long, passionate kiss. They look so ecstatic to be in each other's company. I have never witnessed a happy marriage like theirs.

I continue to watch them out of the corner of my eye as Lauren mentions Robert with derision about being too showy and extravagant with money and how he treated me like a little queen.

"Lauren, that's enough," I say.

"Emma, she cares about you and doesn't want to see you get hurt by all of this again."

Dylan likes having other members on his team, and I admit he plays the boyfriend role well. It would be easy to believe that everything is peachy keen and he is mine and I am his and Robert is history. A clean break with my past sounds ideal, and yet, impossible.

Lauren is about to rub Dylan's head when Leo gently takes her hand in his and kisses it.

"It's true, Em. You've got a great job and a nice guy." Lauren raises her eyebrows at Dylan, who puts a hand to his heart.

"This is a first," he says. "Lauren is paying me a compliment?"

"Dylan, I have always been your biggest fan."

"And one of my biggest critics," he reminds her.

"You deserved it. Don't screw this up." Lauren likes a good argument, so I stay out of this.

Imogene joins us and gives me a side hug. "My sister," she says, referring to our college days when people thought we were related because we have the same dark features, but the similarities stop there. Imogene is voluptuous everywhere; she can pull off any size because she's a walking sex bomb.

"Let's help Jess carry the rest of the dishes to the

kitchen," Imogene says, sounding less bitter than her earlier diatribe. Perhaps Cooper's company has warmed her up a bit.

Dylan shakes his head at me and then nods towards the door. Sure, I would like to leave now, go home and get naked with him, however since this is my first social event, it would be in bad form to depart without assisting the hostess.

Before I leave to help, he bends down close to my ear. "Make it fast; we need to go home."

I help collect coffee cups, dessert plates and stray wine glasses, carrying them to the kitchen where Jess, Imogene and Lauren are picking at leftover pie with their fingers.

"How do you like working at the design shop?" Jess asks me. Her face is still rosy from her romantic encounter with Carson. I envy her assuredness that this is what she wants, and that she has this life at such a young age.

"I like it a lot. Your husband is a great boss, and he's given me some very nice accounts. Everyone there is very easy to work with. I feel lucky to have gotten the job."

"We won't mention my missing guy," Imogene says.

"Jeremy needs time to settle there and then he'll probably ask you to come out or..." Jess's voice trails off.

How does any woman take it when a guy takes off without making any plans for the future with her?

"Don't even try, Jess," Lauren says. "I've gone through every possibility, but Imogene is sure he's dumping her."

"No, I'm pretty sure he's already dumped me."

"Cooper is a cutie," Lauren adds.

Imogene pretends not to hear and gives up using her fingers and starts digging into a pie with a fork.

"Yeah," Jess agrees. "Cooper is a hottie, Imogene."

"Cooper isn't my type and I don't know if I like him. He's too cocky or something," Imogene replies, shaking her head. "I bet he has a tattoo on his ass that says '*Mom*' or something equally lame."

We all laugh at Imogene's snarkiness.

"He's been pretty nice to me," I say without going into further details about our impromptu meeting with Robert where Cooper played a pretty badass bodyguard.

"You've got Dylan, and boy, he sure has surprised all of us. He's really got his shit together," Lauren says. "I've never seen him like this. I don't care how cool he thinks he's playing this, he's totally crazy about you. And I don't mean crazy like last summer when he and Jess went out."

Jess rolls her eyes and laughs. My heart thuds as if it is skidding clumsily instead of beating, and fear rips right through me. I have no idea what they are talking about, but those remarks are enough that I think I am going to be sick.

"Dylan is very different now," Jess says, smiling at me. "He is smitten with you. Carson told me all about it, and seeing him tonight... Dylan looks so healthy and happy."

My face must be frozen. I can't speak. I want to run out of the room, out of the house. I want to go home, but I don't even have my own home. And Dylan? I am his next woman in a long line of them. I suspected as much, but I didn't know I came after Jess. They are all smiling at me knowingly, like we have shared a beautiful bonding moment.

"I have to go, excuse me," I say, leaving the kitchen.

I storm into the living room and interrupt Dylan and Carson. "We have to go," I say, my voice trembling.

Dylan's jovial demeanor with his brother darkens. "Sure, no problem." As he takes my hand firmly in his and escorts me to the door, I mumble my goodbyes to people without actually looking at them.

Outside, the cool spring air slaps my face. That cozy little dinner soiree was a cruel joke. I try to fill my lungs with as much air as possible to stave off my instinct to cry or punch Dylan.

181

"What's wrong?" Dylan questions as he opens the Jeep door for me.

I get in and put on my seat belt, brushing aside his hands that try to help. "Just drive me to the house. I need to sleep."

"Sleep?" Dylan chuckles as if he is reviving our earlier plans.

He gets in the Jeep and starts the engine. Before putting it in gear, he gives me a worrisome look. "I thought you were having a good time in there. What happened?"

"What happened?" I snap. "I found out you haven't been honest with me. I looked like a fool in there. I feel like a fool. Goddamn you!"

Nineteen

Dylan

"Drive already! I want to go home. My fake, temporary home!" she screams at me with her chin held high. Her eyes are wide with anger and fear, and it triggers queasiness—a dull, sick pain in my gut.

"Are you going to tell me what you're talking about?" I yell as I maneuver the Jeep down Carson's driveway and through the dark wooded area then over the bridge from my infamous accident.

"I'm too angry at you to talk."

"If I'm being accused of something, I have a right to know what it is!"

I shift into high gear and speed us home. Emma is silent and stares out the window, so I can't see the tears trickling down her cheeks, though their reflection in the window glistens in the moonlight, and I hear her wet sniffles.

When I park in front of the house, she jumps out of the vehicle and races up to the door to let herself in before I can reach her.

I bound up the stairs two at a time and then pound my fist on her bedroom door.

"Emma, you have to tell me what this is about. You can't just flip out on me and run away. You have to talk to me."

My hands are braced on the door and I am trying to sound as calm as possible. I have a tremendous urge to kick down the door to get close to her, yet that would be something the old me would do, and I can't afford to slip

183

back into that guy for one second.

"Emma," I say in a softer tone. "Please."

I wait quietly and then there's a click as she unlocks the door before coming out into the hallway. Her movements are rigid as she gives herself a wide berth, stepping around me. This is not the girl I kissed in my favorite hidden passageway back at Carson's house. Anger is brewing in her eyes, a sure sign that I've fucked up even if I have no idea what I've done.

"You goddamn prick," she says in a low, steady voice.

I am stunned and completely confused.

I move towards her because my first impulse is to embrace her. She flinches and quickly grabs my arm, turns her body and twists my arm at the same time as she throws all her body weight down on it. Excruciating pain shoots through my trapped limb that she's wrenching.

"Jesus, Emma!"

I don't want to hurt her, but she's about to dislocate my shoulder, so I turn and roll into her twisting motion and topple backwards, bringing her down with me to the floor.

"Get off me!" She starts slapping at my arm that now has her pinned against me and kicking her legs.

I flip over, my face just missing her flailing hands. I grab her wrists and pin them on the floor above her head and use my heavy boots to trap her ankles. She's deceptively strong, and I'm impressed but apprehensive about how to handle this without accidentally injuring her.

"Are you going to try to beat me up before telling me why you're so pissed off?" I shout in her face.

She pants heavily. "Get off me, now," she states icily.

"Do you promise to stop slapping me? Jesus, I can't believe I'm saying this. I'm the one who's had to reform and stop getting in brawls. You don't have a switchblade on you or some other weapon from your buddy, Sean, do you?"

Emma huffs a breath and stares at me. She isn't falling

for my stupid attempts at defusing this with humor.

Our faces are a couple of inches apart, and if I thought this misunderstanding could be remedied with a kiss, I wouldn't hesitate.

Realizing my crushing weight has subdued her, I roll off her and stand up. She won't accept my hand to help her stand, so I move back in case she still feels threatened by me or is inspired to use her Vulcan Grip again.

She folds her arms across her chest and looks incredibly petite and vulnerable with her wild, disheveled hair. I can't believe she could pull off that arm wrench move on me, however the crazy, mean glare she's giving me makes me wonder what I am dealing with.

"Are you okay? Did I hurt you?" I ask. I am genuinely concerned that I could have snapped one of her bony, bird-like limbs.

She looks away, perturbed.

"Okay, since you're the only one here that knows why you're acting like this, you're going to have to talk. So talk," I demand.

She tilts her chin up. "I can't believe you dated your brother's wife! You dated Jess before me! She's one of the women you've slept with!"

"What?" My mind is racing. Lauren has told her about my accident, my hospitalization, and the fact that I slept around. Wasn't Jess a trivial part of that gossip?

"They were talking about it in the kitchen. They said you were going out with Jess last summer and isn't it nice how *smitten* you are with me now," she spits out. "What kind of sick relationship have I walked into? Seriously, you were with your brother's wife?"

I am getting irritated with the way she keeps saying *brother's wife*. "No, I wasn't!" I yell. She steps back, and I berate myself for scaring her.

"This ought to be good."

"Jess wasn't his wife. She wasn't his *anything* when I

went out with her, which was like for five minutes. Really. She'd just moved to town, and… listen, I thought Lauren told you everything about me. I wasn't intentionally keeping this from you. I assumed you knew. Everyone knows."

"Obviously someone forgot to tell me that I'm dating my boss's wife's ex-boyfriend."

"I'm not her ex-boyfriend. Believe me, Jess doesn't think of me in that way. She didn't love me, and I didn't love her. That was one of my bad episodes. I made it worse because Carson did have feelings for Jess, but she didn't know that."

"God, you're not making it sound better."

"Shit, didn't you get the Dylan memo when you moved here? Everyone knows this and it's a non-issue. Carson started dating Jess *after* she dumped me. It's a good thing she did, too. I was in bad shape."

"You don't get to play the crazy card now. No way. You said Robert doesn't get a free pass as an adult, so why should you?"

"Yeah, okay, but I didn't commit a crime. I didn't even commit adultery. It was a fling; short, over and done with."

"And then you went into treatment?" she inquires.

"Yep. I left town and went to Willow Haven where the mentally ill get lessons on how everyone else wants them to behave."

Emma isn't seething, but she doesn't look convinced that this is a minor hiccup.

"I never intended to marry Jess. The ring was a mistake."

"What ring?" she shouts. "You asked her to marry you?"

If I could have asked for a perfect time for my brother to come in and clean up my mess, this would be it.

"Dylan!" she demands.

"No! I didn't ask her to marry me. Calm down,

please." If she doesn't stop yelling, I am going to need a pill, or I'm going to have to bolt out of the house and run ten miles to work off the anxiety attack I'm having over her.

"This isn't the kind of thing people are calm about. This is a big deal, Dylan. At least to me."

"I dated Jess for a few weeks last summer. That's it. We weren't in love and we weren't even good for each other. You said Robert was your mistake, and I would say Jess was mine, but it's the defining act that made me get help, so I can't regret it. I finally got help, Emma."

"Because of Jess."

"No, she was a symptom to a bigger problem. But she is my friend, and my brother loves her. That's it."

"Do you ever think about her? It's a fair question with the way you hound me about Robert."

"I don't think about her as anyone other than my sister-in-law. There's no attraction there, if that's what you're asking."

"I can't compete with a brainiac like her. I don't paint beautiful pictures like her; I knit sloppy blankets. And I suck at math. I can see why you fell in love with her. She's pretty and smart."

I sigh as a headache starts pulsating directly in the middle of my forehead.

"I didn't fall in love with her, for fuck's sake. I stole her from my brother. I was a shit and used her like I used every other woman. When I was with Jess, I did things I shouldn't have done and said things I shouldn't have said, and I barely remember most of what happened. I was up and down; depressed on the inside, wild on the outside. My brain was like a blender. One minute I'd be content, the next I'd be moody and down.

"And I can't give you a name of a single woman I dated in college because I was never in a *relationship*. Lauren told you the truth. There were women, but there were no girlfriends. And the only time I think I was ever in love was in seventh grade when I had a crush on a girl named Anya. All I remember about her is her cute, Russian accent and long, blond hair because she sat in front of me in Social Studies.

"But, I'm telling you the truth—I have no feelings for Jess other than a sisterly affection because she's married to my brother. If she hadn't stayed in town, she'd be another fading memory to me, too. Do you get it now?"

Emma shakes her head dubiously.

It does sound like a farfetched hillbilly story, an unbelievable tale small towns are famous for. I am infamous for.

"This is why I have to take meds and see a shrink. This is why I run and exercise so much. It feels like one big balancing act, but I do have hope that it's helping my brain to recalibrate. My doc says I'm doing well, but a huge part of what I've been doing—staying away from women—is something I can't do forever. I knew that when I met you."

"Uh-huh," she responds. "I'm sure you can't stay away from women. Am I your first test subject? You know, your post-rehab fling?"

"Shit—no," I stammer.

"No? So you failed at your self-imposed exile from women? You're back on the hunt?"

"No. No, there haven't been any other women, and no, you're not a test subject. I'm doing a lousy job of explaining myself." My voice rises in frustration, trying to figure out how to fix this. "I know I have a horrible reputation with women and my past behavior is why I was afraid to get involved with you."

"Don't tell me you've already forgotten my name."

Her sarcasm makes me feel even sleazier.

"Emma, I'm being serious. I'm finally a clear-headed, thinking person, or so people tell me. This is a big deal to me. *You're* a big deal to me. It doesn't matter what Jess is.

You are smart and beautiful, and I'm with *you*."

"What happened to cute, little Anya?"

"No clue. It was a seventh grade crush."

"Okay, so maybe I'm a crush and a good lay because, let's face it, you needed some action, and I'll admit that I was more than willing."

"Except this isn't just sex." I am a little pissed off at how cavalier she's treating this.

"Sure. Tell yourself that all you want. I'm going to bed." She turns to go back into her bedroom.

"Whoa!" I throw myself in front of her doorway and put my foot up on the doorframe to block her. "That's it? You're already writing me off?"

"I think we both acted a little too stupid over the last few weeks. We each have some issues, and we moved fast without really thinking it through. Me and my whole Robert thing; you and your Jess thing."

"What?" I snap. "There is no Jess thing."

"Dylan, move your leg. I'm tired; I'm going to bed."

"So what are you telling me? We're not going to talk about this? Are we going to bed angry?"

"I'm going to bed alone. I don't care what you do. Now move your goddamn leg and let me in *my* room."

"Ah, wait a minute. I thought we were grownups, and for the last couple of weeks, these two grownups have been sharing a bed and everything else. So you don't get to go storming off like a little girl who didn't get a pony for her birthday, princess."

Fuck. I called her princess. I should have known better.

Before I can retract the comment, her knee meets my ribs in some type of crazy maneuver. This woman is like a fucking ninja. I bowl over with the breath knocked out of me and try to catch her leg at the same time. She's too fast, though. She's already spun herself away and brings her elbow down on my shoulder, dropping me to the floor. I sense her jumping over my back to get into her room, and I instinctively reach a hand back and blindly grab her ankle. As she falls to the floor with me, I block her knee before it can ram into my rock hard dick.

Yeah, rough housing with her is giving me a major boner. This isn't how couples fight; this is more like how kids wrestle to get toys away from each other, and her little angry grunts and flailing limbs are turning me on.

I have more than one hundred pounds on her and am able to quickly heave my crawling body on top of her again, pinning all of her moving parts. I bury my head in her neck and go for that sensitive spot that usually makes her go boneless. I kiss her neck then run my tongue up to her ear and suck on her earlobe. This is all out war.

I grind my erection into her, getting some friction going with my chest rubbing against her hard nipples. If I can get her back to the pleasure dome, I can get her to come to her senses about me. Yes, I am resorting to stupid-guy philosophy.

She acquiesces to the ear lobe tactic for about thirty seconds and then the ninja takes over again.

"Dylan, stop it!" she yells.

I crash my mouth into hers, forcing my tongue in. She kisses me back and presses into me, and just when I think I have won her over, she pulls her head away.

"No." She's very clear, and I am not going to be the schmuck that ignores that order.

As I sit back on my knees, she rolls out from underneath me, and when she wipes her mouth, I want back at those pouty lips. I want to wrap my body around her and tell her that not only does her name run through my head all day long like an old-fashioned, stock exchange ticker tape, my insides also ache for her in a way that I have never felt with anyone.

She is so beautiful, and she fights like a warrior. Who wouldn't love that? I want to tell her that I am in love with her, that it is more than sex—it is an all-out soul-crushing love. I have doubted myself when it comes to relationships with women because I haven't ever truly experienced falling in love. I didn't know what I was looking for until Emma slammed into my heart. Thank God she doesn't carry brass knuckles.

"You're kicking me out of the bedroom? Seconds ago, you were kissing me." I hear myself—too much arrogance. I hope she will at least let me sleep in the same bed with her. We don't have to have sex. I just want to be with her.

"You have your own room." She stands up and waits for me to leave.

I am still on my knees like I am about to beg for her to take me back this instant. My pride won't let me stoop to that level, however. No one should have to beg for love. It is plain wrong to put yourself out there like a hopeless fool.

I stand up and tower over her, resisting the urge to push her back on the bed and start the wrestling match all over again. Instead, I back out of the room, watching her eyes ignite with a renewed indignation. I am desperate to come up with a new ploy. Plus, now I know not to turn my back on the fiery, little ninja.

"I'll go to my room, Emma, if that's what you really want. But don't get any ideas that you are moving out of this house. We have two things going on here. Number one, us. Number two, getting rid of your ex."

For a split second, I think I see her doe-like eyes soften. Nope. I am wrong. A cold, glassy reserve takes over her dark eyes when I back completely into the hallway.

"And don't you get any ideas that *us*," she says with air quotes, "is anything more than convenience."

With that declaration, she slams the door in my face.

Unfortunately, there is nothing convenient about this. I still have a major boner for her, so I walk uncomfortably back to my bedroom where I lie in bed and think of how my actions that have happened before I met Emma are screwing up the good thing I've got going here.

191

It's a warm, spring morning, but the deep freeze begins the minute Emma and I meet at the breakfast table. I am ready for our trip into the city, wearing one of my best suits—a designer number Carson made me invest in. I think I clean up pretty good, but she's not taking the bait.

When I put toast, orange juice and cereal in front of her, she helps herself to everything without looking at me. At least she looks like she got as much sleep as I did. Zippo.

I sit down at the little table with her and my knees knock hers under the table. She still won't look at me.

"I'm going for a run with Carson when we get to the office, but you'll have people around, so I won't worry about Rocky showing up."

"His name is Robert," she retorts.

Good, she's talking to me. I'll take whatever crumbs she will throw my way. I can work with this and figure out how to bring her back from the dark clutches of this twisted ideology where innocent men—being me—get lumped in with pond scum.

"And then we can go over the Mercer presentation with Carson."

No response. She's eating her buttery toast as if it is the most pleasurable experience she has ever had in this house.

I am competing with the fucking toast.

"So, it'll be you, me and Carson at the office. Then you and me, working with the Mercer group. Staying in the city for a couple of days. Hotel. You. Me." I am running out of enticing words.

She shoots me a look. "There are two rooms, Dylan. Daisy booked them weeks ago. We won't have any boundary issues about beds. And I'm going to drive myself in to work today."

"Fine. Then I'll follow you on the bike," I add

confidently. "And you and I can go over our own notes on Mercer before we leave for New York. Carson offered us his car to take in to the city later."

"I don't need to go over anything. I already know what I'm presenting to Mercer. Carson has given me carte blanche on this. I can handle my own presentation, you stick to yours."

"Christ, Emma. We're supposed to be a team at work. Don't carry over your irrational grudge about me and Jess to the office."

She looks at me calmly. "I'm not. I'm not about to jeopardize my job or hurt the company. I know exactly what I'm doing."

"Right, I forgot your talents in the wholesale world of automotive goods, and that you're a *people person!*"

Never mimic a woman's own words and throw them back in her face, and never use sarcasm to win an argument. I should just wear a sign that says *Punch Me!* My plan all morning has been to work up to a kiss to smooth things over. At the rate I'm going, I will be lucky to get a handshake from Miss Keller at our next business meeting.

Emma doesn't let my comment ruffle her, though. Even with lack of sleep, she is very composed and poised. Her hair is twisted in some kind of immaculate bun, her black suit and white blouse look perfect on her, and she is wearing tall, black heels. And her perfume makes me want to sink my face in her neck again.

She puts her laptop in her satchel and rolls out her little suitcase from under the table.

"I'm sorry I said that. It was rude," I say, hoping she will give me a forgiving look. Nope.

"It's fine." She rifles through her purse for her keys.

"No, it isn't fine, Emma. We had an argument, and you're still pissed at me. Tell me how to fix it. What do I have to do to make this better?"

"What's done is done. Let's make the best of this meeting. It's important, so let's focus on that, okay?"

"That's it? We're business colleagues, and we're going to erase everything that's happened between us?"

"I've done it before," she says matter-of-factly. "I can do it again."

"Huh." I study her blank expression and consider she may be more fragile than I thought, or she's cunning. "Okay, well, can I at least put my suitcase in your trunk and then we'll switch everything over to Carson's car at work?"

"Of course," she replies.

I follow her outside as she wheels her suitcase with quick, little steps in her heels. At the porch, she is startled when I grab her suitcase and carry it down to her car. She navigates the stairs and rough terrain carefully, meeting me at the trunk.

My mind is scheming, looking around at what I can do to slow her down so I can have a moment with her. She pops the trunk and I put our bags inside. Then she slams the trunk closed without another look at me and turns to walk to the driver's side.

I react without thinking any plan through; all I know is that I want to kiss her. She has her fingers on the door handle, so I grab her free hand and pull her towards me. Her heels cause her to lose her balance on the rocky dirt driveway and she stumbles into my chest. With one arm wrapped around her back, I cup her face and bring her in for a quick kiss before she can protest. It doesn't take much effort to part her clenched mouth and force my tongue inside. I keep her body pressed to me as my mouth firmly locks onto her soft lips and I taste her.

Her initial reaction is a soft squeal and then she lets me take over. She is not exactly joining in, however she is definitely letting me devour her mouth. When I move down to her neck that smells like a place I could get lost in forever, I know I want more. This is the test. Can my lips

194

and tongue run over her soft, smooth skin and make her feel good, or am I going to push the limits and see how far I can go?

While her fingers slide under my suit jacket and graze my chest down to my waist, her other hand runs lightly across my scalp, sending a jolt down my spine and signaling the crew below to go to full mast. I am seconds away from pushing her skirt up and nailing her against the car, not that she would let me take it that far. I don't want to find out.

That is when I stop. That is when I know I have this under control, and that, if I am going to kiss her or do anything else I am fantasizing about, I want her to reciprocate.

"Good." I remove her from my embrace. "That's a good way to start the day, right? And you didn't have to karate chop me or anything."

"You have to stop doing that." She adjusts the collar on her shirt. "You can't kiss me whenever you feel like it."

"Actually, I can. Might not make it right, but it wins every time."

Emma glares at me.

"But you're right. I shouldn't kiss you unless you want me to. And from all your moaning and your groping hands, I guess you're not interested." With that parting shot, I put on my helmet and climb on my bike.

After Emma scowls at me and gets in her car, I follow her to work, grinning every time I catch her looking at me in the rear view mirror.

Twenty
Emma

Thinking about him has me in angry knots. Lusty, angry knots. That was one whopper of a kiss and he knows it. Last night, I had the upper hand by shutting him out and making him go to his own bed. He deserved it. I am not playing second fiddle to someone he claims never to have been in love with, especially with his absurd excuse of never being in love and not remembering women's names.

First, I spend years in love with a guy who can't forget me, and now I am getting swept up by a guy who has the opposite problem. Maybe I am being too hard on Dylan and his bipolar history has left him with a bit of a bullshit memory fog, or maybe he really was never in love before, so he doesn't have any stories of past crushes to share.

Honestly, how is it possible for him to live twenty-four years and not fall in love hard at least once? Not have his heart broken and mangled into a hot mess of despair like the rest of us? Of course, there was his little love, Anya, his seventh grade infatuation. Perhaps that is all there is for guys like Dylan. They remember the quiet beauty that disappears before anything happens and then they hold a torch for them forever.

I don't know if I can handle another guy with extreme issues. I have paid my dues, yet I seem to be good at finding the one guy in the tri-state area who can cause the most problems, and I jump in and fall for him until I am in so deep I don't know how to get out. First Robert and now Dylan.

It is probably not fair that Dylan is being subjected to

my fears about everything that went wrong with Robert, however it goes both ways. I am getting a boatload of unclaimed baggage by getting involved with Dylan. I can pretend all I want about being understanding with regards to his mental health issues, but frankly, I am clueless. Everything I know is based on observations of friends and acquaintances. Some may have shown signs of emotional distress, but I have no formal experience with what Dylan has gone through.

I know plenty of people I think could use professional help, however it's not something that would ever be acknowledged or discussed out loud. I wasn't raised that way; my friends and family would never bring this topic up. Lauren and Carson and others in this town have a different standard of helping those they love, while my father would hand out guns and tell you to watch your back. That sounds rather humorous and unloving because it is. It is also my reality.

I was raised in an uncommon household. I took classes in proper gun training, starting with a basic .22 rifle at age ten and then moved up to semiautomatic handguns. Instead of ballet, there were years of martial arts classes in various forms. We're not a violent family; we're fearful and we've spent too many years living cautiously to the point of being paranoid.

Self-preservation can be a strange thing and comes about in some of most unusual ways. Living like that— loving Robert and expecting change—has just about done me in emotionally. Moving to Hera and meeting Dylan has felt like a rebirth. That's what this all comes down to. Dylan.

When Dylan kissed me, I let him. I want him to kiss me. I want everything the way it was before I knew about Jess and the green-eyed monster reminded me that many women have come before me. I am angry about this Jess story because it never occurred to me that this small town

197

would have the only two women with names Dylan actually remembers!

This is absolutely absurd. Let's not leave out the unforgettable Anya. Dylan remembered she was a cute blond. Good for her, and now I am sounding pitifully bitter about things I cannot change.

I laugh out loud and check out my crazy eyes in the rearview mirror, seeing Dylan tailing me on his bike in an expensive suit that I am guessing is either Armani or Dolce & Gabbana. It is like being followed by James Bond.

I would like to know which woman helped him shop for those nice duds.

Pull it together, Emma. It's time to be calm under pressure.

* * *

I get some peace in the office when Dylan leaves on a long run with Carson. They like to discuss business, and I imagine they do manly things like racing each other up hills and crushing beer cans against their heads. Oh, God.

I put my head on my desk. I just have to get through the next two days in the city—wining, dining and schmoozing with our top rep firm. The fact that my father hasn't been talking to me, Robert is up to his eyeballs in a pile of Fed shit, and Dylan has just dropped a devastating bomb on me, is irrelevant if I don't pull off my new marketing strategy with Mercer. I have to succeed at this job. I have to succeed at something.

I am assembling the last bit of materials and double-checking the PowerPoint presentation and Excel spreadsheets I have created before Dylan returns to the office. Why he wore his suit in to work, knowing he was going to run is beyond me. Unless it was for my benefit. When I saw him in the kitchen this morning, throwing together our breakfast in a perfectly tailored designer suit, my first thought was the suit couldn't possibly look more spectacular on anyone else and he should wear it every day.

The shock of seeing him out of jeans and a t-shirt, looking suave in a suit, made me a little giddy. Though I suppose, if he were always this polished, I would melt again and relish it when I see his ass in jeans. I can't win here. I am attracted to him in every way, and I like him. *A lot.*

After his run, he plans on showering over at Lois's yoga studio, Beyond The Pants, and then he'll change back into the suit before coming back to work. I can picture all those women in their downward dog poses lusting over two hunky guys scantily clad in towels, heading into the spa room to shower. Carson and Dylan have Lois and Eleanor wrapped around their fingers. I seriously doubt other men in town could waltz into the yoga studio and greet the women as they take over their spa. The women probably love it and look forward to some eye candy parading through their classes.

If he put that suit on to placate me, he is really working this. After last night's brawl, I guess he's bringing out the big guns to get my attention, and no matter how much I pretended to salivate over my toast at breakfast and play it cool, it was an obscene test of my willpower not to gape at his beauty. I used to only describe Robert that way and considered other men to be handsome or cute. Dylan is beautiful—the way his body reflects strength and power and his expressive face is either severe or flush with laughter.

It's easy to fall for great curb appeal, though that is not what keeps me drawn to him. More than anything, it is the way Dylan talks to me and what he shares, the secret portals that open up and let me inside. His tender side is heartbreaking, perhaps a consequence of his difficult childhood and his battle with his own emotional upheaval.

That is why I find it hard to believe, or rather, am saddened that he could go all these years without ever being in love. Dylan was made to love someone. The fact that he says he has never been in love worries me and brings out my survival instincts. I don't want to love someone who cannot fully love me in return.

If I want to succeed on my own, it's time to put Dylan Blackard and all those new issues he brings into my life on the back burner for a while. He can simmer there while I get my own life together.

***

Dylan saunters into the office, filling the room with a heady mix of his freshly showered scent and aftershave.

"Hi," he says sheepishly.

I have been working while he has been out chasing the gremlins from his system. He should feel a little guilty, and I should take advantage of that.

"Hi. I'm Emma Keller." I stand and hold out my hand. "In case you forgot my name."

Dylan turns red and his mouth curves into a slight smile. "Funny. Very funny."

"I don't know the extent of your problems with women, so maybe it will help if I reintroduce myself to you every few days. I wouldn't want you to get confused and have a panic attack over some strange woman in your office."

Dylan takes a deep breath and lets his gaze roam from my face slowly down to my heels then he shakes his head and strides towards me. An angry man closing in on me naturally brings out my defensive mode. I sequester those instincts that make me antsy and clasp my hands in front so I don't appear nervous.

"Okay, I got the message," he says tersely. "You don't like what I told you about Jess or how I told you. I'm sorry. I did tell you the truth, and I was being honest about everything. The women in my past. What happened with Jess. And you and me."

"Don't forget cute, little Anya."

"Stop it, Emma. I like what you and I have. I like you." He moves closer.

"It doesn't matter. We need to leave for the hotel, and we need to actually do some work."

His face contorts in disbelief.

"What do you mean it doesn't matter? Of course it matters. We're involved, and you can't decide that it doesn't matter and put the brakes on it just because you're angry about what I did last summer."

"*What I did last summer*. Huh. That sounds like the title of a horror movie."

"It kind of was." He tilts his head and casts his eyes down.

"Dylan, I think that shows how little we know each other. We kind of jumped into this... whatever it is we have—"

"Whatever it is? Man, you're sure doing everything you can to downgrade our relationship to zero, aren't you? We can work on that while we're at the hotel. Time to go."

"We're not going on a honeymoon; nothing is happening at the hotel," I scold.

"Yeah, yeah. Our bags and gear are in the car, so we're leaving now—together—before you think you're doing this on your own."

He hustles me out of the office to the back lot where he has loaded Carson's BMW with our suitcases and laptop bags. Carson is there with Cooper, talking in front of Carson's truck. They turn as Dylan I walk towards them. Dylan takes his hand off my back as we separate and I head for the passenger door that Carson opens for me.

"You two ready?" Carson asks. He glances across the car at Dylan then at me.

The tension between Dylan and me is palpable. Cooper's face goes from us to Carson as if he can tell we have been squabbling.

I remind myself that it is not our job to be friends; we are working on an important project that we have to deliver for the company. This is business, and I have to reassure my boss that I am prepared.

"We're ready," I say.

As I settle into my seat, Carson leans in. "Has Dylan already gotten on your last nerve?" he asks quietly as Dylan opens his door.

"Oh, I believe we are testing each other's nerves." I smile as if this is no big deal.

"Remember what I told you about kicking him. You can keep him in line."

"Thanks for tipping her off," Dylan cuts in, sliding into his seat. "Trust me; she's not shy about using brute force."

"Good," Carson replies and closes my door.

I have broken all the rules; sleeping with someone I work with, moving in with a guy I barely know who happens to be the guy I am working with and sleeping with—was sleeping with. What a mess.

As Dylan backs the car out and drives it out of the Blackard parking lot, his hand grips the stick shift as if he is itching to gun it. We are at the entrance to the main road when he glances sideways at me, staring with his stunning blue eyes and a devilish smile. I can totally read him. He wants to tear down the road.

Before I can admonish him, his cell phone rings and connects to the car's Bluetooth. The display says *Dr. Wang*. Dylan keeps the car idling.

"Hi, Doc," Dylan says. He clicks the speaker off and picks up his phone.

There's a long silence as Dylan listens.

"Yeah, thanks for telling me." He disconnects his call and stares at his phone for a minute before putting it in the console compartment between us.

"Is everything all right?" I ask.

He looks out of the window and then down at his hands on the wheel.

"Dylan?"

As he turns to me, the mirth from a few seconds ago is

gone. He looks stunned before suddenly composing himself.

"Yes, everything is fine."

When he picks my hand up from my lap and kisses it, his warm touch and the tenderness of the kiss sends a pleasant tingle from my fingers to my toes. I want to ask him about the phone call, but that would be opening us up to more personal sharing and only minutes ago I was pledging myself to the job ahead of us.

***

I expect Dylan to be talkative and arrogantly charming as usual with a few good, cocky remarks thrown in, however he is silent on our hour and half drive to the city. He likes to blast AC/DC in the car, but doesn't complain when I switch it to Katy Perry and Imagine Dragons. The loud music blocks out any need to talk, therefore I rest my head back in the comfortable seat and watch the scenery become denser as we enter the city. Once we are in Manhattan, Dylan is still in some kind of disappointed funk and navigates the streets as if by rote, speeding down the West Side Highway, in and out of cars. I close my eyes and hold back my nausea.

"Sorry. Didn't mean to make you nervous," he says, holding my hand until I open my eyes and give a weak smile, acknowledging that I am okay.

We arrive at our hotel in SoHo early enough to take our time. We are not meeting the Mercer reps until a cocktail party later, so Dylan hands the car keys to the valet and lets the bellboy take our bags on his luggage trolley then strides through the hotel lobby, looking every part the confident businessman. He speaks briefly to the concierge as I stand in the lobby and admire the exquisite décor.

It's a luxury boutique hotel, and I can't believe Carson has sent me on this trip in his place. I am excited, yet I feel sort of like a fraud. My father's wholesale business never required me to travel or even dress up. He could run his multi-million dollar business with a rotary phone and a typewriter if he had to. This hotel business event takes my college girl ego to the next level, making me feel more professional.

As Dylan signals me to follow him to the elevator, the bellboy takes a separate elevator so Dylan and I are alone. He pushes the button for the penthouse floor.

"Seriously?" I ask.

"Yes. Top floor, views and all," he replies. "You'll like it. We always use this hotel for business."

"You looked pretty chummy with the concierge. She's very pretty. Do you remember her name?"

He tilts his head and narrows his eyes. "Allison."

"Hmm. You remember her name. I guess you didn't sleep with her, or you just made that name up."

"You're really pushing it." He forces a faint smile. "That's her name, and no, I never slept with her."

"What's wrong? You've been very quiet since we left the office."

"I told you, everything is fine."

"Fine is what people say when it's anything but fine. I say it all the time."

When the doors slide open to a chic, carpeted hallway, Dylan puts a finger between my shoulder blades and walks me out and down the hall. He then removes a card key from his pocket and slides it in the door slot.

"Are our rooms next to each other? This hallway only has a few doors."

"About that. Last week I had Daisy cancel the two rooms and give us this one. Carson usually books this, so I kept it for us."

I stand on the threshold of the room as Dylan pushes the door open.

"Dylan, we're not sharing a bed," I say angrily. "We're in the middle of a major problem, if you haven't noticed."

"Oh, believe me, I noticed, Emma. I can't change the

rooms now—they're booked solid, and this is the best suite in the place. You can have the bed and I'll take the couch."

The bellboy takes that moment to arrive with our luggage so I can't throw a hissy fit. I wander into the room and take in all the beautiful furnishings. There is a king-sized bed with expensive linens I could never afford, a fully stocked wet bar, a desk with a twenty-seven inch iMac monitor, and if that isn't enough to amaze me, frosted sliding glass doors open into a living room with a leather couch, a giant wall-mounted flat screen TV, and views of the Empire State Building.

After the bellboy leaves, Dylan joins me by the corner windows that give us an incredible view of the city.

"We have eight hundred square feet here, so I won't be in your way." He places his hand on the window frame and another on his hip as he somberly looks out at the stunning metropolis.

"What did your doctor say? It was the phone call that's upset you, wasn't it?"

Dylan shakes his head. "I can't talk about that."

"Can't or won't?"

"We need to get ready for drinks with the group. We're meeting in the bar and there will be appetizers, but I can order you some room service now if you like. Or we can order later."

"Okay, you're right. You don't have to answer my question. I was the one who said we need to focus on business."

Dylan's hand reaches out to me, and for a second, I think he's going to touch me, but then he puts his hand down.

"You'll like the spa bathroom. It's better than what we have at home. Why don't you go freshen up? I'm going to change my shirt. Other than that, I'm ready to head downstairs."

He is so formal that I can't believe this is my Dylan.

My Dylan. I am nuts.

"I want to unpack my clothes, and I do want to change. I'm not wearing a suit for the cocktail party. This was for the arrival." I do my best spokes model imitation and sweep my hands down my sides. I don't have Armani or any high-end clothing from Madison Avenue, however I do have some nice dresses I got at the designer outlet in Neptune, New Jersey. I am a Jersey girl after all.

"Take your time." He keeps a noticeable distance between us, either out of respect for my earlier demands or something else is bothering him.

I leave the living area and head back into the bedroom to unpack my clothes and hang my dresses. I have a black, clingy, sleeveless one for tonight's gathering, which is about me getting to know the big players from Mercer. For tomorrow night's party, I am going all out in my bright red, camisole dress. It is shorter and bares so much more skin, even though both are quite skimpy and sexy.

As I take a quick rinse in the shower, I think of Dylan waiting for me on the other side of door and wonder what has gotten him down so suddenly. I am ambivalent about us—too quick, too soon, and too much crappy baggage for both of us. Still, I am torn between wanting to be with him and fearing we may be better apart.

When I say these sentiments out loud to myself, it's much less jarring than seeing it reflected in his demeanor. The first week in Hera gave me a glimpse of his tough exterior before it disappeared all together and we started playing house. Quiet and brooding is the side of Dylan I haven't seen.

I slip on the black dress, apply fresh make-up, and let my hair out of the French twist. I finger my hair so it falls in waves of glossy locks down to the middle of my back. The neckline scoops to the top of my breasts, and I turn to check out my rump. Not bad. On a good day, I give myself an eight out of ten. I suppose I would be more generous if I didn't get sick of looking at my own face and questioning where I fit in on the pretty scale.

It's never mattered in my father's company where most of the men are over forty and sport flabby bellies and balding heads, yet Carson's company has opened a new door to a business that is more artistic and sexy in terms of product and clients. I want to look like I fit the image. He has even mentioned that my role in the furniture part of his business could expand into the eco-home development business he's started. It sure beats tire rims and mufflers. So I am an eight. All I have to do is change the scale from one to eight and that makes me *awesome. That a girl.*

When I come out of the bathroom, Dylan is in the bedroom slipping off his shirt and replacing it with a charcoal gray, fitted one. He looks deliciously handsome. I bite my lip while he pauses and checks me out. His mouth parts into an appreciative *oh.*

"Emma, you look beautiful."

"Thank you. I hope I pass muster with this group. I know I'm a bit younger than all of their reps. Carson told me to act like I own the place. I suppose a little Blackard swagger wouldn't hurt me."

Dylan barely smiles as he shrugs on his new shirt.

"Yeah, that's Carson. Listen to him. He seems tough and confident, but he hates these things. They make him very uncomfortable. He likes being a homebody, and he's really glad to have you doing this instead of him."

"He's had you doing this for a while, too."

"I can't pull off that sexy little number you're wearing, though."

"So I got this job because of the way I look?"

"No. Carson hires people who have talent or potential. You have both. I've listened to you on the phone with some of our biggest jerks. I would have told them to fuck off, and I have in the past. You, on the other hand, are very diplomatic. Our clients like you. Our customer retention is going to go up with you on board."

"That's nice of you to say. Thanks."

I watch him tuck the shirt in his pants and put his suit coat back on without a tie. He is definitely gorgeous. Dylan is complete masculine virility. His scars are subtle enough that they don't distract from his face, yet they are interesting enough to add a bit of rugged, mysterious character.

"I am your biggest fan," he says, straightening his cuffs and collar.

That makes my heart pound against my ribs. I slide my hands up my bare arms as a sudden chill gives me goose bumps and my nipples harden against the black fabric banded snugly across my chest. I cross my arms and look for my evening bag.

"Do you need a sweater?" Dylan gives me his first real, broad smile of the evening.

"No, that will ruin the line of the dress."

"That would be a tragedy. I say no sweater and let's get to the bar. It will be warmer there."

"How noble of you, looking out for my welfare," I say wryly.

"I am looking out for you, Emma."

I believe him when he says that, too.

Twenty-one
Dylan

We walk into the bar and all thirty-two reps and executives from Mercer Group are already here, drinking and mingling. Heads turn to acknowledge me, and all of them give Emma the once over. My arm possessively wraps around her waist as she gives me a wary side-glance.

I have to introduce her to Steve Mercer, the CEO, first. He is a flashy, thirty-five-year-old who gets a lot of press coverage for his appearances on television shows as a design expert. He is cocky and good-looking so he latches on to Emma as I've expected. She is demure when needed and witty when they least expect it. She speaks vaguely about her background with her father's business and concentrates on driving the conversation with her knowledge of latest trends and changes in the industry. I am impressed.

Reluctantly, I let one of the reps, Trish, pull me over to her loud group of sales representatives that I worked with in Los Angeles. I keep glancing over at Steve and Emma. She is being served the hotel specialty, some vodka cocktail, and she hasn't eaten anything. *Damn.* I should have made her order room service earlier.

As the evening wears on, Steve is the one that walks Emma around the bar and introduces her to his sales reps from the West and East Coasts. I was planning on being her host and introducing her to people. However, she looks perfectly at ease with Steve, and I suppose that comes from working with men in her father's business.

As Trish drinks too much and clings to my arm for

several hours, I am basically keeping her upright. I like talking to the sales people—they represent our strongest sales group—however, knowing Emma is hiding somewhere in the bar with Steve Mercer makes me anxious to find her.

Finally, when I locate her, I lean against the bar and watch her from a distance. I hope Steve isn't getting any ideas that he has found his new girlfriend and he will fly her back to his San Francisco home. I have no intention of letting Emma get swept up by any of these smooth-talking, sharp-dressed men. There are quite a few of them, and they remind me of her ex, Robert—always shopping for another woman.

As I sip my seltzer and contemplate how the next two days will go, I'm so caught up in thinking about Emma, I almost forget about the phone call earlier from Dr. Wang. Actually, I want to forget it. His news was upsetting, although not surprising. Months ago, I assumed I would be prepared if I ever received a phone call like that. Nothing prepares you, and it makes you feel weak, agonizingly sad and angry. I think about never telling Emma, another omission that would surly resurface and damage us further.

As if on cue, Emma looks over at me from across the room. That's enough of that.

I cruise through the crowded bar and reach her as Steve is leaning down to whisper something in her ear.

I cup her elbow. "Hey, ready to call it a night? We've got a long day tomorrow."

Emma looks up at me, her big brown eyes a little tired from all the drinks Steve has been plying her with.

"Oh, you're not going to take the lovely Emma away from me now. I thought I'd take her out for a late night dinner," Steve says. "What do you say, Emma?"

"No. I really need to get some sleep."

After a few more sloppy goodbyes from Steve and a some of the other men who gravitate towards Emma, I escort her out of the bar and head to the elevator banks. We get in a car with a couple locked in a tight embrace, kissing without any notice of us. I shake my head and put myself between them and Emma as she suppresses a giggle. I look down at her and can't help smiling at her girlish behavior.

When we get to the room, she kicks off her shoes and runs to the bed, throwing herself on it.

"I love this bed!" she shouts then flips over and watches me as I remove my jacket. "Thanks for getting me out of there. I liked meeting everyone, but Steve was awfully close to asking me up to his room."

"What?" I stalk across the room and throw my arms down on the bed on either side of her. "Did he actually ask you to come to his room?"

"Relax. I didn't go, did I? He kept suggesting we go some place to be alone."

"That asshole." To think I let him handle her all night. I am furious.

Emma looks up at me. I have her in my clutches, almost, and I am paralyzed with wanting to kiss her. She brings her bare feet up and puts them flat against my chest and gently pushes me away.

"I need food. I didn't eat anything down there." She stands up and makes her way to the bathroom.

"I knew it. I'm calling room service."

"Please do," she responds as she goes into the bathroom.

Twenty minutes later, she comes out with damp hair, wearing a clingy t-shirt and lounge pants. I grab my sweatpants from my suitcase then go shower and change. When I come out, the food has arrived and the server is setting up a dining table with white linens and flowers for us in the living area in front of our city view.

Emma seems more excited about this than the cocktail party. Maybe it is as romantic to her as it is to me. I won't get my hopes up, though. Regardless, I put on some

211

Wynton Marsalis jazz selection that comes with the hotel iPod system. As the music fills the whole suite, I turn it down so it doesn't look like I am overdoing it.

"This looks good, Dylan," she says, sitting at the candlelit table.

"I ordered whatever I thought you'd like." I uncover the silver domes to reveal roasted asparagus and cheese sandwiches, truffle French fries, artichoke macaroni and cheese, and a chocolate torte.

We dig in and she eats heartily, moaning over every dish. A wave of contentment rolls over me as I take in this perfect situation. I am sitting across from the most beautiful woman who fires up my soul like no one else, and with the subtleness of the candle light in the dark room showcasing the impressive New York skyline, it gives me pleasure that I can do this for her.

Emma shoves three fries in her mouth and then takes a forkful of chocolate and laughs. "It's so good, I can't eat one thing at a time," she says.

"There are no rules. Take what you want."

I eat more than my share of everything, enjoying it as much as her. I am not allowed to touch her, but she can't stop me from looking. I take in everything about her from the wisps of hair that fall out of her ponytail and frame her face to the single tiny, dark freckle on her left breast exposed by the neckline of her t-shirt.

When she wipes her mouth on her napkin and drinks two glasses of water, I pour more for her. I would like to punch Steve Mercer for trying to get her drunk.

"How did your accident happen? Would you tell me?"

Her question surprises me. I've assumed Lauren has told her everything about that. The details of my truck accident last fall aren't very interesting.

"Sure." I put down my fork and take a gulp of water, figuring out how I will explain what happened—not so much the incident itself, but rather where my head was at.

"I was driving the company truck to Carson's house to deliver some paperwork to him. I can't remember why I didn't have my Jeep at the office." I shake my head, trying to remember that day. "Anyway, I was coming across that little wooden bridge that enters onto his property, driving too fast, probably listening to music or distracted by something."

"That's when you saw Jess driving away from Carson's, right? She had crossed the same bridge," Emma adds.

"Right." I wonder where she is leading with this if she already knows the particulars. "I saw her and then I got to the bridge. I think I remember sliding down the ravine or it could be something I remember from a dream. I wasn't wearing the seatbelt, and I gave the steering wheel a good beating with my head. The rest isn't clear to me. The state patrol came in and an ambulance took me to the hospital. I woke up a few hours later, pretty sedated, and my stitches were done. They kept me for observations, though."

"No, I meant, would you tell me what you were thinking about on that day when you were driving right before the accident happened?"

"Oh. That's when I was in a really terrible place. I wouldn't say that I had a single day of clear thinking. I was very distracted by every negative thought in my head because I was pretty—"

"Depressed?"

"Yeah. I was in a downward swing at the time, and I can't explain to you why that happened. Emma, this isn't easy for me to talk about, especially since I don't have any concrete answers. For years, doctors and therapists have used words like bipolar, manic, mood swings, chemical imbalance and depression—every popular term to describe me. It didn't matter what they called it, though, since no one could fix it."

"I can see that it's not easy to tell me this, but please

213

try. Please."

She's right. I can't tell myself I am in love with her if I won't even talk to her about the worst part of me.

"I was more than depressed. I was thinking about my parents a lot, and nothing Carson did could get me out of that funk. I had been obsessing about my dad more than anyone then because I knew I was like him, and it scared the shit out of me. I inherited this illness from his family. I've refused help in the past, or when I did accept it, I didn't put in my best effort. I always assumed I could handle all of my problems myself. So, that day on the bridge, I was in my own head, depressed and angry over my father as well as angry at myself. I was so sick of being me. I felt so dark and empty inside. I didn't feel love for anyone or anything… not myself, not my life. Basically, I was damn hopeless and didn't give a shit what would happen to me. Then I woke up in the hospital."

In the warm glow of the candle, she looks so beautiful that I dread to think that she's suddenly feeling sympathy for me.

"Except now. You have a doctor and a program that is altering it, right?"

"To a degree. Yes. Don't have any illusions that I'm cured."

She tilts her head and studies me with a kind calmness that goes against everything this little, bossy, aggressive woman has shown me. "Have you ever been suicidal?" she asks without any reservation.

"No. Never. I never had suicidal thoughts, regardless of what some people may have told you. Sometimes I thought it would be better if I just went to bed and never woke up—a natural death in my sleep so I wouldn't have to face myself in the morning, but I've never plotted my own death."

"Nobody talks about you as if you're suicidal. People in Hera say very nice things about you, Dylan. You're quite popular. I just wanted to know for myself. I wanted to hear it from you."

The whole topic makes me uncomfortable. It's easy if I am talking to Dr. Wang or the people I was in treatment with. Not with Emma. This is not how anyone wants to be seen or perpetually thought of by someone who unknowingly owns the deepest part of you.

Brian comes to mind, and his endless worries about his wife and friends having to take care of his mental illness and his inability to cope. He talked about it every day for six weeks straight, through meds and daily therapy. Brian's fear of living with the label as someone who has a mental illness—along with the medical treatments that were ineffective for him—scared the shit out of him. It scared me, too. I was terrified that my future would hold the same fate of a never-ending cycle of failed treatments.

"I don't have any illusions about anyone," she says.

"What about Robert? Why are you still holding on to him?"

Her long, dark lashes flutter as she looks at the candle, and in that solemn moment, she looks like a painting of a sad Madonna from another time.

"It's not him I'm holding on to. It's the few good times I've had that I want to preserve. Seeing him distressed and possibly in trouble makes everything about my life seem phony and sad. I'm not one of those girls who grew up thinking she'd be a ballerina or a princess; I never had the opportunity to truly romanticize life, not much anyway. I saw a lot of ugly things and I can't necessarily blame Robert's family. My father didn't attempt to shield me from anything. Seedy, backroom bargaining deals, the men who came and went from his office, and some of the *special errands* he took me on... I didn't always understand what was going on, but I know my father is a good guy. He's had to do what was necessary to protect his business and us.

"Sometimes, though, his rages and closed office

meetings with dirty people made me wonder what side we were on. Robert was in the same boat, and I kind of pinned all of my last hopes on him. That's what naïve, hopeful teenagers do. It's what I did. I found the one person who understood me, and that's the only part I could romanticize. It wasn't real, though."

"What happened? Why did you break up? Because of his family?" I hate hearing about him, and I want her to say that he is as corrupt as his father and she never loved him.

"Vincent Marchetto controls my father, and my father always controlled me. My father decided who I could hang out with, where I went to college, where we lived, and how much our family participated in that world. Part of me has always resented or maybe even hated him for that. The other part loves him for taking care of us as best he could. I fell in love with Robert years ago, and then—when he came back into my life—I made a conscious decision that he was the one who could change things. At least that's what I thought."

"So then he controlled your life?" I ask, finding it hard to believe that she'd let anyone manage her. She is too strong-willed for that.

"I let him. I thought Robert represented safety and..."

"And?"

"Love." She shrugs.

"So your history was just as mental as mine," I quip and she laughs.

"See? Mental or not, that's how I ended up with Robert. He had the same twisted childhood and understood me." She smiles. "But having these men control every aspect of my life became unbearable and not much of a life at all."

"So then, what do you think of Carson as your boss?" I lean forward on the table and resist the urge to pick up her hand.

"He's a piece of cake. Heaven. Wonderful," she gushes.

"Yeah, women like him. He's good."

"I'm talking about him as a boss. Geez." She blushes.

"I know. I'm just razzing you. You've been giving me a lot of shit about women, and you're making us waste this perfect hotel room."

"Thanks a lot, Dylan," she snaps. "I actually thought we were having a nice time talking. I didn't know this was all about getting me in bed." Emma stands up and slams her chair against the table before storming into the bedroom.

"I was kidding." I follow her. "Since when did you become so sensitive?"

"Since you wrecked what we had." She throws herself on the bed and turns her head away from me.

"Jesus. Is this still about Jess? How many times can I explain that it was nothing to either of us other than a mistake? How can you hold this against me when you've got Robert chasing you down—a guy you said you loved? Maybe you're the one who wrecked what we had."

She flops onto her back and stares at me. "Maybe you're right. Maybe I don't really understand you, and you certainly don't understand the crazy-ass place I came from. So we're even."

"Don't start with that lame excuse."

"Then tell me what the phone call was about, Dylan," she says sternly as she sits up on the bed.

I stand over her, deliberating how I can tell her something that could only create a barrier between us.

"It's not something I can talk about. It's not about you, though. It's something no one should hear."

"And that's why you should tell me. If you trust me, you'd tell me."

She's right of course. In group therapy they kept telling us that we had to share everything with our loved ones and open ourselves up so we don't wallow in pain. It's easier said than done. I can barely talk to Carson about my emotional struggles, and I can't imagine sharing this with a woman I care about. It is not like talking about your day at work. The emotional turmoil makes you feel abnormal and weak, and anyone who has to listen to you day in and day out isn't going to fair much better.

"Emma, it was my doctor. He gave me some bad news. It's not about me, though."

"Yes, it is. It upset you. You were not yourself today, so it is news that has affected you, and I'd like to know what he said."

She crosses her legs and rests her hands in her lap, waiting patiently for me to talk, looking incredibly sweet. I am pretty sure she won't try any offensive hand maneuvers on me if I sit on the bed.

I put one knee on the edge of the bed and slowly sink into the cushiony mattress. "I was in the treatment center for about six weeks, and I made a few friends. You kind of need to. The person I was closest to was a guy from Ohio. His name was Brian, and he really helped me a lot. We became very good friends." I glance up at Emma and her expression is filled with cautious interest, as if she can already read what is going through my mind. "My doctor called to tell me that Brian committed suicide this morning."

She lets out a small gasp. "Oh, God. Why didn't you tell me?"

"Because I can't change what happened."

"You could go to Ohio now. You can still make the funeral, and Carson and I can handle this stuff with Mercer. Or I could go with you to Ohio. We can drive through the night," she rattles off without taking a breath.

Her reaction leaves me speechless. I never envisioned driving with her through the night to see Brian's family.

"No. I can't do that." As soon as the words are out of my mouth, I sense I have failed Brian.

"You can. He was your friend." Emma says in a soft, pleading voice.

"His wife, Katy, is having him cremated because of the

218

damage done to his face by the gunshot, and she's having a private family memorial, not a funeral."

"Oh. Is there anything we can do? Send a note? Flowers? A donation?"

I shake my head. "I don't think it will make much difference."

"And your doctor called to make sure you're okay, right?"

"Something like that."

"Are you going to be okay, Dylan? Isn't this how your father died?"

I am surprised she knows that, or at least that she has cared to remember it from whatever someone has told her.

"Yes."

I don't think I can keep this conversation going without breaking down. I haven't shed a tear since I was fifteen. I suppose it's from years of building up a hard shell of indifference as a defense mechanism. Emma's sad expression pulls some deeper pain anchored in me, and I think I could collapse and bawl if I don't hold it together.

"So, how do you deal with this, Dylan?"

"I don't know. Stick to my program, I guess."

"Meds, therapy and running?" she asks thoughtfully and touches my hand.

"It's all I know. Those are the tools I've been given, and I don't know what else I can do."

"I know, and those are necessary. You can also talk to me."

"Emma, I like you, but you're not my therapist and that's not where I want this to go. Not at all. Understand?"

"I understand that you're stubborn." She pulls her hand back and lies down on the bed. "I need to sleep, so you should go make yourself comfortable on the couch and get some rest, too."

She shuts off the bedside lamp as I head back into the living room. I push the dinner table out into the hallway

219

and then return to search for an extra pillow and blanket in the closet. When I find the items, I make a bed on the couch. I am too long for it, therefore I have to hang my legs over the armrest.

Up until our argument over Jess, I had a lot of brilliant ideas of how this hotel stay would go down. Nothing in my imagination has had me sleeping on a couch and Emma alone in the bed.

I keep the shades open so I can watch the bright lights of the Manhattan night sky. It does nothing to calm my nerves, but it provides some relief that we are far enough from Hera so I am not worried about a surprise visit from Emma's stalker ex, and we're also far enough from Ohio that I only let a few traces of Brian's image enter into my train of thought. There is a brief period where I imagine his wife's grief and his young son asking for his father. I have to block them out, too. I am really thinking about Emma and how she is sleeping ten feet away in a bed that was meant to include me. Her sleep is restless and I listen as she mumbles her way through a dream until her sudden cry jolts me off the couch in a flash.

"Stop it!" she screams.

When I run into the bedroom, she is sitting up in the bed, illuminated by the desk lamp she's left on. Her big eyes flick around the room bewildered, looking like a lost little girl in a very big bed. I rush to her side, and she reaches out to take my arm.

"Bad dream?" I ask eagerly, as if I have been waiting forever to talk to her again.

"I think so, but I have no idea what I was dreaming about." She's fully awake and lucid as she takes in the familiar surroundings of the hotel room. "Someone or something was chasing me, or bothering me in some way. I'm not sure."

"You screamed for them to stop. Pretty loudly."

"I did? I guess I'd had enough," she chuckles and then

looks down at my briefs. "Don't you have pajamas?"

"No, you know I usually sleep naked. I'm wearing underwear for your benefit." I smirk.

She is braless and her nipples make hard points through her sheer, snug t-shirt. I am already thinking about sex and driving away depressing thoughts about Brian. I know I have to get back to the couch before she decides I am a lecherous creep trying to take advantage of the situation.

"Were you sleeping? Did I wake you?"

"No, I can't sleep at all."

"Mmm," she says quietly.

I don't know how to interpret that or her lidded eyes that usually accompany the moan I take as a sign of arousal.

I am about to stand up and go back to the other room when her hand slides down to mine.

"Stay here. You can sleep on that side." She motions to the large, empty space next to her.

"Are you going to put some big pillows between us, so I don't touch you?" I ask wryly. Who am I kidding? I want back in her bed and she knows it by the way my briefs are straining against the prominent bulge I am sporting.

"Nope. No pillows are needed because you're not going to touch me. Remember?"

"Oh, great, so we're still playing that game."

"I'm not playing any game. You're the one who didn't put all your cards on the table."

"But then I did. I've told you everything."

I don't know where she is going with this, and for the first time, I really care what a woman thinks about me. Aside from temporarily obstructing a relationship between Carson and Jess, my short-lived fling with Jess confused the crap out of me. Most of the time, I was also off in my own world. For years it was very easy for me to tune out any woman who tried to engage me in deeper conversations,

221

anything they thought would bring us closer together; especially those post-coital, huggy-feely moments when I was ready to leave. Though, I would do any of that for Emma in a heartbeat and I wouldn't think twice about it. Whatever she wants, I want to be the one to give it to her.

"Stop talking, Dylan. Lie down." She points to the bed.

As I rub the back of my head and walk around the bed, her eyes are on me the whole time, scrutinizing my lower half and letting her eyes slowly roam up to my chest. She's blatantly obvious. Watching her study me in appreciation is both arousing and unnerving, like I am on display as the catch of the day.

Arguments and grudges are one thing, but this is something entirely different. I cannot pinpoint where the change is, yet I am sensing there's been some galactic shift between us.

I stretch out on my stomach next to her, keeping a good ten inches between us so I don't invade her space. The bed is fantastic. I close my eyes and sink into the comforter, stretching out my legs and popping every kink the damn couch has been giving me.

My breath hitches when I feel her fingers dance lightly across my back. I open my eyes and look at her, searching for a sign that we're good and sex is imminent.

"Did you miss me?" I ask, ready to make a move on her.

"Turn over," she says. "Don't talk."

I am already salivating at the thought of ripping her clothes off and putting my mouth on her perfect breasts that seem to be fighting their way out of her shirt. She has me turned on all right, and I am ready for whatever she has planned. I want to forget about all the bad shit, especially friends who commit suicide. I want to block it all out.

I turn over, and as I reach out a hand to cup her face and bring her in for a kiss, she quickly pushes my hand aside.

"No touching," she demands. "Lie back."

I scoff, about to laugh.

"Do you want to sleep on the couch?" Her beauty is inviting, but her tone is severe. "If not, do as I say, Dylan."

At that, I lie back and watch her with fascination.

"Grip the bottom of the headboard," she says. "You can't touch me. At all."

My mouth quirks, ready to protest, however my cock also twitches in betrayal, eager to do as she says. I reach above my head and slip my hands under the base of the wooden headboard.

Emma tugs my briefs down while I lift my hips so she can pull them off. Then she straddles my legs and I become more aroused as her firm tits fall forward when she leans over my cock. She takes it in her hand, stroking it slowly from under my sack to the tip then runs her thumb across the tip until it is slick with wetness. I groan and dig my fingers into the headboard. Watching her do this to me is too hot. I want to throw her on the bed, strip her and fuck her.

She leans over and licks the tip of my cock, and I desperately want to warn her that I could easily blow my load. I think better of saying anything, though. Something about this ninja Tinkerbell ordering me around tells me I better obey her or she will leave me high and dry with a painful boner as my punishment.

Her tongue swirls around the head before she licks my cock with long strokes, going all the way down to my balls. She begins sucking the sensitive skin under my sack, and then sucks her way up to the top again. My dick is standing straight up, ready to shoot. I look at the ceiling, trying to keep my grunting to a minimum. Just when I think I am able to hold out longer, she takes me in her mouth—and this isn't a little bit of sucking—pushing me all the way to the back of her throat.

"Ah, Jesus," I groan as I thrust myself further into her

223

mouth. No sooner do I say that than I feel uncomfortable cool air on my wet cock. Emma is holding my dick in one hand and her mouth is nowhere near it.

"What part about *not talking* do you not understand? If you talk, I stop. And I'm Emma, not Jesus." She looks at me and I want to laugh, but I squash that idea, too.

My desperate cock doesn't have to wait long before it's submerged in her warm wet mouth again. Now she doesn't mess around with tantalizing strokes and licks; she sucks me off hard. She is relentless as her mouth and tongue take over my engorged, pulsating dick. My breath releases in quick pants as I am about to come. My mind is begging for it to never end, and my body is ready to explode.

I pull my hips back to let her know that I am coming, expecting her to let me ejaculate onto my stomach, but she grips my hip and cock harder. She doesn't let go, and I can't stop myself from erupting inside of her mouth. She keeps sucking me off as I thrust and empty myself completely.

I have a few choice words I would like to say right now, however I stick to the code of silence rule. When Emma gets up and goes into the bathroom, I am too spent to move. I close my eyes and my mind plays back what has just happened.

My hands are still gripping the headboard when I feel a gentle tug as Emma pries them off and places my arms at my sides. Her calm expression is strange because this is the girl that loves to talk. She runs a finger down my chest to my stomach and my dick actually twitches again. She chuckles.

"Now you should be able to sleep," she says. "You're relaxed, right?"

"Very," I say hoarsely.

She lifts the comforter from the side of the bed and covers me, tucking me in.

"And you're naked, so you shouldn't have any problem sleeping tonight."

"Emma," I begin to say.

"We're not talking. We're going to sleep. But Dylan, I am very sorry about your friend." Without another word, she goes back to her side of the large bed, which seems really far away from me.

Twenty-two
Emma

Dylan's heavy arm is draped over my waist when I wake up. The comforter is off, and his naked body is spooning me. It feels delicious, and my first thought is to turn into his embrace and kiss him. My second thought is to get out of bed before he wakes up and thinks everything between us is normal and as it should be. Going with the latter thought, I slip out from underneath his arm, strip my clothes off, and get into the hot shower.

I can't believe how brazen I was last night, ordering him around, and this after I threw a hissy fit saying I won't sleep with him. I get to blame some of this on the booze that Steve Mercer kept shoving into my hand, though.

God, I loved seeing the shocked expression on Dylan's face when I went down on him. I actually shocked myself. I didn't plan it, but his insistence on not talking about his grief over his friend's death was hard to take, even though I know it sounds extremely selfish for me to think that way. My ranking on Dylan's list is well below Carson and Dylan's doctor, although I would like to think I am inching my way into his heart and that a time will come when he trusts me.

It was an odd, unplanned strategic move to render him speechless and immobile. He thinks he has control over everything he does, so I gave him a taste of my being in control. It was a powerful feeling to give him pleasure while at the same time boxing him in. He was frustrated at not being able to touch me or talk, but I wasn't going to let him speak if he couldn't share something meaningful

226

beyond sexual utterings.

True, he has admitted what the phone call was about, however he thought he could brush aside discussing the death of someone who clearly was important to him. I can't accept that. Does that mean I can't accept Dylan the way he is? I refuse to believe that since I have no intention of trying to change Dylan. I like him as he is. I may, in fact, love this man who baffles me, so I am sure as hell going to weasel my way into his life, yet this has to slow way down.

Despite my upbringing, I am a romantic at heart. My physical gesture was not a cure for the grief he withholds, but after he shared a brief part of himself, I wanted to do something that didn't involve me begging him to talk when he clearly wasn't going to. Boy, did I find the best way to distract him from his negative thoughts.

I stand under the shower and let the water drown out any residual embarrassment I may have. After all, I pushed the guy away the night before, refusing sex and to share a bed, only to bring him to his knees with my mouth. When I put my face into the stream of water, I feel two hands settle firmly on my breasts, and a large, hard body meets every part of my flesh from my calves to neck. My eyes pop open, and I turn my head to see Dylan smile as he brushes his head against my cheek.

"You left the bed too soon," he murmurs into my ear while his erection pushes into my lower back.

"No. Last night was a one-time thing. I wanted to make you feel better. To make you feel something good. But we're not going to jump back into sleeping together and banging each other at work. I'm sorry if I—"

"I know, Emma. I know what you're doing," he says, turning me to face the shower wall and away from the water before he places both of my hands on the cold tile.

"What am I doing?" I am trembling from both the absence of the hot water and from his firm but gentle hands that glide down to my waist.

"You're showing me who I am," he whispers in my ear. "You're showing me what it's like to go through the motions of being with someone, giving in sexually while managing to be empty inside. I'm not a poet, but I understand you. And I'm not empty inside when I'm with you."

His voice is husky with desire and restraint.

"I sent the wrong message, Dylan." My words are a complete lie, and I am a terrible actress. I have conflicting thoughts about what I've done. Giving him a bit of pleasure because he's become more to me than anyone else, and at the same time, I thought I could act like a heartless sex fiend—a taste of his past. They are contradictory acts, and I've proven that.

"No, you didn't. Don't move and don't talk."

"Oh, please. You can't copy me and expect me to—"

"Hush, woman. It's my turn. This isn't a one-sided relationship." His mouth tickles my neck.

"It's not a relationship, Dylan. Not that kind."

"What kind? Where two people like each other a lot and spend time together, maybe live together and deal with their problems together? If you don't think it's that, then you really don't know jack. And by the way, I get bonus points for remembering your name. Emma."

I can hear the smile in his voice.

"Dylan—"

"No talking." He clamps his hand over my mouth before he grinds his erection against my backside, and I hear the intake of his breath.

His hand slides off my mouth and down my chest where he fondles my breasts as his other hand caresses my butt cheeks before slipping underneath to my sex. His fingers rub me slowly in soft, grazing circles, triggering little sparks of desire that make me shudder.

My forehead presses into the tile wall as he makes me wet, his fingers slipping in and out of me. He kisses the

228

back of my neck and his tongue flicks down across my shoulder. He then pinches each nipple until they are hard, throbbing peaks while his kisses continue down my back to my ass. He actually bites my butt cheek and I whimper. Then he turns me around so my back is flat against the tile. He begins kissing my stomach, and I reach out to touch his head. He immediately clamps both of my hands against my sides and looks up.

"No touching." He grins.

That's when I know I am in trouble.

As Dylan continues kissing my stomach, his tongue leaves a scorching trail down my pelvic bone. His knee pushes my legs farther apart as he nips and licks my center until my body is thrumming with a molten craving for more, then he sucks on my clit and makes my knees feel like goo. I can't fall or move, however, because he is gripping my hands tightly against the side of my thighs to keep me upright.

His tongue slips in and out of me and I moan. I try to squirm as he then adds more pressure, yet I am stilled into a state of euphoric paralysis when he sucks so hard on my clit that an orgasm explodes through me. I can't move as the spasms shoot through my limbs. I gasp and think I am falling when I realize that Dylan is pulling me into his arms and standing up, cradling me.

"Are you relaxed?" he asks with a hint of a smile.

"Perfectly." I'm limp in his arms.

"Good. You get ten more minutes in bed while I shower."

I am amazed that he actually deposits me onto the bed and then heads back to the bathroom with a full-on erection. He didn't even try to get something in return. He has some major willpower, then again, maybe he's going to take care of himself while he's in there.

Twenty minutes later, we are both dressed in fresh suits and my hair is semi-dry and twisted into another bun.

Dylan watches me primp and apply make-up, but says nothing about the hot sexual favors we've given each other.

***

We arrive at Mercer's trendy warehouse style home décor store, a short walk from the hotel. It's before retail hours so the vast space is empty. A pretty store manager leads us upstairs to the corporate offices where there is a spacious conference room with a breakfast spread and large, industrial windows that provide an inspiring view. I expected to be more nervous, yet having Dylan by my side has secured my confidence.

"Oh, my God," I whisper to myself.

"What?" Dylan questions as we unpack our computers.

"I just realized I have spent every moment with you by my side since that night you gave me a ride home."

"You left out the part about kicking me out of bed two nights ago," he says wryly.

No one else has entered the conference room yet, so we are alone. Dylan whisks around me, setting up our gear for our presentations. He is chiseled perfection with the fine suit; his handsome face; the tall, muscular physique that can't be camouflaged by clothing; and those scars that make him even more alluring. He is hot, and my nerves and senses are completely aware of his every movement. My mind keeps drifting back to us in the shower and every moment with him before that.

"I'm serious. It's like we're tied at the hip. This isn't normal even for married people, Dylan."

Dylan stops typing on his keyboard and glares at me then walks briskly over to my side of the table with a marked intensity. He puts his hands on my hips under my suit jacket and turns me away from the conference table.

"Listen to me." His deep voice is strict. "This may have started because I said I wanted to help you—to make sure you're safe from your ex and the shit he's caught up in—but make no mistake, we are tied together. Aside from where we've come from or who we've been with, that was then, this is now. And now we're together. I'm not the most talkative guy when it comes to *sharing,* but that doesn't mean I don't want to tell you what's going on in my head. It means I'm not good at it. But I am trying. For you... I'm trying to do this because of you."

His serious declarations are the most romantic words ever said to me, even more potent than Robert's *"I love you."* To me, Dylan's possessive grip on my waist paired with those powerful statements is an unexpected intimate gesture. I am reeling from his physical and emotional hold on me, and I am no longer falling in love with him. I have *fallen.*

Captivated by his unwavering blue eyes that touch me in a new way, I am about to respond when others begin filing into the room. He lets go of my waist.

"Get something to eat while you can. You need some protein. The buffet has eggs," he says gruffly.

"I'm too excited about our presentation to eat."

"You were very excited this morning, too," he replies with a mischievous glint in his eyes. "You need food. I don't want you fainting on me."

I scoff but blush as I think back to what he did to me in the shower. Dylan chuckles wickedly.

***

Our presentation goes very well over the next four hours. Although I feel like I am high, running on nervous adrenaline, I know my material, and I am very comfortable with the Mercer executives and sales representatives. The only person who makes me nervous is Dylan.

As I stand at the front of the room, explaining the visuals displayed on the theater screen rolled down from the ceiling, Dylan remains across the room, leaning against a wall with his arms crossed as he watches me. When I begin to explain Blackard Designs' new vertical integration approach to our sales minimum, he arches an eyebrow in

231

surprise. It's a plan I've run by Carson but never told Dylan, and he looks amused at my audacity to introduce new sales quotas that are expected to increase our revenues by thirty percent. Through the spiel, the Mercer reps sit around the table and patiently listen. They don't seem upset with the new requirements and sales quotas I babble on about. I expected some pushback and am pleasantly surprised when I don't get any.

When I finish with my presentation, Dylan steps in to impress them with the new designs. Since he still likes to work in the studio and factory as well as work directly with the design team, he knows the furniture lines better than anyone at Blackard, including Carson. Besides that, Dylan is the ultimate showman.

I sit down off to the side and watch him describe the photos of each new piece of furniture. I also notice the female reps watching him as if he is a greased up, half-naked wrestler. Who knew furniture could be so exciting? But Dylan's enthusiasm takes over the room. He is a much better speaker than me, and to his credit, he knows every woman's name in the room. Suddenly, they all have questions for *him.* Dylan points to each one by name and responds thoroughly to each inquiry.

After questions, he ushers everyone out of their seats and takes the whole group downstairs to the store where Carson has had all the new furniture delivered. Gemma and Noelle, our design team, were here the day before to set up the furniture in appealing displays throughout the store, mixing it in with other brands and accessories.

I follow along as Dylan leads the pack, several of the women sticking close to him. I don't blame them. It must be a primal instinct that they want to get as close as possible to the largest, most attractive male. Although, he doesn't seem to notice them and keeps looking for me in the crowd until our eyes meet every few minutes. As I straggle in the back of the group with the men, I roll my eyes to myself. I want to laugh and say out loud, *"It's only furniture, and stop bumping your breasts and girly bits into my guy!"*

It is at that moment that Steve Mercer puts his arm around my waist. "It's going to be a banner year for Blackard, isn't it?"

He gathers me close to him as if this is a prelude to something more between us, and I am stunned that the Mercer CEO is being so forward with me. When he pulls my hip flush with his side and his fingers press into me, a rush of anger fills me and I imagine how I could kick one of his legs out from underneath him and flip him on his back into a painful pretzel.

Before I can react in any way, however, Dylan is in front of us. He pushes right between Steve and me, throwing Steve's arm off my waist to replace it with his own.

"Thanks for entertaining Emma. I've got this." Dylan is very nonchalant about it as well as domineering as he towers over Steve.

I smile weakly at Steve as if it is a thank you for not fondling me I suppose.

Steve looks a little ruffled at Dylan's appearance and quick reflexes, but he adjusts his cuffs in an aloof manner. "She's delightful, but it's time for me to take my crew out for a very late lunch. Are you joining us?"

"No, but we'll be at the wrap party tonight," Dylan answers, holding me tighter against him.

"Great. We could use some one-on-one time together," he says this to Dylan but winks at me. "I look forward to seeing you again, Emma."

When Steve leaves to join his group, Dylan walks me outside to the pedestrian-heavy sidewalk. "Shit," he mumbles. "That guy has been up every skirt. When I saw him touch you, I was so tempted to flatten his face."

"Dylan, this happens in sales all the time. You know

people are touchy-feely in this business. He put his arm on my waist, nothing more."

"Well, Little Miss Ninja, why didn't you throw him to the ground or give him the Vulcan Grip on his nuts like you did to me?"

"I didn't think it would be very professional, especially if I want to stay in this business," I laugh.

"Probably not, but I would have enjoyed seeing that." Dylan stops walking and looks down at me. "That was our first time working together outside of the office, and I liked it a lot. You were great. You blew me away with those new minimum investments. That was gutsy."

"Thank you." I start blushing from the way he keeps staring at me. "Carson knew about it, in case you're wondering."

"I figured. I didn't think you pulled those big numbers out of your cute, little ass. I assumed you had discussed all of this with Carson beforehand. Why didn't you tell me?" He looks a little disappointed, and it pulls at my stomach.

"I wanted to impress you." I sound unsure of myself. "We had a rocky start at work, and I wanted you to be confident with me as a business partner. I didn't want the sex part to cloud your thinking, either."

His mouth drops open as he huffs out a breath while those baby blues don't leave my eyes, and my body begins to tremble a bit. I suppose that admitting to myself that I am in love with Dylan has escalated my worries about working with him and speculating if he sees me as an equal at work or as his little, live-in sex mate.

"I have complete confidence in you. Never question that," he replies. "And by the way, I've had enough of this bun business." He yanks my hair out of the chignon, causing it to fall in thick, tangled waves down my back.

"Dylan, it's a mess." I reach up and attempt to finger the strands into something presentable.

"It's sexy as hell. I think we should go back to the

hotel room for lunch, or are you still freezing me out?"

"Oh, hello, big boy," I say dryly. "What I did to you last night hardly counts as a freeze out."

Dylan grins and runs his hands under my hair and cups my head. He leans in close to my face. "Hmm, I could interpret that in several ways. I'll just say, that was fantastic, and this big boy and his big boy part would like a repeat performance."

"I'll bet. But I was thinking we could talk about what happened yesterday when you got that phone call. I thought we could discuss when you went away to that place."

As Dylan sighs and his warm breath caresses my face, I am inclined to go back to the hotel room and jump into bed with him, but it doesn't seem like the right thing to do. We are prolonging the inevitable, pushing aside the issues that disrupt our lives so they can come back to torture us later. That's the problem with starting a new relationship—it's easy to get caught up in the sex and all the exciting physical aspects and store the potential problems behind an invisible curtain—but the problems always surface, eventually.

"I thought, after last night and this morning, we were good," Dylan says, annoyed.

"We're good at sex. Do you really think I'm still not upset about this Jess thing you had? And that you won't talk about your treatment? Last night, I thought I was…"

"You thought what?" His hands drop from my face in exasperation.

"I thought I was showing you what it's like to get a sexual favor from someone who doesn't give a shit about anything but sex. Like you were with all those women," I say, feeling sick at the thought.

"Then you're a lousy actress."

"I know. I am. Because I do care about you and I thought I could get back at you."

"By giving me a blow job?" he asks loudly.

People passing us on the busy street glance our way with amused expressions.

"I had it planned differently. I wanted to show you what it's like to do what you want and then walk off without a care, but I was torn because I really did want you to feel better," I whisper.

"I don't talk enough so you want to punish me by giving me a blow job? But you feel bad for me, too, and want to make me feel better by giving me a blow job?" he says sarcastically. "I thought I was on to what you were up to, Emma, and I wasn't too worried because we're together all the time. Arguments are normal. I guess this wasn't a typical pissing match, though. You really thought you could walk off and leave?" He's riled.

"Not literally. God, Dylan. I wasn't going to walk out of the hotel. We have a job to do. But I was furious the other night at the dinner party when they brought up Jess and you, and it made me feel really crappy. I spent the last day wondering if I should live someplace else."

"But I thought last night… I thought we were mending fences. I didn't realize you were actually thinking of leaving. I didn't get that vibe at all, Emma. You can't give a great blow job and expect to walk off."

"Would you stop saying blow job?" I whisper angrily as pedestrians continue to watch us.

Dylan shakes his head. "And this morning in the shower, I assumed you were enjoying it because you were with me." There is no affection in his glare.

"I did enjoy it. Obviously. Do we have to talk about this in broad daylight on a busy street?"

Without responding, Dylan grabs my hand and walks me briskly back to the hotel in silence. When we enter our suite, he orders room service and then strips off his suit and puts on those low-slung sweats I love so much. I change into a pair of yoga pants and a t-shirt and then sit on the bed, waiting for him to unload his rage.

236

He huffs and puffs around the room like a caged lion.

"Okay, let's talk," he says angrily.

He doesn't sit down; he keeps pacing.

"Not when you're acting like this. Maybe you should go to the hotel gym and put in a fifty-mile run to work off some of this aggression," I snap back. "Then we'll talk."

"Oh, no. You don't get to *therapize* me, too. You're not my fucking nurse or my shrink."

"You don't even have a name for what I am to you. Exclusive fuck buddy?"

"Fuck buddy!" he shouts and I scramble back farther from him. He is like a giant when he is irate. "Didn't you hear a single thing I said this morning? We're together, and I am trying. You're my girlfriend, in case it hasn't crossed your mind. And how could it not cross your mind? Explain that."

"Um, well, how about we've never even dated. One week you're pretty cold towards me, then I'm living with you, then we start sleeping together, which is something I encouraged, I realize. Then I find out you were involved with my boss's wife and you bought a wedding ring for her. Those are some pretty key details that you left out."

Dylan walks around the bed to stand over me. "We've been through this. I didn't intentionally leave it out. I assumed you knew everything about me already from the town gossip who happens to be your best friend."

"I realize that, and I understand you weren't well then, but that's a really huge thing to leave out."

"So, this whole thing with Jess is a big problem to you even though it happened before I even knew you? Are you going to get over this or is it indefinite?"

"I don't know." I glare at him. "I imagine it's going to be very difficult for me to be around Jess and maybe Carson, too."

His lips curl into thin lines as his eyes widen. My stomach hurts to say I am unsure about us. I know I'm in love with him. I also know that I have never had to deal with such an awkward love scenario.

"Is this a deal breaker?" His voice is low and clipped now.

"Dylan, all I know is that I was falling hard for you and then this news about you and Jess made me think whatever we have or may have was all a lie."

"Do you still feel that way? Because we're not a lie. We're good together."

"Well, before I knew about her, I felt special. It sounds corny and silly because we haven't been together that long, but it's the truth. I thought I was special to you."

Dylan takes that as his cue to sit on the bed in front of me. He then puts his hands on either side of me and leans forward until our faces are less than a foot apart.

"You are special. This isn't about Jess. I had a fling with her. I'm not flinging anything with you, Emma."

Yes, I needed to hear that, however sometimes the words don't erase the bad feelings, and my ego says I am only second-runner up because the first one got away.

"You don't understand," I tell him.

"I don't? How about the recent meeting you had with Robert? You were with him for two years—that wasn't a fling—and I have to sit and watch you console him. It makes your relationship fresh and still perfectly alive when he's undeserving of any affection from you. How do you think that makes me feel?"

"You knew about him before you and I got together. You knew I was trying to get rid of him. It's not the same as being *surprised* after you've already put yourself out there for someone else."

"You didn't answer my question. I'm in this, too. I've put myself out there for you, so how do you think I feel when I see you with Robert? How do you think I feel when I see you worrying about him and dredging up old memories with him?"

I take in his angry eyes that never seem to blink as they lock on me with possessiveness. My heart and ego both remind me that it's a reassuring sign, that he cares about me and I could be the biggest fool. I let my gaze drop down and focus on his bare chest and then down to his abs because I don't know how to respond.

He moves his mouth to my ear with his lips barely touching me. "I'll tell you how I feel. Pissed as hell, jealous that he's trying to take you away from me, and scared that he'll succeed."

On those last words, I look back up and Dylan collides his mouth into mine. It's a fast, aggressive, all-encompassing kiss that's just long enough for him to brand me—to claim me. When he pulls away, my lips feel bruised and swollen.

"If you have any doubts about me, then I'm doing something wrong," he says.

There is a knock on the door so Dylan leaves me to let the room service waiter in to set up another lovely spread in the living room. When he leaves, Dylan doesn't wait for me. He sits down and begins chowing like a fiend. I sit down across from him and pick through the five entrees he has ordered for the two of us.

"I'm going down to the hotel gym to run," he says suddenly, standing and tossing his napkin on his chair. "I don't want you to be alone, but I need to run. I'm feeling jumpy. I wonder why... Will you promise me that you'll stay in the room and not open the door for anyone?"

"You take babysitting to a whole new level."

"I'm serious. I'm not leaving unless I have your word. No going outside, not even a trip to the ice machine."

He grabs a t-shirt off a chair and puts it on along with his running shoes.

"Wow, you saw him. You really think Robert is a danger to me? Because I don't."

"I don't know him and I don't know who else may be

with him, and I don't have a fucking clue what's going on. Until we have more answers, I want you to stay put. Can you do that for me?"

"Sure," I mutter and twirl the pasta around on my plate.

"Good. I'll be back in less than an hour."

"Okay. Go break some records. I bet you can run a mile in thirty seconds, stud." I keep playing with my food.

Unexpectedly, Dylan's large hand is under my chin, and he angles my head up to him then gives me a soft peck on my mouth.

"I knew I could do that," he says with something that almost resembles a smile. "Remember, I've got might on my side, and I'm stronger and faster than you. Now I'm going to go run ten miles. It should only take about five minutes according to your calculations. And before you get all whacked out and think I'm another guy who's trying to control your life, I'm not. I'm the guy that wants to be with you, and I want to keep you safe."

***

I spend the next hour sitting in a chair watching television and staring out the window at the vibrant city below. My chest tightens when I hear the door open and Dylan returns drenched in sweat. He takes off his t-shirt and dries himself off, sneaking looks at me as if he is trying to gauge my mood.

"Are you still angry at me?" he asks.

"Are you still angry at me?" I shoot back.

"I was never angry at you. I was just trying to convince you that I'm not the bad guy. I can't stand that we're dealing with your ex."

"Ditto on your ex. But, no, I'm not angry at you."

"Jess isn't my ex, and she isn't stalking me, and she isn't in trouble with the law."

"You're right."

Dylan eyes me warily. "I'm right about everything?"

"Don't push it." I smile. "You're right about Robert.

And you should know that he couldn't ever win me back. I was done with him last year. This new stuff is about me helping an old friend. Nothing more."

"What else am I right about?" He grins, coming around to my chair and squatting in front of me.

"That we're good together. When we're not arguing, I really like being with you."

"And?"

"And I give great blow jobs."

Dylan's whole face lights up with a boyish grin. He grips the armrests and pulls himself closer to me. "And?"

"What are you fishing for, Dylan? I admit I have had my screw-up moments. I admit I willingly started this with you. I also like working with you. And it's nice when you do tell me things you wouldn't otherwise share with someone. I want more of that."

"I want that, too. I can't share everything with my doctor, like what it's like to get a BJ from an angry girlfriend who thinks she's being vengeful and nurturing at the same time. That would be an interesting topic for my shrink."

I laugh.

"But there's more, Emma." He tweaks my earlobe.

"Yes, Robert is someone I have to deal with, and you'll have to get over that."

Dylan groans then plants a delicate kiss on my nose.

"And Jess is someone who is a permanent part of your life, so I'll have to deal with that on my own I guess. Don't assume it's something I can brush aside so easily, though."

"Fair enough," he replies, knowing he is winning this hand. "What about us living together? And I'm not talking about separate bedrooms with the occasional happy ending, babe."

"I was working up to that one."

"Oh, were you?"

He smiles and it's enough to give me that tingling

feeling from being goofy-in-love.

"I don't know how that will work. It's Leo's house and I'm a temporary guest—"

"Leo isn't living there, and you can share my room. But that's beside the point. You're thinking of an excuse. It doesn't come down to actual geography or which house we live in; it's about sharing a bed wherever we are, even if you choose to live at the Red Roof Inn on the interstate. God, I hope you don't, though."

His face is so close to mine that I can't help myself, I stroke his cheekbone.

"Dylan," I say coyly.

"What, Emma?"

"What time does the party start?"

"In a couple of hours. Why; did you have something in mind?"

His smile exposes perfect white teeth and full lips that I can't get enough of. I zero in on those as I clasp his neck and pull him closer for a kiss.

Kissing Dylan is like being at the top of a rollercoaster as it is about to take the first terrifying and thrilling descent. I can't wait for it to happen and the anticipation of how excited I will be on the ride is intoxicating.

When Dylan puts his arms around my back and eases me forward until I am snug in his embrace, I wrap my legs around his waist as he holds my head firmly to deepen the kiss. The arguing as well as the back and forth accusations of the last couple of days have built a need in both of us that's impossible to ignore. As our tongues duel and my hands run wildly around his head, rubbing his soft buzz and grappling to touch the scruff on his jaw, my body is getting incredibly wound up, like a top that's going to be released and spin out of control.

"Let's not waste the bed," I mumble between our clenched lips.

"I agree, but I really need a shower—"

"No, you don't. Bed, now."

"Yes, ma'am," he replies, picking me up with my limbs wrapped around him.

Still kissing and holding me, he strides over to the other room and falls onto the bed with me, never letting our mouths part. We undress each other, stroking and touching flesh as we expose it with each item of clothing that's discarded. Kisses ensue on hips and stomachs, inner thighs and necks. Our naked, tangled bodies are all that matter now.

All my grandstanding about us not talking enough is tossed out the window along with my personal quibbles on where I stand with Dylan—either as someone he may love or as his short-term girlfriend. I am laughing inwardly because the only talking my body is doing right now is telling itself how primed I am to be screwed out of my mind. I don't want to try to unravel my inane, preachy thoughts. I just want to feel him all over me and inside of me.

At one point, my head is resting on his large thigh and my mouth and hands have his cock, coaxing moans from him while his tongue teases my clit. I've never engaged in this position with any man, and I am completely enthralled and turned on beyond control when we have our heads between each other's legs, bringing one another to volcanic climaxes. As the orgasm shoots a bolt of fire from my center, I moan Dylan's name at the same time he ejaculates onto his stomach and my breasts. The orgasm feels endless and I am crazed with lust.

I turn around and climb on top of him with the stickiness of his semen between our bodies. I need to kiss him again. I can't get enough of Dylan, and I know he can wring more out of my body that is still vibrating. Even after a ten-mile run and an orgasm, he eagerly gropes my ass and breasts while his cock perks and comes back to life. When I lick his small, firm nipples, he is completely hard. I begin

243

rubbing him against my wet sex.

Then we have the *"oh shit"* moment.

Dylan rolls me off him, jumps out of bed and tears through his luggage and drawers searching for a condom. Talk about a lustful fury. I beg him to hurry even though he couldn't possibly move faster or throw more things on the floor. Just when we think it is futile to our sex addled brains—that finding the roll of condoms is like finding the Holy Grail—we both laugh with relief as he discovers one.

Chalk it up to the professional sex fiend, I think. Thankfully, he's got the condom on and is ready to go before the mood or momentum can be broken.

"On your knees," he orders breathlessly, as if he's shaken.

Some poet, but he's mine.

I scramble on all fours and he plunges into me before I can gain stability on the bed. Dylan wraps a strong arm around my waist and holds my body tightly as he mounts me without finesse. He bows over me, putting all of his weight on one arm and thrusts repeatedly with forceful grunts against my neck. I push back, meeting each of his thrusts with my own moans, letting him fill me over and over until my desire is begging for him to quake my body.

"Two days without being inside of you, and this is what you do to me, Emma," he rasps into my ear.

The hand he has splayed against my stomach moves down my rocking pelvis and rubs my clit, fingering the slick folds until I whimper. That magical crescendo of pleasurable sparks begins building quickly. I am impatient for the ultimate explosion to take over totally, knowing it will blind me temporarily and leave me in a glorious stupor of euphoria. I want it now. Just when I hear Dylan's breathing hitch, he detonates my sensitive spot and I climax as he comes, shouting my name.

For a running man, Dylan is breathing rather hard and sweating as if he really did run ten, thirty-second miles. I feel overjoyed that he's completely spent because of me.

After he takes care of the condom, he pulls me down on the bed so we're facing each other and nuzzles his head against my cheek.

There hasn't been any poetic murmurings or tender kisses, it's just been good, old-fashioned fucking. It's exactly what I've needed. It isn't just the physical aspect, either. It is like being doused with a cold bucket of water so I could have the epiphany we all wish would happen at the start of a relationship and not after countless misunderstandings and confused interpretations of mixed signals. Of course, if we didn't have to struggle and suffer a bit in a relationship before we wise up, that would make life too easy.

"I didn't hurt you, did I?" he asks. I find it adorable that a big guy who looks destroyed after shouting through a spectacular orgasm would ask that.

"No, you didn't hurt me." I kiss his cheek and then his nose. "I loved it."

"I loved it, too. I hope I wasn't too rough with you. Seriously."

I smile then wrap my arms and legs around him. Sweaty body and all, I want to be as close as possible to him. He looks relieved and responds by tightening his hold on me.

"Dylan, you can't hurt me. Like you said, we're good together."

"You're just getting that now?"

As I gently stroke the stubble on his chin and let my fingers glide past his ear to his scars, he closes his eyes and groans softly.

"I like tracing your scars. Is that weird?" I chuckle.

"No, it feels good." He opens his eyes and gives me a sweet kiss on my forehead.

Up close, his blue irises are arresting. I wouldn't mind skipping the party and spending the rest of the night here with him. The room is quiet and so decadent that we could easily make up for the lost time spent arguing about other people. It is the first time I feel like we are actually alone and out of reach from everyone in Hera or Jersey.

"Hmm," he murmurs. He stills as my fingers dance along his scalp and neck. "I don't want to go to the party."

"I was thinking the same thing, but my boss wouldn't appreciate me blowing off our biggest client's expensive event. There are hands to shake and asses to kiss."

"Okay, but the deal is, you stick by my side. This place is going to be packed. We go in, shake some hands and pretend to kiss asses and then we leave early and come back here. I want a night with you without all the extra noise and people and all the fucking drama they bring with them. Deal?"

"Yes, sir." I splay my hands on his hard chest and zero in on his lips for another kiss.

"Emma, I'll share something with you... I've had pretty bad insomnia for over a decade—never really got a solid night's sleep before—but I sleep really well when we're in the same bed. You're like a magic pillow."

I laugh. "You can do better than that."

He rolls on top of me, keeping his weight on his forearms so he doesn't crush me.

"I want to be with you all the time. This can't end. We can't end, ever."

Twenty-Three
Dylan

When Emma comes out of our hotel bathroom dressed in a short, body-hugging, strapless red dress, I want to throw my leather jacket over her shoulders or keep her in for the night. It is hard enough watching over her in crowds without her calling attention to herself in a flashy, sexy dress.

I am practically entranced as she sits on the bed with a compact mirror and puts on make-up, outlining her eyes with a dark pencil before she glances at me.

"This takes work; it doesn't just happen," she remarks.

"What?"

"Getting sexy."

"You're already sexy, even without make-up. You're beautiful."

"You are very sweet, but this takes skill. If you're going to wear a dress like this, you walk a fine line between looking like a sex goddess and looking like a hooker. Make-up and hair are the deciding factor."

"Really?" I look at her long, dark hair that has been straightened with some kind of medieval hair iron contraption, and her meticulously applied red lipstick. I don't give two shits about her labor-intensive process; the end product is making my dick twitch in appreciation.

"Don't look at me like that," she says, brushing something on her cheeks.

"Like what?"

"Like you think women are ridiculous with all the time we spend on grooming."

"I wasn't thinking that at all. I was thinking that I'd like to eat you up. You look fucking amazing. You always do, and if you were mine, I wouldn't let you spend all this time worrying about looking a certain way for a bunch of strangers."

She closes the compact and regards me with either amusement or surprise.

Yes, I said *if* she was mine because I still don't know where I stand. She is either very fond of me, or she gets that I am serious about us, and hopefully, she feels the same way.

"Nice sentiment. I'm sure you didn't intend to imply that you'd dictate whether or not I wear make-up or how I dress."

"You know I didn't mean it like that. Shit. You've done it again. Skipped over the good part I was telling you."

"I do know what you said." She puts her make-up in a little bag and zips it closed. "Thank you."

"You don't have to thank me for saying the obvious, it's what you deserve to hear."

***

Mercer is about money and flash, throwing impressive parties. We enter to a massive mob scene at the Natural History Museum, which has been rented out for the evening. As I walk Emma through the crowds of Mercer's wholesale and special retail customers and scores of models and TV celebrities, I zero in on the bars and food stations that are set up around the perimeter. The giant hall is pumped up with loud dance music and flashing purple and pink lighting, making the historic museum look like a funky nightclub.

"Let's get some drinks," I say, looking for an entry into the crowded bar.

"I see some of the Mercer people. I'm going over there. Bring me a glass of wine."

Under the hanging, life-size Blue Whale sculpture, I see Steve Mercer holding court with his admirers.

"Okay, but if Steve so much as touches your elbow, I expect you to put him in a headlock."

Emma pinches my cheek and laughs before walking off to meet the group. *As if I'm joking.* We're finally in a good place, and I have to waste my precious Emma time schmoozing with a few hundred well-dressed drunks who care more about finding a good lay for the night than anything else.

I push my way through the bodies squeezed together around the bar and then signal the attention of a female bartender who ignores the group of women next to me. She delivers my seltzer and wine with a flirty remark about dancing with me later. It has been a while since I played that game with a strange woman—the pick-up lines and sexual innuendoes. I think back to Emma's first day at work and how I treated her, but at the time, I wasn't making a play for her. Sure, all that time I was attracted to her, but I waited for her to make the moves. At least I think I did. I may have forgotten what it's like for a woman to hit on me, and I am fine with that. I'm only interested in getting back to Emma.

I smile and tip the bartender, giving a smile to the women next to me who are commenting about my "sexy scars." Jesus, uncensored drunks. The old me would have jumped at this opportunity; the new me is very uncomfortable.

As I weave my way through the growing mass of people, I can't find Emma and the group. They were directly underneath the massive Blue Whale's mouth, the lowest point of the hanging sculpture. As I look across the sea of heads, trying to spot Emma's red dress, that nasty old enemy—Dread—begins building in me.

As I turn towards the two-tiered staircase where we entered, I see her on the top level by the entrance, speaking to some suit who has his back to me. They are at least a hundred yards from me and I am going to have to go back up the stairs and nudge my way through more people. Something about Emma's animated posture as she speaks to the guy alarms me. I pick up my pace and am less polite to people as I shove my way through to the stairs.

Just then, I see the profile of the guy. Robert. How the fuck?

I slam the drinks on the banister and bolt up the stairs, but not before Robert leads Emma through the diorama hallways. I lose them and start running, backtracking the way we came in. I fly out the front doors where several hundred partygoers are milling around, scanning each one of them frantically. In an unlit area off to the side of the building along 77th Street, I spot Emma and Robert. He's holding her arms by the elbows and it looks like she's arguing with him.

What did I tell her about fucking elbows!

I throw off my suit coat and take off in a full sprint, my brain screaming for that guy to get his hands off my woman. I have no coherent thoughts as sheer brute force takes over and I body check Robert to the ground. Emma screams in surprise, yet even that gives me no inclination to speak and inquire about their conversation, as any normal adult would do.

My fists pummel Robert's face and gut. He is strong and agile, giving back good, splitting my lip and sending a searing pain against my side.

In my peripheral vision, I see flashes of Emma's red dress as she tries to grab our arms and separate us. I block out her protests for us to stop. We're nothing but flying fists as we roll across the grass.

"I was just talking to her, shithead," Robert yells angrily as I wrestle him onto his chest and press all my weight against him, pinning his arms behind his back.

"She only has room for one lunatic in her life and

250

that's me! I'm the one that loves her, and you're just the fucking loser that takes advantage of her generosity," I shout back.

My seething anger is only gratified by the fact that I can out-power this dick. He's a fucking bloody mess, pinned against the ground in his shredded designer suit. Emma is still pleading for us to stop, but her words are drowned out by the rage screaming in my brain.

When I think I have this guy where I want him, I realize my ribs are killing me and my mouth is throbbing where the blood runs out of my cut, swollen lip. I turn to look for Emma. After all, she has to be on my side here; I am only protecting her from an asshole that keeps dragging her back into his fucked up world.

When I turn to speak to her, however, she's gone.

"Get the fuck off me now," Robert hisses.

I push myself off his back and look around frantically again for Emma. I can't fucking believe my shitty luck. As I spot her, Cooper is ushering her onto the back of his Harley. She is wearing his helmet and her red dress is hiked up so she can straddle his bike.

"What the fuck?" I shout as I take off running towards them. I watch as they peal out on 77th Street and head towards Columbus Avenue.

I make it to the curb, looking up and down the busy street, panicking even more when I can't spot them. My head is spinning with how I can get to Emma. Why the hell is Cooper even here? And how did he and Robert both happen to show up at the same time? I check back to where I've left Robert sprawled on the grass, but he's gone.

And Emma's gone with Cooper.

I don't have a car here, and our hotel is about fifty blocks south of this place. I don't know if she's going there or someplace else with Cooper. Panic and anxiety are strangling me.

Find Emma.

I run out into the middle of traffic and stop a cab that is pulling over to pick up waiting customers on the other side of the street. I jump in before they can and shout an address to the stunned cabbie who accepts the hundred dollar bill I shove through the plexiglass window to him.

Going on nothing, I try to formulate a plan to make me feel like I am taking action. I will go to the hotel, get the car, call Carson—

My cell phone goes off.

"Dylan, get everything out of the hotel room and drive out to the address I am going to text you," Cooper's voice says calmly.

"Where is Emma?" I shout into the phone.

The cabbie glances nervously at me in the rearview mirror.

"She's with me. She's safe. You exposed her, buddy. She doesn't need that shit. I got her out of there for her own good. We're at a red light, so I only have a few seconds to talk. I'm taking her out of town to some place safer. Pack your things in the car and meet us. I'll text the address. Room 110. Remember that. I'll explain everything when you get there." With that said, Cooper ends the call.

I look at the blank screen on my phone and estimate how fast I can get to the room and get the car from the valet. *It's going to slow me down*, I think, panicking. The cab is stuck in a traffic clog near Times Square, and since there is nothing I can do to physically move thousands of people and vehicles out of my way, I concentrate on calming down, breathing deeply and silently, counting to twenty each time.

"That's good, slow breaths, relax." My driver nods his head as he watches me in the rearview mirror.

I grip my knees, breathing, counting each street we pass by as we get closer to the hotel. When the cabbie finally pulls in front, the valet reaches for my door, but I am out of the car before he can grab the handle. I fly through the lobby and see that both elevator cars are on higher floors. I don't want to wait, so I head for the enclosed staircase and run up sixteen flights of stairs to get to our room.

I throw everything into our bags, jamming items wherever they'll fit without bothering to change out of my filthy clothes that are stained with Robert's blood—my suit jacket is back at the museum. I don't see any point in packing—I want to get to Emma—however Cooper has sounded very sure of himself, so I will follow his instructions if it means I can get to her.

I keep checking my phone, but there's still no text from Cooper.

I load our bags and computer gear on both shoulders and hoof it down the stairs back to the lobby. For a pretty boy, Robert packs a powerful punch; my head and chest are beginning to ache even more. The same valet sees me barreling through the hotel entrance again, and recognizing my need for speed, takes my valet ticket and races to retrieve my car from the garage a few blocks away.

While I wait, I un-tuck my shirt, using the bottom hem to wipe the blood streaked across my face. I must look menacing.

The valet returns with my car and quickly dispatches the bags from my arms, loading them in the passenger seat as I direct. I hand out another hundred-dollar bill since that is all I am carrying and get into the car when my phone pings with a text from Cooper. It is an address for a hotel in Tarrytown, about twenty-five miles from here.

I break every traffic law getting there.

***

When I stride quickly through the lobby, the receptionist looks uncomfortable with my bloody, disheveled appearance, but I have luggage and give the impression with a fake friendly smile that I am just another guest heading to my room. She is busy checking in other people, so I whiz by the front desk and head for room 110.

When I give the door three hard kicks, Cooper opens it. I glare at him, drop the bags and storm into the room.

Emma is at the far side by the window, wrapped in a hotel blanket. I rush to her and take her into my arms.

"Jesus, Emma. What the hell happened? I thought I lost you," I say with my mouth pressed against her hair. A sudden wave of relief washes over me. I have her.

"I'm okay. I was scared for you. Did you kill Robert?" she jokes and sniffles into my chest.

"No, we fucked each other up. He's worse off than me, though."

"I thought so." She snakes her arms around my waist.

"She needed to be out of there," another male voice says.

I turn to see Sean sitting in a corner armchair. I didn't notice him when I came in; all I could think about and see was Emma.

"What the hell is going on?" I look at Sean and then Cooper.

"I'll explain, but you're going to want to sit down for this one," Cooper replies.

I stare at him. My anger over him taking her is still fresh and a series of new images—namely me laying my fist into his face—crosses my mind. But I'm not that guy anymore. *I can handle this*, I convince myself. My jumpy nerves aren't about to sit down like a good student, but for Emma's sake, I force my tense body and her to sit on the edge of the bed facing Sean. I put my arm around her shoulders while my other hand holds hers in my lap.

"Start talking," I say evenly.

Cooper leans his back against the window and faces me with an apologetic expression. This is not the goof-off Cooper I have seen at work. He is different, and I suspect that I am about to find out more than I want to know.

"In case you don't trust us, Carson knows all about this. After the information I gave him, he wanted me to come

254

get both of you. It happened to be bad timing with the party and all, and Robert showing up."

Cooper's calmness is unnerving to me.

"You said I exposed her. What did you mean and how the hell do you two know each other?" I ask, looking from Sean to Cooper.

Sean is quiet. He looks like a giant side of muscled beef wedged into the chair.

"It's not a coincidence that Carson hired me," Cooper explains. "I used to be an agent for the bureau where I worked undercover following the Marchetto operation."

"You were an FBI agent?" I ask, incredulous at the thought of our office jokester being in law enforcement.

"Agent Cooper Griffin MacKenzie," he replies with a faint smile.

Emma scoffs and shakes her head. Cooper dismisses our disbelief.

"What were you and Robert arguing about?" he addresses Emma.

"He said I have to be careful, that people close to me are lying." She looks up at me with her scared, doe-like eyes.

"Me? He said you can't trust *me*?" I ask.

"Not you. He didn't say. First we were arguing about him asking me to talk outside where it was quieter, then he said someone I trust is not who I think he is. Then you jumped him and Cooper showed up. It all happened so fast. I didn't know who to believe. Cooper seemed like a safe bet."

"Thanks." Cooper smiles.

"Shit, what is going on?" I ask Cooper since Sean is patiently waiting for him to fill us in.

"Okay, here's the story. I was undercover, and at the time, we thought Robert was a key player in the drug ring from two years ago."

"I remember that. Robert and I watched the news about

255

the round-up and arrests on TV, and he mentioned it again when we met him at Rupert's."

"Right," Cooper explains. "It's been really hard to nail his dad for anything. He's very good at using other guys and covering his tracks. After a few years of this bullshit, I resigned from the bureau a few months ago. I wanted to get out of law enforcement all together, but my friends still working in the system gave me the heads up on some shit that Marchetto could implicate himself in."

Cooper turns to Sean and fires a finger gun at him with a click of his tongue.

"We've known each other for a few years," Sean adds. "Even while I was tailing you and Robert for your dad."

"Go on," she says in a sharp tone.

"When I got wind that Vinnie was willing to frame his own kid, I knew Robert would do something drastic. I've followed him for enough years to figure out that he really didn't want any part of his dad's dirty business, though."

"That's true," Emma interjects.

"So why is he after Emma?" I ask.

"He isn't after her. He's warning her," Cooper replies.

"You mean threatening her over whether she talks about something he may have done while she was with him?" I am the loudest guy in the room. Sean signals me with his palm to hold off and wait for the explanation.

"He's not threatening her. I was pretty sure she was never in danger," Cooper says. "Robert was smart enough to get some of his conversations recorded on his phone. He went to some people I worked with in the past and basically gave them all the info on his father's set up in the drug operation. How they were moving the product, to which campuses, to which distributors, and where the cash was funneled. Vinnie has audio and video of Robert in one incident."

"That's the cash transaction Robert told me about. But he didn't know he was being set up by his own father,"

Emma adds.

"Yeah, it was a dumb move on Robert's part, but it's not enough to burn him. He's already cooperated with the Feds and he turned over two audios and then he let them wire him for something that went down recently. That's what Robert was trying to warn you about, Emma."

As Emma casts a wary glance at Cooper and then at Sean, I hold her tighter.

"What went down?" she asks, her voice sounding tiny.

"This whole goose chase isn't about getting you," Cooper says. "Vinnie wants to make his kid pay for the crimes, and they know you're the magnet that leads them to Robert. Old loves die hard, I guess, so they were counting on Robert coming back to you and he did. Vinnie has two of his guys tailing Robert. I saw them in the city following both of you."

"When?" I snap.

"SoHo, when you left the Mercer store. Don't worry; I made those two when they came into town. I was tailing you, found them, and managed to leave a nice package inside their car with a tracker. They're probably heading through the Lincoln Tunnel as we speak, and they'll get a nice stop and frisk on the other side for *reckless* driving. Then they'll get the fun search and seizure treatment. They won't be coming around you again."

"Jesus Christ." I have little patience for this story, and Cooper's seriousness tells me he is leading in to something that is going to be upsetting to Emma.

"And where does Robert go?" Emma asks.

"Into hiding until it's over," Sean answers.

"Until what's over? And what does it have to do with me?" Emma shrieks.

"The Feds want the two biggest fish, Emma. That's Vinnie Marchetto and another guy that has been eluding us for years. Well, he was until Sean put it together and Robert got him on the wire."

"Who?" I demand. "Just fucking tell us."

"Christ on a bike," Sean says. "Emma's father. Sorry, kiddo, but it's true."

"What?" she asks quietly.

Sean looks extremely uncomfortable at giving her this news. "Your dad has been on the in with Vinnie for the past few years. You thought he was still paying out, but he started working with Vinnie and helping with the drug distribution. He's taken a huge cut of the cash and has it socked away under various fake business accounts, and when he travels with your mother to Florida, he always makes a special, private excursion to his offshore bank. He hired me to protect him and you before he got into this shite, before he turned. He assumed I wasn't aware. I couldn't stand by and go along with this load of bollix. I've never done anything illegal, and I wasn't going to let your arse of a father bring me into it now, so I contacted Cooper. We have some mutual friends, so Coop was easy to find."

Emma's face is ashen as she absorbs the news.

I turn to Cooper. "How did you end up in this? At my brother's company before Emma?"

"When we figured out that Robert might go down, we also knew what Vinnie was thinking. He was going to follow Robert's desperation, namely Emma. Robert only cared about seeing Emma, and Vinnie would use that to watch Robert's next move. I went and talked to Carson as soon as Sean told me that Lauren was getting Emma a job at your company. Didn't you ever wonder why your brother hired someone who has no background in your business? Man, I didn't even know how to use a table saw."

"Yeah, and now I see why he hired you while I was out of town. It was a good cover. And he trained you himself and put you on the oven, the easiest job in the factory. So Carson knew about everything?"

"He knew my background and he knew Lauren wanted to help Emma get a job, but he only knew a little about

Robert's situation. I fed it to him on a need-to-know basis. He wouldn't have hired Emma or me if he thought anyone was being put in danger, however I wasn't tricking him into anything. I wouldn't do that.

"And by the way, the job is real to me," Cooper explains. "Since I left law enforcement for good, I actually was looking to do something new, and I like Carson and the company. He didn't hire me on a whim, Dylan, and I wasn't hired just to be a watchdog. I wanted a more easy-going job, and I like the place. Carson and I weren't trying to pull something over on you."

"Whatever," I mutter.

"Listen, I'm serious," Cooper says defensively. "I had no interest in being involved in this shit anymore. That's why I resigned a few months ago. But when the info on Vinnie and Robert came down my network pipeline, I couldn't ignore it. I had to tell your brother, which means I had to come clean about myself."

"I believe you," I say flatly.

Emma's silent sobs tear me away from thoughts about my brother always being one step ahead of me.

"Hey," I say softly to her. "You didn't know, and your dad didn't tell you because he wanted to... shield you from this crap."

Cooper gives me a questioning look. It's dumb to defend her father, but I am trying to lessen the blow, even if it is a lie.

"I can't believe this," she says through a hiccup of tears.

When Sean hands her a box of tissues from the desk, she dries her eyes and keeps her head down.

"Does the FBI want Robert now?" I ask. "Is that why he's running?"

"He's running from Vinnie's thugs," Cooper explains. "There's enough evidence to arrest both Vinnie Marchetto and Emma's father. It would be a plus to have Robert testify in court against them, but they don't need him. Vinnie doesn't know that yet. He still thinks he's safe if Robert is out of the picture. Only a few of us know that arrests are gonna happen in the next forty-eight hours. Robert is smart enough to hide until then. I guess he couldn't resist seeing Emma, and maybe he thought he'd warn her about her dad, or maybe he didn't want to be the one to tell her."

"So what do we do now? We're hiding out, too? Waiting for the arrests?" I feel defenseless without information.

"That's exactly what you're going to do. You and Emma will lay low here while Sean and I go back to Hera. I've already taken Emma's cell phone, including the burners from her dad. I even pulled the phone from this room so she's not tempted to call her dad. And I'm sorry, but I need your phone, too, Dylan."

When Cooper extends his open palm, I reluctantly put my cell phone in it.

"So my father is going to be arrested along with Vinnie. Is this why I couldn't reach either of my parents over the last two weeks?"

"Your dad probably doesn't want you involved. I think your mom knew your dad was up to no good, and that's why she left for Florida weeks ago. She's not involved in this, so she won't be indicted or anything like that if that's what you're thinking about," Cooper explains.

I admit, he is pretty good at playing the good cop, and he sounds sincere. Sean looks broken up over seeing Emma take it all in.

"Won't they arrest Robert, too? For what he did two years ago?" she asks, and I hear the sadness in her voice.

I am not distressed or worried over that. One of the reasons I fell in love with her is because of her big heart, and that isn't something she turns off just because she broke up with the guy. I get that now. I am more concerned

260

about how she will be affected by her father going to prison. I don't think it has fully hit her yet.

"They already cut a deal with Robert. He wore the wire and that absolved him—so to speak—of that cash transaction he participated in two years ago. He has a clean slate. It's up to him if he is going to come in and testify, but you know how that could go down..." Cooper's voice trails off.

"Why didn't Robert recognize you?" she asks Cooper. "If you were an undercover agent, wouldn't he have recognized you when we met him at the restaurant? He saw you."

"Did you recognize me when you met me on your first day of work at Blackard?" Cooper asks.

"No. Why would I?" She looks confused.

When Cooper takes out his cell phone and plays around with it before handing it to her, I look at the photo on the display. A guy dressed in khakis with a polo shirt. Very short, blond hair, shaven, and wire-rimmed glasses. It's Cooper, looking about twenty in the shot.

"That's me two years ago."

"You look like you work for NASA," I say. "Geeky."

"Thank you," he smiles. "I was undercover. I was a fake science grad student. I didn't understand any of the shit going on in those classes, but I saw plenty of Robert... and Emma on campus. You never noticed me."

"Huh," Emma says as she looks more thoroughly at Cooper.

"Robert wore the wire for the Feds after we all met at the restaurant. It's going to help him."

"What's going to happen to him?" Emma is persistent with the questions, I will give her that.

"We'll worry about that when we get to that part. Right now, we need the arrests. Sorry. Carson wants you two here for your own safety. You're not being held by the FBI. This isn't bureau business; it's your brother's doing. He wants to make sure Robert doesn't lead any more of Vinnie's guys your way." Cooper takes back his cell phone from Emma, makes a call and hands me the phone.

"Are you and Emma okay?" my brother's gruff voice asks.

"Yeah. We're stashed in Tarrytown. Nice play, brother."

"As long as you're both safe. We'll talk about it when you come home. Give it a couple of days. Emma is tough, but she may be in shock for a while."

"I got her. Don't worry," I reply as Emma's eyes lock on mine.

"Dylan..."

"Yeah?"

"Sorry shit keeps happening to you. I love you, brother," Carson says and then disconnects the call.

If he only knew that all of this is worth it to have her.

Twenty-Four
Emma

After Sean and Cooper leave, Dylan unpacks our bags. He is quiet, as though he wants to give me my space and time to absorb the shameful information we've received about my father. I never claimed to have a kind or loving father, however I was always the first to defend our circumstances and insist that my father was at least fair. Now I can't even say that. I can't justify what he has done or that, like my mother, I have been complacent about our connection to the Marchetto family. Never did I expect to be in this position, though, and I'm more than sad—I am shocked and angry.

After I take a hot shower and change into more comfortable clothing, Dylan gives me a soft peck on the cheek on his way to the bathroom to shower. I flip mindlessly through TV channels, expecting to see breaking news about the Marchetto revelations with my father's jowly face front and center in an unflattering mug shot. I hold my breath as I switch to every news outlet I can think of. No news yet.

"Don't torture yourself with that," Dylan says, coming out of the bathroom with a towel wrapped around his waist. With the exception of a small, purplish cut on his lip, you wouldn't know he's been in a fight.

As he takes the remote from my hand and shuts the TV off, that's when I start crying. All these weeks I've thought I've been the resilient girl—starting over in a new town, a new job, removed from Robert and my father's business and vile associates. I've felt strong that I could detach myself from those lifelong connections. Now there's a tidal wave of grief surging through me and I weep uncontrollably. Everything I have been holding in— the fear and rage—comes forth, taking with it all that confident power and self-esteem that I've spent years building up.

Dylan quickly embraces me, his damp, warm skin covering and enveloping me so I can cry into his chest. I am not a dainty crier, either. I gasp loudly as the tears blind me and mucous clogs my nose. The entire time, Dylan remains quite, merely putting a box of Kleenex on his lap and continuing to feed me clean tissues.

"I suddenly feel like an orphan," I say between hiccupping cries.

"I know what that's like." Dylan holds me more firmly. "You're not alone, though. You have me, and you have your friends back in town. Whatever happens with your dad, I'm going to be with you. And you have your mom and grandmother."

"I used to be close to my grandma, but she basically stopped talking to me a few years ago when I started dating Robert. The same way she distanced herself from my mother. I think they both knew my father was getting into something, getting in too deep. Getting greedy, I suppose. My mom and her mother have been hiding at Grandmas place in Boca for weeks. It's like they betrayed me, too, by not telling me what they suspected or knew was going on. All of them abandoned me."

"Maybe not telling you was their way of sparing you from this shit. The less you knew, the better. You couldn't be brought in for questioning; you'd be useless to people on both sides if you were completely ignorant. Like Sean and Cooper said, you were only good for leading them to Robert, assuming he'd seek you out. And he did."

"They'll try to kill him. Marchetto and his guys haven't been arrested yet and a lot of the time, these guys get off; the arrests blow up on technicalities. The first thing they'll do, or they're already attempting to do it, is kill the evidence. Robert is the evidence as far as they're concerned."

"You heard Cooper. Robert already turned in audio recordings and the wiretap, so that's done."

"Marchetto doesn't necessarily know that. Just because Cooper is aware of the recorded meetings, doesn't mean Marchetto knows the Feds have possession of them. If Marchettto thinks his son is holding onto this info to use as leverage for himself to cut a deal, Robert is a walking target."

Dylan sighs. "I think Robert knows that, and that's why he's been running."

The waterworks taper off and I clean my face as best I can with the tissues. My skin feels hot and blotchy, and I am overwhelmed with fatigue.

"I'm sorry I compared myself to an orphan. I really don't have any right to feel sorry for myself, especially since you were orphaned as a child. Your circumstances were out of your control. Mine are delusions I've been perpetuating for years, thinking there was nothing wrong with how we lived, and that I was an innocent benefactor to whatever my father provided. I'm such an idiot."

"Hey, you are not to blame for anything your dad did." Dylan pulls my chin up towards him with two fingers. "There's nothing idiotic about trusting your parents. We all want and need that. And there's not much you can do when they disappoint you."

As he leans down and kisses me with barely a sweep of his lips against mine, it's enough to lessen the pain. He moves back slowly, surveying my eyes, as if he looks hard enough, he could see deep inside of me.

"I'm definitely not qualified to give advice on fathers. Mine killed himself when I was a teenager," he says.

"Tell me about that, Dylan. Please," I beg.

Dylan pauses for a moment, and I can tell he's

struggling with how to tell me because sometimes it hurts too much to say these painful things out loud.

"I was destroyed when my dad committed suicide. It was seven years after my mom's death. He had been MIA for most of that time and we only survived because of Carson's strong will and friends like Lauren's family. I assumed my father didn't think twice about leaving Carson and me all alone. And I was hurt that he loved my mother more than us. At least, that's how a screwed up fifteen-year-old saw it.

"For a long time, I mostly felt anger towards him, and I took it out on everyone else. It took a long time—maybe not until I met Brian—for me to understand that my father and Brian were living with a different kind of pain. I can't explain it, and I hope I never know what that's like.

"When I got the call about Brian's suicide, I started feeling angry all over again. I grieve for my friend's pain, but I'm angry that I've had to lose him. It's a selfish feeling because Brian, like my dad, was the one I looked up to. Brian had to succeed in the program because that meant I could succeed. It's pretty scary when the guy you idolize leaves you in the most violent way. First my dad and then Brian."

When Dylan's expression twitches, as if he's holding back tears, I reach my arm up around his neck and bring him closer to me. I force a kiss on him, which is not at all tender. My tongue pushes for more and he returns the kiss with fervor before gently removing his lips from mine.

"You need to rest. It's been a helluva night and it's late. You need real sleep."

He turns down the bed covers and rolls me underneath. I grab his shoulders and pull him down with me, causing him to lose his bath towel in the process. His naked body is glorious and the perfect medicine for anything that ails me. I want to get lost in him and forget about my father and Robert and all the ugly news I expect more of.

266

"Emma," Dylan whispers. He grabs the towel off the floor and covers his perfectly sculpted ass and thighs. "I'm not going to take advantage of you when you're in this... vulnerable condition."

"You could, and I'd let you," I say rather sharply. "I don't want to keep crying. What's wrong with having sex to feel better?" I am thinking of what I did to him the night before and how Dylan submitted to my touch.

"Nothing is wrong with it. I'm trying to be a stand-up guy here—the shoulder for you to cry on—not the guy who fucks the pain away."

"Why can't you be both?"

"You always have a quick answer or a fast fist." His mouth curves into a smile, and my groping limbs retreat and take the hint to relax.

He swiftly pulls on a pair of sweat pants underneath his towel as though he's not allowed to have sex on his mind. "I can go down to the front desk and get a pizza delivered or something. I'll pay cash and have it go through reception so we're not *violating* Cooper's little set of rules. You must be hungry."

I chuckle and cry at the same time. "Oh, Dylan. Thanks for making me laugh. Pizza instead of sex," I mumble. "We both know sex sounds a lot better than pizza."

"Yeah, I do know that, and under different circumstances, I'd be all over you."

"I don't want food. And I don't want you to leave me alone. Okay?"

"Okay," he says softly then climbs under the covers next to me.

When I roll onto my side and hug him, he sighs. He can't tame me, but he sure knows how to calm me.

His hand is under my shirt, splayed against my bare back as he pulls me closer to him.

"It won't always be like this," he whispers with his

mouth pressed against my temple. "Over time, it will get easier to deal with the pain of disappointment and loss. My life has been easier with you in it."

"Really? Thugs tailing us, fights with my ex-boyfriend... This is easier?"

"Believe it or not, yes. I know exactly what I want to do and what I should do, and fortunately, they're the same thing." As he rubs his cheek against mine, his five o'clock shadow scratches my swollen, tender skin in a pleasant way. I wish he'd let me do more than hug him.

"You sound so sure of yourself."

"I am. And that's because of you, Emma."

His baby blues lift and crinkle at the edges when I prop my hands and chin on his chest and look at him.

"And you didn't know anything about Agent Cooper MacKenzie and his background?" I ask.

"No. When I saw you go off with him, I freaked. Seriously, I always thought he was an okay guy, but that move, having you jump on his bike and taking you away from me—I wanted to kill him."

"No, you didn't. You wanted to punch him."

"That, too."

"But you didn't."

"You didn't see the part where I drove over here and walked through the hotel lobby plotting Cooper's demise. I think I counted backwards from one hundred for forty solid minutes, and I took so many deep breaths to calm down that I'm surprised I didn't pass out. My shrink would be proud that he doesn't have to visit me in jail tonight."

I smile at his attempts for me to see past the horrible events of the evening and to realize that what I have with him is genuine.

"What made you trust, Cooper?" Dylan's voice is steady yet nervous.

"Something about his connection to Carson. I've seen it at work. And he was there when we met with Robert the first time at the restaurant. When he told me to get on the bike and that he'd make sure you were with me soon, I didn't doubt him. He knew I couldn't be separated from you for very long."

"Yeah?" Dylan tilts his head.

"Yeah." I plant a kiss on his sternum. "What made you trust Cooper?"

"I didn't have a choice. He had my girl. The only person I wanted was being held hostage by Easy Rider."

"Oh, he wasn't holding me hostage."

"Not knowing what he was doing and where he was taking you almost drove me over the edge. Remember King Kong beating his chest on top of the Empire State Building? If Cooper had called any later than he had, that would have been me up there."

I chuckle and hiccup at the same time, like a scared child who is recovering from a major tantrum.

"And what about Sean?" he asks. "Did you have any indication that he could spring this kind of information on you? I wasn't sure what I thought of him when he came to the house. I didn't know if I could trust him."

"That's because you don't know him the way I do. I always knew Sean was better than my dad. If Sean saw something was wrong, he wouldn't look the other way. That was my father's mistake, believing that anyone who works for him would be loyal if he paid him enough. Sean was willing to lose a very good salary and risk his life, I guess. If my dad is that involved with Vinnie Marchetto, then it is a huge risk to do what Sean did. The only person I'm furious with is my father for doing this to my family... and me for believing all his bull for so many years."

"Maybe our former G-Man, Cooper, is wrong. We don't know for sure if your dad will be arrested—"

"Dylan, don't even try to gloss this over for my benefit. I've lived with this crap for many years. I should have seen the signs."

Dylan strokes my hair and gazes at me with such a loving tenderness. The only man that shocks me is Dylan and his desire to be with someone like me. He has worked so hard to be the opposite of anyone that resembles the damaged, deceitful people attached to me. I don't want him to put his emotional health at risk and jeopardize his progress because he accepts me as I am.

I love him too much to keep him bonded to a destructive family like mine. A father in prison, a grandmother who refuses to talk about our family dirt, and an unstable mother who has legitimate nervous breakdowns... I can't envision Dylan and I going to visit my father at Rikers or wherever he'll end up. And would Dylan feel obligated to help my obstinate mother who would rather pop a Valium with a tumbler of Scotch than seek real help? I don't want to lasso Dylan to that never-ending hell, and I don't necessarily want to be a part of that family anymore, either.

Yet, if I break all my connections with my family and let any lingering love or affection for my parents decay to nothing, can I start clean with Dylan? Is it possible or am I setting myself up for a future of regrets that would also hurt Dylan? How much psychological melodrama can a guy like Dylan handle? Under the circumstances, I could be the worst possible woman for him.

Twenty-Five
Dylan

Carson gets tired of me walking slowly so he sprints ahead of me and makes it to our trailer long before I get there. By the time I get home from school, there are police cars, an ambulance, and Lauren and her parents and a lot of other familiar faces. They are crying, and I hear people mumbling to me and to each other that they are so sorry. I don't want this to be happening, and I hate them all for acting this way.

A policewoman makes me stand by a cop car, and I see Carson come from behind the back of our trailer with some more cops. He's wiping his face as if he's been crying. I have never seen my brother cry. The woman won't let me go to our trailer or anywhere near Carson. They only want to talk to him.

I drop my backpack on the ground and wait for Carson to come get me and tell me what's going on; he's the only one I want to talk to. I know this is bad, especially since it is happening behind the trailer, not inside. I hear the whispers about my dad, but the ambulance guys haven't brought him out; instead, they keep talking to Carson. He is almost eighteen, only three years older than me, but they all know he is in charge because he acts like it.

It may be minutes or hours that pass as Lauren stays with her parents, looking over at me and crying. All I can think is how lucky she is to be standing there with both of her parents. My mom died when I was eight, and we've rarely seen my dad over the years—he barely exists.

When someone slips a warm arm around my shoulders,

271

I look up. It's Archie. I know it is worse than I can imagine because Archie's eyes are watery. No one is talking to me now, they expect me to be quiet and stay still, but I am not an idiot. I am well aware that it is my father behind the trailer, and no one wants me to see him.

A policeman walks Carson over to me, and Archie puts his other arm around him. Carson starts sniffling. I don't know why, but it makes me angry. We are not supposed to have any more bad stuff happen to us. My mother was supposed to get better, and when she didn't, my father said we would all get through her death together, even though he started disappearing on us, and Carson had to take over.

I escape from Archie's embrace with every intention of getting behind our trailer to see what is going on for myself.

"No!" Carson grabs my arm. My brother is strong. He glares at me with tears in his eyes. "You can't go over there, Dylan. Dad is gone."

As he grips my arm tight enough to make bruises, a stretcher comes around the side of the trailer. As I expected, the body on the stretcher is covered from head to toe with a sheet. It still sends waves of sickening shock through me.

I know another parent has left me.

I think I start crying more over my father's death than my mother's because he knew how sad Carson and I were when our mother died. He knew, and he didn't care what it would do to us; he only wanted to stop his own pain.

But he left Carson and me all alone.

People keep leaving me.

***

Working for my brother and taking orders from him is one thing. Taking orders from Cooper and Sean is another. It is only going to last so long with me. I am not about to sit around a hotel room waiting for news from them about what the FBI is or isn't doing with Emma's father and the Marchetto crime family. Even though I feel kind of sorry for the guy, I can't give two shits about Robert when I have

272

Emma bouncing off the walls in this little room, anxious about everyone.

I have her imprisoned in a hotel room with me, and you would think that is all I need. Yeah, old Dylan would be all over this one, making sure we were naked twenty-four seven—screwing, eating, screwing, and watching TV, and then screwing again. My brain used to love those easy agendas, and my body never complained. Thoughts like that make me feel pretty ill about the kind of selfish prick I used to be.

I'm using Dr. Wang's tactic of talking about it in past tense, so I don't confuse that person with who I hope I am today. God, I hope I know what I'm doing. I keep up a good front with Emma, but inside, I still question every move and thought I make.

We are not staying holed up in this place, though. I am getting Emma out for the day, away from the giant TV that looms in our room like a messenger from hell. I saw how tempted she was last night to turn it on again and surf the cable news stations, looking for reports on her father's supposed impending arrest. Nope, I am breaking Cooper's rules; I don't care if they came endorsed by Carson with gold stars branded on Cooper's ass. We are getting out, at least for the day.

I do an hour of sit-ups and push-ups then I finally wake her up from a very groggy sleep. After what she has been through, I should let her snooze all day, however I am getting antsy, and without being able to run or lift weights, I can only do so much exercising in the room while she sleeps.

It is cute watching her drool on the pillow, so I decide to wake her up gently with a few tickles. She sleep-punches me in the shoulder and scissor kicks my chest. Hell, whoever trained this girl prepared her to be ambushed.

Without letting her emasculate me further, I haul her into the bathroom while she apologizes profusely. I make her rush through a quick shower and put on the only clean clothes we have left, jeans and t-shirts, which are fine for what I have planned.

***

"Are you sure this is safe?" Emma asks as I speed Carson's BMW through Tarrytown.

"Absolutely. You're with me." Hiding behind my sunglasses, I give her my best confident smile.

Her face is pale with the kind of fatigue that comes from sleeping after a long crying jag. She's not wearing any make-up, and the way she looks is luminous to me, even on this overcast, gray day.

As we slow down and drive through an open gate, I notice there aren't any other cars. Good—no tourists, so Emma and I have this place all to ourselves.

"Where are we?" she asks, looking up the hill at the gravestones that are shrouded in a surreal, green foliage of trees.

"Sleepy Hollow," I reply.

When I get out of the car and walk around to open her door, she has a befuddled expression as she takes in the lush greenery.

"It's a cemetery." She looks at me questioningly.

"Yes, but it's special. You'll see."

"Are your parents buried here?" she asks softly.

"No. I haven't been here in a long time, but I remember it being nice even though it's a cemetery. And it looks like there aren't any tourists today. Come on."

I hold out my hand and she takes it cautiously. I walk her up Sleepy Hollow Avenue and then turn onto Lincoln Avenue. From up here it is a sea of old tombstones and mausoleums under the cover of ancient trees, blanketing us with a bright green shield from the gray sky.

Emma surveys the vast, dense cemetery. "It's breathtaking. It looks like something out of an old, English novel. You'd never guess we're ten minutes from the

274

interstate. Why are we here?"

I keep her moving on the small paths that weave around the graves.

"It's quiet and peaceful. And it's nicer than the hotel room. We needed to get out of there, and I remembered that this place is close by."

"It's like something out of a storybook, really. The trees are so thick and green, and with the moss on the stones... I almost expect to see werewolves, vampires or trolls."

I laugh. "That doesn't sound very good."

"No, it is. This is like being in a dream, I suppose, because we're here alone. It's nice."

I hold her hand firmly as we walk along the paths, silently reading the tombstones.

"Here, check this one out," I say as we stop in front of a black iron gate that surrounds a small headstone.

"Irving," Emma reads out loud.

"Washington Irving," I add. "As in Ichabod Crane and *The Legend of Sleepy Hollow.*"

Her eyes pop in delightful surprise.

"So you really did bring me to a magical place."

"My mom brought me here a few times. Just the two of us. It was magical to me. I've shared a lot of dismal things with you, and I thought for a change I could show you something good from my past."

"Oh, Dylan. Thank you."

As she wraps her arms around my waist and hugs me, I nestle my fingers in her hair and kiss the top of her head. I have never shared this place with anyone, not even Carson. This was my private place with my mother when she let me play hooky from school a few times and we would come here. She was sick then, but not showing signs of her cancer. She used the time to tell me about growing up and all the things I could be. My mother didn't know I would become sick in my own way and spend years undoing everything she tried to prepare me for.

"It's my pleasure to do something for you. Not everything about my childhood was miserable. There were moments of light and good times. You have those, too, even if it seems really dark right now."

When she sighs against my chest, I hope it is contentment or relief. Then she extricates her warm, little body from mine, still holding my hand, and continues walking, stopping at a fork in the path, contemplating which route to take. As she leads me aimlessly through the maze of curving walkways with no destination in mind, I realize I could do this all day with her, every day.

"This way," I say when I recognize a structure. "There's a mausoleum. We can sit on the steps."

We round the corner of the small building. "William Rockefeller," Emma says, reading the name engraved in concrete at the base of the mausoleum. "No wonder it's the biggest one here."

I sit on the top step and pull her down next to me.

"I remember sitting here with my mom. That's when she told me she was too sick and couldn't get better. I told her to ask the doctor for the thick, pink medicine that tastes like bubble gum because it always made Carson and me better when we were sick."

Emma smiles at that.

"My mom laughed and said it wasn't that easy. We didn't talk about her dying after that. She wanted to pretend that she was a regular, healthy mom, like all the other moms at our school, and my father preferred living in denial."

"Do you and Carson talk about your parents a lot?" She holds my arm, resting her head against my shoulder.

"No. Never. Maybe he talks to Jess about them, though. In a way, it's easier to tell you than to relive it with Carson." I pick up her hand and it looks so small in mine. I turn her palm over and caress it before clasping it in both of my hands. "I like talking to you. This feels good."

She kisses my shoulder. "I like this, too. And you do have some nice memories after all."

"Sure. So do you."

"Some, but nothing that's worth talking about while we're waiting to hear about my father... or Robert. I hate to think about what will happen next."

"You mean if your dad goes to prison?"

"Cooper made that sound like it's a given, and I guess after thinking about this for the last ten hours, I'm not as surprised as I thought I'd be. I'm uneasy about us. Cooper was adamant about us staying put in the hotel room. It's sweet that you wanted to get me out of there and brighten this lousy day, but—"

"Don't you think I can handle this? I'm not afraid of your old entourage from Jersey. I can take anything or anyone that comes our way."

"Dylan, they have guns."

"They don't need murder added to their long list of charges."

"I'm pretty sure Vinnie Marchetto is already accountable for a few deaths," she responds glumly.

"True. And Cooper is probably aware of this, and even so, he wouldn't tell us if he did know."

"So, you think we're safe?"

"Yes. You and I have nothing on Marchetto, and maybe you were their bait to lead them to Robert, but we know that's irrelevant now since Robert has turned over the evidence he has."

"We have to hope Marchetto comes to the same conclusion."

"Emma, Marchetto is not out hunting you down. A bunch of guys aren't going to show up in this little cemetery looking for Carson's marketing assistant." I laugh because the whole idea sounds ridiculous. "I'm staying away from Hera to humor Carson and Cooper, but we're

277

safe. I'd never let anything happen to you, and I'm fairly certain that you'd literally kick the shit out of any guy that tried to attack me."

"I would," she says, proudly. "And if Cooper hadn't confiscated my switchblade, I could—oh, never mind."

"I seriously cannot imagine what defensive skills you have been taught. Someday you'll have to tell me everything. Or show me." I smile.

She shrugs innocently, which makes me chuckle again. She is more at ease and seems to be enjoying our nonsensical excursion. I drag her back off her keister and then press a quick kiss to her lips because I need it and the relief it provides.

"We're not finished. I want to show you something else. My mom always saved the best for last."

We go back down to Sleepy Hollow Avenue which sometimes has a few cars cruising at slow speeds, but today it is empty as we walk along the narrow Pocantico River until we come to an old, wooden bridge.

"Well what do you think?" I ask, looking at the bridge.

"It's a bridge. Are we going to walk across it?"

"Oh, for Christ's sake. Really? Think, Emma. Where are we?"

"Sleepy Hollow Cemetery… because you have a thing for old graves?"

"No. Yes, but whose grave did you see up there? Who wrote that great story—the one my mother would read to me all the time? I was so freaked out; I thought the Headless Horseman was hiding in my closet. I loved that scary shit when I was a kid."

"This is the actual Headless Horseman Bridge?" She lights up and looks across the worn, wooden slat bridge with railings made out of tree limbs.

It is maybe twenty-five feet across the small river, and it opens into a dense forest on the other side. It is a quiet, secluded spot. Emma's right; it's like something out of a kid's storybook. We're alone in this green fortress of solitude with only the sound of the babbling river water a few feet below the bridge.

"Yeah. Well, actually, I don't think it's the original. It looks pretty authentic, though. We'll have to come back on Halloween when they do this place up big with spooks."

She glances at me knowingly, understanding that I am making long term plans with her since Halloween is five months away and I am already scheduling our social events. Then she stops walking in the center of the bridge and leans over the railing to study the shallow water below which really looks more like a wide brook.

"Thanks for bringing me here," she says. "And sharing that story about you and your mother, and for trying to distract me from my bleak thoughts."

I press against her back, reaching an arm around her, right under her chin, kissing the side of her face.

"I wish I could make this better for you, give you back the parents you thought you had, or wanted... I wish I knew what to do for you," I respond, taking in the amazing scent of her skin.

"You are making it better. If I wasn't here with you, I'd be sitting with Lauren and Imogene, blubbering. Lauren would remind me how awful my life was and that I'm better off alone instead of being surrounded by criminals. This is nicer."

She turns around in my arms and pulls my head down for a kiss. Her tongue is light at first as she traces and nips at my lips, but then she's insistent, driving farther into my mouth, hungrily, as if she is mimicking a wild sex romp. Maybe if I'd had my usual morning run, I would have more restraint; however, since I spent the night and morning watching her sleep—my drooling, snoring, beautiful, ninja princess—yeah, I am turned on.

Nothing shows more weakness than getting turned on while the person you desire is grieving or in a state of misery, I think. Then again, I have shown more discipline with Emma than anyone else—ever—and it's not as if we snuck off from a funeral to hook up. I want to keep her safe and make her happy. I also want her, and she has been giving me the green light since last night. I can only say no so many times before I have to say yes.

Her hand rubs the front of my jeans, cupping my groin.

"See? You totally want me." She gives me one of those evil, Catwoman smiles again.

"There was never a question about that. It was about timing," I quip as my hard-on grows under her hand.

I grab her thrill-seeking hand and stalk off to the other side of the bridge, going off the path until we come to a large tree with a massive trunk, something to use as leverage. I have a lot of things on my mind, and by now, I am used to not being able to shut it off, but my libido is the loudest beast in my brain at the moment.

When I push Emma's back gently up against the tree and kiss her thoroughly, it is better than the kiss on the bridge. I am completely taking her mouth as I pin her against the tree with my hard groin. My hands roam up underneath her t-shirt, fondling her nipples that instantly peak, causing her to moan.

We are not about to discuss whether this is the appropriate time as we wordlessly undress. Emma shimmies her jeans and panties down to her ankles and I pull one of her legs up, gripping her underneath her thigh and squeezing her ass. My jeans and briefs are low enough so my cock springs free. Emma pulls a condom from my wallet, and I roll it on in record time while still holding her leg up. She's exposed to me, out here in this mythical forest of ours. She's like a naked nymph, begging me to take her. And I do.

I want possession of her body and heart. I want it all.

As I lift her higher so I can thrust up into her, driving harder, her tight muscles constrict around me, and I stifle my desire to shout as I keep pumping into her. Her hands grip my head and shoulders tightly so my mouth can't escape hers. I am pummeling all of my pent up frustration, doubts and love into her. Everything I feel for her cannot be defined by one solitary event or emotion. It is a culmination of who I am, who she is, and who we are together.

Lust-driven images of Emma excite me. Then thoughts of Brian making the decision to leave his wife and son depress and infuriate me. I can't imagine how I could leave Emma like that. My brain is a fucking blender of these conflicting emotions as I fill her with everything I have. I could never end my life, not with Emma in it.

My arm and hand keep her propped up while my other hand greedily touches her wherever it can, including the sensitive spot buried in her wet, silky flesh. I do everything to elicit a moan from her while she wriggles and arches into me, and I want to profess my love to her, which is something stupid I can see myself doing while we are all hot and bothered over each other. Instead, I say nothing and focus on pushing my tongue and cock into her more to draw out those arousing sounds she makes.

I feel her muscles tightening around me and she whimpers with pleasure, setting off my own shattering climax. I come fast and keep grinding into her, aware that her t-shirt is pushed up and exposing her soft skin to the rough tree bark. She doesn't complain as I continue to batter her against the harsh surface until I am depleted.

As she pulls her mouth from mine and we gulp for air as if we haven't breathed in hours, my head collapses against hers as I take in long, ragged breaths. I feel her arms circle my waist and her hands put pressure on my back as if to reassure me. Being with her is more than comforting; we fuel each other with sustenance. Living apart from one another is not an option. Ever.

"If I said I didn't mean to do that, it would be a lie," I say, out of breath.

"How could you not want to do this? I wanted it. But I think I may need some Bactine for my back. The tree was not kind to my skin." She lets loose a nervous giggle.

"I think a mosquito bit my ass," I quip and laugh with her.

"As long as we don't need tetanus shots."

She dresses and brushes the leaves and twigs off my t-shirt.

"Dylan, I heard what you said to Robert."

I think she is referring to my fist hitting his face and declaring that I am the only lunatic allowed in her life—the only man that loves her. That was a memorable speech. Since she was ready to leave with Cooper, it didn't occur to me that she heard a single word of my hysterical admissions for her and the accusations towards Robert.

"You're not a lunatic," she says emphatically and then turns to take the route back to the car.

Twenty-Six
Emma

When we arrive back at the hotel room, Cooper is there with a huge stash of food from McDonalds spread out on the desk. The whole room smells like French fries. It is a fatty, carb heaven.

"Yum," I say.

Dylan is less polite with Cooper's intrusion.

"I should have known you had your own key. Jesus, the place reeks. Emma is a vegetarian—"

"I would love some fries," I say, cutting Dylan off. "Really, I'm starved." I sit down on the bed and shove a wad of greasy, salty fries in my mouth.

"I was going to order you a real meal," Dylan says, watching me devour the fries.

"Where the hell were you two? I told you to stay put," Cooper says between mouthfuls of his burger.

"Oh, fuck that." Dylan is still watching me as though he can't believe that, after our intense sex scene—where I was loving his body—I can switch gears to where I am loving French fries. "We needed to get outside, and stop making it sound like we're being hunted. No one is after us."

"I promised Carson to keep you two safe. I never said you're being hunted. You need to see this," Cooper responds, polishing off the last bite of a Big Mac.

Cooper gets up, wipes his greasy fingers on a napkin and then turns on the TV. He flips through several cable channels, hitting the news stations all showing the same video of several men being escorted by police and FBI. It's the infamous perp walk, and front and center, is my father, Daniel Keller. I recognize his lawyer, Larry, alongside him. My father has his hands in cuffs as he walks towards the courthouse, surrounded by every media outlet in the tri-state area. The star of the clip is Vinnie Marchetto, who is twenty feet ahead of my father with his own entourage.

I immediately drop the bag of fries, walk into the bathroom and throw up. Dylan races in and murmurs something benign and soothing as he rubs my back and holds my hair up as I violently wretch into the toilet. When it seems nothing is left inside of me, I dry heave while Dylan holds my waist.

"Do you want to go visit him?" he asks, meaning my father, of course. The man who betrayed my mother and me. "Maybe it will help to see him in person."

"In an orange jumpsuit with bullet-proof glass between us? I'll pass," I respond, wiping my lips with a tissue before I rinse my mouth out with toothpaste. "I'm done paying for his sins. I'm done with him."

Dylan hands me a towel after I wash my face then catches my jaw with one large palm and holds me still. "What you heard me say… to Robert. I meant it." His words are sharp and insistent. It's ironic that he won't repeat what he actually said.

"I have no doubt that you're being honest," I tell him.

His eyes wander over my face, giving me a moment to consider formulating a better response. Who wouldn't love this man? He's a bounty of strength and love wrapped up in a beautiful package.

"I want to go home."

Dylan looks confused. "Jersey? To see your dad?"

"Hera. I want to go back to our home."

"Our home," Dylan repeats. "Let's go home."

If he is disappointed that I am not saying more about his confession of love, he doesn't show it. I don't cry over my father, and I say nothing more on the topic. Too many years have been wasted on the Marchettos.

We pack our bags, and Cooper follows us back to Hera on his Harley. Dylan floors it and tries to lose him, but Cooper is a speed demon and deft at weaving in and out of lanes to stay on our tail.

"You two are silly sometimes." I am eager to laugh. "If you really cared about speed, you'd ride a Ducati or Kawasaki."

"We'd rather look cool," Dylan smiles. "Nothing is cooler than a Harley. But I'm still going to lose that prick."

"I don't think so. Cooper seems to anticipate your every move."

Dylan gives me a good, long, hard look before staring back at the road ahead where it's dark and traffic is light. We waited a few hours before leaving the hotel so we could avoid commuter traffic and to give me time to accept what has taken place today.

"We'll be home soon." He lifts my hand off my lap and kisses it then holds it while he shifts the gear.

"I'm suddenly so tired."

"It's finally hitting you, everything at once. You need to sleep, babe."

I love the way he says that. He can spoon-feed me simple, caring words of understanding and it's lovely coming from him. I wish we were already home and he was carrying me in his arms up to bed. I am tired of being strong and playing defense. You can only kick-ass and be tough for so long before you just want someone to bring you your slippers and a cup of hot chocolate. Curling up next to Dylan in bed is all I want right now.

Twenty-Seven
Dylan

She's been asleep for fourteen hours.

Unfortunately, our cable started working again when we arrived home. With constant news coverage on the arrests and watching the replay of her father entering the courthouse too many times, I finally pulled the plug on the TV so Emma would pry her eyes away from it.

She took a long, hot bath in the chipped, old tub and spent most of that time staring at the wall. I had to check on her a few times because she was so quiet. I was nervous about her falling asleep and drowning. No shit. I don't know if it's just excessive fatigue or if she's in shock.

She hasn't said anything about her father or Robert since the hotel, and her mother wouldn't take her phone calls. I thought I had it bad, but she really got screwed in the parent department.

After all of that, I held her until she fell asleep, which wasn't long.

At first, I wasn't sure if I would be enough for her because she is used to a family. Even the parental bickering provides a type of security blanket. But I am not Brian. I am willing to accept my strengths when I have them and ask for help when I don't. I also know I can live without Emma, but I wouldn't be a happy person. She is not my crutch the way I have used others before her. She is the one I love and that's what my life needs. I realize she is still unsure if we have any staying power, however I have all the time in the world for her to figure it out. I sure as hell am not going anywhere.

This morning I leave her tangled in the sheets and comforter, deciding it is safe for me to go on a long run with a stopover at Dr. Wang's office. I figure Emma will be out for a while and I can be home by eleven o'clock before she wakes. I need to clear my head about all of this. Working and living with Emma has been the happiest, and to an extent, the most emotional experience because I have fallen in love with her.

I remember very little about my time with Jess last summer other than complete confusion over what I was feeling. I am perfectly clear-headed with Emma, so sure of what I am doing that I want to throw my arms out and shout to the world that I've figured it out. There's no mystery to me anymore about who I am meant to be with. I am turning into a gushing sap, and I have to remind myself that this is only the beginning. I have to help her deal with her father's incarceration and we have to move on from there.

***

Dr. Wang's expression is hard to read as I am pacing his office, sweaty and tired from my run, but I am too anxious to sit down. I have told him most of what has happened over the last week, leaving out the parts about sex or information from Cooper. I mostly relay details about working with Emma and her father's arrest and how I am trying to help her. As I talk, he types away, glancing at his monitor and then at me.

"Can you sit down now? You're exhausting me," he says.

I slide into the chair in front of his desk. I rest my elbows on my knees, trying to look more relaxed, but my heel taps away loudly on the carpeted floor.

"This is a lot to take on. Last time we spoke, you were talking about living with her and keeping it platonic because you were afraid of your growing feelings for her."

"I never said I was afraid of my feelings for her."

"No. I did." Dr. Wang smiles. "You told me you liked her a lot, but you weren't in love with her. And now?"

"I'm in love with her," I say emphatically. "Yep."

"It sounds like it, and you two have certainly been through a lot together in such a short time. Have you told her how you feel?"

"In a way. She heard me tell her ex that I love her, but I didn't say it directly to her. I've been pretty straightforward that I want to be with her, to keep living together, and I don't want us to think of it as a temporary set-up the way it was initially."

"So you two have skipped over that tedious dating part and you're living together, and you're both in love with each other, but you never talk about it."

I sigh at how inane it sounds. "No one likes a funny doctor."

Dr. Wang laughs.

"I'm just trying to keep the story straight. For months you brought the same news to me every week. You described your workouts, your job, complained about a few clients. You never talked about anything that made you excited. And now, you're practically jumping out of that chair."

"I look that bad?" I hold my jittery leg still.

"You realize there's no right way of falling in love. Just because I told you it is okay to get out there and start dating, and it went another way for you, doesn't mean this isn't going to work out. Is that why you're so nervous?"

"I keep thinking about Brian. He loved his family and he still couldn't escape the reapers. How do I know I won't turn out like Brian?"

"None of us can predict our futures. How do I know I won't have an incurable cancer in five years and leave my wife a widow?"

"Well... crap... I don't want to have to worry about you now, too."

Dr. Wang smiles and shakes his head. "Brian was suicidal even back in high school, Dylan. You're not and never were. He was very ill for a long time, and he was very different than you. You can't get back into that vicious cycle of obsessing about worst-case scenarios. Have you told Emma that you think about this?"

"Not exactly. I told her about Brian's death, and that I'm not suicidal."

"That's good, but you haven't told her everything. Your fears."

"That's the kind of thing that makes people run away from you."

"She's also going through a personal trauma, and you're helping her. You seem to be helping each other. That's good."

"Ah, damn," I mumble. "Excuse me, but Doc, I don't want to screw this up. Tell me what to do?"

Dr. Wang scribbles on his little blue notepad and hands me my prescription refill. "Dylan, you know you must call me—any time, day or night—if you are in trouble. You keep taking your medicine, you keep running because it's good for you, and you keep talking to Emma because that's good for you, too. She really sounds like someone who cares about you. You're afraid she'll run away from you, but you'd be surprised how often a person like that will run *towards* you."

Twenty-Eight
Emma

I walk downstairs, still blurry-eyed from too much sleep, and find Lauren sitting on the living room couch, reading on her tablet.

"Wow, finally. You're awake," she says.

"Where's Dylan and what are you doing here?" I rub my eyes and stretch.

I am still wearing the shorts and tank top I slept in and I feel a slight chill. It looks cloudy and gray outside.

"He went on a run and asked me to sit here until you woke up. I guess he still doesn't want you to be alone because of all the crappy stuff with your dad."

"Geez, I don't think I've had a babysitter since I was nine."

Lauren puts on a frowny face and jumps up to give me a hug. "Hey, I'm so sorry about your dad. I've given you a lot of shit about Robert over the years, but I never thought your dad would do this, and I can't imagine how awful this must be."

Since I don't have any siblings to share this with, I accept Lauren's hug eagerly at first and then wriggle free from her grasp. I am thankful she's said that, yet I'm also afraid I will start weeping again. I am sick of crying. It makes my head hurt and my body tired. When it comes to being sad and furious over my father, I am emotionally depleted. I have to get off this really lousy merry-go-round of putting so much stock into my father. It's over, he's done, and I am finished when it comes to depending on him.

"I'll be okay. Thanks for coming, although it really wasn't necessary for you to babysit me."

"Well, Imogene and I haven't gotten to spend any time with you since you moved here and I feel bad about that. We've been so focused on our jewelry business and covering shifts at the diner, we never really made any time for you."

"I was busy with my new job, too."

"And Dylan, right?" she sighs. "I've known him forever, and I would have never fixed you two up. I didn't even think he'd be your type—definitely not the way he used to be—but you two really hit it off, didn't you?"

"You could say that." A warm smile blooms across my face thinking about Dylan.

"Oh, God," Lauren says, seeing me flush. "You're in love with him."

"Yes."

"And, he feels the same?"

"Yes, it's mutual, but we haven't really gone there because we've had a few hiccups along the way. Aside from my father's dirty dealings and Robert showing up, I didn't know about Dylan and Jess until the dinner at Carson's house. You forgot to tell me that part, Lauren."

"I'm sorry. I guess I'm not good at keeping track of my gossip, and I never thought you'd be hooking up with Dylan. Maybe it's a good thing I forgot to tell you about Jess because, if you had known, you wouldn't be with Dylan now. Right?"

"Nice save." I give her another hug, and she wraps her skinny arms around me.

"So, is this going to work out, having to see your boss's wife at every family and social function?"

"I really like Dylan. I'm trying not to think about him and Jess, and he insists they were never in love, and it was nothing."

"You *like* him?" Lauren scoffs. "You love Dylan. No

woman would live in this dump with that stinky couch and those stupid weights in the living room if she weren't totally gaga over the guy. And Dylan's right. Jess was always mooning over Carson. It just took a while for those two to get their act together. Forget about what happened between them last summer. Dylan is crazy about you. I can't believe what you two have gone through already, either. Most guys would feel threatened by Robert showing up. Not Dylan. Cooper told us about the fight and Dylan tackling Robert. Good thing no one got arrested."

"Well..."

"Oops," Lauren covers her mouth. "I'm sorry. I meant other than your dad. This whole thing sucks, and I haven't been a very good friend when it comes to your relationship with Robert, but I'm here for you now. And I guarantee I'm going to scream at Leo and Dylan about fixing this dump up. Dylan needs to at least bring in some new furniture. He's got a lady living here, not Sasquatch."

I laugh.

"Okay, I have to get to the diner, but we're going to have you over for a girls' night soon. You, me and Imogene."

I walk Lauren out to her rusty, little car and watch her drive off. Before I turn to go back towards the house, another car comes from the other direction. I don't recognize it, but it pulls into the dirt driveway that leads up to the house. As it gets closer, I see Robert at the wheel. He parks the car behind Dylan's Jeep and gets out wearing jeans and a leather jacket. He pulls off his sunglasses as he walks towards me.

"Robert," I struggle to say.

His face is badly bruised from the beating he took from Dylan. He still radiates a special handsomeness, yet I can see the weathered exhaustion under his façade.

"Emma," he says my name with a relieved happiness, the way a boy named Robby once did. "I wanted to make sure you're okay. You must be devastated about your father."

"I'm doing okay." I reach out to touch one of the purple bruises on his cheek and then think better of it and pull my hand back.

"I don't want you to hate me and think badly of me for the rest of your life."

"I don't. I think badly of our fathers," I say somberly.

Out of the corner of my eye, I see a flash of movement. It's Dylan running up the driveway, barreling towards us like a running machine. He is bare-chested with his t-shirt draped around his neck and his thick, muscular hamstrings are pumping ferociously as he picks up speed, running straight for Robert, his eyes ablaze with anger. My first instinct is to move Robert out of the way—he hasn't even noticed Dylan.

I reach out my hand to Robert's arm, and in a scene that unfolds before my eyes in slow motion, I watch as Dylan throws his two hundred pound plus body down on Robert. As their bodies collide to the ground and skid across the gravel-strewn dirt, I hear Robert grunt in pain and see his Glock fall from the inside of his jacket.

"I told you to stay the fuck away from her!" Dylan shouts as he yanks Robert's hands behind his back into an arm lock.

I run over to pick up the gun, and just because I am pissed that these two are fighting again, I shoot the gun once into the ground to get their attention and then point it at their feet.

"Emma!" they both shout in unison.

"Both of you stop it," I demand.

"Emma, you don't know what you're doing," Dylan says. "Put the gun down."

"Don't taunt her. She knows exactly what she's doing. She's a very good shot," Robert grunts as he struggles against Dylan's weight on top of him.

"Both of you shut up and get up."

"Emma, give me the gun," a familiar voice says from behind me. I turn around and there's Cooper, holding his hand out with a little smirk.

"You again? How do you keep showing up?" I screech.

Dylan gets up and yanks Robert with him.

"I've been watching Robert. I saw him head this way," Cooper explains. He is very calm and waves his palm upward at me, waiting for me to turn over Robert's gun. "Come on; you're not going to shoot anyone."

"Of course not. I was only trying to get them to listen," I say as I release the magazine from the gun, eject the round from the chamber, and shove both parts in the back waistband of my shorts.

As if things aren't getting interesting enough, Carson's big, black truck comes up the driveway followed by Sean's car. Dylan and Robert glance in their direction before turning back to me. Dylan's eyes go wide as they settle on me.

"Did you just put a gun down your pants? You can't keep that!" Dylan shouts.

"Stop shouting!" I shout back.

"Both of you calm down," Cooper says in his steady, laid-back voice.

"What's the problem?" Carson questions as he and Sean approach.

"Emma?" Dylan asks.

"Well, Cooper took my knife, and maybe I need something for self-defense. The gun doesn't have serial numbers anyway. It's not registered. I could keep it for my own protection. Right, Sean?" I turn to him and he sighs. "You were the one who gave me the knife. You taught me how to defend myself."

"Jaysus, Emma. You don't need the fecking gun. Give it to Cooper," Sean responds.

Huffing out a sigh, I pull the gun and magazine from

my waistband and slam them into Cooper's palm. I am surrounded by five hulking, controlling men. This is bull, again.

"I want my knife back," I mumble to Cooper and cross my arms.

Dylan stares at me, his composure collapsing momentarily as he recognizes my fear. Then he turns his anger back to Robert. "Why the hell are you here?"

"To say goodbye to Emma." Robert's tone is clipped, but his eyes land softly on me with regret.

"Oh, fuck you and your goodbyes," Dylan yells. He pushes Robert back with that I've-had-enough-of-this-bullshit expression before he strides towards me.

"Why do you need a knife, Emma?" His tone softens as his hand gently cups my face.

I look at Sean.

"No, don't look at him for answers. You tell me," Dylan urges. He is perspiring and breathing hard. I watch a drop of his sweat fall from his chin to my wrist.

"I'm a little freaked out over everything. I feel like I need something for protection, and that knife once saved my life," I say softly to him, self-conscious that the others can hear me.

"What?" Robert asks.

"What happened? Tell me all the shit now," Dylan says calmly.

"When Robert and I started... dating... I was attacked in the parking garage at a mall near my parents' house."

I have everyone's attention now. Sean looks very uncomfortable, and I can tell by the stunned expression on Robert's face that he has never heard about this.

"Tell me," Dylan says, taking my hands. Everything, from his loving eyes to his tender touch, tells me that he wants to be the one to save me from these men that have let me down over the years. He wants to be my hero.

I stutter for a moment, trying not to cry as I retell the

incident. "The guy came from behind and grabbed me. No one was around to help or hear my screams, so I hit him in the groin and may have broken his nose, just like Sean taught me. When the guy started to buckle, I swiped his face with the knife to scare him off. It worked. He was wearing a ski mask, but I could see the blood seeping through where I slashed him. He took off."

"Jesus, what if he'd had a gun? He could have killed you," Dylan argues.

"So I was supposed to do nothing and let him rape me? He wasn't trying to mug me. I recognized his voice. I knew who it was. He was there to rape me, and when a guy's private parts are searing in pain, he generally loses his ability to use a gun."

Dylan grimaces. "You're very brave," he says quietly to me.

"No. I'm very scared. That's why I react the way I do." I wish the others weren't listening; I feel so exposed. "Bravery is about risking your life for someone else. I was only protecting myself. I'm not afraid to fight back if it means I get to live."

"Did you press charges against him?" Dylan asks, knowing what the answer will be.

"No, he was one of Vinnie's guys. I heard he left town."

"Who was it, Emma?" Robert inquires angrily. I can tell he is tired of being pushed in the background by Dylan, and he's shocked. I know he's thinking it was an incident that happened on his watch and he's going to feel guilty about it. That's why I never told him.

"It was Michael Pasculli," Sean says wearily.

I turn to Sean. "I suspected you knew my secret, but… how did you know?"

"Because the fecking bastard didn't disappear," Sean replies. "That day, when I asked you about that bruise on your neck, you said it was nothing, but I heard you mumbling Pasculli's name. I paid him a visit and he had a major cut on his face, courtesy of you. All I did was spread the word that one of Vinnie's own guys tried to rape his son's girlfriend. I didn't have to do anything else. The problem took care of itself."

"Emma, why didn't you tell me?" Robert looks sickened.

I don't want to dredge up some old boyfriend-girlfriend drama in front of Dylan.

Dylan squeezes my hands and pulls me closer to him, making it clear to Robert that Dylan is in charge now.

It's an ugly topic, and although I am relieved to have told Dylan, I never wanted to share it with others.

I look at Robert with reluctance. "Because you would have hunted him down and killed him. I didn't want you to be that person—a murderer. Besides, he left town."

Robert shakes his head. "No, he didn't. That's when he went missing."

"Emma, Vinnie took care of Pasculli," Sean adds.

"Jesus Christ. You people." Carson shakes his head.

"Wait a minute." Dylan turns to Robert. "Your dad is willing to kill you, but he gets revenge for Emma?"

"This was more than two years ago," Robert explains. "It wasn't about protecting Emma. My father was protecting his reputation. He couldn't let Pasculli sully our family's *great* reputation, so I'm sure my father had him disposed of."

Robert, not intimidated by Dylan's hold on me, steps closer to me. "I can't believe you didn't tell me this. I would have done something about that guy. If you had never let it slip to Sean, Pasculli could have come back and done something worse to you."

"Forget it," Dylan says to him. "I'm watching over her now. You two say your goodbyes. You've got thirty seconds, and then, Emma, you're going inside with Carson. You're not a part of the rest of this business."

My mouth drops open, yet I don't know what I can or should protest. I am honestly tired of this *business* as they refer to it.

Dylan suddenly leans down to my ear so the others can't hear. "You're mine, Emma," he whispers forcefully.

"Em…" Robert begins to say.

Dylan releases my hands and waves me towards Robert. "Go ahead. Say your goodbyes. Thirty seconds. I'm being generous." He says this directly to Robert.

Robert doesn't waste time with words he has said over and over. As he steps forward and embraces me—hard—I close my eyes and take in his familiar scent and breathe deeply to soothe myself, thankful that he is alive.

"Goodbye, babe," Robert whispers and gives me a peck on the cheek.

"Be careful," I say into Robert's warm gaze and then Carson's arm circles around my waist and we turn to walk slowly back to the house.

Twenty-Nine
Dylan

Cooper follows me into the house where Emma and Carson are sitting silently at the kitchen table. When she sees me, her mouth falls open as if she wants to ask me a lot of questions about what's just happened, and then she looks as if she's afraid to know.

"So?" Carson asks. "Everything squared away?"

Cooper nods and hoists himself up on the kitchen counter.

"What?" Emma asks. "Is that He-Man code that you've killed Robert?"

"Funny," I say, but I am happy to see that my spunky, little ninja is back. "Don't worry. He's gone, and he's safe."

"Seriously, where is he?" she insists.

"Robert had two options," Cooper says to her. "He could participate in the trial and help the prosecutors and go into protective custody, or he could disappear."

"He'd be killed in protective custody," she says.

"Most likely," Cooper agrees. "And Witness Protection wasn't looking like a safe option to him, either, so he chose to disappear."

"How?" she asks.

"Cooper has a large network of friends in and out of law enforcement," I say, putting my hands on her tense shoulders. "They will move Robert out of state and then out of the country."

"Sean is taking him to his first checkpoint." Cooper smiles as if he does this all the time. "I can't tell you more than that, Emma. The less you know, the better."

"How very clandestine of you," Emma says to Cooper. "But, thank you for helping Robert."

"Thank Dylan. It was his idea. He convinced me to call in favors, and he convinced Sean to help get Robert out of here with the necessary papers and such."

She removes my hand from her shoulder and looks up at me with something between gratitude and bewilderment.

I shrug. "We had to help him get out of here so he could get his life back, a better life. Besides, the further away from you, the better."

"Thank you." She can barely get the words out without her eyes misting up.

Shit, I don't want her to start crying over that guy again.

"Well, that's enough for me," Carson says, standing up. "I need to go home and try to forget this little nightmare."

"I'm so sorry I got you involved in this mess," Emma says to him.

"Don't be. I'm glad it's straightened out, and it wasn't the worst that could have happened. I'm just relieved no one got injured." Carson kisses Emma on the cheek and pats her back. "I'll see you very soon, and... I'm really sorry about your father."

"Thank you."

"You and Dylan will have to come up to the house for dinner in a few days. I know Jess would like that."

Oh, fuck. Why did he have to mention Jess? I know my brother means well and he doesn't know about my argument with Emma over Jess. Carson is always so clueless about these things. He lives in his own little, happy bubble. I can't blame him, but Jesus, now he has Emma thinking about Jess again.

"I have to get going, too," Cooper says. "There's this snarky brunette I love having wait on me at the diner. I'm going to have to convince her that she likes me."

300

"Imogene?" Emma asks, surprised.

Cooper chuckles and then pulls Emma's switchblade out of his jeans and places it on the table. He slides it towards her with a smirk.

"Wait," I say to Cooper. I hold out my hand to him. "Thanks. Thank you for everything," I say as Cooper slams his palm into mine for one strong handshake.

Then Carson and Cooper leave together. When I hear the front door close, I pull Emma out of her chair and gather her in my arms.

"It's done," I say. "No more looking over your shoulder. Do you understand that?"

She nods against my chest.

***

Emma spends most of the day sitting on the couch and staring out the front window. I don't know if she is daydreaming about her past with Robert, agonizing about his future, wondering about her father, or thinking about us. All that bravado I put on for everyone earlier in the day is gone. Despite telling Dr. Wang that I would open up to Emma more, I am afraid to ask her what she's really thinking about.

I lift weights while she observes me through several sets with a cautious interest. She still has that distant expression of someone who has been thinking long and hard. This woman has had way too many things to reflect on. I'm still upset over her near-rape incident, although it explains a lot about her defensive nature and inclination to respond with physical force when she's scared. I do know more about her, and I don't think I could ever get tired of learning about Emma Keller.

"Lauren says this place is a dump," she says suddenly.

I put the barbell down and turn to see her smiling at me.

"It is. Well, not the structure, but I'm aware that the furnishings downstairs are atrocious."

"She was awfully offended and said she's going to

301

have a word with Leo and you."

Emma stretches out her long, bare legs on the couch. I want to thank the creator of those short shorts that reveal the lace rim of her underwear and the bottom of her butt cheeks. I can't let her leave the house in them again, though. She gave Cooper an eyeful and that guy is on the prowl. Of course, he's also handed back her switchblade, so I don't think I have to worry about her being able to take care of herself if any guy crosses her.

"You're not blinking," she states. "What are you staring at?"

"Your legs. You. You're beautiful." I sit up on the weight bench and catch a whiff of myself. "Christ, I smell like a barn."

"Worse."

"Yeah, I need to go take a shower." I pause and study her innocent yet sultry pose. "Do you hate this place? It's not really very nice."

"I like living here, Dylan. My room is beautiful. *Our room*," she adds.

***

When she turns in before nine, I don't bother to ask or question where I belong. After a long, hot shower, I skip shaving and put on some freshly laundered sweats and join her in our bedroom. I move to the center of the bed and she curls herself into me. I know what I would like to do, but I intend to let her rest and not make any moves on her. At least, I think I am trying to be thoughtful and considerate of her emotional state, however all my good intentions tend to go out the window whenever she responds with her own sexual advances.

"So this is our bedroom," I say, waiting for confirmation.

"Yes, this is the nicest one."

"I guess Leo can turn my bedroom into the guest room. Anyway, I think he may be moving in with Lauren permanently, so maybe I should buy this place and finish fixing it up. What do you think?" I am fishing because I want to hear her say those three little words when, ironically, I haven't said them directly to her.

She runs her feather light touch across the stubble on my chin and I bury my hands in her soft, long hair. Her belly pushes against my erection, so I pull back.

"I think you could do amazing things with this house."

"I'm going to say this so we're clear, and you're not obligated to say anything." I cup her face.

"I love how you build up so much drama to everything," she responds and her lips touch mine.

"I love you. That's all I wanted to say."

"That's *all*." She laughs and kisses me again. "That is a big deal... Make love to me, Dylan."

Damn. My cock heard her, and now it's happening.

"Sleepy Hollow was lovely, but that tree did a number on my back. I just want you to make love to me in this bed."

"You don't have to ask twice," I say, moving gently on top of her. "I'm on it."

It is the first night we are truly alone. No mysterious prepaid phones ringing, no ex-boyfriends making unexpected visits, no cryptic calls or appearances from her father or men from her former life, and no revelations from well-meaning friends who light the fuse for more misunderstandings.

We have each other in the only place that feels like home for both of us. So much for good intentions. I make love to her for hours, exploring every part of her like she is new to me all over again while she whispers sweet, tender declarations... *"I love your arms, I love your shoulders, I love your eyes, I love Freedom,"* she kisses the small tattoo on my wrist, and she even shouts, *"I love your body"* during a climax, but not the words I am waiting for. It's all right. Through therapy, patience is one of the things I have acquired in small measures. Well, unless an ex-boyfriend is anywhere in the vicinity, then I lose it like a rabid dog. I'm working on that.

Thirty
Emma

Another day of waking up in an empty bed, and another day of realizing how much I dislike not having Dylan's large body next to me in the morning. Thinking of Dylan makes me hurt with need; the wanting grows with each day, and I decide that this is how love should be.

I shower and put on jeans and a flower print blouse that makes me feel pretty. I am so tired from Dylan's insatiable, sexual appetite that the extra sleep does nothing to hide my fatigue. *But this is a good kind of exhaustion,* I remind myself.

When I stumble downstairs, the kitchen has a fresh pot of coffee and pancakes on the stove. I pour syrup on Dylan's homemade flapjacks and eat the food right off the griddle. My guy is an unbelievable cook.

The sound of a large truck rumbling in front of the house makes me put my coffee down to go inspect. I open the door and stand barefoot on the porch, watching Dylan jump out of the Blackard Designs delivery truck before he walks around back to open the doors and pulls the ramp out. When Carson's truck pulls up alongside the delivery vehicle, I see Jess in the passenger seat. They get out and have a short discussion with Dylan. Then Carson and Dylan disappear into the truck. While they carry a large dining table and make their way towards the house, Jess scolds them for not wrapping everything in plastic to protect the wood. As Dylan comes up the porch steps first, grinning at me, his exuberance is contagious.

"Hi," he says, and I feel a little fluttery and excited.

"Hi." I stare right at him, blushing as I think of what we did all night.

"I brought a few things for the house." He disappears inside the house with Carson and the heavy furniture. "But I don't want you to see it until I have it set up," he shouts from the living room.

I stay on the porch and Jess joins me. I can't help but size her up and compare myself to her. She's pretty, she's a genius with job skills I could never master, she's creative and talented enough to sell her paintings, and she grew up in a more sophisticated culture than me. And she's slept with Dylan. Yes, that makes me ill to think about.

"Can we talk?" She looks extremely uncomfortable asking me that.

"That doesn't sound good," I say.

She laughs to break the tension. "No, it never sounds good to start a conversation like that."

"I have an idea what it's about."

She nervously brushes her voluminous red hair off her face and looks at the ground. It's then that I realize she has her own social awkwardness.

"Lauren and Dylan both told me about you not knowing... can we step over here so we can talk privately?"

Oh, this is going to be painful if she's afraid to talk to me. She's already stumbling through each sentence.

I follow her to the end of the porch so the guys can make the back and forth trips to the truck and house without hearing us.

"We don't know each other very well, and I'm probably not the person you'd like to see, but I think I should say something."

"Shoot." I am hoping she can spit it out; she looks frazzled.

"A year ago, Dylan was very different. He was very sick, and I didn't understand that, and I was too stupid to listen to everyone who knew better."

"I already know that. Lauren told me about his illness and the accident," I add.

"I know they told you about him being bipolar. I want to tell you that he did not love me. We were never in love, but two good things came out of that bad year. I fell in love with Carson and Dylan got help. Dylan is getting better every day. He's not perfect—none of us are—but he's remarkably different, and this is the first time I've ever seen the *real* Dylan."

"Okay." I seriously don't know what to say to her. Should I thank her for trying to put me at ease even though I don't feel any different? Should I be polite because she's my boss's wife?

"What I'm trying to say is that Dylan is very happy and I wish you could see him through everyone else's eyes, especially Carson's since he's known Dylan the longest. Dylan is a strong person and so caring, and... and he's just so good. And he's in love with you. He's fighting for you. You're smart and probably know this already, but I think it's good to hear it out loud. I don't want you to think his feelings have anything to do with what happened with me, or that he's trying to prove himself to Carson. It's all about you. Dylan is all about you. In a good way, not his obsessive, bipolar way."

I snort a nervous laugh at that last comment.

Jess smiles and looks more confident about what she's saying. "I thought you should know that."

"Thank you."

"Dylan once told me that as Carson's brother he was obligated to tell me how great Carson is and that I should... you know... love Carson. I'm Dylan's sister-in-law, so I'm obligated to tell you how great Dylan is."

Her kindness coaxes a small smile from me. "How did you know you were in love with Carson?"

"Ah, well, whenever he was near me, I had the

proverbial butterflies in my stomach, and I wanted to vomit. I mean, my insides were in terrible knots and I really wanted to barf. A lot."

I laugh.

"I didn't really know anything about being in love until Carson. I think, when you're with the person you're meant to be with, you do everything possible to be the best part of yourself, and you bring out the best in each other. I see that in Dylan. He's a better person with you."

"That's very thoughtful of you to say. Thank you."

Jess smiles uncomfortably. "Well, sometimes I talk too much. Let me try to sum this up… I was not Dylan's first love. You are. And you can be his one and only if that's what you want."

"We're done," Dylan shouts from the living room. "Come on in!"

Jess smiles at me. "He's not making this house pretty for Leo, and everything he did for Robert was because Dylan loves you. You realize that, right?"

"Yeah."

"Good. Now, let's go see your beautiful new furniture."

Thirty-One
Dylan

While I set our new dining table for lunch and put out some sandwiches, Emma wanders around the living room trying out the new leather couch, the lamps, the chairs and end tables. She opens and closes all the doors on the entertainment system that hides the large flat screen TV. Then she tries out the drawers and shelves in the buffet cabinet in the dining room.

"Are you going to sit down and eat?" I ask, amused.

"Did you steal all this furniture from the showroom?"

"No, I paid cost for everything. Some of it, like the lamps and accessories, were on loan from Mercer's store, but I paid for those, too."

"It must have cost a small fortune. Remember, I work there, and I had Carson raise the prices on everything?"

"I know, and he said you've brought in a nice bundle of revenues, so we'll be getting bigger commission checks. But I paid for this. It's a gift for you."

"It's very generous. I never expected you to spend this kind of money, though. It wasn't necessary."

"I don't want you living in a dump. And, Emma, I don't think you're aware that I have equity in the company. Not as much as Carson, of course, but I have a percentage as an investor, so I do make a nice living. I'm not rich, but I'm not broke, either. I can afford the furniture, and I plan on buying the house from Leo. He and I already discussed it... unless you'd rather find a different house."

"Oh. No, I like this house," she says with an uncharacteristic shyness.

I can tell she's fairly surprised by this news and is most likely thinking that there is now a shift in the income paradigm, and that we will be owners instead of renters. She liked thinking we were on equal footing, financially, therefore I'll have to figure out how to convince her that what's mine is hers.

When I go back into the kitchen to take my meds with a glass of water, for a split second, I have a bad sense that she is not really here. That I've imagined falling in love with this remarkable girl that turned my world upside down. I put the water glass down on the counter and walk back into the dining room. She is very real. She's standing behind her chair, patiently waiting for me.

"I forgot to tell you something. It's something you should have heard from me a while ago, *out loud*," she says.

"Uh, huh." As I walk slowly towards her, her ramrod posture makes me a little suspicious. I don't have the energy if she's going to surprise me with one of her Bruce Lee moves.

"I love you, Dylan Blackard. Very much."

That stops me. I guess I didn't expect to hear it any time soon. I thought it would be a long, drawn out work-in-progress, like therapy with Dr. Wang.

"Well?" She tilts her head and smiles at what must be my odd, confused expression.

"Yes," I respond. "I agree completely."

She laughs. "You should see your face. You're so cute."

"You surprised me," I reply, closing in on her in one long stride and eagerly putting my hands on her waist.

"Oh, I'm not done. There's more."

"Is it as good as the first part?"

"Yes."

"Are you going to propose?" I laugh.

"Not yet. We just got new furniture. Let's start with that." She strokes my cheek.

"Tell me." My confidence is bolstered enough that I don't care what she says next. It could be an admission to having five ex-husbands, and I wouldn't care.

"When I broke up with Robert, I thought he loved himself more than me because we couldn't seem to get away from his family. I knew I could never accept his situation, and I blamed him, *unfairly*. It turns out that I come from the same crappy kind of family. I want to put all of that behind me, though. I want a guy who loves me more than anyone or anything. I may sound selfish, but I know I want someone who is devoted to me and can't see his life any other way."

"That's me, baby. All the way."

"Good, because I can get kind of ornery and rough when things don't go my way."

"I like that about you, but we're also going to have to agree on some issues."

"I'm listening."

"You can't avoid your family and pretend they don't exist. When you're ready, we're going to see your dad in prison—you need to talk to him. And we're making a trip to Florida at some point so you can spend time with your mom and grandmother. I'll be with you, babe, through it all."

"Oh," she groans skeptically. "Okay. And that means you're going to call Brian's wife, Katy, and you're going to talk to her because you need it, and it would be nice for her to hear from someone that cared about her husband."

"You're right. I'm going to do that."

I maneuver her rear end against the edge of the table and keep her in a snug embrace.

"And I want you to be sure you understand what you're getting into with me." As I kiss her cheek, her big, brown eyes are filled with acceptance.

"The pills and the doctors are forever. I will never be cured. I'll be better, but don't assume this all goes away

311

sometime. It never does. I have to live with my illness and manage it for the rest of my life. You make it easier to do that, in every way. I love you beyond belief, and that helps me, but there may be a time when I need more help. I hope not, but you should be aware that it's a possibility. If this is too much of a burden for you and you don't want to be a part of this, I understand."

"Okay, well, it's official. Dylan Blackard, you are crazy. If you think I can't handle being with you because of your illness, you've sorely underestimated me."

My breath escapes me in a rushed sigh of relief.

"I have to make sure you understand me, Emma. Do not offer me sympathy. Do not pity me or my past in any way. Love me. That is all I want—it's all I need."

There's a heavy silence.

"I love you." Her stare is unflinching.

"Good." I lean in to give her a long, slow kiss and then she pulls back.

"And you forgot about my burden that you'll inherit. I'll forever be associated with mobsters. As long as there is easy access to the information on the Internet, my name will come up, linked to the Marchetto family and Daniel Keller. Eventually more people will know, and I'm not talking about the nice people in Hera. It will probably haunt me forever, and people will want to ask a lot of questions."

"You can change your name."

"You mean, do away with Emma Keller all together? Or I suppose I could go by one name, just Emma. Like Beyoncè or Cher." She laughs.

"Or you could be Emma Blackard." I smile when she gapes.

"It's too soon for that, Dylan." Her voice is soft like she's singing to me. "But I love you, and I want that to be part of our future. I do."

"Me, too." I can barely speak as my heart swells and pounds against my chest. I didn't think I'd turn into a sap over this, but I am. "Why me, Emma? Why do you love me?"

"You're easy to love. I feel amazing when I'm with you. You know what it's like to walk outside into the warm spring sunshine after a long, bleak, cold winter? That feeling of the sun new and hot on your skin as it warms your cold bones, and suddenly the darkness is gone. You feel really good... It's pure happiness... You're my sun, Dylan."

"I love you, too," I say more assertively. "But I'm not a poet. I can't match your words unless you want me to sing something from Bon Jovi, maybe 'Shot Through the Heart'?"

Emma laughs and shakes her head.

"No, that's probably not the best choice. Maybe 'Living On A Prayer'?"

"No, no singing." She grins.

"Really? I could recite the lyrics to one of those Katy Perry tunes you like. I got the eye of the tiger, a fighter, dancing through the fire," I deadpan.

Emma laughs. "Please, no."

I kiss her neck.

"I like the kissing," she adds.

"I think we should christen the table," I say, trailing kisses down her neck.

I lift her onto the table and slowly lay her down on her back with part of my weight on top of her. As she's about to speak, I catch her mouth in a slow, deep kiss. She moans and tugs at my clothing. While I pull off my shirt, she wriggles out of her jeans and unbuttons her shirt.

Suddenly, I am slightly nervous. It hasn't occurred to me that this would happen so soon with Emma. I didn't really believe that I could tell her I love her and that I come with a lifetime of an unpredictable illness, and that she would then agree to this so easily. I assumed she would be encouraging and willing to give it a try, which wouldn't be

313

difficult since we are already living together. From my perspective, I counted on it being a long-term relationship that could end badly if I blew it by getting in another fight, a bout of never-ending despair, or worse, she would realize she could never really love me.

I have underestimated her and us. I've definitely hit the mother lode with her. She loves me and she considers marriage as part of our future. And I have her naked, spread eagle on our new table. *Hell, yes.*

Epilogue
Dylan

This year has gone by too fast. I've tried to savor every moment and memory with Emma, but it seems we're always making new ones.

We made several trips to the prison in New Jersey to see her father. They spent a good portion of their time staring at each other, saying nothing. It wasn't hostility that separated them—it was disappointment. Eventually, Emma's father made a request for some books he wanted to read, and that little mission of assembling his reading list gave her something relevant to do for him. Over several months, they began to talk about her job, living in Hera, the books she was reading, and working with her growing list of wholesale customers. They were very careful, however, never to discuss anything related to the Marchetto family to spoil their father-daughter time together, which seemed like something new and precious to them.

I also booked two separate weeks in Boca and went with Emma to visit her mother and grandmother in Florida. Grandmothers love me, and true to form, I discovered I could do no wrong in her eyes. Emma's mother was kind to me, but much more closed off. I fixed things around her mother's new condo, cooked some nice meals, carried their umbrellas and gear to the beach, and drove them to the mall. I was the all-around handyman and chauffer. On top of that, Grandma Rose kept pinching my ass, saying I was so handsome that Emma better snatch me up and marry me now. I gave Emma pointed, little amused looks over that.

I would marry her in a second, but I think Grandma

Rose really likes me because she knows I'm not going anywhere. Emma is it for me.

Emma gave me a few surprises of her own. One day I came home to find that a commercial range and fridge had been installed. She had Carson take her out to shop and negotiate a price on the restaurant quality equipment, and she used her new bonus to pay them off. She said she wanted to make sure I would stick around because she really liked having a personal chef. All I know is, I was cooking non-stop for that woman, whatever she wanted. Sometimes, I had eight gas burners going and the commercial-grade fridge with glass doors was fully stocked and organized the way I wanted. So I started taking Dr. Wang's advice, and we began entertaining people at our home. We had the furniture, the kitchen equipment, and the annoying, adoring hosts who can't keep their hands off each other.

It didn't end there, either. Each day, week and month got better and better. I fell more in love with Emma. On Halloween, I took her to the evening festivities at Sleepy Hollow where we did the scary night tour through the cemetery. Then we went to the nearby Philipsburg Manor for the Horseman's Hollow event with the creepy, dark creatures that shifted in and out of the nighttime special effects landscape. Emma let out a blood-curdling scream when the Headless Horseman rode through, and I laughed as I held her. I knew she was mine, I had no uncertainties anymore. That evening was when I began to think of us in terms of being married.

That piece of paper won't change much considering we're already spending twenty-four hours a day together, yet it is important to me to let the world validate what I have with Emma. I am stubborn or maybe old-fashioned that way.

***

And now, it's late spring again and our one-year

anniversary of living together is tomorrow. Lois is holding one of her big garden parties, a casual event where half the town comes out to gush over her elaborate architectural masterpiece of a garden. It is like a mini version of the gardens at Versailles except hers are next to a cottage instead of a castle. Only Lois and Archie know what Emma and I have planned for the party.

After everyone enjoys getting lost in the garden mazes and eating plates of barbeque ribs and chicken, drinking under the white lights Lois has strung across the trees, she asks everyone to shut up. Most are laughing at Lois's direct approach, but that stops when they see Emma and I walking hand in hand up to the porch where Archie's friend, a judge from a nearby town, is waiting on the top step. Lois comes forward with a bouquet of flowers for Emma to hold. It's in that moment that we hear gasps from the guests.

I am dressed like every other guy here—in jeans—but I have at least worn a white button-down shirt instead of my usual t-shirt. Emma is wearing a white, cotton dress that falls below her knees along with sandals.

We walk to the base of the stairs and the judge stands just a few steps above us with Lois and Archie behind him. Out of the corner of my eye, I see Carson stand up from his table. He reaches for Jess's hand and they walk over to stand behind us. Everyone else follows their lead until we have about two hundred people standing up to witness our wedding.

There is no introduction, everyone knows what is happening. The judge gives the standard vows because Emma has insisted she doesn't want flowery words, especially since I struggle with attempts at being poetic. She only wants simple gold bands and *"I do."*

When I bend down for our kiss to seal the deal, the crowd begins cheering and applauding. I am caught up in the fervor, and instead of a simple kiss, I pull Emma into a bear hug and give her a proper kiss that shows how I really feel. After she's released, she launches her bouquet somewhere and stands on tiptoe to wrap her arms around my neck. Camera flashes begin going off and surround us with blinding light before we finally part and face our admirers.

"Let's toast the couple!" Archie exclaims, raising a champagne flute.

"To the sexy couple!" Imogene screams drunkenly, waving the bridal bouquet and a bottle of champagne with joy.

Emma smiles at me, and I am lost in a liberating rapture. I believe this is what it feels like to walk towards freedom. It won't always be like this—I expect some dark with the light—but I am going to try like hell to breathe life into every single day I get to share with Emma.

Acknowledgments

Much love and gratitude goes to my family for supporting my writing endeavors, even when I become unbearable.

A big thank you to my early readers: Jooge, Trisha Hudson, and author, Nikki Young. I appreciate the time they put into my book and their enthusiastic encouragement.

A very special thank you goes to Emma Corcoran, my lovely Irish friend, book reviewer, and all around special person. She has been the biggest cheerleader of Dylan's story since its inception and helped with every step, all the way down to the cover design image. Emma's suggestions along with her unbelievable support kept me going daily, and I couldn't resist putting her colorful Irish expletives in Sean's dialogue.

Zoe York, a wonderful romance author, played a key role in helping me move forward after my first novel, FEARSOME, was published. Zoe and all the writers at Romance Divas have been an incredible source of information and support.

I have a fantastic editing team at C&D Editing, and I get tired just thinking of all the work Alizon Duckwall and Kristin Campbell put into my books. Honestly, they are so amazing.

Aaron Campbell gets all the credit for my website because I'm inept in that area, and he knows it.

Damon at damonza.com created the perfect cover for Dylan's story; he absolutely nailed it. I appreciate both his talent and patience.

A funny note of recognition goes to Clarice Wynter, an author who made me laugh hysterically with a personal story she once shared. It inspired the "beeping scene at the dinner party," which is probably only hilarious to me because we experience this in our home quite often.

About the Author

S. A. Wolfe lives with her husband and children in New York City. When not writing or reading, she loves hanging out with family and friends. Unfortunately, she is also great at procrastinating.

Dear Reader-

If you enjoyed FREEDOM, please consider leaving a review on Amazon, Barnes & Noble, or any book blogs you participate in. I would really appreciate it.

Also, I love interacting with readers, so please visit me at:

www.sa-wolfe.com
https://www.facebook.com/sawolfe24
https://twitter.com/sawolfe
sawolfe24@gmail.com

JOIN MAILING LIST

To receive information about upcoming releases, opportunities to be an ARC reader (Advanced Reader Copy), or excerpts from upcoming books, please join my mailing list at:

https://www.facebook.com/sawolfe24/app_100265896690345

Thank you!

S. A. Wolfe

CPSIA information can be obtained at www.ICGtesting.com
Printed in the USA
LVOW08s2003110716

495869LV00009B/1282/P